Unconscionable

Unconscionable

A Rich Coleman Novel

Volume 3

BY

William Manchee

TOP PUBLICATIONS, LTD.
DALLAS, TEXAS

Dedication

To all the millions of Americans who tasted the dream of home ownership only to have it turn into a nightmare of unfathomable grief and despair.

Unconscionable
A Rich Coleman Novel
Volume 3

© COPYRIGHT
William Manchee
2012

Top Publications, Ltd.
Dallas, Texas

ISBN 978-1-929976-98-0
Library of Congress: 2012946643

TABLE OF CONTENTS

PRELUDE

Having a son graduate from law school should have been a proud moment for Rich Coleman, but he had an ominous feeling as he watched the line of SMU Law School graduates in their blue caps and gowns make their way to the folding chairs lined up in front of the stage. His decision to become an attorney, rather than a stockbroker as everyone had expected, turned out to be a huge mistake. The graduates were all smiling and talking excitedly now that law school was behind them. Rich remembered his own graduation a little over thirty years earlier. He remembered how relieved he had been, so full of hope for the future. He was engaged and looking forward to a long life with Paula, the woman he loved and cherished more than the air he breathed. Rich thought his life was perfect . . . for a while, anyway. He had made partner in record time and his dreams of becoming a successful attorney seemed to be coming true. But it had been too good to last, he supposed. Every Sunday at mass he'd thank God for all his blessings, particularly for bringing Paula into his life. But in one shocking and horrific twist of fate she was taken away by a drunk driver who'd run a red light and broadsided them. Rich never saw the car—just felt the impact and heard Paula's neck snap.

For months he was a wreck, dreaming each night of the car wreck and hearing horrific crack of Paula's neck over and over. Depressed and unable to sleep for more than an hour or two at a time, he was mentally and physically exhausted and barely able to drag himself to work each day. It wasn't long before his casual drinking became a frequent crutch to get him through each day. He found if he drank enough he'd pass out and wouldn't dream. Of course, he suffered with nausea and dizziness at night and headaches in the morning, and his productivity at the firm came to a standstill. He often wondered why the other partners

1

hadn't fired him. By all rights they should have, and probably would have, had it not been for the intervention his college roommate, Joe Weston.

Joe had been a business major and gone on to get his MBA. After graduation he'd joined a major investment brokerage firm and Rich had been one of his first clients. Joe had been the best man at Rich's wedding and was nearly as devastated as Rich when Paula was killed. He warned Rich not to drink too much, but his warnings fell on deaf ears.

One weekend Joe called Rich to see how he was doing, and when he didn't answer, Joe went over to his apartment to check on him. He found him drunk and passed out. After that Joe insisted he get some counseling. Rich resisted, of course, as drunks usually do, but eventually he came around and started seeing a counselor. Over a period of a year and a half, she helped him learn to cope with his loss. She told him part of his problem was survivor's guilt. *Why had God taken Paula and not me?* It was a question for which there was no answer, of course, but she finally got Rich to accept that fact and move on.

About this time Rich met Erica Fox. She was the teenage daughter of one of the firm's good clients, a millionaire named Franklin Fox. At the time he was the only one in the firm with any financial expertise, so he ended up being appointed Erica's trustee in the event of Franklin's death. Franklin was in good health and nobody expected him to die any time soon, so Rich thought nothing of the appointment until he got a frantic call one night from Erica with the news that her father had died in a skiing accident in Switzerland.

Since Erica had no family (that she was speaking to, anyway), Rich had to fly to Switzerland to take charge of her person and arrange for Franklin's body to be returned to the States. When he left Dallas he thought of Erica simply as a client in need, but as they spent time together getting Franklin's affairs in order, they fell in love. It wasn't because Rich was irresistible or anything like that, but more likely due to the fact that they had both recently lost someone they'd dearly loved and had opened up to each other in a way only two grieving souls could. Even though he'd fallen in love, he didn't acknowledge it to Erica and had no intention of acting on his feelings. He knew their relationship was wrong and forbidden, but Erica didn't care about that. She was a millionaire's daughter used to getting her way, and as it turned out, Rich didn't have the strength to resist her.

For a while they were able to keep their illicit affair a secret, but eventually they were discovered by Erica's estranged aunt, Martha Collins, and one of the firm's partners, Peter Phillips. It got ugly after that and Rich lost his job at the firm, but that wasn't the worst of it. Erica's aunt Martha was murdered, and of course Erica and Rich were the prime suspects. Erica claimed she hadn't killed Aunt Martha but insisted on pleading temporary insanity nonetheless. She claimed to be protecting Rich by admitting to be guilty and forced him to make a pact that if either of them were convicted they'd commit suicide together as a show of their love.

Rich thought it was pure insanity, but he loved Erica and felt he had no choice but to accept the pact or lose her forever. Fortunately, she put on quite a performance at trial and was acquitted. Rich was greatly relieved, since he really didn't want to take the cyanide pill Erica had prepared for him. He didn't make out as well with the State Bar of Texas, however, even though he and Erica had gotten married by then. He'd breached his fiduciary duty to Erica by entering into a personal relationship with her, not to mention the fact that she was a minor at the time. So, he had to accept a public reprimand and agree not to act in a fiduciary capacity again for five years. This was pretty light treatment for his transgressions and could only be attributed to Erica's refusal to cooperate in the State Bar's prosecution and the fact that he'd made Erica over a million dollars since being appointed her trustee.

His eldest son, Matt, had even worse luck when he started his bankruptcy law practice in 2005. He had met a SMU student named Lynn Lakey at a New Year's Eve party at the Hotel Continental in Dallas. It was love at first sight, and within six months they were happily married. Lynn was a marketing major, and she got this crazy idea about getting rich by setting up a bankruptcy mill. It wasn't a new idea, but she took it to a new level. She thought with so many Americans over their heads in debt but afraid to file bankruptcy that the right marketing approach would bring them in in droves.

It took a little fine-tuning but Matt and Lynn finally came up with an effective TV campaign, and the Debt Relief Centers of Texas took off. Much to their delight, within just a few months, bankruptcy filings in North Texas were up 13 percent. Unfortunately, this sudden increase in filings got the attention of Frank Hill, chairman of MidSouth Bank, a subprime lender in Houston with thousands of customers in North Texas.

Hill immediately launched an investigation, which eventually determined that the Debt Relief Centers of Texas and their unique marketing approach was responsible for the unprecedented rise in bankruptcy filings in North Texas. In response Hill enlisted Douglas Barnes, a corporate troubleshooter, to devise a strategy to put the Debt Relief Centers out of business. At first he went to the State Bar and lodged a complaint. When that didn't work, he played some dirty tricks on Matt designed to embarrass and discredit him. Finally, when the dirty tricks failed he hired an ex-marine thug named Hans Schultz to coerce one of Matt's employees into setting him up for bankruptcy fraud. At first Matt was going to fight the indictment, but while he was in jail awaiting his bond to be posted, he was visited by several inmates who told him to plead guilty or they'd kill his wife, Lynn.

Matt took the threat seriously and, against the advice of counsel, pled guilty. But Frank Hill broke his promise and had Hans Schultz kill Lynn anyway, just hours after Matt had been locked up and it was too late to back out of his plea bargain. Matt was obviously devastated losing Lynn and vowed to get even

4

with Hill one day. As soon as he was released from prison he made good on his vow. Not only did he get the banker indicted for ordering Lynn's murder, but he tricked MidSouth Bank into issuing thousands of credit cards to penniless prison inmates all over the country. Needless to say, the bank regulators came in rather quickly after that and seized control of the bank.

So, both Matt and Rich had tried to dissuade Ryan from going to law school. It had been a perilous profession for them, and they didn't want him to get hurt like they had. Unfortunately, he wouldn't listen, since he was hell-bent on becoming a criminal defense attorney. The more Rich and Matt argued against it, the more determined he became to take that perilous career path. Finally, they gave up and just prayed his luck would be better than theirs had been.

Ryan's motivation for wanting to be a criminal defense attorney was fairly obvious. He'd seen his brother wrongfully accused of bankruptcy fraud, and it outraged him that an innocent man could be framed and end up in prison. Rich told him that it happened all the time and that one more criminal defense attorney wouldn't change the fact that powerful people usually got what they wanted. Being idealistic, as most new attorneys are at that age, he couldn't accept that perception of reality. Somehow he'd find justice for his clients no matter what the cost. But he was wrong, and they all paid a dear price for his stubborn quest for justice.

Chapter 1
Graduation

It was a pleasant day on the SMU campus in Dallas. The ceremony was being held outdoors in the law school quadrangle. It was a small and intimate crowd, as the graduating class was just over a hundred students. Erica, her mother, Matt, and Rich were the only ones there supporting Ryan. Erica's father was dead, and Rich's parents lived in California and were too elderly to travel.

Since Rich had graduated from SMU some thirty years earlier, he had been afforded the privilege of delivering Ryan's diploma to him. Ryan smiled broadly when Rich handed it to him and shook his hand. Rich had done the same thing for Matt and, as Ryan walked off, Rich worried that he might have jinxed Ryan. He wasn't a superstitious person, but he couldn't help but wonder if somehow he had passed on his bad fortune to Matt and now he was doing the same thing to Ryan.

After the ceremony was over they went inside the administration building where there was to be a reception. While they waited for Ryan to join them, Rich went and got everyone a drink. When Ryan finally showed up two drinks later, he had a girl in tow.

"Mom, Dad. This is Amanda Sherman. She and I were study partners."

Rich gave Amanda a quick look and then grinned at Ryan. She was a looker, and he wondered how much studying they'd actually done when they were together. He stifled a laugh.

"Oh. So nice to meet you," Erica said. "What a nice ceremony. Your parents must be very proud of you."

"Yes. They are."

Unconscionable

"I'm just glad it is over," Ryan noted. "I can't wait to actually start practicing."

"Well, you still have to pass the bar," Rich reminded him soberly.

He shrugged. "I know. Wouldn't that be a kick in the ass if I failed the bar after three grueling years in law school."

Amanda shook her head. "Yeah, like you have something to worry about. You always ace the tests. I'm the one who barely passes."

"Don't worry," Rich interjected. "I barely graduated from law school, but I did pretty well on the bar—top ten percent."

Amanda's eyes lit up. "Really?"

"Yes, the bar exam is more practical than academic. I'm not a scholar, so it was a breath of fresh air to be given some real-life cases to analyze rather than be asked to remember the details of a bunch of irrelevant historical cases."

"Well, that makes me feel better," Amanda said.

"So, what type of law do you want to practice after you pass the bar?" Erica asked.

"My undergraduate degree is in English literature so I was thinking of something related, like publishing or literary rights."

"She wants to be a literary agent," Ryan said, rolling his eyes. "She's going to waste her law degree."

Rich shrugged. "It may not be as glamorous as being a criminal defense attorney, but if she signs some good talent she'll be making more money than you will pleading out drug dealers."

Ryan frowned. "I'm not going to represent drug dealers. I'm only taking on clients who are innocent or who had a good reason for the crimes they committed."

Again Ryan's motivation was obvious. Matt had committed a number of criminal acts in his quest for vengeance against Frank Hill and MidSouth Bank, but Ryan considered them all justifiable considering that Hill had hired Hans Schultz to kill Lynn and three other people that Ryan knew about. In Ryan's mind, his brother's actions were just and right and he would have been proud to defend someone like Matt seeking justice as much as revenge.

"You'll starve, then," Rich noted. "Very few criminal defendants are innocent."

Ryan shrugged. "Then I'll have to do bankruptcies for you for a while until I get established."

"That's fine," Rich said, happy to hear for the first time that Ryan was considering practicing with him. "I just don't want you to get your hopes up. If you really want to practice criminal law you should go work for the DA for a while and learn the ropes."

Ryan shook his head. "No. I'd never be a prosecutor. They don't give a damn about justice. All they care about is their conviction rate."

"You don't have to make a career of it," Amanda interjected. "It's just a good way to learn how the system works."

Ryan shook his head again. "The system doesn't work. That's the problem."

"So, how do you think you can change it?" Amanda asked.

"I don't think I can change it, but I plan to become good enough to beat it."

"Well, I have to admit you have the cocky confidence of a criminal defense attorney," Rich said. "Just be sure you can deliver what you promise."

"Don't worry, Dad. I'll do whatever it takes to win."

Ryan's attitude scared Rich. Matt's and Rich's experiences had hardened him and given him a jaundiced view of the world. Rich thought back to when they were fun-loving teenagers. The one thing Matt and Ryan had in common was their love for fantasy, warfare, and science fiction. They spent countless hours engaged in mock combat, whether it was Risk, Dungeons and Dragons, Civilization, or countless other games. To get an advantage over the other, they studied the theories and exploits of Machiavelli, Alexander the Great, Genghis Khan, Napoleon, and Field Marshall Rommel. Although Ryan held up better than most, Matt almost always prevailed, not so much due to his ruthless, relentless attacks, but more on account of his thorough preparation for battle. Now Ryan was thinking like Matt. Rich guessed he'd learned from his brother not only what it took to win, but the preparation necessary to annihilate his opponents. Recalling the last time he'd seen Matt, Rich realized he hadn't followed them into the reception. That upset him because he had planned to take everyone to dinner after the ceremony was over.

"Where's Matt?" Rich asked.

Ryan and Erica began scanning the area for Matt.

"I don't know," Ryan said.

Rich grimaced. "I guess I'll go look for him. He looked kind of in a daze, so he might not have noticed that we had left."

Ryan rolled his eyes. "What's with him? He seems so out of it lately."

"He's depressed," Erica replied. "He's still grieving."

"It's been over two years. It's time he got over her."

"He'll never get over her," Erica explained. "That's the way love is—eternal."

"Oh, give me a break," Ryan spat. "If he'd just start dating again he'd find someone else to fall in love with. It's just chemistry, for godsakes."

Rich smiled. "Well, as interesting as this philosophical debate is becoming, I think I'll pull myself away and go find him."

Rich left as Erica was about to rebut Ryan's assertion that love was just a matter of chemistry. He went outside to make sure Matt wasn't still in his chair where he'd last seen him. He wasn't there, so Rich assumed he'd followed the crowd inside. It was a big room so he started in one corner and began searching in a grid pattern. That would work if Matt were standing still, which he thought to be the most likely case. After searching half the room he spotted him at the bar with a gorgeous blond in a short cocktail dress. She wasn't a graduate or a mom, so he was curious who she was and approached them tentatively.

"Matt. There you are."

"Oh, Dad. Where did you guys go? We've been looking for you."

"Over there," Rich said, pointing in the general direction of their party. He smiled at the young lady.

"Oh, this is Candy Kane. We're going out after the ceremony. I told her to meet me here."

Rich stifled a laugh. He wondered what kind of a sick parent would name their little girl that. "Oh . . . good. Can she join us for dinner?"

Matt frowned. "No. Sorry, Dad. We have other plans."

"Hmm. That's too bad," Rich said. "Well, at least come over and introduce your friend to everyone."

Matt looked at his watch. "Actually, if you don't mind I think we'll take off. The ceremony is over, right?"

Rich nodded, showing his disappointment by his facial expression.

They got up and Candy extended her hand. "Nice to meet you, Mr. Coleman. Matt has told me all about how good you are at investing."

"Not now, Candy," Matt said irritably.

"Wait a minute," Candy insisted. "Matt said you didn't do that anymore, but I thought maybe you might make an exception."

"Do what?" Rich asked, although he already knew the answer. During Erica's trial it came out that he had parlayed $50,000 into a million dollars in less than a year. Ever since that publicity he had been hounded by people, mainly women, wanting him to invest their money.

"I've got a nice stash of cash set aside from, you know, my work, and I'd be honored if you would manage it for me."

Rich smiled. "Well, Matt was correct. I'm not a licensed

11

stockbroker or money manager."

Candy gave him a wounded look as Matt took her arm and guided her away. As they were going out the door Matt looked back and shrugged apologetically. After a minute of processing what Rich had just seen, he went back to their group.

"Did you find Matt?" Erica asked.

"Yes. I did. He was at the bar."

"Oh. Is he going to join us?"

"No. He left with a hooker."

Ryan turned his head. "What did you say?"

"He was with a woman. I think she was a hooker or an escort. Anyway, they had other plans."

"Oh, my God!" Erica exclaimed. "He brought a hooker to his brother's graduation?"

"Well, I not sure what her line of work is, but she did admit to having quite a large sum of money. She wanted me to invest it for her."

Ryan's mouth opened but no words came out. Erica just shook her head. Amanda looked confused.

"What's he doing?" Erica asked.

Rich shook his head. "Grieving, I think, was your diagnosis."

Erica looked at him and frowned. "You'd better have a talk with him. I'm worried."

Rich took Erica's hand and squeezed it firmly. "I will. I'll go see him tomorrow and find out what's going on."

Erica took a deep breath and gave him a worried look.

"Okay," Rich said. "Who feels like some dinner? I've got reservations at Del Frisco."

The next day after mass Rich made good on his promise and went to see Matt. He lived in an apartment in a suburb of Dallas called Richardson. Rich had never actually been to the apartment before, and the complex was a maze of buildings, so it was no simple chore finding his unit. When he finally found it and knocked on the door there was no answer. He hadn't called ahead because he wanted to catch Matt by surprise. If Matt was into hookers and escorts, Rich was sure he wouldn't want to talk about it with his father. Rich wondered if he was inside hiding or actually out somewhere.

There was no way to look inside from the front, so he went through the garden gate back to his patio. When he looked inside he gasped. Candy was lying naked on the carpet, and Matt was slumped in a corner passed out. An empty bottle of Jack Daniels sat next to Matt's feet. For a moment Rich pondered whether to go in. If they were just sleeping off drunkenness from a night of partying it might be best to leave them alone and come back another day for their talk. But then he noticed bloody vomit next to Candy's mouth. With that discovery he started banging on the glass door.

The banging made quite a racket, but neither one of them stirred, so Rich took out his pocket knife and started playing with the lock. The door gave a little so he slid it open. It hadn't been locked. The room reeked of a combination of vomit, blood, and cigarette smoke. Rushing in, he checked Candy for a pulse. She had one, but it was shallow. He went to Matt and began shaking him. It took a minute but Matt finally began to stir. He went back to Candy and tried to shake her into consciousness as well but she didn't respond. He got out his cell and called 911.

"Hello. Nine-one-one. What is your emergency?"

"I have a young woman who is unconscious and not responding to my efforts to wake her up. She's consumed a great deal of alcohol. I'm not sure if she's taken any drugs, but she's vomited blood."

"An ambulance is on its way. Do you see any bottles of drugs anywhere nearby?"

Matt was struggling to his feet so Rich asked him. "Did Candy take any drugs?"

He pointed to Candy's purse. Rich grabbed it and dumped its contents out on the ground. A large prescription medicine bottle fell to the carpet. Rich picked it up and read the label.

"Yes, there's a prescription bottle of Percodan. It's got about a dozen pills in it."

"Okay, she may be bleeding internally from the combination of the Percodan and alcohol. Is she on her stomach or back?"

"Stomach."

"Turn her over, put a pillow under her head, and make sure she's breathing."

She was breathing, so Rich gently turned her over and put a pillow from the sofa under her head.

Glaring at Matt, Rich screamed, "What in the hell are you thinking? You let her take drugs and alcohol? Are you nuts?"

Matt swallowed hard. "I swear I didn't know anything about the Percodan. She takes those for anxiety. All I saw her do was drink."

"You drank a entire bottle of Jack Daniels in one night?"

Matt shrugged. "I guess. I wasn't counting the shots."

"What's gotten into you? What happened to your ministry?"

Matt slumped into the nearest chair and took a deep breath. He had established a ministry in prison and had joined a church after he got out. Since he couldn't practice law, he was going to study to be a minister so he could preach against materialism, which he considered to be man's greatest weakness. Initially when he started the Debt Relief Centers of Texas it had been the result of his and Lynn's desire to get rich quick so they could have anything money could buy. But along the way Matt realized the high price people paid for their greed. He had a lot of time to think about it in prison and decided that once he'd brought MidSouth Bank down he'd devote his life to turning people away from greed and materialism.

"I shut it down. It's a hopeless cause!"

"What do you mean? I thought you were visiting all the churches and raising a lot of money?"

14

"It worked for a while, but when my notoriety wore off, the big crowds dwindled and money dried up. Once I wasn't raising all that much the board of trustees told me I had to come up with some new ideas or they'd take me off the circuit. They said I was a good speaker but people got tired of hearing the same message."

"Well, that kind of makes sense."

There was a knock at the door. Matt got up and let the paramedics in. Rich reiterated to them all he knew about Candy's condition. They checked her vitals, put her on a gurney, and rolled her to the ambulance parked outside. Matt and Rich followed the ambulance to Richardson Medical Center. After checking in with the emergency room nurse, they took a seat and waited.

"So, when they asked you to come up with different material, you just gave up?" Rich asked.

"I wasn't accomplishing anything. The church wasn't interested in curbing greed or materialism. They were greedier than their congregations. All I heard about was how my message wasn't working anymore. Contributions were down and they couldn't have that."

Rich laughed. "That figures. No matter what line of work you're in it all ends up being about money."

"Not when Lynn and I were working with the Debt Relief Centers. I really felt like I was accomplishing something. And when I was plotting to bring MidSouth down I felt the same way."

"It's too bad you don't have your law license anymore. I've got a crusade for you."

"A crusade? What kind of crusade?" Matt asked.

"The mortgage industry. It's a fucking nightmare. People are getting screwed a dozen different ways and don't know it until it's too late. I must get a four or five calls a day from angry consumers who have been foreclosed or are about to be."

The door opened to the waiting room and a nurse came

out. "Is someone here with Candy Kane?"

Matt stood up. "Yes, that's me."

"You can go back. She's in room E216."

They got up and followed the nurse to Candy's room. She was groggy but awake. An IV hung from a hook attached to her bed, and a heart monitor was beeping beside her. Matt went over to her.

"Are you all right, Candy?" Matt asked gently.

She smiled faintly. "I think so."

"Why did you take the pills?" Matt asked.

"Oh. I had a terrible headache. The pills usually stop it."

"That's because Percodan has aspirin in it," the nurse said. "If you'd have just gotten an aspirin you would have been all right, but Percodan and alcohol don't mix. That's why you were vomiting blood. The combination of the Percodan and the Jack Daniels did a number on your stomach."

"Will she be all right?" Matt asked.

The nurse nodded. "Probably, but the doctor wants her to stay overnight so they can do some more testing."

Matt sighed, feeling greatly relieved.

"Okay, we are going to move her to a room now. So why don't you go to the third-floor waiting room? Her room number will be 324."

Matt nodded then leaned down and gave Candy a kiss. As an orderly was coming in to transport Candy to a room, they went back into the waiting room.

"Want to get something from the cafeteria?" Rich suggested. "It will be a while before they get Candy situated in her new room."

Matt nodded. "Sure, let's go."

The cafeteria wasn't busy, so it didn't take long for them to get a couple of sandwiches, potato chips, and soft drinks. After paying for the food they took a seat at a table.

"So, why are you out with a hooker?" Rich asked.

"She's an escort, not a hooker. She just goes out on dates.

16

Or she used to, anyway."

"Well, she was naked on your floor, so I would say she was more than an escort to you."

Matt nodded. "Yes, I've been a regular for quite a while. I don't like going places alone but I'm not really ready to date yet. It was a perfect situation."

"Right, but—"

"But after being with her a lot we became friends. She doesn't charge me anymore. We just hang out."

"But you have sex, too?" Rich noted.

Matt shrugged. "Sure. We both have our needs, but we're not in a committed relationship or anything."

With Rich's history with women he wasn't about to judge Matt's behavior, so he kept his mouth shut.

"Well, I'd better get home. Your mother will be worried. Can you take it from here?"

"Sure, thanks for checking up on me. If you hadn't shown up no telling what would have happened."

"Yeah. Well, I'm glad it wasn't more serious. Call your mother when you get a chance. She's worried about you."

They stood up and embraced, and Rich left. When he got home Erica and Ryan were anxiously awaiting his arrival. He filled them in on what had happened and his conversations with Matt.

"Is there any way we can get Matt's law license reinstated?" Ryan asked. "He needs to get back to practicing law."

"Yes, that would be the ideal solution. I could get him all the foreclosure work he could handle. Unfortunately, I've been so busy with bankruptcies and estate planning to take any of it in myself. You wouldn't be interested in that, would you?"

Ryan gave him a look. "Are you kidding? I don't know anything about real estate and I'm not interested in learning about it. I hated that class in law school."

Rich sighed. "Well, the only way we could get Matt's

license back is to appeal his conviction and get it set aside."

Ryan perked up. "Well, he was innocent. Couldn't we file an appeal and ask the court to reverse the conviction?"

Rich shrugged. "The problem is everyone knows he helped all those inmates get MidSouth credit cards. They didn't charge him with it since MidSouth was taken over by the feds and the conspiracy to kill Lynn came out."

"Still, it would be worth a shot. Don't you think?"

Rich nodded. "Sure, it's probably exactly what Matt needs right now. I'll call Matt's attorney, Bruce Pierson, tomorrow and ask him about it. But don't get your hopes up."

After Ryan left, Rich began to consider the possibility of getting Matt reinstated. It was a long shot but well worth the effort if there was any chance of success. The thought occurred to Rich that Senator Goss might even help out if he asked him. Senator Goss had been an ally in Matt's efforts to get Congress to do something about predatory lenders before Matt was sent to prison. For the first time in months Rich was feeling optimistic about the future. Would it be possible to have both his sons practicing law with him? Coleman & Sons PC. That had a nice ring to it. Somehow he had to make it happen.

Chapter 2
Intervention

On Monday Ryan went to Richardson Medical Center to see Matt. He found him asleep in the waiting room. He sat down beside him and shook his shoulder gently. Matt woke up with a start.

"What the—?" Matt exclaimed.

"Hey, big brother. Sorry to wake you, but I heard about your friend's accident. I was worried about you."

Matt sat up, rubbed his eyes, and looked at Ryan warily. "It's okay. It's almost visiting hour, so I had to wake up anyway."

"How is she? What's her name?"

"She's going to be okay. And you know her name is Candy Kane."

"Right. Candy Kane?" Ryan snickered.

Matt smiled. "It's not her real name. She keeps that a secret. It was her stage name when she was a stripper. She runs an escort service now—but there's no sex involved in her business."

"Except for you?"

"I'm not a client anymore and, yes, if we feel like it we have sex. So what? I'm not going to marry her."

"Does she know that?"

"Yes. We've had that conversation. She understands. She can't get married anyway. It would ruin her business."

Ryan nodded. "Okay, so Dad told me you quit the ministry. What's up with that?"

Matt shrugged. "I'm burned out. It was just bullshit. I wasn't accomplishing anything—other than raising money for the church coffers."

19

Unconscionable

"So . . . The church does good work, doesn't it?"

"I guess, but being a fund-raiser for the church isn't my idea of a career."

"Good. I never liked your ministry, no offense. It just wasn't you."

"Right. It was a good cover for a while and I even started believing myself for a while, but I just don't have my heart in it anymore."

"So, what now?" Ryan asked.

Matt shrugged and looked away. "I don't know."

"Well, Dad and I have an idea."

Matt looked back at Ryan. "I figured that's why you came by."

"Well, we're all worried about you."

Matt sighed. "You don't need to be. I'll figure things out."

"Uh-huh. Like you did last night?"

Matt sucked in a deep breath. "That was an accident."

"Right. But Candy may have died had Dad not come by."

"Okay!" Matt spat. "Just spit it out. What's your great plan for my life? I'd like to hear it, 'cause right now my life pretty much sucks."

Ryan hesitated. "Well. How about coming back to Dad's firm? It will be great—Coleman & Sons PC, Attorneys at Law. That was always Dad's dream, but he never told us. He wanted it to happen but he didn't want to force it on us."

Matt laughed. "That's your great idea? Give me a fucking break! You know that can't happen," he said angrily, tears welling in his eyes. His voice softened. "It would be nice but, as you know, I don't have a license anymore."

"Dad's talking to your lawyer today about getting an appeal started. He thinks it may be possible to set aside the conviction. If it is set aside, you'll be able to reapply for your license."

Matt sighed. "What about the credit card fraud? I've been

waiting for that hammer to fall for a long time."

"Well, if it was going to happen don't you think it would have already? I doubt any of the prisoners will rat you out."

"Some won't, but there will be at least one of them who will want to cut a deal to escape prosecution. You can bet on that."

"If the DA was anxious to indict you, that may be true. But I think they all feel sorry for you since you lost Lynn. I don't think they will ever come after you."

Matt took a deep breath and let it out slowly. "I hope you're right."

"So, are you on board with this?" Ryan asked hopefully.

Matt shrugged. "I guess. It's a waste of time, though. I'll never get my license back."

"Maybe not, but you should at least try. Dad said to report for work tomorrow."

"Tomorrow? Is he a magician or something?"

"No, he'll hire you on as a paralegal until you get licensed again."

"A paralegal." Matt chuckled. "Isn't that a kick in the nuts."

"Well, it's better than drinking yourself into oblivion," Ryan replied. "Anyway, Dad has some big crusade he wants to put you on. Apparently there will be a lot of research and investigation to do before you can start suing people. So, that will keep you busy for a while."

Matt chuckled. "What do you know about this crusade?"

"Not much. Something about mortgage servicing companies or some shit. I don't know."

"Yeah, he brought it up to me already. I'll check my calendar and see if I'm free tomorrow."

Ryan laughed. "Yeah, why don't you do that." He stood up to leave. "See you tomorrow, then?"

"Right . . . You want to meet Candy before you go?" Matt asked.

Ryan nodded. "Sure, that's really why I came. You don't think I came to see your ugly face, did you?"

Matt grinned, stood up, and pushed Ryan toward the door, causing him to stumble. "Hey, watch it!"

"Clumsy?" Matt chided, putting his arm around his brother. "Thanks for coming by, you little turd."

Inside Candy's room they found her eating lunch. Obviously in a good mood, she smiled when she saw them enter.

"Hey, there you are, and you brought the graduate," Candy said.

"Yes, that's right," Matt agreed. "Another attorney has been unleashed on the world. God forbid."

"Sorry I missed the graduation," Candy said. "A client held me up."

Ryan shrugged. "Well, you should have come to dinner with us anyway. My mom would have loved to meet you."

"She wanted to," Matt said. "I was the one who wanted to bail. I just didn't feel like facing Mom. You know how she can be."

"Right. Well, she knows everything now, so you won't have to explain anything to her."

"Good," Matt replied.

"So, tell Candy the good news," Ryan suggested.

Matt smiled. "Well, it appears I'm going to work for my father. He's got some big crusade he wants me to start working on. Mortgage servicing or something."

"That's wonderful," Candy said. "But I thought you couldn't practice law anymore?"

"I'll start out as a paralegal. You don't have to have a license for that."

"And we're looking into getting his conviction overturned," Ryan interjected.

Candy raised her eyebrows. "Wow. That would be wonderful."

"It's a long shot, believe me," Matt said dejectedly, "but

22

it can't hurt to try. It will keep me busy."

"That's good. . . . So, what kind of law will you be practicing, Ryan?" Candy asked.

"Criminal defense."

"Really? Huh. Well, I may need your services."

Ryan frowned. "How's that?"

"I run a dozen or so girls in the escort business, and every week it seems like one of them is getting picked up for prostitution. It's a bullshit charge. None of my girls have sex with their clients, but the police like to harass us anyway. I've got an attorney who usually gets the girls off without much trouble, but he's an asshole and I wouldn't mind dealing with someone I liked."

Ryan shrugged. "Works for me. I haven't passed the bar yet, but as soon as I do, I'd be happy to handle your cases for you."

"Excellent. Looking forward to working with you."

"Of course, Amanda won't like it," Matt interjected.

"Why not?" Ryan asked.

"Being around all those pretty girls all the time."

Ryan shrugged. "They're just escorts, I thought."

"But they'll be grateful escorts," Matt explained. "You'll be their hero. It will be quite a temptation."

Candy gave Matt a wry smile. Ryan raised his eyebrows. "Huh . . .Well, that's the kind of problem a man likes to have, right?"

Matt laughed. "Yeah, right."

When visiting hours were over Ryan said good-bye and left to go back to the office. He was in a good mood and couldn't wait to tell his father that Matt had accepted his offer. Not only had he convinced Matt to come back to work, he'd lined up his first client. Not a bad day's work.

Chapter 3
Insider

It was a hot day for this early in June. Rich was on his way to see Bruce Pierson, Matt's former criminal attorney. He had told him briefly what he wanted to talk about over the phone, and Bruce seemed intrigued but noncommittal. As he walked across the street from the parking lot that he usually used in this part of downtown Dallas, he wondered if he was being unrealistic in thinking Matt could get reinstated. He sighed as he pushed through the circular doorway into the thirty-four-story Bryan Tower Building, a magnificent light green reflective glass skyscraper. He took the odd elevator bank to the twenty-third floor and walked into the reception area of Bradley, Pierson & Jones LLP. The receptionist looked up.

"Good morning," she said.

"Hi. I'm here to see Bruce Pierson."

She nodded. "Yes, have a seat and I'll tell him you're here."

Rich took a seat and picked up the *People* magazine that was sitting on the coffee table in front of him. He leafed through it without seeing anything, his mind still focused on the upcoming meeting. A door opened and Bruce Pierson emerged.

"Rich," he said, extending his hand. Rich stood up and shook it energetically. "Come on back to my office," Bruce said.

They walked down a long corridor to the corner office. The office had a modernistic decor and a fabulous view north all the way to LBJ Freeway and beyond.

"So, how have you been?" Bruce asked.

"I'm doing fine. The bankruptcy business is booming, as usual."

"Yeah, I bet it is with all the credit the banks are throwing at people these days."

"Right."

"So, how is Matt? You said he's been a bit depressed lately."

"Yeah, he's been kind of drifting here lately so Ryan and I thought maybe we'd try to help him out."

Bruce shook his head. "I was completely devastated when Matt insisted he plead out on the bankruptcy fraud charges. I told him I thought we could beat them."

"I know. It wasn't your fault. I just wish Matt would have confided in us. He fell right into Frank Hill's trap."

"I was sick for months after Lynn and her sister were murdered. What a tragedy. I know how much Matt loved Lynn."

Rich nodded and looked away, trying to keep his composure. He'd held up pretty well during Matt's ordeal. He had to for Matt's sake, but after the conviction he fell apart and became so depressed that he had trouble focusing at work and spent hours just staring out the window.

"Right," Rich agreed. "Anyway. We want to look into getting the conviction set aside."

"Sure. I was expecting you to come in sooner, frankly," Pierson said. "With Hill's conviction of the three murders, that corroborates Matt's story that he was coerced into the plea deal."

"Yes, well, when Matt got out of prison I'm afraid all he had on his mind was taking down Hill and MidSouth Bank, and he wasn't worried about how many laws he broken to do it."

"Right," Pierson said solemnly.

"He was prepared to live outside the country if things hadn't worked out. Fortunately, things cooled down and he was able to come home."

"Well, you're right. If we file an appeal that will force the US attorney to look again at Matt's involvement in the credit card scam that led to MidSouth's failure, we'll force them to either prosecute Matt or close the investigation. It's a terrible crapshoot."

"I know, but there is really no other choice. If we do nothing Matt will never be able to practice law again, and that's why I think he's been so depressed."

"Well, it's his decision. I can get the appeal going right away."

"If I get Senator Goss to talk to the Justice Department, do you think that would help?"

"Actually, that's a good idea. Let him feel them out. Tell them Matt is thinking of appealing his conviction so he can practice law again, but there is no point in doing that if they have Matt under investigation on the credit card scams."

"Okay. I'll go see Senator Goss and see if he'll help us. I feel confident he will."

Rich left Pierson's office feeling optimistic. If Goss talked to the Justice Department they couldn't really discuss the case, but he could probably tell by the reception he got whether there was any danger of Matt being prosecuted. Either way that information would be invaluable to Matt.

When he got back to the office, Suzie, his secretary, advised him Shelly Simms was there to see him. Rich had noticed the woman in the reception area and wondered who she was. She was well dressed and middle-aged and seemed a bit uneasy. Rich went out to greet her.

"Ms. Simms?"

She nodded, grabbed her purse, and stood up.

"I'm Rich Coleman. Come on back."

Simms followed him back to his office, and Rich motioned for her to take a seat in a side chair. Suzie stepped in and asked if she would like water, coffee, or a soft drink. She declined.

"So, it's a scorcher out there today," Rich noted to break the ice.

"Yes. I can't believe it's already over a hundred degrees."

"I know. Wait till August rolls around."

"Isn't that the truth?"

"So, what can I do for you?" Rich asked.

Shelly took a long breath. "Well, I'm afraid I'm going to have to file bankruptcy."

"Oh, really? Personal or business?"

"Personal. I got laid off about six months ago and I haven't been able to find a new job."

Rich sighed. "Well, the job market's kind of tough right now. What did you do before you were let go?"

"I was a customer service manager for North American Servicing," Shelly advised.

Rich nodded. He knew North American Servicing very well. They were one of the largest mortgage servicing companies in the country and the target of many governmental investigations into their alleged illegal practices. He'd heard horror stories about them from a number of his clients.

"Oh, I see. So, why did they let you go?"

"The two major partners in the business got at odds and one of them, Lucius Jones, left and set up a competitive company, Reliable Mortgage Servicing. I had been in Lucius's division when the split up took place, so I was let go. Lucius offered me a position in his new company, but he's a jerk so I didn't accept the offer."

"A jerk?" Rich chuckled.

"Yeah. Among other things."

Rich smiled. "So, you didn't want to be associated with him?"

"No. Walter Savage was his partner and while they were together he kept a leash on him, but now that he's on his own there's no telling what he'll do."

"What was the cause of the split up?" Rich asked curiously.

"You've probably heard about the problems mortgage companies are having with their paperwork these days?" Shelly asked.

"Right. They are buying and selling mortgages so often they don't always transfer the liens properly."

"Exactly. So, several of the big lenders came to NAS and asked them to clean up the mess for them."

"Right."

"But that would require going back and creating a bunch of documents and backdating them."

Rich nodded.

"So Walter refused, because he's not going to be a party to fraud, right?"

"Uh-huh."

"But Lucius wanted to do it because there's lots of money in it."

"I see."

"So, these mortgage lenders told Lucius that if he splits off they'll give him all their business if he can solve their paperwork problems."

Rich shook his head. "Well, it sounds like you made the right move. You wouldn't want to get involved in any of that nonsense. I can't believe the mortgage lenders think they will be able to get away with blatant fraud."

"Lucius has promised them he can handle it very discreetly."

Rich rolled his eyes. "Well, he may get away with it for a while, but eventually he'll get caught."

Shelly nodded. "Anyway, I'm way behind on my bills and need to get a fresh start."

Rich nodded and pulled out a bankruptcy packet. He started working on a legal services contract while Shelly filled out the bankruptcy questionnaire. Before she left he gave her some checklists to fill out and an instruction sheet explaining everything he would need to file her case. She agreed to put it all together and bring it back in a few days.

Rich pondered what Shelly had told him. He couldn't believe some of the largest mortgage lenders in the country would be involved in outright fraud. The documents Lucius Jones would be creating would be used in court to prove up foreclosures or as proofs of claims in bankruptcies. Every time one of those documents were filed somebody would be breaking the law. He couldn't wait to tell Matt that he'd met someone who'd actually had verified what had been rumored in legal circles for months. He found Matt setting up in his new office.

"Hey. How's it coming?" Rich asked.

"Okay. It feels strange sitting behind a big desk again. I got used to working on a table in the prison library."

"Well, that's all behind you now. You can start living like an attorney again."

"So, how did it go with Pierson?" Matt asked as he sat down in his new executive chair.

Rich took a seat and leaned forward. "He had an interesting idea," Rich told him and then explained about their plan to have Senator Goss feel out the Justice Department before filing his appeal.

Matt sighed. "Senator Goss is a wimp. I doubt he'll do it."

"Well, it won't hurt to ask, will it?"

Matt nodded. "I guess not. . . . But I'm not going to get my hopes up. I'll work on your crusade because it sounds interesting and I don't have anything else to do, but if I don't get my license back you'll have to hire someone else to put it in motion."

"I know. But I'm confident that won't be necessary."

"I hope not. So, tell me more about it. What do you want me to do?"

Rich smiled and leaned back. "Okay. Well, in the past year or so I've been barraged with calls from people in trouble with their mortgages. I've put a lot of them in chapter 13 to stop pending foreclosures, but most of these people never should have been given a mortgage."

"How's that?"

"For the last five or ten years lenders have been giving out mortgages to anyone with a pulse and with no money down. Then they sell the mortgages to securitized trusts and make a killing in the process."

"A securitized trust?"

"Yeah, a pool of mortgages administered by a trustee. Everyone in the pool shares in the profit or losses of all the mortgages in the pool. It evens out the risk."

"Hmm."

"Now, due to the recession, a lot of these new home owners can't afford to pay their mortgages, and home loan defaults are at an all-time high."

Matt nodded. "That makes sense with unemployment at ten percent."

"Exactly. So, everyone loses if there is a foreclosure. The consumer loses his house. The mortgage companies take a beating financially when a house is foreclosed. And the government loses if it has guaranteed the loan. Plus every time there is a foreclosure sale in a neighborhood all the home values do down. If home values go down pretty soon you have a bunch of mortgage loans that are underwater, which means the home owners can't sell or refinance them."

"Okay, so what can we do about it?"

"Well, the government is putting a lot of pressure on lenders to offer forbearance agreements, short sales, or modifications to cure defaults. Now the mortgage companies are so swamped with customers wanting to take advantage of these programs the servicers can't handle the volume, so instead of ramping up their operations to deal with it, they are just going through the motions to satisfy the government with no intention of helping the home owners."

Matt grunted. "Sounds like your typical greedy lender."

"Unfortunately. So, the moment I put the word out that we're taking mortgage cases we'll be inundated with clients and can start suing the mortgage companies and their servicers."

Unconscionable

Matt shook his head. "Sounds like fun. I wouldn't mind kicking a little mortgage company ass, but foreclosures aren't illegal as I recall."

"No. Not if they do them right and don't cut any corners. But with the volume we're looking out right now there are lots of mistakes being made. Plus, they are luring clients into a false sense of security by letting them fill out modification applications when they know the modifications will never be approved."

"Well, we can't let them get away with that," Matt said with a grin.

Rich smiled. "My thoughts as well. Anyway, I got some new dirt on the mortgage industry today. A client came in for a bankruptcy, and it turns out she worked for NAS."

"NAS? Is that a mortgage company?"

"No, North American Servicing. It's probably the largest mortgage servicer in the country and, apparently, some mortgage lenders recently came to them wanting help with some paperwork deficiencies."

Rich told Matt what Shelly had told him.

"Wow! That could generate some serious punitive damages if we could prove they were filing fraudulent documents with the court."

"Yes. If we file a lawsuit and they respond with fraudulent documents, they'll be in serious trouble."

"It's too bad your lady didn't go to work for Lucius Jones. She could be a spy for us."

Rich thought about that. "That's true. She is unemployed. I wonder if we could convince her to take the job that was offered her."

Matt's eyes lit up. "Oh, my God! Could you imagine what we could do to them with a mole inside their organization?"

Rich nodded. "Yeah, but there would be nothing in it for Shelly."

"We can pay her a percentage of each verdict," Matt suggested.

32

"No," Rich objected. "That wouldn't be ethical, and if that leaked out, her credibility would go down the toilet."

"Maybe she'd do it just to put the asshole out of business."

"Perhaps. I'll discuss it with her and see what she says."

Rich could see that he'd piqued Matt's interest in his mortgage company crusade. He knew Matt would spend endless hours now learning everything he could about his enemy. Matt was relentless at research and preparation and once the game began, God help his opponent. Rich chuckled to himself at the thought of it.

A few days later Shelly returned with her paperwork to complete her bankruptcy. Rich went through it with her and together they finished up her schedules and statement of financial affairs. When they were done Rich broached the idea of her becoming an informant.

"Listen. We are about to start taking mortgage cases. The demand is pretty high and my son Matt is coming back to the firm to handle them."

Shelly smiled. "That should be a pretty lucrative business."

"I think so, particularly if what you told me the other day is true."

"It is, believe me."

"You know, you could do the world a big favor by helping us nail Lucius Jones and putting his company out of business."

Shelly shrugged. "Sure, but I don't have any direct knowledge of this. Everything I know is hearsay."

"That's why you should take the job he offered you. That way you can keep us apprised of what's going on."

Shelly just stared at him. "You want me to be a spy?"

"Exactly. You hate the asshole, you said. So, help us put him out of business."

"What's in it for me?"

"Well, unfortunately we can't pay you anything or you'd lose all credibility. But I'm sure Jones will pay you handsomely, and you need a job."

Shelly laughed. "So, he'll be paying me to spy on his operation and won't even know it?"

"Exactly," Rich replied.

"What if the feds come after him? I might get prosecuted."

"If that looks like a possibility you can turn state's evidence against him and get immunity. I'll vouch for you—tell them you were trying to help us take him down."

Shelly took a deep breath. "I'll have to think about it. If Lucius found out what I was doing he'd probably have me killed."

Rich nodded. "You're right. So, don't do it unless you really want to. We'll nail the bastard anyway; we just thought you might want to help us accelerate the process."

"No, it's a great idea. Just let me sleep on it. I just don't know if I could pull off the charade. I'm not such a great actress."

Rich felt good after Shelly left. He knew she really wanted to take Jones down and just needed time to get up the courage to take the job. He felt a little guilty, though. What if she was discovered and got hurt? Would Jones really kill her if he found out what she was up to? He finally decided they'd just have to be very careful so he wouldn't find out.

Chapter 4
The Manuscript

A week after graduation the bar review course began. Ryan left his office early and picked up Amanda on his way to the Crown Plaza Suites at Park Central where the course was being held. A rare cold front for this time of year had passed through Dallas, and there was a cool breeze from the north. Amanda didn't know what was going on, but Ryan seemed oddly cheerful in light of the fact that he was facing three grueling hours of bar review. She had asked him about it, but he had failed to provide any explanation other than it was a beautiful day.

The bar review course was as intense and unpleasant as they had anticipated, but somehow they got through it. Ryan suggested they have dinner at the hotel's Café Biarritz, because he was famished. Amanda agreed so they took their study materials out to the car and then returned to the restaurant. It was a Monday night so it wasn't crowded. The waiter brought them some bread and Ryan ordered a bottle of wine.

"So, that was a lot of fun," Amanda said, rolling her eyes.

"Actually, it was better than class. At least everything they went over was straightforward and didn't require any interpretation. I hate it when a professor throws three or four different explanations of the same issue and you have to figure out which one is correct."

"None of them are correct. That's the problem," Amanda complained. "The courts often disagree on the same issues."

"So, what did you do today?" Ryan asked.

Unconscionable

"Oh. I checked a book out of the library called *Literary Marketplace*. It lists all the literary agencies in the country. I'm researching which ones I want to approach for a job."

"Are there a lot of them?"

"Hundreds, but only about ten percent of them would be worth working for."

"So, are you going to call them or write letters?"

"Letters at first and then follow up with a phone call. I could go to work for the agency I interned with last year here in Dallas but they are rather small."

"I didn't know you interned with an agency last year. What agency was it?"

"The Colson Agency. Brenda Colson is a family friend. She said to come see her after I graduated, but she only has a few major authors. Most of her clients are midlist. I wouldn't make a lot of money there."

"What does a literary agent get paid, anyway?" Ryan asked.

"Usually fifteen percent of what the author gets."

"How much does an author get?"

"An author will get a royalty anywhere from ten to twenty percent of net revenue."

"So, if the author gets fifteen percent, you get fifteen percent of his fifteen percent, right?"

Amanda nodded. "It's not much so you don't want to represent too many midlist authors. The real money comes from movie deals and other subsidiary rights."

"It doesn't sound all that lucrative to me," Ryan said.

"If you represent a prime client he or she might get a million-dollar advance, so you'd get $150,000."

"Right, but how many contracts like that are you likely to place each year?"

"Probably not that many."

"I'll stick to practicing law, I think."

The waiter brought them their wine and took their orders.

Ryan ordered the Tuscany steak and Amanda got seafood pasta.

"So, most of the agencies are in New York, right?" Ryan asked.

Amanda sighed deeply. "Yes. I'm afraid so."

"What if I don't want you to go to New York?"

Amanda gave Ryan a hard look. "Are you telling me not to go?"

Ryan shrugged. "Yes. Don't go. Go to work for your friend. If you don't make as much money it won't matter. Between the two of us we'll have plenty of money."

"So, what are you saying?"

"Move in with me. We'll pool our resources and you won't have to be worried about money while you're looking for a potential best-selling author to represent."

"So, what if I want more?" Amanda said cautiously.

Ryan shrugged. "More what? More money?"

"No. More than just a roommate."

"Oh. Well, we'll probably end up getting married eventually. I can't imagine myself with anyone else but you. But the time isn't quite right. We need to wait a couple of years and get established in our professions."

"Why?" Amanda asked. "If we're meant to be together why not get married now?"

"A wedding would be too much pressure on us right now. We should do it when our lives are more stable and we know what we want."

Ryan's words didn't sting her as much as they should have. Most men had difficulty with commitment while women usually knew what they wanted. But she wasn't sure about Ryan, either. She liked him a lot, but did she love him? She wasn't sure. Her career was important to her, and most literary agents worked in New York.

Amanda sighed. "You're probably right. No need to rush things. We have plenty of time."

"Don't worry. I'm not going to bail on you down the

road. I love you," Ryan said earnestly.

"You do?"

Ryan laughed. "Isn't it obvious?"

"Not always."

"Well, I do love you and that's not going to change."

Amanda struggled not to pledge her love to Ryan. It would have been the natural thing to do, but she couldn't bring herself to do it. Luckily, Ryan hadn't noticed or didn't want to pressure her into saying it. Did that mean she didn't love him? She didn't know what it meant, only that she was glad she hadn't said it. But was she willing to postpone her career for a while and move in with Ryan? She guessed she owed him that much. She'd give it a year, she decided, to discover if what she felt for Ryan was love or infatuation. Being in New York wasn't absolutely necessary. At least in the beginning. She was young and didn't want to make any mistakes, so she'd be patient. Life was too short to be consumed with regrets.

"Okay. If you're sure you want to support me while I build up my client list."

Ryan nodded. "Hey. My father has a manuscript. It's a true crime. The story of how he met my mother and when she was tried for murder."

Amanda perked up. "Seriously, he wrote a book about it?"

"Yeah. I haven't read it. My mother won't let me. I don't know why. It's been over twenty-five years since it all happened. My mother was found not guilty by reason of temporary insanity although she claims she was innocent."

"Your mother temporarily insane? I seriously doubt it."

"I know. It's a stretch but I guess she put on quite a performance. Some psychiatrist prepped her. My grandmother even testified."

"Oh, I'd love to read it. Do you think she'd let me?"

"Not likely, but I know where it is—up in the attic in her cedar chest. You could borrow it and I doubt anybody would notice it was missing."

Amanda's eyes lit up. "Let's go get it."

"Right now?"

"Yes. Now that you've told me about it I won't be able to sleep until I read it."

Ryan laughed and then became silent while he thought about it. "We'll need an excuse to go up in the attic. You'd like to see my college yearbooks, wouldn't you?"

"Absolutely. Let's go."

"Okay. That will be our cover story if my mom asks."

"Sure."

Amanda was ecstatic about the manuscript. Ryan had told her the story earlier and it had been fascinating. She prayed Rich was a good writer. Even if it needed work she could help him rewrite it and then it could be submitted to the editors that Brenda knew. True crime was very popular, and if the book did well she could pitch it to Hollywood for a movie. Amanda could barely contain her excitement as they pulled up in front of Ryan's parents' home, got out of the car, and went inside.

"Hello!" Ryan said as they walked in the door.

Erica came in from the kitchen and smiled. "Hey. Come in. I'm so glad you stopped by. I have a peach pie in the oven."

Ryan grinned. "Good timing?"

"So, how was the bar review class, Amanda?" Erica asked.

"Scary. They covered so much material I could hardly keep up."

Erica smiled sympathetically. "So, did you two come to visit or do you have something on your mind?"

"Amanda is moving in with me," Ryan announced.

Erica raised her eyebrows. "Wow. That's wonderful."

Amanda shrugged. "He's too cheap to marry me."

"No," Ryan said, sounding hurt. "That's not true. We'll get married down the road. It's just premature right now."

A bell rang in the kitchen.

Unconscionable

"Oh, there's my pie," Erica said.

"We're going up into the attic," Ryan advised. "Amanda wants to look at my college yearbooks."

Erica nodded. "Okay, I'll have your pie ready when you finish."

Amanda gave Ryan a guilty look. He motioned for her to follow him. They climbed up the stairway, went down a short hallway, and stopped. Ryan reached up, pulled down a folding staircase, and began climbing up. Amanda followed him. The 14' x 18' attic was cluttered with dusty boxes, old furniture, and rolls of carpeting. Ryan pointed to a cedar chest at one end.

"There it is."

Ryan pushed away a cobweb and walked quickly to the box with Amanda on his heels. He opened it and breathed in the strong cedar scent. Inside were a number of quilts, some baby clothes, and what appeared to be a box of white typing paper. Ryan picked up the box and handed it to Amanda. "Here you go. Knock yourself out."

Amanda took the box reverently and opened it. Inside were 220 single-spaced, typed pages of *The Pact* by Richard Coleman. She closed the box and smiled up at Ryan gleefully.

"This is so exciting. I can't wait to start reading it."

"Take it out to the car while I keep my mother busy."

Amanda nodded and they got up to leave. "What about the yearbooks?"

"Right," Ryan said, looking around the room. He spotted a bookcase, went over to it, and took out two yearbooks. While Ryan was doing that Amanda went to close the cedar chest and noticed an envelope. She picked it up and read a note on the front of it: *Revisions to The Pact by Richard Coleman*. Figuring it was changes Rich wanted to make in the manuscript if it were retyped, she slipped the envelope into the box.

As Ryan had suggested, Amanda took the manuscript and put it their car and then came back inside. When she walked into the kitchen Erica was just setting two pieces of peach pie on the kitchen table.

"You want coffee or a soft drink?" Erica asked.

"Coffee," Amanda replied.

"Me, too," Ryan agreed.

"Who were you looking up in the yearbook?" Erica asked.

"Ah. Nobody in particular. She just wanted to read what people wrote about me."

Erica laughed. "Yeah. There were a few gems in there, if I remember correctly."

"Where's Dad?" Ryan asked.

"He went to a Rangers game with Joe. He won't be back until after eleven."

They talked while they ate their pie, but Ryan could tell Amanda was anxious to leave so she could start reading the manuscript. Just as soon as they'd finished eating he stood up.

"Well, thanks for the pie, Mom. We've got to hit the road. We need to get a couple of hours of studying in before we go to bed."

Erica got up and started cleaning off the table. "Well, come by anytime. It was nice to see both of you. Don't study too hard. You need your sleep."

Ryan leaned over and gave his mother a kiss on the cheek. She smiled and gave him a hug. Twenty minutes later Ryan dropped Amanda off at her apartment.

"You want me to come in?" Ryan asked.

"No. I won't be good company. I plan to read a good chunk of the manuscript tonight."

"Why? What's the rush?"

"I'm excited. If it's good maybe your dad can be my first client."

Ryan sighed. "Well, good luck talking him into publishing it."

"If I negotiate a big advance, how can he refuse?"

"I don't know. I'm just saying. Don't get your hopes up."

Unconscionable

Amanda kissed Ryan good night and then went inside. She put the manuscript on the coffee table in front of her sofa and opened the box. After lifting out a handful of pages she began reading. Several pages into the manuscript she was hooked and didn't stop reading until she was finished at 4:03 a.m. She stood up and stretched, knocking the box off the sofa. The envelope with the revisions fell to the floor, and when she shuffled her feet to bend down and pick up the pages she accidentally kicked the envelope under the sofa and out of sight. Bending down awkwardly, she retrieved the box and carefully placed the manuscript back in it.

She yawned and looked at her watch. With only a few hours of sleep she didn't know how she'd make it through the next day, but she didn't care. She was sure *The Pact* would be a best seller and now all she had to do was convince Rich Coleman to let her represent him. She felt confident that with Ryan's help he wouldn't refuse. *But why hasn't he already published it? It doesn't make any sense. He has to let me find a publisher. He just has to. I won't take no for an answer.*

Chapter 5
Unconscionable

Matt sat at his desk and began reading with only mild interest some materials Rich had given him about the mortgage crisis. Real estate had never been something that appealed to him much. He had taken basic property law at SMU but it seemed so mundane and boring that he had learned just enough to pass the course and move on to more exciting things like personal injury where an attorney could make some serious bucks. Unfortunately, tort reform in Texas had made a personal injury practice less lucrative, so Matt began searching for something else. That's when he and Lynn discovered the potential of a bankruptcy practice in a credit-driven economy. It had worked well—too well, in retrospect.

From his reading he learned that home mortgages were now bought and sold like stocks and bonds. That meant the notes and deeds of trust had to be standardized so that they could fit into a portfolio and be sold in bulk. The problem with this practice was the effect it had on the mortgagor or consumer. Often these loans would be transferred between different investors several times a year and new servicers would be appointed to collect the mortgage payments and make sure the property was properly insured and the taxes paid. Of course, each time a new servicer came into the picture there was a new opportunity for error in the accounting of the loan.

Matt learned that trading in mortgage loans was so lucrative that the mortgage companies had drastically lowered their minimum requirements to be a home owner in order to increase their loan portfolios and their profits. This seemed good for the consumer since it meant a family could get into a new home with no money down, greatly reduced personal income requirements, and only modest credit. It was good for the construction industry, too, because it meant increased housing starts, greater sales of lumber and building materials, and more jobs. It seemed like everybody profited, so Matt wondered how there could be a crisis.

The intercom squawked, and Suzie advised him that a new client had arrived for a consultation and that his father wanted him to join them. Grabbing a legal pad, he got up and walked briskly to the conference room. He walked in and observed a young woman in her late twenties shuffling through a large stack of letters and documents. She looked upset and profoundly sad.

"Matt, this is Cindy Sharp."

Cindy nodded but didn't get up. Matt took a seat next to Rich and started taking notes on his legal pad.

"Okay," Rich said. "You said over the phone that your husband recently committed suicide."

"Yes, we had the funeral last week."

"I'm very sorry. Did I understand you to say that you blamed his suicide on your mortgage company?"

Matt looked up in surprise, his interest piqued.

"Yes, Reliable Mortgage Servicing. They took over from North American Servicing, our original servicer."

"So, how did they cause your husband's suicide?"

"They promised not to foreclose, but it was a lie. They kicked us out of our house, removed all our furniture, and left it all out on the front lawn."

"Really?"

"Yes. Tony got very angry and attacked one of the constables who was taking stuff out of the house. They arrested him, took him to jail, and charged him with assaulting a police officer. He was so humiliated by the foreclosure and the arrest that he wouldn't even let me visit him while he was in jail—said he just wanted to find a hole and crawl in it."

Matt grimaced in disbelief. "Wow, I can't believe they arrested him."

"Well, they did and when I got word he was being released I came down to the county jail, but they'd already let him out and he was gone when I got there. They found him that same afternoon back at our empty house hanging by the neck from the staircase."

Matt looked at Cindy in horror. "Oh, my God!"

Rich shook his head. "How did he get in?"

Cindy started to sob. "He broke a pane of glass out of the back door and unlocked it. Then he went upstairs, tied a noose around his neck, tied the other end to the railing on the stairs, and then jumped off."

Matt felt a chill go down his spine.

Rich got up and retrieved a box of tissues for Cindy.

"So, who found him?" Matt asked.

"Ronald Goddard, the bastard who evicted us from our home. I hope he rots in hell!"

"Somebody from the mortgage company?"

"No. The real estate agent they hired to evict us."

Matt nodded.

"So your home was recently foreclosed," Rich continued.

"Yes," Cindy replied. "Just last month."

"Okay. Why don't you start from the beginning. Tell me when you first got behind on your mortgage."

"Tony, my husband, was a bricklayer for Arrow Construction Company. He worked for them for fifteen years before they filed bankruptcy last year. As you probably know, there hasn't been any new construction in this area for a couple of years."

"Right," Rich acknowledged. "The real estate market has pretty much collapsed."

"So, he had to go on unemployment, but that's only about a third of his normal pay. I'm a schoolteacher and my pay isn't enough to support the family. We have three children under

45

seven."

Rich shook his head and Matt continued to take notes.

"We had to cut our expenses way back to make ends meet, and we were doing okay until Tony's unemployment ran out. Then we began to get behind on our bills."

"So, that's when you got behind on your mortgage payments?" Rich asked.

"No. We got behind on our credit cards but we kept the house note current. What happened was our mortgage company, North American Servicing, sold our note to Reliable Mortgage Servicing—they call themselves RMS on their letterhead. We got a notice to make our payments to RMS but we had already sent the payment that month to North American. We paid by money order so we couldn't stop payment or anything."

"Okay. So, what did you do?" Rich asked.

"I called North American and told them what had happened and they said not to worry about it, as they would forward the money to RMS."

"But that didn't happen?" Rich said, shaking his head knowingly. He'd heard this story time and again. It was ridiculous how the mortgage servicers treated people. *They should know that when they take over a loan and the note is a month late it's probably their fault, yet they immediately come down on the consumer and treat him like a deadbeat.*

"No. In fact we immediately started getting late notices and telephone calls claiming we were a month behind."

"So, what did you do?"

"We called North American again, and they acted like they'd never heard from us before. We had to start all over again and explain what had happened. It was so frustrating I could have screamed. I told them that we had sent our payment to them and they were supposed to forward it, but RMS hadn't gotten it yet. So, they checked their computers and finally acknowledged that they had received the check but that the funds hadn't been remitted to RMS yet. When I asked them why, they had no explanation but assured me the payment would go out the following day."

"Okay, so what happened next?" Rich asked.

"We kept getting late notices and each time they'd charge us a late fee. Then we got a notice that they had paid our property taxes and were increasing our house payments."

"Why did they do that?" Matt asked.

"I don't know. We've always paid it in the past when we got our income tax refund. But they said since our account was delinquent they assumed we wouldn't have the money to pay the property taxes so they paid it for us. That meant now we owed a payment of $1,212 plus one-twelfth of the property tax amount, or $1,572 per month."

"So, when you got your income tax return why weren't you able to get caught up?" Matt asked.

Cindy sighed. "That's when Tony was diagnosed with prostate cancer and had to have surgery right away. He was out of commission six weeks. During that time I had to put the kids in after-school care. Between that expense and the deductibles on Tony's treatment I missed another house payment."

Matt shook his head. "Boy. Talk about bad luck."

Cindy nodded. "I was at wits' end about missing a house payment, so I called them and explained the situation. They passed me around for a while until I talked to a Joan Londry of the modification department. She said they had a hardship program for people in situations like ours and she didn't see why I wouldn't be eligible for it.

"She said the way the program worked was they would take the delinquency and tack it on to the end of the note so once the modification took place I would be current and only responsible for regular monthly payments. I was so relieved because that was exactly what I needed.

"So, when they sent me the paperwork, I filled it out and sent it in along with other documents they wanted. They said it would take thirty days to process and that I didn't need to make any mortgage payments while the modification was being considered."

"Let me guess," Rich said. "You didn't hear from them about the modification within thirty days?"

"No, so I called them and it was like I had never talked to them before. They said they couldn't find my modification application, but not to worry because they would note in the computer that a modification was in process. So, this time when I sent them my mortgage modification package I sent it by FedEx and tracked it to make sure they got it. Then, just to be sure, I called them and they confirmed that they had the application and supporting materials.

"A week later I was shocked and dismayed when I got a letter from an attorney advising me that I was sixty days past due on the mortgage, had an escrow shortage, and that they were considering accelerating my note and foreclosing. Tony went absolutely crazy when he saw the letter. He was recovering from surgery and already a mental wreck. This undid him."

"I can imagine," Matt said, shaking his head.

"He was angry at first, then became depressed, and finally quit talking. He'd just sit on the sofa all day with a somber look on his face. He quit shaving, hardly spoke to the children, and would only get up to go to the bathroom and go to bed. I wanted him to see a psychiatrist but he refused. I told him he had more time to deal with the mortgage company than I did, so he should call them, but he didn't. When I finally found time to call them myself a man named Ahmad Sheik said not to worry about the attorney letter as it was just routine. He said the computer sent any account over sixty days to their attorneys automatically but as long as they were processing a modification, they wouldn't foreclose.

"By this time I didn't trust them, so I asked for something in writing. In response I got a form letter acknowledging the receipt of my modification package and stating that as long as it was being processed they would not foreclose. Obviously, this letter eased my concerns and I put the foreclosure out of my mind, concentrating then on getting Tony out of bed and functioning normally again.

"Another few weeks went by and, not hearing anything, I called the modification department again and, for the third time, they acted like I had never called them. I asked for a supervisor and a Lois Ross came on the line. She said they had no record of my modification application. When she said that, I was so outraged I could hardly breathe. I told her I had a FedEx tracking number showing the package had been received and RMS's own confirmation number acknowledging receipt. But that didn't matter to her. She insisted they didn't have it and asked me to send it in again. I was flabbergasted at this, but I had no choice but to do as she requested.

"The next day I faxed the packet to them and got a confirmation that it had been received. Later that day when I got the mail I noticed there was a certified mail notice. The notice scared me but it was impossible for me to get to the post office until the next morning. When I finally opened the certified envelope I discovered it was a default letter and a notice of trustee's sale. When I got back home I immediately called the supervisor, Lois Ross, who I had talked to the day before, and she acknowledged that she had the paperwork and not to worry about the foreclosure notice. She assured me the modification application would stop the foreclosure."

"But it didn't?" Rich interjected.

"No. Several weeks later Tony noticed a man taking photographs of our house. That upset him, so he confronted the man, who identified himself as Simon Artis and told Tony that RMS had hired him to do an appraisal of the property. When he asked him why they would do that, he advised him that our house had been foreclosed and the RMS was putting the property on the market for sale."

"Jesus!" Matt said. "I can't believe they did that to you."

"It happens all the time," Rich replied. "I told you most

mortgage servicers are totally incompetent and don't care about their customers. Their only concern is to maximize the fees they can charge the mortgage lender."

Matt just shook his head in anger. "So, what did your husband do then?"

"He told them we had a modification in progress and that they'd promised not to foreclose. Artis just laughed at him and said we had ten days to get out or they'd go to the justice of the peace and file an eviction suit."

"How did Tony react to that?" Rich asked.

"He told the guy that if anybody set foot on our property he'd shoot them."

"Was he serious?"

"No. He doesn't own a gun. Tony wouldn't hurt a soul, but he was very upset and worried about what was going to happen to us. We had no money and if we were evicted we'd be out on the street. We have relatives but they are out of state and I'd lose my job if we left Dallas."

"So, What did you do?" Matt asked.

"I called Lois at RMS again and asked her why they had foreclosed when we had a deal. She told me to send them a letter explaining what had happened and asking for them to set aside the foreclosure sale."

"So, did you do it?"

"It seemed like a colossal waste of time, but I did what she suggested. Unfortunately, they still filed the eviction suit and set it for hearing in ten days. At the hearing we told the judge what had happened, but he said his hands were tied and gave us seventy-two hours to get out of the house."

Matt couldn't believe what he was hearing. He realized now the mortgage lenders were just as greedy and underhanded as the credit card companies that he had been up against before he went to prison. The more he heard the angrier he became.

Cindy continued. "We slept that night at the Kamona Motel. It was a really sleazy place but it was cheap. The next day when we went to the house to start packing we found it padlocked. We called Simon Artis, but only got his voice mail. We slept another few days at the motel, but the fourth night we were out of money and slept in the park. On the fifth day we went by the house and the constables were there removing everything and placing it in the yard. When Tony saw them throwing our stuff out on the grass he became outraged and started yelling at the constables and getting in their faces. They told him to back off, but instead he took a swing at one of them, and they arrested him.

"The kids and I slept in the park again that night. In the morning I took them to school and then went to work. Later that day I got a call from someone at the jail informing me that they were letting Tony out and that I should come pick him up. When I got there he was gone. He hadn't waited for me. I drove around looking for him, but I never thought of going back to our house. The police called me in the late afternoon and told me Tony was dead."

"Did he leave a suicide note?"

"Yes. He apologized to me and the kids for letting us down and said we were better off with him dead."

Matt looked at Rich and then at Cindy. "I can't wait to sue those bastards," Matt said angrily.

"Do you think we have a case?" Cindy asked.

"Yes. I can think of several legal theories that should work—unfair debt collection, breach of contract, and fraud."

Cindy nodded. "Good. I want them to pay!"

Rich explained the standard contingency fee contract that stipulated that if they settled the case without filing a lawsuit they got 25 percent of the recovery, 33 percent if they had to try the case, and 50 percent if the case was appealed after trial. Cindy thought that was fair and signed the contract. Matt said he'd start working on a petition immediately and when it was ready he'd have her come back in to make sure he had the facts correct before they filed it. After Cindy had left, Rich asked Matt what he thought about the case.

"I can't believe how she was treated. It's so outrageous; it's hard to believe it really happened the way she said it did."

"Oh, I'm sure RMS will have an entirely different story, but I'd bet on Cindy's version," Rich said.

When Matt got back to his research into the mortgage crisis he found himself much more interested and focused. He wanted desperately to make RMS pay for Tony Sharp's death. What they had done to Cindy and her family was unconscionable and he vowed to do whatever it took make them pay.

Chapter 6
Selling Her Soul

Shelly Simms, a trim brunette, was stunningly attractive and boys were always trying to flirt with her, but she was more interested in personal achievement than sexual gratification. Because she spurned these advances she had a reputation of being stuck-up and conceited. Her attitude can be explained by the competitive environment in which she was raised. Her father was a colonel in the United States Marines Corps stationed at Camp Pendleton, California, her mother a registered nurse working the ER at Sharp Memorial Hospital in San Diego, and her twin elder brothers had been accomplished athletes. Consequently, Shelly had to fight for attention and lived for any opportunity to outshine her brothers. Since they were two years older than her that opportunity didn't come often, but when it did she was equal to the task. In practical terms, however, what this meant was she was always at the top of her class whether it be sports or academics.

Although her father had pushed her toward a military career she resisted, having had enough of the migrant life of a military brat. Instead she opted for a business career and got her MBA from the University of Dallas. She liked San Diego, but by the time she graduated her parents had moved to Quantico, Virginia, and her brothers were in medical school in Chicago. So, she interviewed in Dallas and landed a job as a loan processor with North American Servicing in their Dallas offices.

Being intelligent and quite competent, she climbed the ranks at NAS quickly and in less than five years found herself as loan acquisitions manager. It was in this position that she met and got to know the two partners of NAS, Lucius Jones and Walter Savage. The two partners were the exact opposite of each other. Walter was older, low-key, and conservative while Lucius was aggressive and ruthless and a compulsive gambler. Since Walter had put up the money for the venture he had a 51 percent majority in voting rights. This worked pretty well as Lucius was never happy and always looking for ways to improve the bottom line, but Walter was there to block the more outlandish schemes Lucius was constantly conjuring up.

It was when the mortgage crisis came to a head that it became apparent that Lucius and Walter could no longer work together. It wasn't unusual for the two of them to argue a lot, but the situation had become unbearable. Liberal lending practices had finally caught up with the industry and foreclosures were at an all-time high. If this wasn't enough, many lenders woke up one day to discover that they had been trading their mortgage portfolios so quickly that their attorneys and document processors hadn't been able to keep up. Consequently there were often serious gaps in titles and lien transfers, which caused problems when their mortgagors filed bankruptcy or it became necessary to foreclose.

Lucius's answer to the problem was to go back and create the missing documents out of thin air to cure the gaps and holes. This, of course, would have been illegal and fraudulent, so Walter would have nothing to do with it. Eventually, the pressure from the mortgage lenders to do something became so intense, it was too much for Lucius and he demanded Walter buy him out. Although it wasn't a good time for Walter to be raising money for a buyout, he was sick of fighting with Lucius, so he sold everything he had and offered it to him. Lucius wasn't happy with the offer since it was barely half what the company had been worth just a year earlier, but he knew in the current economic climate it was the best he could expect. They closed the deal and went their separate ways.

Lucius hadn't directly supervised Shelly's department, so she hadn't had to deal with him, but when their paths had crossed Lucius had often flirted with her and even asked her out once. He was married, and she could tell by the look on his face that his only interest in her was getting into her pants, the thought of which made her shudder in horror.

When she was promoted to customer service manager she became aware of his aggressive and amoral approach to business and didn't like it at all. Her staff was constantly barraged with complaints about billing errors, escrow issues, and slow modification processing, but they couldn't get any straight answers from the departments involved so that the issues could be resolved. This was not only frustrating but she felt guilty giving people the runaround all the time. Finally, the situation became untenable and when the company split up and technically had to terminate all its employees, she opted to look for a job in another industry—an industry with a brighter future.

Rich's suggestion that she go to work for Lucius had intrigued her. She had no desire to get within a thousand yards of the man, but the idea of helping to bring the bastard down excited her. The fact that she'd get paid handsomely while she did it was the icing on the cake. She picked up the phone and called Rich.

"I'll do it," she said, trying to hide her glee.

"Really?" Rich replied. "That's awesome. I actually didn't think you would go through with it. Most people don't have the guts for anything the least bit dangerous."

"Well, I need the job. The only reason I didn't take it before was the fact that I hate Lucius and the way he does business. So, since I'm doing it to help take the asshole down, I can live with it."

"Good."

"So, how's this going to work?"

Rich thought a moment. "Actually, we can't have any formal agreement or strategy. I can't promise you anything for the information you provide. Nor can I influence your testimony if you are ever called to testify. You always have to tell the truth. But, since you are my client we can get together from time to time and talk. Everything we talk about will be privileged so you'll never have to testify about our conversations. But we can't talk by telephone. No emails or letters. Only face-to-face meetings in a secure location."

"Okay. So, I just go to work and do whatever they ask of me."

"Right. But if they ask you to do something illegal or unethical I would object and go on the record as being against it, for your own protection. But if they insist, follow their instructions."

"Okay."

"In other words, we don't want them trying to blame any of these schemes on you."

"Right. But what if they do it anyway?"

"Well, you are protected by the corporate veil. It would be unusual for anyone to go after you since you have no assets for them to seize if they got a judgment against you. Normally, only the company is at risk and the owners and principals. If there are any criminal prosecutions you should be able to cut a deal with the feds in exchange for your cooperation and testimony."

"You're sure they'd cut me a deal?" Shelly asked.

"Yes. It would make no sense to go after you. You're just hired help."

"All right. I'll call Lucius and see if he wants to hire me." She laughed. "Although, I don't think that will be a problem."

"Why do you say that?" Rich asked.

"The guy's got a hard-on for me. He can barely keep his hands to himself when we're together."

"Really. How are you going to handle that?"

"I'm a military brat and I've taken every self-defense training course the military offers, plus I have two older brothers."

"Still, be careful. I don't want you to get hurt."

"I'll be careful. Don't worry."

"Thanks, Shelly, for doing this. You're doing the right thing. Keep me posted."

"I will."

Shelly hung up and took a long breath. She wondered if she was making a big mistake getting involved with Lucius Jones. But before she lost her nerve she picked up her phone and called him. After several minutes of being transferred through his various levels of screening, he answered.

"Shelly? I didn't expect to hear from you. What's up?"

"Well, I may have acted rashly in declining your job offer. I haven't been able to find a job and I'm kind of desperate. Is your offer still open?"

Lucius sighed. "Sorry, Shelly. I've filled the customer service manager's job."

"Oh. Okay. I knew it was a long shot. I guess I didn't appreciate what I had."

Lucius was silent for a moment. "You know. I may have another job for you, if your attitude has changed."

"It has. I promise you. I know now that sometimes you have to do drastic things to survive."

"Yes. It's a cutthroat world out there and only the strong and bold survive. And I'm a survivor as you know."

"Yes. You are. So, what kind of job is it?"

"It's too complicated to discuss over the phone. Let's get together next week and discuss it. I'll buy you lunch."

"Sure," Shelly agreed, stifling a gag.

"I'll have my secretary call you and arrange it."

"Okay."

"See you next week, then," Lucius said and hung up.

Shelly disconnected, suddenly feeling dirty. She got up, walked to the bathroom, and turned on the shower. She undressed, got in, and began washing herself vigorously. After a few minutes she felt a little better and started to wonder what project Lucius had in mind for her. She hated having to wait a week to find out. That was too much time to worry and imagine the worst. She wondered if she'd done the right thing. *Oh God, what have I gotten myself into?*

That night, in her empty apartment, Shelly sat and worried. She lived alone in northeast Dallas having been divorced a year earlier. They'd wanted children, but one of them wasn't fertile, apparently, since she hadn't gotten pregnant during their three-year marriage (notwithstanding considerable effort to do so). Whether or not this was the root cause of their drifting apart she didn't know, but it clearly was a contributing factor. Her current marital status was another reason she opted to go back to work. If she did end up in trouble, nobody would get hurt except her. The final factor was the sheer boredom she felt sitting at home. At least if she went back to work she'd be kept busy and wouldn't have so much free time to lament her miserable existence.

On Tuesday she got a call from Lucius's secretary. She was to meet him the following afternoon at the Canyon Creek Country Club. She breathed a sigh of relief when she got the call because she had been concerned that Lucius wasn't serious about the job or had already filled it. She arrived about fifteen minutes early the next day and was shown to a table. Right on time Lucius showed up and took a seat across from her.

"This isn't the most exclusive country club in town but I like it. It's small and intimate."

"It's very nice," Shelly said.

The waiter brought them a menu and some bread. Shelly ordered a lunch salad; Lucius got a turkey sandwich and ordered some wine.

"So, have you talked to Walter lately?" Lucius asked.

Shelly shook her head. "No. Not since I was laid off."

"Me either. The poor bastard's going to run NAS in the ground within a year. Take my word for it."

"You think so?"

"Yes, we were losing thirty grand a month when I split

58

and the situation has to be ten times worse now. What an idiot he was to buy me out."

"It was your lucky day, I guess," Shelly said evenly.

"Anyway. Let me tell you what I need and you can let me know if it something you're willing to do."

"Okay."

"As you know, NAS had some serious problems with loan documentation if a property is involved in litigation, foreclosure, or bankruptcy. We got some bad advice from our attorneys and the people over at MERS. They assured us their electronic registration system was sufficient for documentation of lien transfers and foreclosure sales. Unfortunately some of the courts don't agree. For instance, when a loan goes in default and we have to foreclose we have to prove we own the note and deed of trust to go forward. This can't always be done so as the note may have been transferred a number of times since its origination."

"I'm familiar with that problem," Shelly said.

"So, something has to be done. We lose money if we can't foreclose right away or file a proof of claim in bankruptcy court."

"So, what do you want me to do?"

"I would like to hire you as vice president in charge of loan documentation. Your job is to produce whatever paperwork is necessary to show a clean chain of title. You'd have to provide assignments, deeds, affidavits, or whatever documents are necessary to prove in court that we own the note and the deed of trust."

"So, I do research, track down the proper paperwork, and gather it together quickly?"

"That may work sometimes, but a lot of time the paperwork doesn't exist. We know we own the note and the deed of trust, we just can't prove it. So, you do whatever it takes to properly document quickly, no more than thirty days. Can you handle that?"

Unconscionable

Shelly just looked at Lucius. He was asking her to prepare fraudulent documents to be filed in court proceedings and as official public records in counties all over the country. She knew Lucius did this kind of thing, but she didn't expect to be put in charge of it.

"If it insults your sense of morality, then forget it. I thought—"

"No, no. I'll do it. I'm just not sure how to go about it."

"Oh, don't worry about that. There are companies out there who will actually prepare the documents for you. All you have to do is provide them the specifications for each document. That way you or your staff won't have to do any of the forgery yourself."

Shelly swallowed hard. "Well, that's a relief."

"So, are you on board?"

"What's the salary?"

"A hundred and twenty grand plus bonuses."

Shelly stifled a gasp at the number. She had been making $80,000 when she was laid off.

She nodded. "Of course. When do I start?"

"Eight o'clock a.m. tomorrow. I'll show you around and introduce you to your staff."

Shelly forced a smile. The waiter brought their food and poured them a glass of wine. While they ate, Lucius filled her in on his new company, Reliable Mortgage Servicing.

"I got the bulk of the servicing business when we broke up. You know how I did it?"

"No."

"I promised the lenders I'd clean up their messes. It will cost them, of course. But when you screw up you have to pay. Walter wouldn't promise shit. He just told them he'd help them in any way he could to straighten things out. No guarantees."

"Walter is a straight arrow."

Lucius laughed. "Right. That's why he's going straight out of business."

Shelly forced a smile and took a drink of her wine.

"You know, I almost went to law school. It's a good thing I didn't. I've talked to our lawyers. If they make two hundred grand a year they're lucky. You know how much I made last year?"

"No," Shelly replied. "How much?"

"One point two million. This is a very lucrative business."

"I can see that."

"You have to work all the angles. There are a dozen ways to make money in this business."

They talked for another half hour, and then Lucius left to go to a meeting. By the time Shelly got to her car she had a splitting headache. The pain began in her left shoulder and radiated up the left side of her neck, through her mouth and gums, all the way to her temples. She massaged her neck and shoulders trying to relieve pain but with little effect. *How am I going to do this?* She was already a wreck and she hadn't even started. On the way home she emailed Rich from her mobile phone to set up a meeting. They'd set up anonymous email addresses and a simple code so there would be no discernible record of their contact. When Rich got the message he would know where to meet her. They met at the Starbucks near his office several hours later.

"I thought I'd get the customer service job again but I didn't expect this," Shelly said.

"I've heard of this type of thing, but it's hard to believe it actually happens," Rich replied. "The bankruptcy judges will be very angry when they find out there have been fraudulent documents filed in their courts."

"I don't know the name of the company that actually produces the paperwork, but I'll let you know as soon as I find out."

"Don't write anything down. Just memorize it and tell me about it when you can. I don't want anything left around that could arouse suspicion."

"Okay."

"Lucius wasn't suspicious at all given your previous objections to his tactics?" Rich asked.

"No. He bought my story that I was desperate. Plus I wore a cocktail dress so he'd have trouble concentrating on anything but my breasts."

Rich laughed. "Well, you do need the job, so if he checks that out there won't be any surprises."

"To be honest, though, I am a little scared. Not of Lucius but of getting in trouble for what I'll be doing for him."

"There's still time to back out. You don't have to do this."

"Yes I do. I need the job. It's pretty pathetic when you have to sell your soul to get a job."

"You're not selling your soul," Rich argued. "You're helping me attain some justice for one of Lucius Jones's victims."

"Right."

"Like I told you. Just do whatever he tells you. You don't need to gather evidence or anything. I'll do a production request for anything you tell me is out there. So there shouldn't be any risk to you. When the time comes to take RMS down I'll subpoena you and all you have to do then is tell the truth."

"Okay."

"We'll meet every couple of weeks but only if it is safe. If anyone sees us together you just tell them I'm your chapter 13 attorney and you just ran into me."

Shelly nodded.

"Thanks again for doing this."

"Well, at least I won't starve now."

Rich laughed. On the way home Shelly went shopping and picked up a couple of new outfits so she'd look decent on her first day on the job. Although she was still a little nervous, she was starting to feel better about what she was doing and, like Rich said, she didn't have to do anything other than her job, so there really wasn't any risk at this stage of the game. When it became time to testify, however, things might change. Lucius Jones wasn't the type of man to let betrayal go unpunished. Oh, he might be in Club Fed for a few years and she'd be safe. But when he got out he would be looking for vengeance.

Chapter 7
Representation

Amanda's alarm clock went off, interrupting a pleasant dream. She had been in a studio with Rich getting him ready to go on *The Late Late Show* with Craig Ferguson. Ferguson was her favorite late-night talk show host and one who actually appreciated good literature. She, like millions of other women, found him irresistible and had experienced a "Fergasm" more than once. She was irritated that her dream had been interrupted.

After her mind cleared she remembered her task for the day—enlist Ryan's help in getting his father to let her represent him as his literary agent. She had to be given the opportunity to place *The Pact*. She didn't know if she liked that name. It was too ordinary for such an extraordinary book. She pondered several alternative names—*Death Pact*, *Suicide Pact*, *Extreme Love*. She liked *Extreme Love*, but love by nature was extreme. It wouldn't work. *Death Pact* was accurate but not very romantic, and this was the ultimate in true romance—not just physical love but a love so strong neither Rich nor Erica could live without the other. There was no going on if one of them died. *All or None.* Would that work? No. Maybe *Deadly Pact*? No, it didn't convey the romance. *Extreme Sacrifice*?

She sighed. For the first time she realized how difficult it was to pick the right title for a book. But she was getting sidetracked. The important thing was convincing Ryan to help her. He'd have to read the book to understand why it had to be published. It pained her that they wouldn't be able to meet until after bar review class, and then they'd be distracted and it would be difficult for them to talk. Lunch. She'd have to convince him to have lunch with her. She went to her purse, got out her cell phone, and punched Ryan's speed dial number.

"Hey, girl. You're up early."

"I've got to meet you for lunch. This manuscript is awesome! You've got to read it and then help me persuade your father to let me represent him."

Ryan laughed. "You want me to read a manuscript right in the middle of bar review?"

"Yes. Meet me at lunch and I'll give it to you."

Ryan sighed. "Okay. Come by the office at noon. I'll only have time to go downstairs to the deli."

"Thank you. I'll see you then."

Amanda thought for a moment. She should make a copy of the manuscript to give Ryan. She didn't want the original out of her sight. She'd stop at Kinko's on the way to Ryan's office and make copy. She'd have to make sure Ryan didn't let his father see him with the manuscript. She had to plan carefully how to make her pitch. Then she thought of Brenda Colson. If she was going to stay in Dallas she needed to meet with Brenda and accept her offer of employment.

She wondered if Brenda had been serious when she made the offer. It had been made at a cocktail party and she was sure Brenda had been a little drunk at the time. *She might not even remember the conversation, but she's Mom's best friend. How could she turn me down? If I came in with a manuscript, that couldn't hurt, either. It would be nice to know what she thought of it, too. If she likes it, that will give me ammunition to convince Rich to allow me to represent him.* Amanda called information and got Brenda's number. The information operator connected her.

"This is Brenda Colson."

"Brenda. This is Amanda Sherman."

"Amanda! How are you?"

"Fine. I've just graduated from law school and you said to give you a call when that happened."

There was a moment of silence; then Brenda replied evenly, "Right. So, you still want to be a literary agent?"

"Absolutely. And I already have a manuscript that I think will be a best seller."

Brenda laughed. "I wish I had a dollar for every manuscript I thought would be a best seller, but it's good that you're passionate about it."

"So, were you serious about hiring me or has the situation changed?"

"Yes, I was serious. I loved the way you dug into our slush pile when you worked here as an intern. We actually placed a couple of your discoveries."

"Did you? That's great."

"But you realize I can't pay you but minimum wage plus your commissions. It wouldn't be much until you placed some business."

"I understand. My boyfriend is going to support me until I get established."

"Okay. That's wonderful. He must be quite a guy."

"He is. He's not crazy about my career choice, but he wants me to be happy."

"Sounds like a keeper. I'm anxious to meet him."

"Yes. I've told him all about you, and he's anxious to meet you, too."

"So, when will you be available?"

"I'm available right now and I'm anxious to show you this manuscript."

Brenda laughed again. "Okay, I've got some time around three this afternoon. We're still in the same offices."

"Thank you, Brenda! I'm so excited."

"Me, too. See you soon, honey. Looking forward to it."

Amanda closed the connection and smiled broadly. She knew everything would work out. She could feel success in her bones. But as much as she tried to ignore them, negative thoughts began to creep into her mind. *What if Rich is adamant about not publishing the novel? What if Erica is the problem? Maybe digging up all of those memories would be too much for her to handle.* She sighed with worry.

When Amanda got to Kinko's she decided to make two copies of the manuscript. She'd give one to Ryan and one to Brenda and keep the original in a safe place. At lunch Amanda dropped off the manuscript to Ryan. She didn't stay to eat as she wanted Ryan to read the manuscript and not talk to her. After she left Ryan she went to Barnes & Noble to kill time until her meeting with Brenda. Once she was there she realized she could use the time to study the true crime that was currently being published. She'd need to know this if she was to going to be negotiating with editors in the future.

When she got to the Colson Agency at three p.m., memories of her internship came rushing back. She wondered which manuscripts had been placed. She had been amazed at how many good writers there were out there trying to get published and how few actually made it. The competition was brutal. She began to wonder if Richard Coleman's novel was as good as she thought. Perhaps in her excitement to start her new career she hadn't been terribly objective. She was afraid Brenda would think it was crap and question her decision to hire her.

The receptionist took her back to Brenda's office right away, which she saw as a good sign. *Maybe Brenda really thinks I do have a future as a literary agent. But it could just be because of Mom. Who knows.* Brenda welcomed her and told her to sit down. There was a stack of papers in front of her.

"Well, this was an unexpected surprise," Brenda said. "Your timing was good; I was just about to rent out our empty office."

"You weren't going to hire anyone?"

"No. The way the market is with publishers concentrating on their A-list authors and letting significant numbers of their midlist go, it didn't make sense to take on the overhead."

"So, why are you showing pity on me?" Amanda asked.

Brenda smiled wryly. "Because you already have a best-selling manuscript. How could I turn that down?"

Amanda rolled her eyes. "You're mocking me! You don't believe me."

"No, I'm just teasing you. Where did you find this manuscript, and what makes you think it has best-seller potential?"

"It's true crime and it comes with an incredible love story. It's called *The Pact*, but I'm not sure about the title. We might be able to come up with something better."

"Who's the author?" Brenda asked.

"My boyfriend's father, Richard Coleman."

Brenda's eyes lit up. "This isn't the story of Erica Fox's murder trial, is it?"

"Yes. It is."

"I didn't know Richard had written a book about it."

"He wrote it while they were sailing in the Caribbean just after it all happened. He is a very good writer."

She looked at the box Amanda had in her lap. "Is that it? Can I read it?"

"Yes, but I haven't gotten a contract yet. I've got to convince him to let me represent him. If you like it and think the odds are good that someone will pick it up, then Ryan and I should be able to convince him to sign a contract."

"So, I may be wasting my time," Brenda mused.

"Possibly, but with Ryan's help I think I should be able to convince him."

"All right. Leave it on my desk," Brenda instructed as she stood up. "Let me show you your new office and while I'm reading this you can attack the slush pile."

Amanda stood up and smiled. "Sounds good."

Her new office was only eight by ten feet but it had a small desk and several bookcases. In one corner hundreds of manuscripts were stacked up nearly to the ceiling. Amanda looked at the stack warily.

"Sorry about that. We're a little behind. I was considering just returning them since I'll never have time to tackle all of them."

"It's a good thing you didn't. There may be some good stuff in there."

Brenda handed her a file. "You'll need to fill out the employment application and all the government and insurance forms in here."

Amanda took the file and put it on her desk. Brenda left and Amanda started to straighten up her new home. She was excited about her new job and, after completing all the employment forms, picked up the manuscript on top of the slush pile with alacrity. It was a political thriller that the author promised would shake up Washington. She laughed at such naïveté but immediately got engrossed in the book. She was half-finished with *Force of Freedom* when Brenda stuck her head in her office.

"You were right about Richard Coleman's novel. It's good and it's been long enough that most people will have forgotten the story. I'm not sure it will be a best seller, but I think one of the New York publishers will pick it up. It will be a good start for you."

"Thank you," Amanda said, a little disappointed with Brenda's assessment of the prospects for the book. But she was glad that Brenda thought it was good enough to place.

Amanda looked at her watch and saw it was time to leave for her bar review class. She stood up and began packing up her backpack. As she was about to leave Brenda's secretary, Julie, walked in and handed her a manila envelope.

"What's this?" Amanda asked.

"It's a contract for Richard Coleman. Congratulations!"

Amanda nodded. "Don't congratulate me yet. Wait until I get him to sign it."

Julie smiled. "Good luck, then, and welcome aboard. It was getting a little too quiet around here. It will be nice to have someone to talk to when Brenda's in New York."

"Thank you, Julie. I appreciate that."

Julie left and Amanda made a quick exit. She had a thirty-minute drive to her apartment and wanted to be there when Ryan stopped to pick her up. Ryan was walking up to her door when she drove in the parking spot in front of her apartment. She got out quickly and retrieved her backpack.

"Where have you been?" Ryan asked as she caught up with him.

"Brenda hired me. I've already started working."

Ryan smiled. "That's awesome. I didn't even know you had an interview."

"I told you I had a job there if I wanted," Amanda said as she unlocked the door. She pushed it open and walked inside with Ryan on her heels.

"And you weren't kidding," Ryan said, relieving her of her backpack and setting it aside. They embraced.

"Did you have a chance to read any of your father's manuscript?" Amanda asked, looking up into Ryan's face.

"I read the first chapter, but that's all the time I had."

"What did you think?"

He nodded. "It's good so far."

"Well, Brenda liked it. She wants me to sign your father."

"Seriously? She read it already?"

"She's a fast reader. She reads two or three books a day. She had it finished in the time it took me to read half of the book I was working on."

"Wow! That's impressive."

"So, can you read the rest of it tonight? I'd like to go visit your mom and dad Friday night. We don't have bar review on Friday."

"Hmm. I'm a slow reader. It will take me a couple of days to read it."

Amanda let out a long breath. "How could you be a slow reader? You've got a doctorate degree."

71

Unconscionable

"I have lazy eye, so my eyes fight with each other while I read. It's really annoying."

Amanda laughed. "That should be interesting to watch."

Ryan shrugged. "I doubt it. They fight very quietly."

Amanda shook her head and rolled her eyes. "We'll get takeout tonight so you'll have more time. I brought a manuscript of my own to finish so we can have a reading party."

Ryan grimaced. "Okay, but let's not make a habit of it. Reading isn't my idea of a party."

"Well, the party starts when you've finished the book. We'll break out the booze and get naked."

Ryan's face brightened. "Okay. Now you're talking."

After bar review they stopped at Panda Express and got Chinese takeout. Amanda marveled at how quiet her apartment was with both of them reading. Usually it was quite noisy with the TV blaring and both of them talking. She liked the library-like silence. At midnight she was done with her manuscript, but Ryan still had a third of his book to finish. He yawned.

"Almost done, big boy?" she teased.

"Yeah, well, I'm going to be too tired to party when I'm done."

"Oh, I doubt that. What do you think so far?"

He shrugged. "Well, since it's my mother and father all the sex is a little hard to take, but it's definitely a good story."

"Any reason why your father would object to it being published?"

"I can't think of anything. Mom's more likely to be the obstacle. She might not like her suicide pact or claim of insanity to be public knowledge."

"You've got to help me convince her to let it be published. I already have a contract ready for your father to sign."

"Boy, you're a fast worker. How did you manage that?"

"Brenda tried to downplay the book's potential a bit, but the fact that I have a contract in my backpack leads me to think she likes it more than she is letting on."

"How much will he make if it sells?"

Amanda shrugged. "It could be as little as $5,000 and as much as a million. It just depends on how good the publisher thinks it is and if there is competition."

"How would there be competition?"

"If we really thought it was an extraordinary book we could send it to several editors and tell them we were having an auction and that the contract would go to the highest bidder. If that happened, then the sky's the limit."

"All right. I'll keep reading."

When Ryan was done two hours later Amanda made good on her promise to get naked and, remarkably, Ryan's exhaustion seemed to disappear as they made love for over an hour. When they were spent and Ryan finally turned over to go to sleep, he wondered what had gotten into Amanda. She had never been so full of fire and passion. He hoped it was her new career because he wanted as much of that action as he could get!

On Friday Amanda had the jitters. She wanted to sign Rich so badly she could scream, but she feared one misstep and all would be lost. Ryan had called his mother and told her they wanted to come over, so Erica invited them for dinner. She said she'd boil lobsters, which was Ryan's favorite. When they arrived at around six thirty, Rich was in the living room watching the evening news. He shut off the TV as they walked in and sat down.

"So, how's the bar review coming?" Rich asked.

"Good," Ryan said. "It's a bit tedious but it's been a good review."

"So, you'll be ready for the bar exam coming up?"

"As ready as ever, I guess."

"So, Amanda. Ryan tells me you want to be a literary agent?"

Amanda nodded. "Yes. I know it probably sounds stupid since I'll soon be licensed to practice law, but I never intended to practice. I just wanted the degree. It puts me a notch above the average literary agent. In fact, I got hired this week by the Colson Agency."

"Congratulations!" Rich said. "That was fast work."

"Yes. Brenda Colson is a family friend and told me many times to come see her when I graduated. So, I guess she wasn't kidding."

"She's a good judge of talent, obviously. And it helps to know the right people."

"Yes. That's right. And, in that regard, today is your lucky day."

"Huh?" Rich said, looking a bit confused.

"When I told Ryan I had decided to become a literary agent he told me about your manuscript. Of course, I insisted upon seeing it immediately, so when I was up in the attic the other day with Ryan he showed it to me."

Rich stiffened and looked at Ryan. "He did?"

"Yes, I'm afraid I took a peek at it. I hope you don't mind."

"Ah—"

"It's really good, you know. And since now you have a literary agent in the family, I could help you get it published. Have you tried to get it published yet?"

"No . . . So, you've read the entire manuscript?"

Amanda nodded. "Yes. Don't blame Ryan. There is no stopping a determined woman."

Rich looked at Ryan irritably, then laughed. He knew the truth of Amanda's statement. He lived with a determined woman. He sighed. "I don't know. It was a difficult time in our lives and I'm not sure it would be a good idea to dig up all those memories."

Erica walked in and smiled. "What memories?" she asked.

"Oh. Amanda has read my manuscript and wants to represent me."

Erica's face went pale. "Really? How—"

"I told her about it," Ryan said, "and she was curious, so I took her up to the attic. The bottom line is, the story is a real page-turner and Dad should publish it. It's not like there are any secrets in there."

"You've read it, too?" Rich asked.

"Yeah. I really liked it. You're a good writer, Dad."

Erica swallowed hard. "You should have asked permission."

"If you didn't want us to read it why did you leave it lying around?" Ryan asked. "In fact, why in hell did you write it if you weren't going to publish it?"

Rich looked at Erica and shrugged. "You're right. At one time I wanted to publish it, but—"

"We decided against it," Erica interjected. "I'm not particularly proud of being declared temporarily insane."

"Ms. Colson really loves it. She thinks one of the major New York publishers will pick it up. If so, there would be an significant advance."

"Brenda Colson has read it?" Rich asked.

"Yes, and she loves it."

Erica gasped. "Rich. What is wrong with you?"

Rich ignored her. "How significant an advance?" Rich asked.

"It's hard to say, but maybe six figures."

Rich looked at Erica. "Maybe we should help Amanda out."

Erica raised her eyebrows then turned to Amanda. "You just read the manuscript, not my revisions?"

"Right. Were there revisions?"

Amanda remembered picking up an envelope marked *Revisions*. She racked her brain trying to figure out what had happened to it. She remembered taking it but didn't remember seeing it after she'd gotten home. She detected a bit of concern about the revisions. She wondered what was in them that had them upset.

"No. I just did a little critique, but the manuscript is fine the way it is."

"Would I have final approval over the content?" Rich asked.

"Of course. It's your book."

"So, we'd see a final galley before it was published."

Amanda nodded. "You'd have about fourteen days to make any final corrections before it went to print."

After exchanging a look with Rich, Erica said, "Well, I guess if you want to do it. Just don't make any commitments for me. I don't want to be interviewed."

"You won't have to," Amanda said. "Rich will have to do a book tour and a few TV interviews, but I'll make sure you're not dragged into it."

"Good. I don't think I could handle it."

Amanda smiled broadly. "Thank you so much. You don't know what it means to me to have this opportunity. I'm going to work very hard on this project and make us some serious money."

Rich laughed. "That sounds good to me."

Amanda couldn't concentrate while they ate dinner. All she could think about was how she'd market Rich's book. She'd get Brenda's input and use her contacts, of course, but she wanted to do it herself. She didn't want Brenda stealing her first client and taking the credit for placing his book.

The revisions that Erica had made bothered her, too. It seemed there was agreement that the revisions should not be made. This made Amanda wonder why. What was in the revisions that was so secret? She didn't want this one issue to torpedo the deal, though. She'd have to find the revisions and somehow get them back into the attic in case Rich or Erica went looking for them.

She racked her brain for an excuse to come back the next day. She had a contract all ready for Rich to sign, but she had thought it a little premature to give it to him then. She decided delivering the contract would be her excuse. After dinner she broached the subject.

"We'll drop by tomorrow afternoon with a contract. Around two p.m. maybe? I can't start marketing the manuscript until it's signed. I can fax you a draft in the morning, and if you have any questions you can give me a call. Hopefully we'll have ironed everything out and you can sign it tomorrow night. Of course, if you need more time that's fine, too."

"No," Rich replied. "I'll be in the office tomorrow until noon. Your plan should work."

Amanda smiled. "Excellent. Thanks again for giving me this opportunity."

Rich nodded. "Well, I just hope you find some editors who like the manuscript as well as you do. I've heard it's not easy to get a publishing contract from one of the majors."

"It's not, but I've got a good feeling about this book."

When Amanda got back to her apartment she retraced her steps and found the envelope under the sofa. She let out a sigh of relief when she found it. Then she wondered if she should open it and see why Rich and Erica were concerned about the revisions. They didn't want the revisions made to the book, so she didn't need to open it. But her curiosity got the best of her, and she opened it and began reading.

She gasped midway through the revised story line. She couldn't believe what she was reading. Was Rich's manuscript a lie? Was Erica's version the real story of how Aunt Martha was murdered? Her heart began pounding. The revised story would be worth ten times the original version. Could it be true? Had Rich Coleman gotten away with murder?

Chapter 8

Demand

After the meeting with Cindy Sharp, Matt began researching what legal theories might be applicable to the facts of her case. The promissory note and deed of trust were contracts, as was the forbearance agreement. If there was a defect in the foreclosure process, that could be a breach of the deed of trust. If it could be shown that the parties entered into a forbearance agreement, then that was obviously breached by the foreclosure. A contract required an offer, acceptance, and consideration. It could be oral or written unless it couldn't be performed in a year; then it had to be in writing. The forbearance was only for the period it took to approve the modification. That was clearly less than a year so an oral contract was okay. The problem was consideration. Cindy had not paid any new consideration because she was told not to make payments, as past due amounts would be added on to the end of the note.

Without new consideration the contract wouldn't stand up, which left a cause of action called promissory estoppel. This was the situation where there was an offer, acceptance, no consideration, but the plaintiff had fully performed the terms of the contract, and it would be a gross miscarriage of justice not to honor it. Matt liked this theory and thought he could prove it. He also planned to look into RMS's foreclosure of Cindy's property to see if there were defects, the most obvious one being a break in the chain of ownership of the note or defects in the lien.

Unconscionable

Texas had another law called the Unfair Collection Practices Act that he thought had promise. This statute provided a cause of action for misrepresentations that were made while trying to collect a debt. Matt thought this had possibilities because the early collection letters misrepresented that the account was delinquent when it wasn't. He also thought that RMS's representation that it would not foreclose while a modification was pending was a lie and a misrepresentation that would be actionable under the statue.

Once he had his legal theories developed, he turned to the question of Cindy's damages. They had lost the equity in their house, Cindy had spent a lot of time moving and resettling the family and would be entitled to damages for her lost time and toil, and she'd be entitled to recover her attorney's fees. These were her economic damages and they would be fairly easy to prove. More difficult were her mental anguish damages and the damages associated with her wrongful death claim.

Mental anguish, to be recoverable, had to be severe and accompanied by physical injury or symptoms such as headache, insomnia, nausea, depression, and so forth. Matt didn't think he'd have a problem with that, as Cindy's own testimony alone would be enough to prove it. More difficult would be establishing the causal connection between the foreclosure and Tony's suicide. That would be a stretch but not an impossible one. If this connection could be made, then Cindy would be entitled to recover medical expenses, funeral costs, loss of consortium, Tony's mental anguish, loss of his future income, her mental anguish associated with his death, and the list went on and on.

Once he had his legal theories and damages set Matt called Cindy back in to discuss making a demand. In a breach of contract action it was required to make a demand before filing a lawsuit in order to be eligible for attorney's fees if the demand was not met. It made sense to try to settle anyway since litigation was expensive, time consuming, and traumatic for the client. It was always better to settle for a little less than one might think

80

one was entitled to and avoid the chance of getting nothing. Cindy took a seat across from him.

"So, the reason I called you in is to discuss what amount of money you would be willing to settle for rather than going to court."

Cindy took a deep breath. "How much do you think I can get?"

"That's hard to say. There are a lot of variables we have no control over, like, what judge is assigned to us, what kind of a jury we draw, how you and the other witnesses perform in court, and so on."

"Hmm. So, how do we figure out what to demand?"

"Well, you want to get the equity in the house back. I've calculated that at about $50,000."

"Right."

"You're going to be entitled to something for the mental anguish you have suffered. That's a very difficult amount to calculate. How much do you think you should get to compensate you for what you went through—not considering your husband's death. Just what you went through up to the time of his death."

"A couple hundred thousand at least."

"Okay, you'll have to testify as to what you went through and convince the jury that it was severe enough to warrant that kind of an award."

"I can do that," Cindy said.

"Then you have lost time, out-of-pocket expenses, loss of credit from the foreclosure . . . so I'd add another $50,000. So, that is $300,000 plus attorney's fees of one-third."

"What about Tony's suicide?"

"Well, you are at $400,000 right now. That's a pretty healthy demand. If you ask for more, I think your changes of settling pre-suit are nil. But if you could live with $400,000 less our third, then that's the demand I would make. We can stipulate that this demand doesn't take into consideration any claim you might have for punitive damages or wrongful death. That way if we don't settle we can demand a lot more later on after the suit is filed."

"I don't know. I would really like to get at least $500,000."

"Okay, we can demand that and see what happens. They might go for it considering you could recover another million if we can get punitive damages or get you wrongful death damages."

Cindy nodded. "Okay, that sounds good."

After Cindy left Matt drafted up a demand letter demanding $500,000 and sent it to RMS. He wasn't very optimistic that RMS would accept it, but it was a necessary part of the process and got them one step further on the long road to justice. Now all he had to do was wait thirty days for a response. But that time wouldn't be wasted. He would use it to draft the original petition so it would be ready the moment RMS rejected his demand.

Once the petition was filed they'd have to wait another thirty days for a response before they could start doing discovery. Litigation is a slow process and takes a lot of patience. Matt figured it would take a year and a half to two years before they got to trial. A lot of clients couldn't handle that, so Matt was careful to warn them not to expect anything exciting to happen for quite a while. He didn't need clients calling him every week wanting an update when nothing was happening.

Matt had learned to be patient in prison. He had nothing but time to kill so he learned how to make himself busy when it seemed there was nothing to do. Since he hadn't been reinstated yet, his father couldn't assign him any other cases to handle, so Matt planned to spend every minute on the RMS case even though there was nothing technically that needed to be done yet. This was his father's advice: *Act as if the case is about to go to trial and prepare accordingly.* In doing so he'd get a much better perspective on what evidence he would need to prevail at trial and be able to adjust his discovery plan accordingly. His father also promised he'd be much calmer and confident because everything he would need during the prosecution of the case would already be done. Oh, he'd have to make changes and conform his work to the actual facts as they developed, but those tasks would be a lot easier with the basic work done.

"I've always wanted to handle litigation this way but never was in a position to do it," Rich said one day. "But you have that opportunity and should take advantage of it."

"I will," Matt promised. "So, I heard from Ryan that you're going to publish your true crime book."

Rich shrugged. "Yeah, I kind of got pushed into it. It wasn't my intention to ever publish it, but I didn't want to alienate my future daughter-in-law."

"Why did you write it if you didn't want to get it published?"

Rich sighed. "Well you see, my recollection of what happened to Aunt Martha and Erica's aren't the same."

This shocked Matt; he'd never known this. He had only heard his father's version of Aunt Martha's murder and his mother's trial. He didn't know Erica had a different version.

"How are they different?" he asked warily.

"I have never told anyone, nor has your mother, but she seems to think I killed Aunt Martha."

"What? Why would she think that?"

"I don't know. I have no memory of what actually happened that night. I thought I'd been mugged and was out of commission when the murder took place, but your mother says she found me hovering over Aunt Martha at the motel and hit me over the head not realizing it was me. She says she and Joe carried me to the alley behind the bar where the police found me."

Matt's eyes widened. "So, you can't let any of this get out."

"No. It's okay. We're going to publish my version of the murder, and it's not a lie because it's what I remember. No one will be able to contradict it except your mother and Joe, and that would never happen."

Matt just stared at his father. "Does Ryan know?"

"No. I'm only telling you because I know I can trust you. I can't tell Ryan because of his relationship with Amanda. Amanda can't know anything about this. She'd probably like the revised version better because it would make it look like I got away with murder."

"Did you?" Matt asked.

"Like I said, I have no memory of what happened that night."

"Does Joe confirm Mom's story?"

Rich nodded. "I'm afraid so."

Matt sighed deeply. "Shit!"

Rich laughed. "Exactly."

"So, why don't you tell Ryan the truth and tell him to get Amanda to back off?"

"No. She's already shown the manuscript to her boss and if I try to back out now, they will know I'm hiding something. I think the best thing is to just publish my version and after a few months it will all go away."

Matt shook his head. "I hope you're right."

"Me, too," Rich said.

"Did Mom write her version down?"

"Yes."

"Where is it?"

"Still up in the attic."

"Are you sure?"

Rich suddenly got a worried look on his face. "Well, that's where it was the last time I saw it."

"You'd better find it and shred it," Matt suggested. "You don't want that getting into the wrong hands."

"Okay, I'll do that tonight when I get home."

"Good."

Matt went back to his office, still reeling from the revelation that his father might be a murderer. It was so out of character he had trouble accepting it. Yet his mother would have no reason to lie about it and Joe was his best friend, so it almost had to be true. But he still couldn't believe it. There just had to be some other explanation.

Chapter 9
The VP

Shelly got out of the elevator on the ninth floor of One Main Place in downtown Dallas. She looked to her right, saw the offices of Reliable Mortgage Servicing, and walked over and through the glass doors. The receptionist looked up, and recognition showed on her face.

"Shelly. I heard you'd be in today."

"Hi, Sally. Yes, I decided I needed a job worse than my moral integrity."

Sally laughed. "Ain't that the truth."

Sally Sterns had been the receptionist at NAS, and she and Shelly were good friends. Lucius Jones's unethical business practices had been the topic of many conversations in the lunchroom at NAS. In fact, most of the employees talked badly about him behind his back.

"You can tell him I'm here."

"Will do, sis. Oh, I'm so glad you're coming on board. It's been a little gloomy around here with the Lizard in charge."

Lucius Jones had been dubbed "the Lizard" by his staff at NAS for obvious reasons. A wave of dread washed over Shelly as she took a seat to wait. A few moments later he walked in with a broad smile on his face.

"At least you make him smile," Sally said under her breath. "That's the first one I've seen in a week."

Shelly stifled a laugh. "Good morning, Lucius."

"Good morning," Lucius said, extending his hand. Shelly shook it warily and immediately regretted it. He locked onto it with both hands and squeezed it like it was a prized possession.

"Get Shelly some coffee," he said, still holding on tightly. She jerked her hand free while he was barking out the order.

"So, I like your new offices," she said to distract him.

He nodded. "Yeah, we went first class. You've got to impress the clients. If you don't look successful they won't have confidence in you."

"So, where is my office?" she asked, looking around.

He pointed down the hall from the direction he had come. "At the end of the hall, right next to my office."

She looked over at Sally and grimaced. Sally turned her head and coughed so Lucius wouldn't see her laugh. Shelly followed Lucius down the hall and into an office. It was small but had a nice view over North Dallas.

"This will do nicely," Shelly said.

"Good. You have a half hour to get settled. Then at ten o'clock we have a meeting with Consolidated Document Retrieval in the conference room."

"Okay," Shelly said, taking a seat in her executive chair. "Thanks, Lucius."

He nodded and left. Shelly took a deep breath and swiveled around to look out over the city. *The view will be good for daydreaming,* she thought. Not that she'd have much time for that. Sally walked in and put a cup of coffee on her desk. Shelly turned around and smiled.

"So, what's your job going to be here?" Sally asked. "We already have a customer service rep."

"I know. I'm going to be VP of document retrieval."

"Oh. Our forgery division."

They both laughed hard.

"Right. So, where's the supply room? I need to get organized."

Sally led her to the supply room and helped her gather together what she needed. At ten she walked into the conference room. Three men were seated on the opposite side of the huge conference table. Lizard was at the end of the table. He motioned for her to sit next to him. Her stomach turned, but she managed to force a smile and take the appointed seat. The three men stood up.

"Gentlemen, this is Shelly Simms, our new VP of document retrieval. She'll be coordinating the work with your company."

"I'm Sanford Ross," the blond man said. "I'm the owner and founder of CDR." He pointed to the men next to him. "This is Roger Stafford and Juan Rubio. They have been assigned to work with you on supplying whatever you need."

"Excellent," Shelly said and took a seat.

"Okay, let's get started," Lucius said. "We have a huge amount of work to do, but our first priority is accounts in foreclosure. We only have a short period of time to file proofs of claim and lift stay motions. In order to do that we have to document the lender's secured position. Currently we have about two thousand accounts in bankruptcy around the country without a clean paper trail."

"Two thousand?" Shelly gasped.

Lucius nodded bleakly. "So, you're going to have to go through each file, determine what documents are missing, and give Roger and Juan the specifications for creating new ones."

"Specifications?"

"Yes. The type of document needed, the parties, the date of execution, the person or persons who should have signed the document. Then within seventy-two hours of submission CDR will deliver to you the needed documents."

Shelly looked at Roger. "How will you be able to create the documents so fast?" Shelly asked.

"You don't need to know that," Lucius interjected. "You just accept the documents, check them for quality and conformity, and then send them to the law firm that needs them."

"Does the law firm know where the documents are coming from?" Shelly asked.

"No. Nobody knows where they come from except the

people in this room, and I want it to stay that way. As far as the rest of the world is concerned, you simply dug through the files and found the documents requested. Is that clear?"

Shelly nodded. "Absolutely."

Lucius sighed. "Now, I cannot stress enough about security. There will be no emails, telephone calls, or use of the US mail. Everything going back and forth between our two companies will be by messenger or overnight courier. All packages are to be stamped confidential for the recipient only, and no one is allowed to open documents not addressed to them. No exceptions."

Shelly swallowed hard. She quickly calculated in her head the number of documents she'd likely need for two thousand accounts. It could easily be five thousand individual documents, all with different mortgagors, dates, and officer signatures.

"How about my staff?"

"You'll have to recruit what you need but no one who works for you must ever know where you're getting the missing documents."

"What do I tell them when they ask where I found it?"

"Just that our law firm had it or the original mortgage company forgot to forward it with the original loan file. Use your imagination."

"Okay. Who will be certifying the documents as the custodian of records?" Shelly asked.

"Georgia Jenkins," Lucius replied. "She's our custodian of records and we pay her enough that she'll sign whatever affidavit you put in front of her."

She swallowed hard. "Right."

"Okay. Any questions?" Lucius asked.

"No. I think we're clear. We got your documents samples, so we are working on finding the right grades of paper and inks necessary to make them look authentic."

"What about notaries?"

"We have actual notaries for every state of the Union.

They work for one year but never renew their commissions. That way no one will ever be able to find them to testify."

Shelly was glad the meeting was over. She had a splitting headache just thinking about the enormity of the task she had in front of her, not to mention the ethics involved. She wondered if she'd ever be able to sleep again. When she got back to her office she was shocked to see that twenty-two boxes of loan files had been delivered to her. She sighed and opened the first box.

As she went through the files she found the original documents were in place but after that it was hit or miss. Many of the transfers had been made en masse by computer and there was nothing in the file documenting the transfer of the notes or the liens on the real estate that secured them. For each file she'd have to figure out its history and then be sure the proper documents populated each file.

Her immediate problem was staffing up. There was no way she could possible handle this job alone, so she got on the phone with the personnel firm she'd used with NAS and arranged for them to send over a half dozen prospective employees with some real estate experience. After she'd hung up the phone rang. She picked it up.

"This is Tim Simpson over at Jones, Stratford and Simpson."

"Okay," Shelly said.

"I understand you're the person I need to talk to about getting some documents."

"Who are you?"

"Your attorneys in Austin. We handle your bankruptcy cases."

"Oh. Right. What can I do for you?"

"We're running up on deadlines for filing a half dozen proofs of claim. I was told you were working on getting us the documentation?"

"Yes. Okay. Can you email me a list of what you need and I'll get right on it?"

"Sure, but we've got less than ten days to get it filed or the claim will be disallowed."

"Right. I'll get right on it."

Shelly hung up the phone and looked at the twenty-one boxes of files she hadn't even inventoried yet and sighed. Her computer beeped, indicating she'd just gotten her first email. She opened it and saw it was from Tim Simpson. She looked at the list, then at the boxes, and wondered how she'd been talked into taking on such a horrible job.

Chapter 10
The Contract

Ryan and Amanda languished in bed on Saturday morning. They'd made love when they first woke up, like they did every Saturday morning, and then ate breakfast while they read the morning paper. Amanda lived for the weekends because she had Ryan to herself. She loved to hold him after they'd made love and feel the energy flow between them. It was as if their bodies were being recharged. It felt wonderful. She made them bacon, eggs, toast, and coffee and as she took the first bite out of her toast a thought crept into her mind.

"Oh, shit. I've got to fax your father the contract."

Ryan laughed. "You should have just had him sign it last night."

"I know. But that would have seemed presumptuous."

Ryan rolled his eyes. "He wouldn't have cared."

Amanda put her breakfast aside and stood up. "It will just take a minute."

She ran into the second bedroom that she used as an office and rummaged through her backpack. She found the contract and fed it into the fax machine. A few minutes later she was back eating her breakfast.

"So, Dad seemed excited about having his manuscript published," Ryan noted.

"Not your mother, though. She seemed a bit upset."

"Well, having everybody read about her sticking cyanide up her vagina could be a bit embarrassing."

Amanda sighed. "True, but they were so much in love. It's not often you find a commitment that strong."

Ryan raised his eyebrows and decided it was time to change the subject before Amanda started asking him about *his* commitment. It wasn't that he didn't love Amanda, but he personally thought his father was crazy to commit to dying rather than living without Erica.

"So, now that you have a contract, what are you going to do?"

Amanda sighed. "Hope like hell I get a few editors interested. Fortunately, Brenda can get me in to see them. If I were on my own it would take years to develop those kind of relationships."

Amanda didn't hear from Rich about any problems with the contract she had faxed, so promptly at two p.m. she and Ryan showed up with the original to be signed. Erica was conspicuously absent, apparently deciding she needed to go grocery shopping. Rich showed them into the dining room.

"So, I looked over the contract and didn't see anything too onerous."

Amanda smiled. "No, it's the standard literary contract that all the AAR reps use." Amanda pulled out the contract and handed it to Rich. He signed it and gave it back to her.

"Fantastic. I'll keep you posted on how it goes. It may take a while. Editors are not known for their speed in reading submissions. We probably won't get any feedback for ninety days or more."

"Well, I've waited this long. I guess a few more months won't matter."

They got up.

"Oh," Amanda said. "I need to put these yearbooks back in your attic. I'll just be a moment."

"That's all right," Rich said. "I'll put them back."

"No, no. I took them out, I'll put them back," Amanda said, rushing out of the room.

Amanda heard Rich ask, "So, are you ready to take the bar?"

94

"Ready as ever, I guess," Ryan replied.

The bar is the last of my worries, Amanda thought as she pulled down the attic staircase and climbed up. Putting the yearbooks and envelope back where she had found them, she thought about the copy she'd made at Kinko's and wondered if there was any way she could convince Rich to publish Erica's version of the story, but she knew that was unlikely. A few moments later she was back downstairs. Ryan was inching toward the door because they were on the way to Lake Lavon for some water-skiing. They said their good-byes and left.

On Monday Amanda found Brenda in her office drinking a cup of coffee and poring over a manuscript. She gently knocked on the door, contract in hand.

"Here it is," Amanda proclaimed proudly.

Brenda looked up and smiled. "Oh. Wonderful. Come in. Sit down."

Amanda handed her the contract and then took a seat. Brenda flipped to the signature page and nodded. "Wonderful. So now the fun begins."

"So, who do you think we should show it to first?"

"Oh, I've already promised it to Sheila Samson at Thorn. She's dying to see it. Call her and maybe she'll have lunch with you."

"She's in New York," Amanda noted.

"Right. You'll have to grab an early flight. It will be a great experience for you."

Amanda could hardly contain her excitement. On her very first day on the job she would be calling one of the most influential editors in the publishing industry to set up a meeting! Rich was right about knowing the right people. She was on the fast track to success. She could just feel it.

"Okay. I'll go give her a call and set it up."

Amanda went back to her office and began reading the manuscript again. She'd have to know it inside and out if she was going to pitch it to Sheila Samson. As she read, she corrected a few typos and began noting portions that might need some rewrite. In the afternoon when she was done, she took it to Julie.

"We'll need this manuscript put in electronic format and sent to a proofreader."

Julie took the manuscript and set it down. "Okay, it will take a few days."

"Can they put a rush on it?" Amanda asked.

"Yes, but it's a twenty percent markup on expedited service."

"How much will that be?"

"Probably a couple hundred bucks," Julie replied.

"That's okay. I'll spring for it."

Julie nodded. "Okay. I'll take care of it."

Amanda figured they probably wouldn't get the manuscript back in time for her to go to New York that week, so she called Sheila Samson and made an appointment for the following Tuesday, since the bar exam was on Monday. While she was waiting for her meeting she worked on a synopsis of the story and a short pitch. There were so many manuscripts being peddled to the big publishers that it was critical to be able to give a two-minute pitch that would pique the interest of the listener. Once an editor was interested, then she'd have more time to discuss the details of the book. Because of Brenda's relationship with Sheila Samson she probably didn't need a pitch, but she would need it later, so it wouldn't hurt to be prepared.

Over the weekend she saw Rich and told him she was going to New York to discuss his book with Thorn Andrews Publishing. He was impressed and excited to hear Amanda was already talking to a publisher. Erica was less enthusiastic but seemed resigned to having the book published.

Amanda and Ryan took the bar exam on Monday, and when it was over Amanda was worried she hadn't done well, since all she could think about was her Tuesday meeting. The next day Amanda took a six a.m. flight to New York and caught a taxi to the Thorn offices in Manhattan. When she walked into

Sampson's office thirty minutes before her appointment, Sampson was in a meeting.

"That's fine. I'm early," Amanda said to the receptionist. "Is there somewhere I can freshen up?"

She followed the receptionist's directions and found the ladies' room without difficulty. Once inside she took a long look at herself in the mirror. Her hands shook as she freshened her makeup. She hadn't remembered ever being so nervous. When she was done she took a few deep breaths to try to relax. Finally, when she felt her heart rate had subsided a bit, she went back to the waiting room.

"Ms. Samson just got out of her meeting," the receptionist advised. "She said she'd join you in two minutes."

Amanda nodded and looked around the plush office. As she was waiting a tall young man walked up.

"Hi. You must be Amanda," the tall man said.

Amanda stood up. "Yes. That's me."

The tall man extended his hand. "I'm Robert Todd, VP of marketing. I'm going to join you for lunch, if you don't mind."

Amanda shook his hand tentatively. "Not at all. That would be great."

Robert smiled wryly. "So, this is your first placement?"

"Yes, I just started working for the Colson Agency last week."

"Well, I hope Rich Coleman is a good writer. I know the story was quite a sensation at the time."

"He is good. I'm going to encourage him to do some more writing."

A middle-aged woman in an expensive-looking suit walked up. She had a stern, all-business look on her face that filled Amanda with anxiety.

"So, you found Amanda, I see," Sheila said.

"Yes," Robert said. "I was just telling how hopeful we were that Rich Coleman was a good writer."

Sheila nodded. "Yes, I'm anxious to read the manuscript

and find out. Let's get some lunch. I want to hear all about how you managed to get him signed."

They left and walked several blocks to a busy Italian restaurant. The waiter took them to a booth in the corner. Amanda drew in a breath of the wonderful aroma of fresh bread being baked and smiled at Sheila.

"So, Brenda has told me a lot about you," Sheila said.

"Really?"

"Yes, she has high hopes for you and, so far, you haven't disappointed her."

"Well, I'm afraid I got lucky with Rich Coleman. I'm dating his son."

"How did you find out he had a manuscript? That was a pretty well-kept secret."

"Ryan ran across it in the attic. He mentioned it to me when I told him I wanted to be a literary agent."

"Hmm. Lucky for you," Robert said. "Does Rich like to travel? We'll want to do a national book tour, of course."

"Yes, I've mentioned that to him. He's fine with it."

"What about his wife?" Sheila said. "Would she go with him?"

"No. She said to keep her out of it."

"Too bad," Robert said. "She'd be a big draw."

Amanda shrugged. "I'll talk to her some more, but she was pretty adamant about it."

"So, I assume you brought the manuscript?" Sheila asked.

"Yes," Amanda said, grabbing her backpack. She took out the manuscript box and handed it to her. Sheila took it and set it next to her. "There's a summary and blurb in there, too."

"Good. I'll read it tonight and call you tomorrow."

"Can I read the blurb now?" Robert asked. "I kind of know the story, but I was very young when it all happened."

"I've got it memorized," Amanda said. " 'Richard Coleman has made partner in his law firm in record time. Despite his success there is little joy in his life, having recently lost his wife in a tragic car accident. It's been a year now and he's tried to adjust to the loneliness and emptiness in his life with little success. Then he meets Erica Fox, the seventeen-year-old daughter of a high roller, Franklin Fox. Mr. Fox is divorced and needs someone to be trustee over Erica's affairs should he die. After eliminating all potential candidates for the job, Rich ends up being recruited for the task. When Franklin dies just weeks later, Rich assumes his duties but soon is drawn into an illicit affair with Erica, his ward. When they are discovered by a meddlesome aunt she threatens to blow the whistle on them and have Rich thrown in jail. When she is later found dead, the two lovers are prime suspects. Eventually Erica is charged with the murder, but Rich doesn't think she did it and sets out to prove it. What he doesn't realize is how perilous the search for the truth will be. . . .' "

Brenda smiled. Robert nodded. "Very good. You've got my attention," Robert said.

"It may a bit long," Sheila noted, "and it doesn't mention the death pact. We'll work on it."

After lunch Robert drove Amanda to the airport. He told her the fact that he'd been called in at this early stage was a good sign. It meant management was very interested in the concept even without actually reading the manuscript.

"If they don't like the manuscript, they may hire a ghostwriter to edit it to make it commercial," he told her.

Amanda didn't like that idea. That would delay the project for a year or more, and she was hoping to have the book in print in a year.

"Right. I've read a lot of books and gone through a lot of manuscripts, and I really don't think you'll need to do much editing. Rich is a lawyer and a good writer."

"I'm sure he is, but legal writing and creative writing are very different."

"But this is true crime," Amanda argued.

"You still have to make it read like a novel so people will

be entertained."

"Well, let me know what you think after you read it," she said as they pulled up to the curb at LaGuardia Airport.

She got out, thanked Robert for lunch, and went straight to her gate. Her flight wasn't for an hour, so she pulled out another manuscript she had been working on and began reading. After about five minutes her mind began to wander. She wondered what Sheila would think of the manuscript. Sheila hadn't taken her personally to the airport because she had said she wanted to start reading it. By the time Amanda got back to Dallas, Amanda knew Sheila would probably have it read if she was as fast a reader as Brenda, which was a safe bet. She wondered how long Sheila would make her wait before she called back. Usually, you had to give an editor at least a month's exclusive look at a manuscript. The publishing business moved at a snail's pace. Amanda cringed at the thought of having to wait that long. She wondered if she had the patience to be a literary agent.

She sighed. The secret, she knew, was to get a lot of projects in the pipeline so you would always have something coming to fruition to keep your spirits up and your pocketbook full. She thought about the manuscript from the slush pile she was reading. It had started off strong but began to drag in the middle. She knew as soon as she lost interest in a manuscript it was time to cast it aside and start a new one, but she also knew she had been distracted and shouldn't let her distraction affect the hopes and dreams of a would-be author who had put hundreds of hours and his or her heart and soul into a manuscript.

She thought about Rich and wondered how he would feel seeing his book finally published. Would he be as excited about it as she was, or would reliving the pain and sorrow of the past detract from the exhilaration an author would usually feel? Would Erica's discomfort ruin it for him, or would she come around when the book was released and the royalties started coming in?

Amanda didn't have to wait long for an answer from Sheila. On Friday Brenda got a telephone call. Sheila was faxing a proposed contract and wanted them to consider it over the weekend and get back with her on Monday. Amanda read the contract as it came off the fax. It was the standard Thorn contract, but a couple of provisions bothered her. Along with a ten-city book tour, appearances at Bouchercon and Book Expo in LA, Rich had to commit to two late-night talk shows. The kicker was Erica had to appear with Rich for the TV shows and the advance was only $50,000. That would mean her commission would only be $3,750 after she gave half of it to the Colson Agency.

Although Amanda was disappointed, Brenda told her not to lose any sleep over it because it was only an opening offer. But Amanda was fearful that if Erica wouldn't agree to do the talk shows, there wouldn't be a contract at all. When she and Ryan went over to his parents' house that night her stomach was in knots. They sat at the kitchen table and Erica served them iced tea and brownies.

"So, you've got an offer already," Rich said excitedly. "That was fast."

"Yes, but it's just an opening offer, so don't be disappointed. Brenda thinks we can do better," Amanda explained as she handed Rich the contract.

Rich began reading to himself. "A hardback edition tentatively scheduled to be released six months from contract execution," he summarized. "That's good. A $50,000 advance, ah hah, book tour, TV shows—hmm."

"What's wrong?" Erica asked.

"Ah. They want both of us to be guests on two talk shows to be determined at a later date."

Erica stiffened. "No. No way. I told you to leave me out of it. I'm not going on TV to be humiliated."

Rich sighed and looked at Amanda. "Didn't you tell them Erica wouldn't make appearances?"

Amanda shrugged. "Well, when you meet an editor you don't want to start dictating terms before they read the manuscript. We'll just have to tell her tomorrow. Hopefully it won't be a deal breaker."

"You're not going to make much of a commission on that advance," Ryan noted.

"I know. But hopefully the book will do well and there will be royalties down the road."

"Well, aside from Erica's participation I don't see anything wrong with the contract, if you're happy with it."

"The advance is a little light, but like I said, we can make a counteroffer. I'm going to talk to Brenda about it tomorrow and then we'll probably get Sheila on the phone to discuss it."

"Well, I'm not doing this for the money," Rich said. "Erica and I have done very well and our lives are not driven by financial gain anymore. Actually, we're doing it to help you out and, I'll admit, to gratify my ego a bit."

They all laughed.

"You know," Rich continued, "everybody thinks they have a novel or story to tell the world, but only a very few have the opportunity to actually get it out there. You're giving me that opportunity and I appreciate it. And if it helps kick-start your new career, well, that's just a bonus."

"Thank you, Mr. Coleman," Amanda said appreciatively. She was glad Rich was being so amenable but disappointed Erica hadn't even considered appearing on the talk shows. She could have understood her position if Erica's version of the story was being told, but it wasn't.

The next Monday she and Brenda got Sheila on the telephone to continue negotiations. Brenda took the lead.

"Sheila. We took the contract to our client and he's happy with most of it, but there are a few issues."

"Like what?" Sheila asked.

"Well, of course, that's not a spectacular advance. What kind of a print run were you thinking of?"

"Well, it's difficult to predict the market these days with so many independents going out of business and even the chains in trouble. This economy hasn't helped, either. We would probably start off modestly with maybe twenty thousand copies. If it does well we can get a second printing out fairly quickly."

"That small a run, huh?"

"Yes, like I said, the book business is in turmoil right now. We're taking quite a risk since this is kind of an old story and not of any historical consequence."

"Well, a bigger problem is Mrs. Coleman's participation. She doesn't want to do the talk shows. She's not crazy about the media dragging up all the sordid details of her past, but she can insulate herself from all that by not going out or watching TV for a few months."

Sheila sighed. "Well, I'm afraid that's a deal killer. The only way I could talk my manager into a contract offer on this deal was if Erica and Rich did the talk shows together. We contacted producers at *The Tonight Show* and *The Late Late Show*, and they liked the joint appearance idea, but weren't so sure if just Rich appeared alone. The idea of two lovers willing to die rather than live without the other is appealing, but without Erica there to explain her point of view it wouldn't work."

"So, you're saying if Erica doesn't appear there is no deal at all?" Amanda asked.

"Yes, I'm afraid so, but I'll tell you what we can do. We can increase the advance to $75,000. Maybe that will help convince Erica to get on board."

Amanda didn't say anything.

"Okay. We'll take that to our client and get back with you, Sheila. Thanks for getting on this so quickly."

"No problem. Hope you can talk some sense into Erica."

"Me, too," Brenda agreed.

Amanda was sick after the telephone call. She knew there was no chance Erica would change her mind. She had made that perfectly clear. It was so frustrating to be on the verge of her first placement and have it blow up in her face. She began to get angry. Why was Erica being so difficult? Would it kill her to be on a talk show? Most people would give their first child to be a guest on Jay Leno or Craig Ferguson. But not her future mother-in-law—*the bitch*.

She couldn't handle another face-to-face with Rich and Erica, so she called Rich and told him about Thorn's sweetening of the offer. He told Amanda he didn't think Erica would budge but that he'd try one more time to get her to change her mind. A few hours later Rich called her back with what he said was good news.

"What do you mean?" Amanda asked.

"Erica says she'll do one talk show, and that's it."

A flood of hope washed over Amanda. She wondered if that would be good enough. She prayed it would. The next day she and Brenda got Sheila on the phone again.

"So, Erica has agreed to do one talk show," Brenda said. "Do you think your people can live with that?"

"I don't know, Brenda. They were pretty adamant about two shows. You get a gold mine of publicity from those talk shows. Jay Leno has over three million viewers and Craig Ferguson has a million and a half. You can't turn down that type of publicity. Unfortunately, they both said having Erica there was the main draw. After all, she was the one who went on trial for murder and almost died from the cyanide poisoning."

After the telephone call Amanda stormed back to her office. She was so angry and frustrated she could scream. How could this be happening to her? It wasn't fair. She was on the verge of tears when an idea came to her. She knew how to close the deal, but she'd have to be very discreet about it. She got back on the telephone with Sheila, this time alone, and made one last pitch. She made Sheila promise not to tell Brenda what was going on. Sheila said she'd run the idea past her bosses and give Brenda a call if it was a go. An hour later Brenda came into Amanda's office with a puzzled look on her face.

"What's up?" Amanda asked expectantly.

"Ah. I just got a strange call from Sheila. They've reconsidered and will do the deal—$75,000 and just one talk show appearance."

Amanda feigned surprise. "Oh, really?"

"Yes. And they decided to do an initial fifty-thousand-print run."

"Seriously?" Amanda said, swelling with pride. "That's wonderful."

Chapter 11
Reinstatement

Rich walked into Matt's office with a big smile on his face. Matt was concentrating on the final draft of his original petition against RMS and didn't notice him.

"Got good news," Rich said.

Matt looked up. "Oh. I didn't see you there, Dad. What's up?"

"I just got off the phone with Pierson. The Fifth Circuit Court of Appeals has granted you a new trial."

Matt leaned back in his chair and raised his eyebrows. "Oh, that's awesome! I can't believe it."

"Yes, and Pierson has talked to the assistant US attorney on the case and he says it's unlikely they'll prosecute a new trial."

Matt got up and went around his desk to Rich and gave him a hug. "Thank you, Dad. I feel like a massive weight has been lifted off my shoulders."

Tears welled in Rich's eyes. "I know. The nightmare is finally over and now you can get on with your life."

"Well, I still have to reapply for my license, but that should just be a formality, don't you think?"

"Yes, now that your conviction has been set aside there is no reason not to reinstate your license, particularly if the US attorney isn't going to retry you or bring any new charges against you."

While they were talking excitedly, Ryan walked in. "So, what are you two so happy about?"

"The Fifth Circuit just granted Matt a new trial," Rich said.

"Oh! Wow! Congratulations, big brother. That's great news. We'll have to celebrate tonight."

"Good idea," Rich agreed. "I'll call Erica. She's good at arranging parties."

"I'm sure Amanda will help," Ryan said. "I'll have her call Mom."

After the celebration broke up Matt went downstairs to get the mail. When he brought it back up he noticed there was a letter from Richmond & Richmond, a law firm that Matt knew often represented RMS. He tore open the envelope and read it carefully. It was exactly what he expected. RMS denied any wrongdoing and warned that it would seek recovery of the mortgage deficiency and attorney's fees and costs if they filed a lawsuit. Matt dialed Cindy Sharp's telephone number. She answered on the first ring. They exchanged greetings.

"I just wanted to let you know that we got a response from RMS and they are denying liability."

"Did they offer anything?"

"No. In fact, they threatened to countersue for the money they lost when they foreclosed, plus their attorney's fees and costs if we filed suit."

"Could they recover all that?"

"Yes. It's possible. If we sue for breach of contract the prevailing party would be entitled to recover their attorney's fees. Also, they could ask for a declaratory judgment, and if they prevailed they might recover attorney's fees under that theory as well."

"How much would that be?"

"It could be twenty-five to fifty thousand dollars or more, but our case would have to totally fall apart for that to happen."

"So, what are the odds?"

"I can't give odds. It's a crapshoot. We could win big, we could lose big."

"So what if we lose and I have to pay $50,000?"

"Then you'd be probably forced to file bankruptcy."

"Wonderful," Cindy spat. "They drive my husband to suicide and I end up owing them fifty grand."

"I won't lie to you. That could happen, but I'd be shocked if it did."

Cindy sighed. "So, now what?"

"Well, you have to decide if you want me to file the lawsuit. You could just walk away and there'd be no risk."

"I'm not going to let them get away with killing Tony. They have to pay for what they did."

"Okay. So, you want me to go ahead and file the petition? I sent you a copy last week. Did you read it?"

"Yes, but I'm not sure I understand it completely."

"Well, the important thing is that all the facts alleged are accurate. Nobody expects you to understand all the legalese."

"The facts are accurate. Go ahead and file it."

"All right. I'll do it tomorrow."

"Thanks, Matt," Cindy said. "Sorry I yelled at you, but I'm just so pissed off at those bastards I can't stand it."

"I know. No problem," Matt said softly. "I'll let you know when they answer the lawsuit, probably in about thirty days."

"Okay, thanks."

Matt hung up and then read the petition one more time before taking it to Rich to sign. Technically he hadn't gotten his license reinstated yet so he couldn't sign as the attorney of record. After Rich signed it, Matt took it to Suzie and told her to get it ready to file. Now it was a waiting game. After the suit was filed the clerk had to issue citation and get the constable to serve it. This could take weeks and then the defendant had three to four weeks to answer it.

To short-circuit the process Matt took the petition to the district clerk's office and walked it through. This meant he filed the case and then waited while citation was prepared. The employees in the clerk's office didn't like attorneys who couldn't wait their turn, but Matt didn't care. This was the only case he had to work on, so he needed to move it along. After he had the citation in hand he walked it over to the constable's office and was assured a deputy would try to serve it that very day. When he arrived back at his office Suzie informed him that the constable had called and confirmed that Lucius Jones had been served.

Twenty-eight days later RMS's answer came in over the fax machine. Much to Matt's chagrin RMS had made good on its promise to countersue for a deficiency on the note, plus attorney's fees and court costs. When Matt told Cindy about the countersuit she was livid.

"They're suing me for $67,000?"

"Yes, $67,000 plus attorney's fees, but the court's not going to give that to them unless all of our causes of action fail."

"Still, the nerve of those bastards to sue me after what they did."

"I know it's frustrating. Don't worry about the countersuit. They just filed it to upset you. I doubt they expect to recover anything."

"I'd dive into the pits of hell before I'd give them a nickel," Cindy spat.

Matt stifled a laugh. "We'll get some discovery out right away and put the case on a fast track. They'll be doing everything in their power to delay and obstruct our prosecution of the case."

"Can they get away with that?"

"Yeah. They're experts at it. It's a good defensive tactic plus it allows them to run up their bill without the client screaming. Don't worry, though, we will keep the heat on them and make them sweat."

"Good. Make them sweat blood."

Matt hung up the phone, shaking his head. Cindy was really out for revenge, which meant the case wasn't likely to settle. They'd be going to trial and he knew the road there would be a difficult and costly one. He could feel his stomach begin to twist, so he took a deep breath and tried to relax.

That night they all went out to Texas Land & Cattle to

celebrate Matt's successful appeal. Along with the family they invited the office staff and several close friends. All together there were twenty-five of them sitting together in the back room of the restaurant. When they had finished eating, Rich ordered champagne for everyone and offered a toast.

"Matt, I know you have suffered immeasurable loss and endured much pain and sorrow these past few years, but all of your sacrifice hasn't been in vain. You've accomplished a lot in waking up Congress and forcing them to deal with predatory lenders. Some important laws were enacted on account of your actions. And now you are embarking on a new journey to shake up the mortgage industry and make them accountable for their transgressions against the American consumer. So, here's to Matt—may God and Lady Liberty shine upon you and guide you on your new endeavors."

"Hear! Hear!" someone said as everyone raised their glasses and drank in Matt's honor.

Matt stood up and thanked them all. He didn't give a speech, since he really didn't have anything to say. Everyone knew what had happened to him, so there was no need to go into that. Besides, he was trying hard to forget the past. And the quest to make the mortgage companies accountable was just in its infancy, so there wasn't much to talk about there, either. So he just sat down and smiled at Candy, whom he had invited to accompany him to the party. It just seemed natural to bring her. In the past they'd only gotten together on the weekends or at night and kept a low profile. But now that the family knew about their relationship there was no need to hide it anymore.

Candy had recovered fully from her accident with the Percodan, and Matt hadn't brought the subject up again. Fortunately, Candy had cut down on her own personal escorting as she was kept busy managing the growing number of girls under contract to her. She got 30 percent of their take so it was a pretty lucrative venture. Since most of the managing was done by telephone she could do it quite easily from Matt's apartment or out on the town if they decided to go out.

Because Matt hung around with Candy so much, he got to know most of the girls who worked for her, and it wasn't unusual for one or two of them to be hanging around at Candy's house or Matt's apartment, depending on where they were sleeping that night. Matt found the girls to be a great escape from the stress at the office and looked forward to going home at night to see who would be there with Candy. Most of the girls liked Matt, so the moment he came in they would be hovering over him, anxious to make him comfortable after a long day at the office.

After the family party was over they went to Candy's place, a restored mansion on Swiss Avenue, where a real party was under way. Candy's girls liked Matt a lot, so they had planned a night that he wouldn't soon forget. Ryan and Amanda had been invited, too, since Ryan was now officially their criminal attorney. Many of the girls had brought their boyfriends and Candy had invited some of their best customers, so the house was rocking when they arrived.

When Candy and Matt walked in, an escort named Sharon Sparks was the first one to greet them. Candy gave her a double take.

"I thought you had a date tonight," Candy remarked.

Sharon shrugged. "The guy turned out to be an asshole. All he wanted to do was grope me. I told him to keep his hands off but he ignored me, so I went to the ladies' room and never came back."

Candy nodded. "That's too bad. He seemed like a nice guy when I booked him."

"I thought so, too, until he got me alone."

"So, what do you do if one of your dates tries to force himself on you?" Matt asked.

"Pepper spray," Sharon replied. "I had a can ready in case I needed it."

Matt laughed. "Have you ever had to actually use it?"

Sharon nodded. "Yes. It's pretty nasty stuff. I almost felt sorry for last bastard I sprayed with it. He was in terrible pain and agony, the poor bastard."

Two blonds, who looked to be twins, strolled up on each side of Matt and latched on to him. "I'm sorry, but we're in charge of taking care of the guest of honor tonight."

Matt looked at Candy and she nodded. "Go with Gina and Jenni. Enjoy yourself. I've got to go deal with Sharon's date. I'm sure he's going to want a refund."

"You're going to give it to him?" Ryan asked.

Candy shrugged. "Yeah. It's better than worrying about him attacking one of the girls or coming here and torching the place."

"Do your clients know where you live?" Ryan asked.

"They're not supposed to, but they could find us simply by following one of the girls here."

Gina and Jenni took Matt to the bar where the cute brunette bartender gave him a long kiss and then a rum and Coke to wash it down. They then whisked him away to the kitchen where there was an impressive array of appetizers and desserts. They sat him down at the kitchen table and proceeded to feed him a little of everything. Matt was loving every minute of this royal treatment as Ryan looked on, a little jealous. Ryan wondered if they'd throw him a birthday party like this. Amanda must have sensed his thoughts because she pinched him hard.

"Ouch! What are you doing?"

"Get that smirk off your face," Amanda said.

"What?" Ryan complained.

When Matt was full, Gina and Jenni took him to the foyer where they had cleared out the furniture to create a dance floor. A live band set up in the corner was playing an assortment of classic rock, jazz, and hip-hop. Gina and Jenni danced with Matt at first, but then the other girls started cutting in. When Candy finally made it back from her crisis management she reclaimed Matt and they danced a few slow numbers together. The other guests were enjoying the evening as well, dancing, eating, talking, running off to a bedroom for more intimate activities, or going outside to smoke or get some fresh air.

It was nearly two in the morning when guests started leaving. Matt and Candy were exhausted and were heading for the master bedroom when Gina and Jenni intercepted them.

"Can we sleep here tonight? We're too drunk to drive home."

"Sure," Candy said, too tired to fight with anyone.

"Me, too," Sharon said, stepping in their path.

Candy stopped abruptly. "Fine. Let's have a slumber party."

"Great idea," Sharon said, running off to tell the other girls.

Candy had been joking, but she was too tired to take back the invitation. When they finally made it to the bedroom Matt took off his shirt and pants and climbed under the covers. Candy unbuttoned her dress and pulled it over her head. Matt lay back and watched her attentively as she took off her bra and slipped in beside him. As he was about to wrap his arms around Candy he heard giggling. He looked toward the door and saw Gina, Jenni, and Sharon coming to join them. He looked back at Candy nervously. She laughed.

"This is your lucky day, hot shot. I hope you're up for it."

Matt swallowed hard. "Me, too."

During the next week Matt got the first round of discovery out to RMS's attorney, Marvin Richmond. It was the standard requests for production, admissions, and disclosures. The purpose of the production was to get all of RMS's documents. The admissions helped him determine which facts were contested and which were not. The disclosures would tell him damage calculations, what defenses or counterclaims to expect, and who had knowledge of the facts of the case.

Unfortunately, Matt knew RMS would do a half-assed job of answering the first round of discovery and he'd have to file a motion to compel to force them to fully respond. It was annoying to him that Richmond wouldn't cooperate in the first place but there wasn't much he could do about it other than complain to the judge. When the responses came back thirty days later it was even worse than he'd expected. Richmond had objected in every conceivable manner to every request and each interrogatory.

Matt immediately put together his motion to compel and faxed it to Richmond. He had an obligation under the rules to try to work out discovery disputes without a hearing before the court if possible. Then he had his new secretary, Melissa Curry, get Richmond on the line.

"What can I do for you, counselor?" Richmond said gleefully.

"Ah. I got your discovery responses, and I don't agree that your objections have any merit. I've faxed you a draft of a motion to compel that sets forth my problems with your responses. Can we talk about them now or would you like to schedule something after you've had a chance to study my motion?"

"Every one of those objections is valid and I stand by them. I don't have to study your motion to know whether I oppose it."

"Okay. You don't want to go over each item and discuss it as the local rules require?"

"I know the rules. Although it will be a colossal waste of time, I'll read your motion and get back with you next week. I'm kind of busy right now."

"Can we set a time for a conference now? I'm not going to wait too long to file this motion. The discovery period is running and it will be over before we know it."

"I don't have my calendar right in front of me. I'll get back to you."

Unconscionable

"Right. Sure you will," Matt said and hung up.

Although Matt was obligated to give Richmond a reasonable amount of time to respond, he didn't have to wait forever. He programmed his calendar to remind him to follow up in one week. In the meantime he decided to go through the documents and evidence that Cindy had brought in to determine what could be used at trial. It was a very tedious process reading and studying each of the hundreds of documents including notes, deeds, mortgages, statements, letters, and emails. Matt was exhausted when he finally left the office at six thirty.

He went to Candy's place, since she had called earlier and told him the girls were cooking spaghetti if he wanted to come for dinner. When he knocked on the door, Sharon answered wearing shorts and a halter top. Memories of their slumber party a few weeks earlier came rushing through his mind. It was all a blur now, but he did have a vivid memory of Sharon's impressive breasts.

"Just in time. Gina and Jenni are just draining it now."

Matt walked in. "Good. I'm starving."

"You want some wine?" Sharon asked.

"Absolutely. Make it a double."

Sharon grinned. "Tough day?"

"Yeah. You could say that."

Candy came around the corner and smiled at Matt. "There you are."

Matt walked up to her and they embraced. "Thanks for the invitation," he said, letting her go and heading for the kitchen. He took a deep breath, savoring the pleasant aroma of tomato sauce, meatballs, and garlic bread. "I hope you made plenty," he said to Gina, who was cooking in her bikini. He surmised she'd been working on her tan earlier in the afternoon.

Gina nodded. "Get a plate and I'll fill it up."

Matt gave her a plate and she gave him a huge portion. After he'd gotten some garlic bread and refilled his wine glass he sat down at the kitchen table. Candy followed suit and joined

116

him. Soon they were all eating, laughing, and having a good time.

"So, you had a tough day, Matt?" Sharon said.

"Oh, just a bit tedious. Pouring through records can give you a headache in a hurry."

"What are you looking for?"

Matt told them about how Cindy and her late husband had gone through a foreclosure and how it had driven Tony to suicide. "So, I'm looking for the forbearance agreement or evidence that there was one. Cindy swears there was but hasn't been able to locate it. I'm sure RMS has a copy, but they haven't produced it and may not unless we put a lot of heat on them."

"Can they do that?" Gina asked. "Don't they have to turn over everything?"

"They are supposed to, but who's to know if they do or don't."

"Mmm. That sucks," Gina said. "You want some aspirin?"

"Thanks, but I took some before I left the office."

Gina got up, came around so she was directly behind Matt, and put her hands on his shoulders. "Oh my God. You're as tight as a hooker's jeans."

Matt started to laugh, but his laughter turned to moans of relief as Gina gently but firmly massaged his neck and shoulders. "That feels great."

"It should. I spent six months in massage school. Never did get my license, but it comes in handy on a date. It's not quite as good as sex for them but most of my clients will settle for it."

"I'd hire you," Matt said softly. "This *is* almost as good as sex."

Candy watched Gina work, feeling a bit jealous. Matt was officially her boyfriend but she had decided to share him with her girls. They all liked Matt. He was good looking, easygoing, but more importantly, he was a good listener. If one of the girls had a bad date and needed someone to talk to, Matt would sit down with them, look them in the eyes, and listen attentively until they were done. Few men would do that and the girls needed a man to talk to whom they could trust and respect. It didn't hurt either that Matt was an ex-con. For some strange reason, women were attracted to bad boys, and it was particularly true for Candy's crew. Since they walked the fine line between escorting and prostitution, they felt Matt was one of them.

Matt and Gina took their massage therapy to the blue leather sofa in the living room. Matt took off his shirt and lay facedown while Gina climbed on his back so she could apply some serious pressure to loosen his tight muscles. She worked hard, and before long Matt had forgotten about Richmond, RMS, and all the other problems he faced. All he felt at that moment was pure, unadulterated pleasure.

Chapter 12
Loose Ends

Six weeks after Rich signed his contract with the Colson Agency, Amanda got a big package in the mail. It was the preliminary galley ready for Rich's review. It essentially was a handmade copy of the book, complete with a proposed cover design. According to the contract Rich had fourteen days to review it, correct any errors, and approve it subject to the corrections that were noted. Amanda spent two days going over it and then took it to Rich's office. Suzie showed her in and they embraced.

"So, you got the galley," Rich said.

"Yes. They got it back to us pretty fast."

"I should say so. Are they going to release it early?"

"No. It's just that there is a lot of work involved in launching a book so they have to have it completed and advance copies printed four or five months prior to its release."

"So, they're right on schedule, then?"

"Yes. So, it's important that you go through it and make any corrections within the next twelve days. I've gone through it and marked the corrections I saw, but you need to do the same thing and make any corrections I missed."

Rich nodded. "I'm not the greatest editor, but I'll go through it slowly and hopefully I'll notice anything that is awry."

"Good."

"So, will I see it again before it's finalized?"

"No. It will go immediately into production once you've put your final stamp of approval on it. They'll make your corrections, proofread it one more time, and then send it to the printers."

"So, have they given you a release date yet?"

"I don't know, but the sooner you can look it over, the better."

"Okay, I'll get right on it."

"Good," Amanda replied and stood up. She started to leave and then turned back to Rich. "Is Erica getting used to the idea of being on TV yet?"

Rich shook his head. "No. She's pretty worried about it. She's a pretty private person so she won't enjoy the publicity."

Amanda shook her head. "I'm sorry. I hope she isn't mad at you, or me, for making her do this."

"She is, but she'll get over it. Don't worry. Family is important to her, so after it's over she'll move on."

Amanda left feeling rather sick inside, knowing what she was about to do. The television interview was going to be much more traumatic than either of them expected. She was on her way to see a college friend at the *Inquisitor* to set in motion a media storm that would send *The Pact* straight to the *New York Times* Best Seller list. When she had proposed it to Sheila, she was stunned and questioned whether Amanda would have the guts to pull it off. Amanda knew Rich and Erica would be upset at first, but when the royalties started rolling in, they'd thank her. At least she hoped that would be the case. They claimed that the money didn't matter, but she thought that was pretty much bullshit. Of course they were doing it for the money.

She wondered how Ryan would react to her clever little stunt. Would he ever forgive her, or would it mean the end of their relationship? Amanda thought a lot about their relationship, but for some reason a breakup didn't worry her all that much. Did that mean she didn't love Ryan or that her career was more important than their relationship? She supposed it did, and maybe it would be better if they split up now and not invest any more time in a relationship that had no future.

Sylvia Sams had been the editor of their high school newspaper. She was the gossip queen and knew everything that went on socially at the school. Her ambition in life had been to become an entertainment journalist, but that hadn't worked out since she didn't have the raw beauty needed for someone in front of a network camera. For a while she had worked at the *Dallas Morning News* and contributed to their entertainment department, but she was laid off when a steady drop in circulation mandated a reduction in the newspaper's staff. She went on unemployment, but when it was about to run out and she was desperate, she went to the *Inquisitor* and applied for a job.

In her job interview she dazzled them with her knowledge of the entertainment industry and its stars. In fact they were so impressed they hired her on the spot, and she'd been working there now almost five years. Sylvia met Amanda in the reception area, and they went down the street to a sports bar and had lunch. After going through the buffet line and getting couple of beers they found a large booth in the corner where they could spread out.

"So, you got a new job, huh?" Sylvia asked.

"Yes. Can you believe it? I'm actually a literary agent now."

"That's wonderful. I knew you could do it."

"Look at you. I read your magazine every week and love your stories. You're a talented writer."

"Yeah, well. It's not that I'm such a great writer. The key is getting good stories and I'm the master at that."

"I believe you, and that's why I wanted this meeting."

"Really?" Sylvia said.

"Yes, I've got a great story for you. One that will spark a media storm once it comes out and you'll be right in the middle of it. It should do wonders for your career."

Sylvia gave Amanda a skeptical look. "Where would you get a story like that?"

"Well, I kind of stumbled into it."

Unconscionable

She and Sylvia had not been close since graduating from high school. They'd kept in touch and ran into each other from time to time, but that was about the extent of their relationship, so for next half hour Amanda brought her up to date.

"So, when I told Ryan I had decided to be a literary agent he told me about a manuscript his father had up in his attic. I asked him if his father had ever tried to get it published, and he said no."

"Hmm."

"Anyway, I was intrigued, so I talked Ryan into letting me read it."

"Really?"

"Yes. And it was an awesome story. It took place some twenty-five years ago, so I wasn't familiar with what had happened, but the gist of it was that Rich was appointed trustee over Erica's estate and when her father died Rich stepped in and handled everything. She was seventeen at the time and Rich was nearly thirty. Apparently Erica had a crush on Rich and seduced him into a illicit affair, although Rich didn't put up much of a fight. They were madly in love."

Sylvia nodded. "Okay."

"So, everything was fine until Erica's aunt, Martha Collins, found out about the relationship and threatened to have Rich disbarred and prosecuted for statutory rape. Of course, they couldn't let that happen, so Erica tracks down her aunt and goes to the motel she's staying at to try to convince her not to prosecute Rich, except when she gets there Aunt Martha is dead."

"Sounds like a good story, but I don't see why the media will be interested in it now," Sylvia said.

"Well, Rich's new book, *The Pact*, will be coming out soon and, of course, it will follow the official story line—no surprises. Erica is charged with Aunt Martha's murder but is found to be innocent by reason of temporary insanity. The problem is, the book is a lie."

"A lie?" Sylvia asked.

"Yes, when I was up in the attic I found some revisions to the book in Erica's handwriting. She rewrote several key parts of the book. In her version she found Rich at the motel unconscious next to Aunt Martha's body. So, she and Rich's friend Joe move Rich from the crime scene and dump him in an alley behind a tavern near his old office. When he starts to wake up she smacks him over the head with a brick and leaves him there in the alley to be found later. This provides him with an alibi."

"So, Rich was the actual killer?"

"Yes, and he got away with murder because Erica took the fall for him. That's why Erica made him commit to the suicide pact. She wanted to be sure he really loved her before she took the fall for him."

"Wow! That quite a story."

"It gets better. When the book comes out, Rich and Erica are scheduled to be guests on Jay Leno."

"Seriously?"

"Yes. So, if the true story came out the same day, Jay Leno would have no choice but to confront them with it," Amanda said.

Sylvia nodded excitedly. "Uh-huh. And the next day it would be the top story on the entertainment front and I'd own it."

"Yes, you'd be the focus of everyone's attention since you broke the story."

"Okay, but how do I know what you're telling me is true? How do I verify it?"

"Do you really have to verify it? Can't you just say your information came from a reliable source?"

"Well, maybe, but it would be better if I actually had some proof that it's true. Our lawyers might not approve the story without a little credible evidence of its accuracy."

"How about if I let you read Erica's handwritten revisions? Your people can do a handwriting analysis to prove its validity."

Unconscionable

"Where would I get a sample of her handwriting to compare?"

"In her trial some of her letters were introduced into evidence. They should be archived somewhere. I'm sure your people could find them."

Sylvia nodded. "Okay. Your plan might work, but why are you doing this? Rich and Erica are going to know you were the leak, don't you think?"

"I'll deny it. Erica left her notes just lying around in the attic for years. Matt or Ryan or any of their friends who went up there over the years could have found it and read it. Anyway, don't worry about me. I've got a plan to deal with that."

"Right. And all the media attention won't hurt the sale of Rich's book?"

Amanda smiled wryly. "I shouldn't think so."

They both laughed hard.

"Okay, I'm in," Sylvia said. "When can I get an advance copy of the book and see Erica's revisions?"

Amanda grabbed her backpack. "Right now," she said and pulled out a manuscript box. "This is a copy of the galley that Rich is reviewing right now."

"What about Erica's revisions?"

"I'll give them to you just before the book is released."

Amanda could have given her Erica's notes then, but she was afraid the story might leak out prematurely if she did. She couldn't take that chance.

"This is what I love about this job—the anticipation of breaking a scandalous story."

Amanda laughed. "I bet."

Sylvia rose her mug of beer. "Here's to Rich and Erica, may God help them when this story breaks."

Amanda smiled guiltily and rose her glass to Sylvia's. "And may we all survive their wrath."

They both drained their beers and left separately to put their plan in motion. Amanda, on an adrenaline high when she left the bar and got back in her car, had to stifle an urge to ignore the thirty-five-mile-per-hour speed limit downtown. She felt good about her meeting with Sylvia and could almost see Erica's and Rich's faces when Jay Leno confronted them. Sales would go through the roof, and movie producers would be in a frenzy to sign a movie deal. Her career would skyrocket!

As she was driving back to her office, she forged a plan to explain how Sylvia obtained a copy of Erica's revisions to the manuscript. She'd have to enlist someone to break into Rich's home, go to the attic, and steal the revisions. She wondered how that could be done without compromising herself. She didn't want to end up in jail. Then she figured it out. She'd find some unsavory people, inadvertently let them know there was something of great value in the Colemans' attic, and let their devious minds do the rest. It wouldn't matter that they didn't steal the revisions. The press would just assume the robbery was a ruse and the culprits photographed the revisions but otherwise left them undisturbed.

Rich had insurance, Amanda reasoned, so if they took other things it would all be replaced. She'd just have to be sure it was done when they weren't home. She didn't want anyone getting hurt. When Rich and Erica were off on Rich's first book tour would be the perfect time. She'd have to time it very carefully and make sure the robbers knew they had to hit during the weekend while her future in-laws were out of town. She felt good when she got to the office with that loose end ironed out. Her plan was going to work, she just knew it.

Chapter 13
Summary Judgment

Matt was in a good mood because he'd just received a letter advising him that his application to be reinstated with the State Bar of Texas had been approved. Finally he could put his name on pleadings and appear in court. It had been a long, painful journey back, and he was glad it was finally behind him. He just prayed the future would be brighter. He called Candy and told her the good news.

"Oh, that's fabulous, honey. God, what a relief, huh?"

"Yeah, it really is."

"We'll have to celebrate tonight."

"Sounds good to me."

"The girls are going to be thrilled. Maybe we should have another slumber party."

Matt thought about that for a moment. The last slumber party had been memorable but also a little overwhelming. "Nah, how about just you and me. You're the only one I want to be with tonight."

"Wow! Turning down a slumber party?"

"Yes, but don't tell the girls. I don't want to hurt their feelings."

"I won't. I don't really want to share you, anyway."

"Good. Then I'll see you later."

"Okay. Call me."

After he'd told the good news to his secretary, Melissa, and his father, he returned to the task of answering his mail. It was a tedious process that a lot of attorneys delegated to staff, but not Matt. He wanted to see every piece of mail that came through the office. That way he couldn't be blindsided by something that his secretary might not have thought to be important. His brow furrowed as he spotted a letter from Richmond. *Now what's he up to?* He picked it out of the pile and noted it was heavy. Some kind of pleading. He thought maybe it was discovery responses, but it was too early for that. He opened it warily and read the title. *Motion for No Evidence Summary Judgment. What the hell?*

It was premature to be filing a motion for a no evidence summary judgment, as most judges wouldn't consider one until the discovery period was over. The plaintiff couldn't be expected to have all his evidence put together until he'd finished sending out his discovery and taken depositions. This was a bullshit motion designed for one purpose only—to harass him and waste his time. Anger welled inside him as he read the voluminous document. It would take him weeks to respond to it and distract him from more important work on the case. Worst of all, he'd have to spend hours with his client putting affidavits and evidence together for the response. He cursed Richmond for his underhanded tactics. As he was lamenting this development Ryan walked in.

"Hey! I heard the good news."

Matt smiled and stood up. The two brothers embraced.

"Yeah, thanks," Matt said.

"I've got good news, too!" Ryan said excitedly.

"Really? What's that?"

"I got my bar exam results back. I passed!"

Matt forced a smile. "Oh. That's great. Congratulations, little brother."

"Thanks," Ryan said, a little disappointed by Matt's less-than-enthusiastic response. "What's wrong? Something happen?"

"Yeah, look at this bullshit motion for summary judgment."

"What? From Richmond?"

Matt nodded. "That's right, and he's already got it set for hearing."

Ryan shrugged. "Well, that's standard procedure for the

defense bar these days, from what I've been reading in the *Bar Journal*. Any way to run up their bills. You know with tort reform cutting down on the number of lawsuits a lot of firms are hurting for business, so they compensate by billing the hell out of every file they have."

Matt didn't respond.

"So, are the girls throwing you another party?"

Matt shook his head. "No. I think Candy and I are just going to go out to dinner or something. No slumber party tonight."

"*Slumber* party? Is that what happened after Amanda and I left? You never told me."

Matt chuckled. "Yeah, well, some things are private."

Ryan frowned. "No, no. You've got to share with your brother. You don't get to keep secrets. When I left, Sharon and the twins were still there. Did they stay the night?"

The guilty look on Matt's face answered Ryan's question. "Okay, spit it out. I want all the sordid details."

Matt sighed. "It was nothing."

"Nothing, my ass. Did you have sex with anyone other than Candy?"

"I take the Fifth," Matt replied.

"Oh, my God. So, you did, you little rascal. Who'd you do it with?"

"Sharon was first."

"First?"

"Sharon and then Candy cut in."

Ryan shook his head. "So, that was it? Sharon and Candy."

"That's all I could handle. I was half-drunk. The twins got me in the morning—in the hot tub."

"Oh, you're such a liar."

Matt laughed. "It's the truth. I promise you, but believe what you want. I don't care."

Ryan left Matt's office rolling his eyes. Matt sighed when

he was gone, recalling that memorable moment of seeing the twins there naked in the hot tub beckoning him to join them. He wondered if he'd made a mistake in declining another sleepover. His intercom broke that nagging thought. The receptionist announced that Cindy Sharp was on the line. He blinked to bring himself back to reality.

"Cindy, hi," he said.

"Mr. Coleman. I was just calling to see if you heard anything."

Matt took a deep breath. Clients were always impatient, and Cindy was worse than most. Even though he'd explained that litigation took years, she would call every week for an update. "Well, actually something has come up."

"What?" she asked worriedly.

"RMS has filed a motion for summary judgment."

"What does that mean?"

"It means they claim we don't have a case—insufficient evidence to prove all of the elements of our causes of action."

"So, are they right?"

"Well, maybe right now, but we haven't conducted discovery yet. The judge will never grant it. It's premature."

"But they might win?"

"No. I don't think so, but we will have to respond and it's going to take a lot of time and hard work to respond to it. I'll be needing your help to gather information and prepare a response."

"I can't believe this shit! They're going to make us go through a bunch of hoops like a circus clown. The bastards killed my husband. You've got to make them pay."

"We will. But it will take time. You've got to be patient."

"Yeah, well time isn't on my side. I'm destitute," she said, starting to cry.

"Listen, remember the lady we told you about on the inside?"

"Yes," Cindy said.

"Well, apparently Lucius Jones is involved in document

forgery. We don't know how it works quite yet, but there is a chance the affidavits attached to this motion may be forgeries."

"What? The bastard is making up his own evidence?"

"Yes. That's what it looks like, but I haven't had a chance to study the affidavit or verify the title to the loan yet. But don't worry, we're on top of it."

"Don't worry? Right. That's easy for you to say. Maybe I should go find the bastard and put a bullet in his head."

The line went dead. Matt shifted nervously in his chair. Was she serious? He didn't think so. She was just angry and for good reason. He called her back just to be sure, but she didn't pick up. He wondered if he should do something, but what could he do? Finally, he decided he was overreacting and went to lunch.

When he got back he took a closer look at the motion for summary judgment and, in particular, the exhibits to it. One of them was an assignment of the original note from Southern Atlantic Mortgage Company to RMS dated July 11, 2005. It was signed by Robin Stuart, executive VP. He wondered if Stuart had actually signed the assignment. Still worried about Cindy hanging up on him, he called her again. She picked up this time.

"Hello."

"Cindy. This is Matt again. We were cut off. Are you all right?"

She sighed. "Yeah, I'm fine."

"Good. I took a closer look at the motion, and I'm going to check the signature on one of the documents. It may be a forgery. If it is it could blow the case wide open. I just wanted you to know."

"Thank you," Cindy said, seeming dejected. "I'm sorry I hung up on you. It's just been hard with Tony gone. I miss him so much.'

"I know it's been hard on you, but I want you to know that Jones is going to pay for what he's doing. In fact, I'm devoting every waking hour to figuring out how to take him down along with all the other scumbags in the mortgage business like him."

"Yes, Lucius Jones will pay," Cindy said evenly. "Thanks for calling me back, Matt. I'm okay. You don't have to worry about me. Everything is under control."

"Okay," Matt replied, but he wasn't sure Cindy was okay. She was different somehow—like she'd had a few drinks or taken a sedative. Finally, he decided she was still grieving and her mood swings were just part of the process. Perhaps after she got angry with him, she took her doctor's advice and took a sedative. *That's probably it,* he convinced himself.

Chapter 14
Doc Shop

It took about a week for Shelly to get her new division staffed, organized, and under way. It was a monumental job to go through the thousands of files, figure out what documents were missing, determine what each document would look like had it been generated properly at the time of the transaction, furnish the information to the CDR, or the "Doc Shop" as Shelly called it, and then review it for accuracy.

It was a stressful job, too, because there had to be 100 percent accuracy. Most of these documents would be introduced in court or in deposition and scrutinized very carefully by opposing counsel. Any error could lead to the document being discredited and a foreclosure being set aside or a proof of claim being denied. Further, such an error could raise a red flag and lead to a more extensive inquiry.

To complicate matters more, nobody in her division could know that the documents were being produced after the fact from a company not even affiliated with RMS. It had to look entirely legitimate, a division devoted to tracking down missing documents rather than producing documents that never existed. So nobody on Shelly's staff knew Sanford Ross, Roger Stafford, or Juan Rubio.

Since Shelly was the only one who could interact with the Doc Shop, she spent long hours each day on the job. Unfortunately, even though her department was well organized, she had no control over the Doc Shop, which, as the volume grew, was taking longer and longer to produce its documents. On account of this she was getting a lot of complaints from the company's attorneys who were getting bombarded with discovery

Unconscionable

requests in pending litigation or trying to clear titles on foreclosed properties.

When the situation got to a critical state Shelly asked for a meeting with Sanford Ross and his staff. She had to find out why the Doc Shop couldn't keep up. At least that's what she told him. Her real objective was to get a closer look at the operation to see how it worked in case she'd ever have to testify. Ross agreed to her request and invited her to come to their offices the following afternoon at three p.m. for a tour.

The next afternoon she drove up to CDR's offices located in an office-warehouse district off Midway Road in Carrollton. CDR's operation took a third of the office building, and there were about a dozen cars parked in front. For anyone driving by it looked like a typical document storage or shredding operation. Shelly parked her grey Honda Accord, walked in, and introduced herself to Melba, the receptionist. Melba said she was expected and that Mr. Ross would be out momentarily. She took a seat and began absently thumbing through a magazine. A few minutes later Sanford Ross appeared. She had only briefly met him before at RMS's offices. At the time he seemed a pushy and bit arrogant. She wondered how best to handle him—she needed him to open up to her. He extended his hand, and she shook it warmly.

"It's nice to see you again," Shelly said.

"Yes, I'm glad you finally decided to come out and see our operation."

"Well, I've had my hands full getting my department organized and under way. Can you believe the volume of business we've been sending your way?"

Ross nodded. "Lucius warned us he'd keep us busy, but you're right, it's been a bit more than I expected."

"Right. That's why I wanted to come out. You know, find out how you operate, so maybe we can coordinate our efforts a little bit better."

"Okay. Follow me and I'll give you the nickel tour."

"Where are Juan and Roger today? I thought they were

134

running the operation for you."

"Juan is on vacation and Roger is sick, so I'm filling in today."

Shelly doubted that was true, but she didn't say anything. Apparently Ross didn't trust Juan and Roger completely or he'd have let them give the tour. She followed him into a large room filled with computer workstations and high-volume printers. He walked into one of the cubicles where a young woman was working. She looked up when they walked in and surrounded her.

"Okay. This is Stephanie. She prepares the assignments. She has every format ever used by RMS or any of the former servicers. There is also a database that provides the names every employee of the servicers who would have been authorized to sign the assignments and randomly picks one to be listed as the authorized representative. The program is so good it knows when employees were on vacation or sick and makes sure their names don't appear on any documents during that time period."

"Wow. That's impressive," Shelly agreed.

"Stephanie, how many assignments do you do in a typical day?" Ross asked.

"Two hundred or so on a typical day," she replied. "I have to manually input the data or it would go much faster."

"Thanks."

Ross led them over to one of the high-speed printers. "This printer can reproduce just about any document in black and white or color. Document forms can be scanned in and then made into master templates for mass production. We can duplicate state emblems, corporate logos, or letterheads, you name it."

Shelly frowned. "You mean you create government documents?"

"Not for you guys, but we could do it if you needed it."

Shelly couldn't believe what she was hearing. She wondered if they did driver's licenses and passports, too. She followed Ross as he took her into the next room. Here there were eight long worktables with dozens of men and women signing

135

documents. Each had two stacks and would routinely pull a document from the first stack, sign it and put it on the second stack, and then repeat the process.

"Sergio. Who are you right now?" Ross asked.

Sergio smiled. "Russell Thompson, vice president of acquisitions for Trinidad Mortgage Company," he replied.

Shelly looked at the document and saw where Sergio had signed in perfect script the name *Russell Thompson*. Shelly frowned.

"So, how do you get people to do this? Aren't you worried they'll go to the authorities and tell them what you are doing?"

"No. Most of these people are ex-cons, homeless people, or illegal immigrants. None of them want anything to do with the government. As long as we pay them promptly in cash they'll do whatever we tell them."

Shelly was shocked and found it difficult not to show it. This was blatant criminal activity and she was a party to it. Her stomach started to twist, and she felt nauseous. She decided it was time to leave. She looked at her watch and feigned alarm.

"Oh, look at the time. I'm going to be late for an employee interview. I'm afraid I'm going to have to go. Thanks for the tour. This has helped me understand the logistics of your operation. Do you expect to be expanding to keep up with the demand?"

"Yes, the lease on the space next to us is up soon, so we'll be doubling our size in the next ninety days."

"Great. That should help a lot. I'll come back and take another look after the expansion."

"Excellent. We'll be looking forward to it," Ross said.

Ross showed Shelly to the front door, and she forced a smile as she left. On the way back to the office she stopped by Starbucks, where her meeting wasn't with a prospective employee, but rather a prearranged meeting with Rich and Matt. Rich had wanted Matt to meet Shelly since he would be handling the mortgage cases now that he had gotten his license back. They got a table in the back and sat with their backs to the front window.

"You won't believe where I just came from," Shelly said.

"Where?" Rich asked.

"The Doc Shop."

"The what?" Matt asked.

"The offices of Consolidated Document Retrieval. I call it the Doc Shop. You know, since they produce documents to order." She told them about her tour of the facility and how they could forge just about any kind of document.

"So, let me get this straight," Matt said. "They have hundreds of people forging documents?"

"Yes, it's mind boggling. I'll admit."

"But nobody at RMS knows about it except you and Lucius."

"Well, the lenders know about it. That's part of Lucius's sales pitch. He promises to create a paper trail so they can prove up their loans."

"Do you have any contact with these lenders?"

"No. Not so far. Lucius does all his negotiations in noisy restaurants or strip clubs where he is sure nobody is listening."

"Did he tell you that?"

"No. His secretary did. She overheard him tell some clients that nowadays you couldn't talk about anything sensitive except in your lawyer's office or at a strip club where it's too noisy for anyone to overhear you. But, who knows, they could just as well go to a bowling alley or mall parking lot, who knows?"

"Yeah, I'm not sure a restaurant's a good idea. I just listened to a news report that a lot of restaurants have listening devices at each table. They say it's so they can monitor the employees' interaction with their customers, but can you imagine the things they overhear that have nothing to do with their employees."

"That's outrageous," Shelly said. "There's no privacy anymore."

"So, is there any way to tell if a document is a forgery?" Matt asked.

Shelly thought for a moment. "Yes. The signatures won't match the original officer's signature. If you can get true samples of the officer's signature and compare them, it should be obvious."

Matt shook his head. "Nobody would ever think to do that unless they knew the document was a forgery."

"Exactly," Shelly agreed. "Nobody would ever dream there is such widespread fraud going on in the mortgage industry. And those who suspect it don't care that much because it's only done to correct sloppy business practices. The consumer owes the money so they are not really getting hurt."

"Except people who buy property and then later find out they don't really own it because of someone's sloppy paperwork. Or, somebody invests in these securitized trusts and then their investment craters when it turns out the trust can't prove it owns half of its inventory of notes," Rich remarked.

"I may have one of those forged documents," Matt said. "Could you check it out?"

"Sure, what do you have?"

"An assignment from Southern Atlantic Mortgage Company to RMS dated July 11, 2005. It was signed by Robin Stuart, executive VP."

"Do you have a copy?" Shelly asked.

"Right," Matt said, pulling out an envelope. "It's in here."

Shelly opened the envelope and examined the document. "No problem. I'll find Mr. Stuart's actual signature, compare it, and let you know."

"Thanks."

They continued to talk for another few minutes and then the meeting broke up. Shelly felt better after she had spilled her guts to Matt and Rich. It made her feel cleansed knowing that she was only getting her hands dirty so Lucius Jones and his kind could be brought down and the integrity of the mortgage industry could be restored. She didn't know exactly how that would come about, but she trusted Matt and Rich to make it happen.

When she got back to the office it was nearly six thirty p.m. and the office was deserted. She went to her office to check her messages and emails before going home. She frequently got frantic messages from attorneys or customer service representatives that she had to deal with immediately and couldn't wait until the following morning. As expected, there were a few brush fires she had to put out, and the next time she looked at the clock it was nearly eight thirty.

It was dark outside, and except for a few security lights the offices were dark. She turned off her light as she was leaving but noticed Lucius's office was still lit up. She wondered if he was still working. She hadn't heard him, but she'd been pretty focused on what she was doing, so he could still be working and she wouldn't have realized it. The building manager had asked all the tenants to be sure all the lights were off when they left at night, so it was the rule that the last person to leave turned off all the lights.

Shelly detoured by Lucius's office to see if he was there and, if not, to turn off his lights. As she stepped into his office she looked around but didn't see him. When she started to turn off the lights she smelled a strange odor. She sniffed the air and then noticed an overturned wastepaper basket. She took a step toward it, wondering if Lucius had thrown away some food that was decaying. As she was leaning over and sniffing one more time, Lucius's body came into view. Her eyes widened as she saw him lying in a pool of blood with a crystal-handled letter opener protruding from his neck. She screamed several times and almost fainted. Finally, when she started to regain her composure, she looked around frantically, wondering what to do. She knew nobody was around, so she took her cell phone out of her purse and called 911. Twelve minutes later there was a loud knock at the door.

"Dallas police! Open up."

She rushed out of Lucius's office, went to the front door, and opened it. Two detectives rushed in followed by a uniformed policeman.

"Where's the body?" the first detective asked, thrusting his badge in front of Shelly's face. It read DETECTIVE GIL JENSON.

"Back here," Shelly replied and led him to Lucius's office.

Detective Jenson told her to stay put, and he went in and looked around. His partner followed him in and quickly scanned the room.

"Nobody in or out of this office until the crime scene unit arrives," Jenson barked to the uniformed officer.

"Yes, sir," he replied.

Several more uniformed officers came through the front door along with a building security officer.

Shelly took a seat in Lucius's secretary's chair. She watched anxiously as the room quickly filled with more detectives, policemen, and crime scene personnel. Fear swept over her as she tried to fathom the ramifications of Lucius's murder. She feared all the dark secrets that she had become involved in would now be exposed, and with Lucius gone, she'd take the fall for all his sinister activities. She wondered who had killed Lucius and why. Her mind raced trying to make sense of it. Should she get an attorney? Should she keep her mouth shut or talk openly to the police? If she clammed up they'd think she killed Lucius. She didn't know what to do. Tears began streaming down her cheeks as she began to sob.

Chapter 15
Under Suspicion

At nine thirty p.m. Rich got a high-priority text message on his cell phone from Shelly. This surprised him as he couldn't imagine what could be so urgent at that time of night. He apologized to Erica and left. When he got to Starbucks about thirty minutes later, Shelly was seated with her back to the front window in their usual spot. He rushed over and sat down next to her.

"Shelly. What's wrong?"

"Lucius is dead. I just found him with a letter opener stuck in his neck."

"What? Are you serious?"

"Yes. I've been at the Dallas police station up until a few minutes ago giving them my statement."

"Do they know who did it?"

"They asked me that same question. I told them I only knew of two people who hated him enough to kill him—his wife and his ex-partner."

"I know about his ex-partner, Walter Savage, but I didn't know he had marital problems."

"Yes, his wife hates his guts. She caught him cheating on her about six months ago. The only reason she hasn't divorced him is RMS isn't worth much right now. She's hoping he'll turn it around and it will become more valuable. Then she'll file for divorce."

"It doesn't sound like she did it, then," Rich said.

"Unless she's given up and decided to go for the insurance money," Shelly said thoughtfully.

"How much insurance does he have?"

"A quarter million group insurance and I'm sure he had some personal policies as well."

"That could be the motive, but killing your husband and getting away with it is no simple proposition. She'll be the number-one suspect unless she has an airtight alibi. If she doesn't, the insurance money will be tied up until her name is cleared and that could take months if not years."

"I could see Savage doing it," Shelly said. "Lucius screwed him when they split up the business and he didn't even realize it until it was too late."

"I wonder who's going to run the company now that Lucius is dead?"

Shelly sighed. "I have no idea. I hope it's not his wife, Samantha. I'd hate to have her as a boss."

"Could she run it? Does she know anything about it?"

"Yes. She ran the insurance department at North American Servicing before they split up. I don't know why she didn't come to work for RMS. I guess it was about the time she discovered the affair so she decided to find a new job."

"Does she know about the forgery department?" Rich asked.

"Probably. Before she caught him with his pants down, they worked together pretty closely. When it happened he begged her to forgive him, but she wasn't interested. I don't think she was all that upset, but saw it more as an opportunity to extricate herself from a bad relationship and end up with some serious cash in the bank."

"What makes you think that? Did she say something to give you that impression?"

"No. It's just office gossip, but I'm pretty sure it's true."

"Well, I don't know that there's much we can do about the situation now. Why don't you go home and get some rest. I'm sure tomorrow will be an interesting day for you. Let's meet tomorrow night about this same time and you can fill me in on what's going on."

Shelly agreed to the meeting and then left. Rich finished his coffee and then called Matt on his cell phone. He filled him in on the murder and Shelly's situation.

"I hope this doesn't screw up my case. What if RMS falls apart with Lucius gone and ends up in bankruptcy? Our claim would be wiped out if that happened."

"Shelly thinks Samantha Jones is capable of stepping in and running the business."

"If she's not in jail," Matt noted.

"Maybe she'll have an alibi and be able to step in and take over."

"Even so, it's not likely she'll be able to run it as well as Lucius did."

"Well, you never know. She might be a better manager than Lucius or she might realize her shortcomings and hire someone to run it for her. There's no reason to worry about it now. We just have to assume the company will continue in business and our lawsuit is still viable."

There was a beep on Matt's phone. "Hang on. Someone is trying to get through to me."

The phone went temporarily dead and Rich took a deep breath. He wondered how Lucius's murder would affect their lawsuit. Was it the beginning of the end for RMS? If Samantha Jones didn't want to run the business she'd likely put it up for sale and the assets might disappear before they could get their case to trial. As much as he had disliked Lucius Jones he wished he were still alive. His death had made things much more complicated.

Matt came back on the line. "Dad. That was Cindy Sharp. The police are looking for her. They came by her house but she wasn't home. Her babysitter was there and told them she was out. She wants to know what to do. Should she and the kids get a motel so the police can't find them?"

"Jesus. Why are they after her?"

"The police said they just wanted to talk to her."

143

"About what?" Rich asked.

"They didn't say. Do you think it could be about Lucius Jones's murder?"

"Possibly, if they came across the lawsuit and read the petition. They would have seen that Cindy blamed Lucius for her husband's suicide. Does Cindy even know Lucius is dead?"

"Yes. It's made the TV news, but she claims to know nothing about it."

"Where was she tonight? Why did she need a babysitter?"

"She said she had a shopping date with a girlfriend but she didn't show up."

"So, she has no alibi?"

"No," Matt said. "Apparently not."

"We'd better call Ryan and tell him he's got a new client."

"Do you think he can handle it? He's just barely out of law school."

"We'll give him any help he needs. I'm sure he'll be fine."

Matt sighed. "I don't know."

"He'll be fine," Rich repeated. "I'd rather not farm Cindy's case to another law firm. It's going to be complicated enough as it is."

"All right. I'll call him and give him the good news."

"And tell Cindy to meet us at our office. I'm going there right now. We'll all meet with her tonight and then one of us will call the detective handling the case tomorrow and arrange a meeting."

"Okay."

Rich hung up the phone, walked out to his car, and took off for his office. He was worried about Cindy's civil case if she were a person of interest in Jones's death. If the jury thought she had anything to do with his murder they would figure she'd gotten her revenge and not award her a dime. Ryan would have to prove her innocent of Jones's murder before the civil case went to trial, otherwise they'd be screwed. Luckily criminal cases were put on the fast track so it was likely it would be over long before the civil case came to trial. That was assuming, of course, that they charged someone right away.

Rich unlocked the office, went inside, and turned on the lights. He figured it would be a long night, so he made a pot of coffee. Ryan showed up about ten minutes later and they went into the conference room. Matt and Cindy came in a few minutes later.

"Okay," Ryan said to Cindy. "I hear you had detectives looking for you?"

"Yes, Detectives Jill Finch and Tom Morin. They left their cards."

So, where were you tonight?" Ryan asked.

"I was supposed to meet a girlfriend from work at Stonebrier Mall. We were going to do some shopping and then get dessert at the Cheesecake Factory, but she didn't show up," Cindy replied.

"Do you know what happened?"

"Yes. I got a text from her about ten minutes after we were supposed to hook up that her son was throwing up, so she had to cancel."

"So, what did you do?"

"I went shopping alone. I'd already spent money on a babysitter, so I figured I might as well take advantage of it."

"Did you buy anything?"

"No. I was in a bad mood and didn't see anything I liked that much."

"Did you go to the Cheesecake Factory?" Ryan asked.

"I thought about it, but it's embarrassing to go in there alone and eat a big piece of cheesecake by yourself. People would think I was a real loser."

Matt laughed. "Oh, I doubt that, but I understand what you're saying. I hate to eat alone myself."

"The problem is you left no paper trail. We can't prove

you were even at the mall," Rich said.

Cindy shrugged. "Sorry."

"Did you see anybody you knew or talk to anybody at all?" Ryan asked.

Cindy shook her head. "No. I'm afraid not."

"Did you get gas that night?"

"No."

"Do you know where Reliable Mortgage Servicing's offices are located?"

Cindy looked away and closed her eyes. Then she took a deep breath and looked at Ryan. "Yes, I'm afraid I do."

"How?" Rich asked. "The modification was all handled by mail, wasn't it?"

"Yes, it was, but I looked them up online and got their address. Then I paid them a visit to give them a piece of my mind."

"When was this?"

"Months ago. When they were threatening to foreclose."

"So, were you able to talk to Jones at that time?"

"No. He was out but I did leave a message with his secretary."

"Really? What was in the message?"

"I told him that he wasn't going to get away with taking our house and that he would pay one day for the way he treated people."

"So, did you ever make good on your threats?" Rich asked.

"No. What could I do? File a complaint with somebody? I just figured eventually we'd win our lawsuit and I'd get my revenge that way."

"So, you didn't go over to his office today?" Ryan asked.

"No. Like I said. I was at the mall. I never got close to downtown Dallas."

"Good," Ryan said. "At least there won't be anybody who saw you down there."

"So, do they really think I had something to do with Lucius Jones's death?" Cindy asked.

"Well, they probably have no idea at this stage, but they have to check out anybody with a motive. When they talk to you and you don't have an alibi, that's going to put you high up on their person-of-interest list."

Cindy groaned. "Shit! That's all I need."

"What I'm more worried about," Rich said, "is the impact Lucius's death will have on your lawsuit. The fact that the owner of RMS is dead takes some of the wind out of our sails as to punitive damages. The jury isn't going to be anxious to hurt a grieving widow—Mrs. Jones—and her children. Not to mention that RMS may not be viable if new management doesn't step in quickly and take charge."

"So, what are we going to do?" Cindy asked.

"Well, it depends if you want us to represent you in this matter. It's not part of your lawsuit, so we'd have to charge you by the hour."

Cindy rolled her eyes. "You know I don't have any money."

"I know and normally we wouldn't touch a murder case with less than a $50,000 retainer, but we might be willing to take your case due to the special circumstances that exist right now."

"What special circumstances?" Cindy asked.

"Well, we feel pretty good about your civil case so we might agree to let you pay us from your share of the proceeds of the recovery. The problem with that is if you lose, then we'd get nothing."

"But you said you felt good about the case?"

"We do, but that's a hell of a gamble, which we wouldn't usually take, except for one thing."

"What's that?" Cindy asked warily.

"We have in our firm a brand-new attorney who has his mind set on practicing criminal law."

Cindy looked at Ryan. "So, you want me to let Ryan

represent me. So, I'm like a guinea pig?"

Rich laughed. "Well, it won't be that bad. Matt and I will keep a close eye on your case and make sure he's doing a good job. We're not criminal attorneys, but we know plenty of good criminal attorneys who we can call on for help if need be."

"Well, that's probably better than a court-appointed attorney," Cindy reasoned.

"If I were in trouble, I'd trust my little brother," Matt said sincerely.

She sighed. "Okay. I can live with that, I suppose."

"Good. Ryan will fix up a contract and have you sign it before you leave so we can represent to the detectives assigned to the murder investigation that we indeed represent you. Tomorrow, Ryan and I will arrange for them to come here and ask you their questions. Hopefully, from their interview we'll learn a little more about the murder. We have someone at RMS, too, who will keep us apprised of what's going on there, so hopefully we'll be able to stay out in front of the situation."

Cindy nodded. "Okay. When should I be here?"

"Just keep your cell phone on and we'll call you the moment we have a firm time."

"Okay," Cindy said and got up to leave.

Ryan escorted her into his office where he had her sign a contract for the criminal defense in the event she were charged. Ryan was excited to think he might have a murder case, but deep down hoped it wouldn't come to pass. He was smart enough to know it would be better to start off slow and work his way up to the big leagues, but he also knew it wasn't wise to pass up a golden opportunity. He'd just have to work doubly hard to make sure Cindy had the best defense possible.

The next day Rich called Detective Jill Finch at the number printed on the card that he had been left at Cindy's place.

"Finch here," she said.

"Detective. This is Rich Coleman. I'm an attorney representing Cindy Sharp. She says you left your card at her place last night."

"Oh, okay. Yeah. We need to talk to her in regard to a homicide last night."

"Who was killed?" Rich asked.

"Lucius Jones. CEO of Reliable Mortgage Servicing."

"Right. I saw something about that on the news."

"Yes, and we did a search of the county records and found out your client has a lawsuit going against RMS."

"Yes, she does."

"So, we need to talk to her."

"How about this afternoon, say, two o'clock p.m. at my office?"

"Sure, where are your offices?"

Rich gave her directions and then hung up. He called Ryan and told him to contact Cindy and have her in their offices at one thirty. It was always good to prep a client before they were interrogated. Detectives could be extremely intimidating, and she needed to know how to respond to them. When she arrived they took her into the conference room.

"Okay, Cindy. Don't let these guys scare you. They are just here for information. You didn't have anything to do with Jones's murder and they don't have any evidence against you, so this should just be routine."

Cindy nodded. "Right."

"Now, a couple of rules you need to follow. One, listen carefully to each question. If you don't understand it don't try to answer it. Just ask them to restate it. Okay?"

"Okay."

"Two. Just answer the question they ask you. Don't volunteer information. In other words, if they ask you what time you had lunch yesterday don't tell them you went to Wendy's and got a hamburger about two p.m. Just say two p.m."

"Right."

"Three. If you don't know the answer to a question just say so. Don't speculate or tell them what you heard. If you don't know the answer to the questions just say, 'I don't know.' "

"Uh-huh."

"Four. If they keep asking you the same question, over and over again, just keep giving them the same answer. Don't feel like you have to change your answer just because they don't like it. Stick to your guns. Remember they are here to get evidence against you. They are not your friend no matter how polite and amiable they may seem."

Cindy nodded.

"Five. If you get flustered, scared, or just want to confer with me a minute before you answer a question just say, 'I need a minute with my attorney.' Then we'll step outside and you can ask me whatever question you have. It's better to confer with me privately than answer a question you're not sure about."

"All right."

"So, have you thought of anything since last night that we need to know?" Ryan asked.

"Like what?" Cindy asked.

"Have you thought of any other contact you may have had with Jones—other letters, emails, telephone calls, or face-to-face encounters?"

"No. Not that I can remember."

"All right, then," Rich said. "Just sit tight until the detectives get here and we'll get started."

Cindy relaxed in her chair as Rich and Ryan left her alone. When Rich got back to his office he saw there was a message from Richmond. He wondered what he wanted so he called him back.

"This is Marvin Richmond," Richmond said.

"Marvin. Rich Coleman returning your call."

"Oh. Yes. I guess you heard about Lucius Jones's murder."

"I did. I was sorry to hear it. Do the police have any leads yet?"

"No. Nothing solid yet."

"So, who's going to run RMS now?"

"That remains to be seen. Ron Seward is the VP. He's taken over the day-to-day management until there is a board meeting."

"Right. Well, what can I do for you?"

"I'd like to move all our deadlines back by ninety days due to Mr. Jones's death. It's going to take a while for his replacement to be selected and get up to speed on the case."

"Sure," Rich replied. "That shouldn't be a problem as long as you don't set your summary judgment for hearing in the next ninety days."

"No. I'll wait."

"Okay. I'll have to confirm it with my client but it shouldn't be a problem."

"Good. I'll send you an order."

Rich hung up. He couldn't remember Marvin Richmond ever being so amiable before. He wondered what was up with him. Did he have a trick up his sleeve? As he was thinking about this Suzie came on the intercom.

"Detectives Finch and Morin are here."

"Okay. I'll be right with them."

Rich got up and stepped into the reception area. They all shook hands. They engaged in a little small talk, and then Rich led them into the conference room. Ryan stood up but Cindy didn't move.

"This is Cindy Sharp," Rich said. "Cindy, these are Detectives Tom Morin and Jill Finch."

Detective Morin was about six feet tall, heavyset, with dark hair, and had a scowl on his face. Detective Finch was much shorter, blond, and robust and seemed amiable.

"Pleased to meet you," Cindy said.

"So, how can we help you, Detectives?" Ryan asked.

Morin looked at Ryan. "Well, like I said on the phone, we searched the records at the courthouse and discovered this lawsuit your client has going against Mr. Jones."

"Well, it's against his company RMS," Ryan said.

"I know but in your complaint you allege that RMS was responsible for Tony Sharp's suicide. Is that what you think, Ms. Sharp?"

Cindy nodded. "There is no doubt in my mind about it. RMS is responsible."

"Did you know the decedent, Lucius Jones?"

"No. I've never met him," Cindy replied evenly.

"Did you know he was the CEO of Reliable Mortgage Servicing Inc.?"

"Sure, I read about him in the newspapers."

"Didn't you also write him a letter complaining about how his company was treating you and your husband?"

"Yes, when I couldn't get the customer service department to respond to me."

"In fact, you hand delivered the letter, didn't you?"

"Yes. I wanted to be sure he read it. I figured if it came in the mail someone would just file it without him seeing it."

"Did you read the article in *Forbes* last week about RMS's policy of dual tracking?"

Cindy looked at Ryan.

Ryan frowned. "What does that have to do with your investigation?" Ryan asked.

"It's a simple question," Detective Morin said. "Yes or no?"

"I may have skimmed it," Cindy admitted.

"So, you knew that Lucius Jones had implemented a policy of dual tracking at RMS."

"You mean screwing with people?" Cindy replied.

"Well, that's the net effect. I think that policy is the gist of your complaint—the government mandated that RMS consider modifying your loan rather than foreclose, but what they did was process your modification at the same time they were processing your foreclosure. The problem was they weren't really interested in modifying your loan and were only going through the motions to satisfy the government. So, all they had to do to get what they wanted was lose your paperwork and delay the modification process to give them time to foreclose."

"Okay, so you can read," Ryan said. "What's that got to do with anything?"

"It's called motive. Your client knew Lucius Jones had just started RMS and was responsible for adopting the policy of dual processing, which ultimately ended up costing your client her home and her husband. Isn't that right, Ms. Sharp?"

"Don't answer that," Ryan said. "Do you have any other questions?"

"Yes. Where were you last night between six and eight o'clock p.m.?"

Cindy sighed. "At Stonebrier Mall."

"Were you with someone?"

"No. I was alone. I was supposed to meet a friend but her kid got sick and she canceled."

"So, how long were you at the mall?"

"From about six to seven thirty."

"Did anybody see you?"

"I wouldn't know, but I didn't see anybody I knew."

"Did you buy anything or use your credit card?"

Cindy shook her head. "No."

"So you don't have a confirmable alibi?"

Cindy shrugged. "I guess not."

"Did you see Lucius Jones last night?"

"No."

"You didn't go over to his office for any reason?"

"No. My attorney gave me strict instructions not to contact RMS or any of its employees while the lawsuit was pending."

"All right," Detective Morin said. "That's all I have for now. If you're telling the truth, then you'll probably not be hearing from us again, but if we find out you've lied to us we'll definitely be paying you another visit, and it won't be as pleasant as this one has been."

"Okay. There's no need to threaten her," Ryan said. "She's telling you the truth."

"I hope you're right, counselor. For her sake I hope you're right."

Detective Morin and his partner left, and Cindy let out a sigh of relief. "What an asshole."

"Yeah. Don't let it get to you. He was just trying to intimidate you so you'd be too scared to lie. You did fine."

"What if I didn't lie but I left something out?"

Rich and Ryan looked at each other. "Left something out?" Ryan repeated.

"Well, he didn't ask where I was before I went to the mall."

"Where were you?"

"I was over at the Bureau of Vital Statistics near Parkland Hospital getting copies of Tony's death certificate."

"So, you weren't too far from Jones's office at RMS?"

"Right. In fact, I may have driven right past it about the time of the murder. Should I have told Detective Morin that? I wasn't sure."

Ryan shook his head. "No. With a little luck he'll never know."

But Rich knew better. In this day and age with surveillance cameras everywhere one of them would have surely caught Cindy's car in the vicinity of RMS's offices and eventually Detective Morin would find that tape and be back to confront them with it. Rich's stomach began to twist, and Ryan shifted nervously in his chair.

Chapter 16
Release

Amanda was ecstatic when she received five advance copies of *The Pact* in the mail. She immediately sat down and inspected one of them carefully from beginning to end. Delighted with how it had turned out, she called Rich.

"I've got it!" Amanda said gleefully.

"How does it look?" Rich asked.

"It's beautiful. I love the cover, and the layout is very professional yet a bit unique. They did a good job."

"So, when can I see it?"

"How about I drop a couple of copies over to you during the lunch hour?"

"That will be fine. Do you want to have lunch?"

"No, but we should get on the line with Robert Todd to talk about your promotional tour and TV appearance."

"Sure. That sounds good. I'll see you at noon."

Amanda hung up and immediately called Sheila Samson at Thorn.

"The book looks fabulous," Amanda said excitedly.

"Yes, doesn't it?" Sheila replied. "We're getting good feedback from our sales reps. They say the book buyers like the look of the book, and the story line, but they're not sure if the public will be interested in a twenty-five-year-old murder."

"Well, we know that will change, don't we?"

"Indeed we do," Sheila agreed. "How is that aspect of your marketing plan coming along?"

"Well, after I see Rich I'm going to see my contact at the *Inquisitor*. I'll give her a copy of the book and let her read it first, then I'll visit her again with the real story."

"Sounds good. Just be sure the timing of the story is right."

"Oh, I will. Don't worry. It will be in everybody's best interest to get it right."

"I told the people at Leno to expect a lot of buzz on the day of Rich and Erica's appearance."

"What did they say?"

"They wanted more specifics, but I just said there would likely be a lot of controversy about the book and that Jay should be ready for it."

"Good. I'm going over to Rich's office right now to give him a couple of copies of the book. I'll get him on the phone with Bob to coordinate his book tour. Do you have a date for Leno yet?"

"Check with Bob to be sure."

"I will. Talk to you later."

"Bye."

Amanda stuffed three copies of *The Pact* into her backpack and headed off to Rich's office. It was a cool fall day, but the trees hadn't begun to turn yet. In Dallas they didn't turn until late November, as it was often eighty-five to ninety degrees during October. She parked in the visitor parking in front of the building and took the elevator to the seventh floor. Rich had nice offices, and the view from his office of downtown Dallas was breathtaking. Suzie showed her into his office but didn't leave.

Amanda gave her a look. "Hey, I've been waiting twenty years to see this book. Come on, let's see it," Suzie said.

Amanda laughed and dug out two copies from her backpack. She handed one to Suzie and one to Rich.

"Wow! This is impressive. Aren't you glad you finally dug that manuscript out of your attic?"

Rich shrugged. "You can thank Amanda for that. It would still be there had she and Ryan not conspired against me."

"Ah, come on," Suzie said. "You've been dying to get this published since the day you wrote it. Admit it."

Rich cracked a smile. "Well, you may be right."

They all laughed.

"All right, I'll leave you two to your business," Suzie said and left the room.

"So, what do you think?" Amanda asked.

Rich held the book up and opened it. "It's incredible. I can't believe I'm a published author."

"Soon to be a best-selling author," Amanda added.

"Well, that remains to be seen."

"I don't know. I talked to Sheila and she says the book buyers are pretty excited about the book hitting the shelves."

"Really? That's good to hear."

"Well, let's get Bob on the phone. I've got meetings all afternoon with media people about your book."

Rich raised his eyebrows. "What kind of media people?"

"A couple of book reviewers and a magazine editor. I'm trying to make sure there are plenty of people reviewing it."

Rich nodded and sat down at his desk. "Okay, I'll get Mr. Todd on speakerphone."

Amanda sat down and took a notepad out of her backpack while Rich dialed the number. The operator at Thorn came on the line, and Rich asked for Robert Todd.

"Hello, this is Robert Todd."

"Mr. Todd. This is Rich Coleman and I've got Amanda here. You're on speakerphone."

"Hi, Rich . . . Amanda."

"Hello, Bob," Amanda said. "So, what do you think of the book?"

"It looks great, and everybody I've sent it to is excited about its release."

"Good," Amanda said. "Well, Sheila said when the advance copies came out to get in touch with you to work out a promotional campaign."

"It's all worked out. I just need to get your approval on the dates."

Unconscionable

"I'm at your disposal," Rich said. "That's the advantage of having two sons in the practice—they can cover for me if something comes up."

"Well, good. I've got a six-stop tour lined up the last week of the month. We're going to start you at the New England Independent Bookseller's Association Trade Show in Boston on Friday. It will be an informal meeting with independent bookstore owners and then a signing."

"Sounds interesting."

"Then a couple of book signings, one at the Manhattan Barnes & Noble in New York City on Saturday, and another one at Borders in Philadelphia on Sunday."

"Okay."

"Then we'll go to Chicago, then Dallas, then on to LA for *The Tonight Show* to wrap up the tour."

"Wow. That sounds like a lot of traveling," Rich noted.

"It won't be so bad. You'll be traveling first class," Amanda said.

"We put Dallas just before LA so you could pick up Erica for *The Tonight Show*," Bob said.

"Oh, that wasn't necessary. She's going to travel with me; she just won't be going to the signings."

"What will she do while you're tied up? You may be gone for four or five hours at each appearance."

"She said she'd catch up on her shopping."

Bob laughed. "Well, you'd better sell a lot of books, then."

Rich smiled at Amanda. "You got that right."

"So, do I have your approval, then?" Bob asked.

"Yes. Absolutely. I'm looking forward to it."

"Okay, then I'll email your itinerary to Amanda and we'll have someone pick you up at the airport at each city. That way you won't have to worry about cabs or navigating in unfamiliar cities."

"I appreciate that. I hate having to mess with rental cars,

and cabs are so expensive you've got to carry a fortune with you to make sure you have what you need."

"I hear you," Bob agreed.

They ended the call, and Amanda excused herself and walked to her car. Her next stop was Sylvia Sams at the *Inquisitor*. A wave of guilt washed over her as she drove. She worried that her scheme would backfire and Rich and Erica would find out what she had done, but it was too late to back out now. She'd made promises to Sylvia, and her career as a literary agent would take a nosedive if she didn't deliver what she'd promised to Thorn. She'd called ahead, so Sylvia was waiting for her in the reception area.

"Hey, Amanda. Come on back to my office," Sylvia said.

Amanda nodded and followed her down a long hallway to her office. They took a seat across from each other at a round table.

"So, let me see it."

Amanda grinned and pulled the book out of her backpack. She handed it to Sylvia, who took it and rotated it around to take a good look.

"Impressive," she noted.

"Right, except it's a lie."

"So you say. When do I get the revisions?"

"The night before Rich and Erica go on Leno."

"Not until then?" Sylvia complained. "I'll have to pull an all-nighter to have a story ready for the afternoon edition."

"Sorry, but timing is critical. If Erica gets wind of the leak, she won't show up for *The Tonight Show*."

"Oh, all right. I guess it will be worth it."

Amanda smiled. "I promise you it will."

Amanda left the book with Sylvia and then headed to Barnes & Noble at Lincoln Park, across from Northpark. This was the site of Rich's Dallas book signing, and she had an appointment with the store manager and a columnist for the *Dallas Morning News*, Steve Sawyer, who was going to cover the story. Amanda went to the information counter and told them why she was there. A few moments later two people walked up.

"You must be Amanda. I'm Jill," the bookstore's community relations manager said.

"Yes, Jill . . . nice to meet you."

"This is Steve Sawyer."

"Nice to meet you, Steve," Amanda said. "Thank you for agreeing to cover this event."

"It's my pleasure. I covered the Martha Collins murder trial way back when it happened, so I was the natural choice for the assignment."

"Well, I've been told the wholesalers will have books by the end of the week, so you should be getting yours shortly thereafter."

"Good. I've got the display all ready," Jill said.

"So, will there be any surprises in the book?" Steve asked.

"Well, I don't know about surprises, but for the first time the public will get the inside story of what happened. Although the press covered the store pretty well, neither Erica nor Rich ever gave the press an interview."

"So, when do I get a copy?" Steve asked.

"I think the plan is to send out advance copies to the media about a week before the book's release. I'll make sure you get one."

"Can you tell me why it's taken so long for Rich to publish his story?"

"Well, the whole thing was embarrassing for Erica, so she made Rich promise not to publish it."

"Until now."

"Right. As you know, Rich and Erica's son Ryan and I are dating. So, since I was just starting out as a literary agent, I asked them if I could represent Rich and as a favor they both agreed."

"Wow. So you're the one to thank for the story finally

160

being published."

"Yes. I guess you could say that."

"So, when can I interview Rich?"

"I'm sure he'll be happy to talk to you before or after his signing."

"Before would be better. No telling how long the signing will last and I'll want to get the story out."

"That's probably wise. He'll be tired after the signing, too, and may not have much time before he has to head for the airport."

"Okay, I'll see you soon," Steve said.

Steve and Amanda said good-bye to Jill and walked together out of the store. They talked a few minutes outside and then went their separate ways. Amanda wasn't sure about her next errand. She needed someone to break into the Coleman house while they were away, so there would be an explanation how the *Inquisitor* got a copy of Erica's version of Aunt Martha's murder. She'd given this problem a lot of thought. One option, she thought, would be go to a bar where thugs were known to hang out, pretend to get drunk, and let the word out that the Coleman house would be empty for a week. The only problem with that was she didn't particularly want to go into a sleazy bar.

Another idea would be to hire a homeless person or some teenagers to break in, but then the break-in could be tracked back to her if the burglars were caught and decided to implicate her in order to reduce their sentence. Finally, she remembered Rich telling her about a ring of thugs who routinely watched the obituaries so they would know when a decedent's home would be unattended while everyone was at the funeral. She wasn't sure that would work, but it was the best idea she could come up with, so she went with it.

She went to the public library, logged on to one of their computers, and found the *Dallas Morning News* website. There she placed an order for an obituary, making up a name but giving Rich's address and giving the time of the funeral at two p.m. with a reception following from three to six o'clock. This she thought would give the burglars at least five or six hours to do their business. She didn't want to use a credit card, so she wrote a note that she would pay by check and it would be put in the mail the following day. She planned to use a money order so it couldn't be traced back to her if anyone saw it and recognized the Colemans' address.

Amanda wasn't entirely confident that the obituary ad would work, so she made a point to tell everybody she came in contact with that Rich and Erica would be away from their house for at least a week. She felt bad about what she was doing but felt she had no other choice. If someone didn't break into their house, it would be hard for her to disavow leaking the alternate version of the story. She reasoned that the Colemans had insurance so whatever was taken would be replaced.

Amanda and Ryan took Rich and Erica to the airport to fly to Boston for the first book signing. Amanda was nervous and distracted knowing that her carefully worked out plans were starting to play out. She avoided eye contact with Rich and Erica for fear her face would betray the emotional turmoil she was feeling. She was glad that security protocol would not allow them to accompany them to the gate. After they'd let them off and driven away she let out a sigh of relief.

"What's wrong?" Ryan asked.

Amanda shook off a little nervous tremor. "Oh, nothing. I'm just worried about how the book will do and how Erica will handle being on Jay Leno."

"Don't worry. Everything will be okay. The book looks great and I think Mom is getting used to the idea of being on TV. She's never been the shy type."

Amanda took a deep breath, trying to relax. "I know. There's just so much at stake—not only the success of the book but my career. If the book bombs, my career may be over before it ever got off the ground."

Amanda began to sob. Ryan grabbed her hand and

squeezed it. "Come on. It will be okay."

Tears began streaming down Amanda's face. She wiped them away with her hand. She wished she could tell Ryan why she was really crying, but she knew that would blow her plans if she did. Could she get away with this? Was she insane to even try it? The urge to confess to Ryan was so strong she could hardly stand it. But everything she had worked so hard for would all be over in an instant if she did. Ryan would dump her, Rich would find a way out of his contract, and she'd lose her job at the Colson Agency. It was too late. She had to go through with it and learn to live with the pain she suffered for her betrayal.

Chapter 17
Person of Interest

Ryan was worried about Amanda. He'd never seen her so nervous as she was when they were taking his parents to the airport the previous afternoon. Amanda had never been the emotional type, yet she'd actually cried after they dropped them off. Ryan realized this was Amanda's first book placement and there was added pressure because her client was her future father-in-law, but still, it seemed there was something else going on. He wondered if it had to do with their relationship. Their relationship had been strained lately with the bar exam looming ahead, the book placement taking so much of Amanda's time, and Ryan's new murder case. He finally decided it was a combination of all those things that had Amanda so stressed.

A couple of days went by with little change. Amanda seemed preoccupied and distant. After a good trade conference in Boston with the New England booksellers, Rich's New York book signing was less than spectacular. Initially there were quite a few spectators, but after Rich spoke they quickly dispersed and he sold less than fifty books. That night Amanda had seemed depressed and although Ryan tried, he couldn't do anything to cheer her up.

Finally, when Rich and Erica were almost due back in Dallas for their book signing, Amanda seemed to snap out of the doldrums and come alive. All day she'd been a flurry of activity in preparation of the event. Ryan was relieved with her transformation and began to focus again on his new criminal practice, which amounted to only two clients so far, Matt's friend Candy and Cindy Sharp. Neither of these clients had anything going when Ryan walked into his office on Tuesday morning, but that changed in a hurry. The receptionist announced that Cindy Sharp was on line two. Ryan picked up.

"Ryan Coleman."

"Ryan. This is Cindy. I need your help."

"Where are you?"

"At police headquarters."

"Police headquarters? What happened?"

"They just brought me in for questioning. You were right—they discovered that I'd driven by the RMS offices."

"Oh, shit! Okay, where exactly are you?"

"Dallas Police Department, downtown."

"Okay. I'm on my way. Don't say anything to them."

"I won't. I told them I wanted my attorney."

"Good. See you soon."

Ryan was nervous as he headed downtown to the police station. His father was out of town, and Matt hadn't gotten to the office yet and he apparently had his cell phone off. He told himself it wouldn't be a big deal. Just sit there with Cindy and make sure Finch and Morin didn't beat up on her too much. He could do that. Traffic was heavy, as it was the tail end of a busy rush hour. Ryan cursed a driver who cut him off on Central Expressway. Thirty minutes later he parked his car in a lot across from the police station and went inside. At the dispatcher's desk he asked for Detective Finch or Morin. She told him to take a seat and wait.

Several minutes later Detective Finch walked up and said to follow her. Ryan did what he was told, and soon they were in a small interrogation room. Cindy smiled when Ryan took the seat beside her.

"Are you okay?" Ryan asked.

She nodded. "Fine, now that you are here."

They talked a minute and then Detective Morin walked in with a scowl on his face. "So, I told you the second interview wouldn't be pleasant."

166

Cindy looked away.

"So, what's this all about?" Ryan asked.

"It's about your client lying to us," Detective Morin spat. "She said she didn't go to Lucius Jones's office on the day he was murdered, but that was a lie."

"It was not," Cindy protested. "I didn't go to his office."

"Oh, yeah. How come I got your car on a video parked a block away from RMS's office at 5:07 p.m.?"

Cindy frowned. Ryan looked at her worriedly. "I don't know how that could be," Cindy said, and then her face lit up. "Oh, you mean at the bank? I stopped at the ATM to get cash to go shopping."

"Wasn't that convenient," Detective Morin said. "Why didn't you get your money at the mall? They have ATMs there."

"Yeah, but they don't belong to my bank. I don't have to pay an ATM charge if I withdraw money from my bank's ATM."

"So, you stopped to save a buck?" Detective Morin questioned.

"The bucks add up," Cindy noted.

"Well, in our last interview we established that you had a motive to kill Lucius Jones. Now we know you were in the vicinity, so you had opportunity, too."

"Just because she was down the street doesn't prove she went up to his offices," Ryan argued. "It was after hours, so how would she get in?"

"Well, that's a question we haven't figured out yet. If we had, we'd be arresting your client right now. For now I just want to let you know that we've bumped your client from a person of interest to a prime suspect."

Ryan nodded. "Okay, so Cindy is free to leave, then?"

"For now. Don't leave town, and make arrangements for someone to take care of your children in case we find that last piece of evidence we need to charge you with Lucius Jones's murder."

Ryan stood up. "Come on, Cindy. Let's get out of here."

Unconscionable

Cindy quickly wiped a tear from her eye and stood up. She glared at Detective Morin. "I didn't kill him. I'm not that kind of a person."

"That's enough, Cindy," Ryan said. "Come on."

Ryan took her arm and ushered her out of the interrogation room. When Ryan looked back the detective had a big grin on his face. Ryan shook his head and turned away. When they got outside Ryan pointed to his car.

"I'll give you a ride home."

"Thank you. I left my kids at a neighbor's. What an asshole to tell me to find someone to watch my children when I'm arrested."

"I know. He seemed to be enjoying it, too."

"Do you think it will happen? Me getting arrested, I mean?"

Ryan shrugged. "You know, Cindy. You can't hide things from us. Why didn't I know you went to that ATM?"

Cindy looked down. "I don't know. I guess I didn't think anybody would find out."

"We told you there are surveillance cameras everywhere and every ATM has one."

"I know. I'm sorry. I won't hide anything from you from now on."

"Good. So, the detectives aren't going to find any evidence that you went up to Jones's office, are they?"

"No. I got my money and left," Cindy replied.

"So, you really used that ATM to save a buck?"

Cindy laughed. "Partly. I also wanted to use it because after the money comes out, I get a receipt with my account balance printed out. That helps me keep track of how much money I have at any given time."

"You don't use a check register?"

"No. I'd always forget to write in the checks, so I never knew what my balance was. Now I get it automatically when I withdraw money, or I can request it without taking any money.

Sometimes I check my balance before I take any money out so I know how much I can ask for. I did that the night I went to the mall because I wanted to have as much money with me as possible. It's embarrassing if you see something you like but can't afford to buy it."

Ryan left Cindy off at her neighbor's and then went back to the office. Matt was there and wanted to know how things had turned out with Cindy. Ryan explained what had transpired and they talked awhile about it. On the way home that night Ryan went by his parents' house to pick up the mail and take in the newspaper. When he got inside he took everything into the kitchen where he had been leaving it for his parents who were returning briefly the next day. He felt a draft as he walked into the kitchen and looked up. Much to his shock and dismay, someone had thrown a brick through one of the windowpanes and let themselves in.

He started looking around to see if anything was missing but found everything in the kitchen to be in its place. Then he went into the living room and inventoried the TV and stereo—still there. He thought of his mother's jewelry in the master bedroom, so he rushed down the hall and threw open the door. Every drawer had been pulled out of both chests of drawers and the contents dumped. When he looked around for her jewelry box, he saw that it had been turned over and was now completely empty. He cringed at the thought of having to tell his mother that she'd been robbed.

He didn't think there was anything worth stealing upstairs, but he decided to go check anyway just in case he'd forgotten about something. When he got to the top of the stairs he noticed some wood chips and attic insulation on the floor. After looking around in all the upstairs rooms and finding nothing missing, he pulled the attic ladder down and climbed up into the attic. It was dark, so he flipped the switch at the top of the stairs and a single sixty-watt bulb illuminated. He looked around the attic but could find nothing missing. The only thing out of place

169

was the cedar chest that hadn't been completely closed. Going over to it, he remembered it was where his father had kept the manuscript. He opened the chest and saw the manuscript was gone, but that didn't surprise him, as he knew Amanda had taken it. He sighed, took one more look around, and went back down into the main house.

When he got back to the kitchen he used his cell phone to call 911. Twenty minutes later two police officers came by and took a report. They said there would be an investigation but doubted they'd find the burglar since he hadn't left any evidence and none of the neighbors had seen anything. Ryan said he understood and the two officers left. Then he called Amanda to explain why he wasn't home yet.

"They broke into your parents' house?" Amanda said, feigning complete surprise.

"Yes. They took Mom's jewelry."

"Oh, no!"

"Mom will be completely devastated when she finds out. She'll want my father to put in a security system, I'm sure."

"Well, at least they weren't at home."

"Yeah, thank God."

"Well, come home. I'm suddenly feeling very insecure myself."

Ryan laughed. "Okay, I'll see you in a few minutes."

When Ryan got home Amanda was at the door to greet him. They embraced and Amanda wanted to know what the police had said. Ryan told her they didn't think there would be an investigation since none of the neighbors had seen anything.

"They're going to check local pawnshops to see if any of the pieces show up. Mom will have to give them an inventory."

"I hope she was insured," Amanda said.

"I don't know. I would assume so, but I don't know for sure."

"I'm surprised that's all they took. Your parents have a lot of nice stuff."

"I don't know. Maybe something scared them away before they had a chance to steal anything else."

"Could be. . . . So, I talked to your father. The book tour hasn't been going so well. They're anxious to get home."

"Really? What happened?"

"Bob, Thorn's marketing guy, says that it's been too long since the murder trial and not that many people remember it. But he's hoping the *Tonight Show* appearance will help."

"I'm sure it will," Ryan agreed.

The next day Amanda and Ryan drove to the airport and picked up Erica and Rich. They were tired and Erica was in a bad mood. Ryan hated to bring up the break-in but felt he had no choice in the matter.

"Yesterday someone broke into your house," he said evenly.

"What?" Erica said. "What did they take?"

"Your jewelry. I think that's all, but you'll have to check everything carefully when you get home."

"There was only costume jewelry in that box. We keep anything of value that I don't wear regularly in a safety deposit box."

"Well, that's good," Amanda said, feeling greatly relieved.

"How did they get in?" Rich asked.

"They threw a brick in the window, unlocked the door, and then entered the house. I imagine they searched every room but there's no way of telling. Your bedroom was the only room they ransacked. They did check out the attic, though. I didn't see that anything had been taken."

"That's all junk up there," Rich said.

"What if they come back?" Erica said. "We'd better have a security system installed. I don't want someone breaking in while I'm home alone."

Ryan grinned at Amanda.

"Yeah. I've been meaning to get one put in, but just

haven't got around to it. I guess we could buy a dog. I heard they are a good deterrent to burglars."

"I don't want a dog," Erica moaned. "They are too much trouble."

"Maybe we shouldn't go to LA. Can we postpone it because of the break-in?"

Amanda shook her head. "No, you can't reschedule it. Getting the *Tonight Show* appearance is a one-shot opportunity."

"But they might come back to the house."

"I'll call ADT in the morning," Rich said.

"Ah, I doubt you'll have time," Amanda noted. "You've got promotional events all day. Maybe Ryan could take care of it for you."

Ryan looked at Amanda and then shrugged. "Sure, I guess you should get it put in right away."

"Would you do that, honey?" Erica said. "I would really appreciate it."

"No problem. I'll call them tomorrow. I don't think it takes that long to install. Oh, by the way, Dad. They picked up Cindy and took her in for questioning. I had to go down and sit with her while they interviewed her."

"You're kidding."

"No."

Ryan filled Rich in on the details of the interview.

"I'm sorry I wasn't home to help you out."

"It's all right. It was no big deal."

After they'd left Ryan's parents at home, Amanda and Ryan went back to their apartment. Before they made it, however, Amanda got a call on her cell phone. It was Robert Todd.

"What!" Amanda exclaimed. "Why? . . . I can't believe this. . . . I know. It probably won't make any difference. . . . Okay."

Amanda hung up and took a deep breath.

"What was that about?" Ryan asked.

"We got our time cut on Leno. There's going to be a third

guest."

"Who?"

"They didn't say."

"Well, that's not so bad, is it?"

"No. I guess not. It's just less time to talk about the book."

While they were driving, Ryan again sensed something was wrong with Amanda. She'd been better, but now she seemed very nervous and preoccupied. He knew there were things going on in her pretty little head that he obviously knew nothing about. He felt hurt that Amanda wouldn't tell him what was bothering her so much. If they were eventually going to get married they shouldn't have any secrets.

"You know, if something is bothering you, I'm a good listener."

Amanda turned and looked at him. "What did you say?"

"Tell me what's bothering you. It's better to talk about it than let it get all bottled up inside you."

She shook her head. "Nothing is bothering me."

Ryan shook his head as he pulled the 2005 Lexus into the carport next to Amanda's 2003 Honda Accord. Amanda was stubborn and often reacted emotionally rather than logically. Ryan tried to think of another approach to try to win her trust, but nothing jumped out at him. Finally he decided it was temporary and he'd just have to wait it out until this book launch was over. Then life would get back to normal—at least he hoped so.

Chapter 18
Showtime

Amanda knew that Ryan went by his parents' house each night to take in the mail and the newspaper. She had hoped that one night he'd come home with the news that there had been a break-in, but that hadn't happened. None of her attempts to make the premises vulnerable to a burglary had worked. Now she was getting panicked, because time was running out. With Ryan's parents coming home the next day she decided to take matters into her own hands. It would be risky. If she were spotted, she'd be in serious trouble. She rubbed her neck, which was already starting to tighten from just thinking about it.

On the way home from her office she detoured to Rich and Erica's neighborhood and drove slowly through the alley that wound behind their house. It was dark and she didn't see anyone around, so she parked a few houses away and walked to their back gate. She had been at Rich and Erica's house enough times to know the gate was left open so the lawn service could get in and out. Once inside she picked up the brick that Rich used to hold the gate open when he was working in the backyard, and walked to the back door.

Lights suddenly flooded the alley, causing Amanda to duck down, although it would have been impossible to see her in the backyard. The car drove by slowly but didn't stop. She wondered if the driver would pay attention to her car parked on the side of the alley. If they took down her license plate number she could be tied to the burglary. She kicked herself for not renting a car that couldn't be traced back to her.

Amanda knew that Rich didn't have an alarm service. He

had told her the story of how years earlier, when they did have a security system, Erica had burned some bacon, which had caused the smoke alarm to go off. In Rich's haste to disarm the alarm so the fire department wouldn't come, he accidently set off the panic alarm. Before he knew it there were two fire trucks, an ambulance, and a SWAT team coming down the street toward their house. An hour later, after he'd finally convinced the cops and the firemen that it was just a false alarm, Rich ripped the alarm system out of the wall and vowed never to use it again.

He had said many times it was the best move he'd ever made since worrying about the alarm going off caused him more stress than the fear of a burglar. Smiling at the thought of Rich ripping the alarm system out of the wall, Amanda broke one of the glass panes out of the door, reached in, and unlocked it. She was wearing gloves so she wouldn't cut herself or leave fingerprints. Quickly, she went upstairs, pulled down the attic staircase, and shook it so some attic insulation would fall to the floor. Then she let it close back up and went downstairs. She thought she should steal something to make it look like a legitimate burglary but hated to do it. After thinking about it long and hard and finally deciding she had no choice, she went into the master bedroom, tore open every drawer, and spilled the contents onto the floor. When she found Erica's jewelry chest she emptied the contents into a plastic grocery bag and stuffed it into her pocket.

On the way back to her Honda another car drove by slowly. Taking cover behind two trash cans, she hunkered down low and held her breath while the car went by without stopping. She wondered if it was the same car that she'd seen earlier. As she was driving home she wondered what to do with the jewelry. *Surely anything of value would be insured,* she reasoned. Her best bet would be to get rid of it. If she kept it there would be a chance Ryan might find it and she'd be exposed. So, when she saw a Thom Thumb grocery store, she drove through the alley and threw the bag of jewelry in a Dumpster.

When she got home Ryan was waiting for her and wanted to know where she had been. She blamed her tardiness on a meeting with the CRM at Barnes & Noble to help her set up the book display for the upcoming signing. Ryan accepted the explanation without comment, and Amanda quickly changed the subject.

The next morning Amanda drove to the Dallas Public Library and browsed the fiction aisles. After a few moments Sylvia Sams appeared, and Amanda let her read Erica's revisions to Rich Coleman's novel. When she was done she had lots of questions.

"Let me get this straight. Erica is saying Rich actually killed Martha Collins?" Sylvia asked.

Amanda nodded. "Exactly. She found him at the motel next to Aunt Martha's body."

"Wow!"

"Then she and Rich's best friend took Rich to an alley and left him there so it would look like he'd been mugged and thus provide an alibi."

"And Rich has no memory of this?"

"Right. He truly believes the manuscript is an accurate account of what happened."

"Okay. Let me just compare the handwriting on these revisions to some samples of Erica's handwriting that we were able to obtain. Then if they match I'll go write the story."

"No problem."

She let Sylvia do her analysis, and when she was satisfied the document was real she left to go write the story. Amanda lingered at the library another fifteen minutes and then went to her office. There was lots to do before she and Ryan had to pick up Erica and Rich at the airport. She called Sheila at Thorn to check on any new developments.

"Sheila. This is Amanda."

"Hi, Amanda. How are you?"

"A little nervous."

"I bet. Well, it won't be long now. How did your chance meeting with Sylvia go?"

"She's writing the story as we speak. Needless to say she was delighted with the scoop."

"Is she good with the timing?"

"Absolutely—she understands Rich and Erica have to be totally surprised by the story. If they find out about it before the taping starts at NBC they'll probably cancel."

"Well, we can't let that happen. It's not easy to line up these appearances on late-night talk shows."

"So, if everything goes well how do you think it will impact book sales?" Amanda asked.

"I think it will shoot to the top of *New York Times* Best Seller list in no time. We've alerted our printers to get ready for a new print run."

"Obviously, Rich won't do any more book signing after this."

"He won't need to. Every time he has an encounter with the media the publicity will be like twenty book signings."

"I know. This is so exciting!"

"Aren't you worried about your relationship with Ryan when this comes down?"

"Sure, but I think I've got that angle covered."

Amanda hadn't told anyone about her burglary and didn't plan to. There was no reason for anyone to know about it and much safer for her if they didn't. Her biggest worry was Erica. If Erica didn't buy the burglary explanation, she'd blame Amanda for the leak, and that would threaten her relationship with Ryan. She was sure in that event Erica would try to prevent their marriage and Amanda might lose Ryan as the result. But she knew it was too late to worry about that now.

Amanda arrived at Barnes & Noble thirty minutes before the seven p.m. signing. The store was pretty quiet, which was a little bit unsettling. She knew that Rich hadn't been attracting big crowds, but this was Dallas, his hometown, where the Martha

Collins murder had been big news in the early eighties. She expected at least a modest crowd for the event, particularly after Steve Sawyer's nice article in the *Dallas Morning News* that morning. In the article he'd recounted the illicit love affair between Rich and Erica and how it had driven them to make a suicide pact in the event either was convicted of Martha Collins's murder. He gave the book a generous review and suggested that anyone who wasn't sure what true love was all about ought to read it.

Amanda took the escalator upstairs to where the book signing was to take place and was pleased to see a dozen people had already taken seats for the event. When she spotted Jill she went over to her.

"So, everything ready?"

Jill nodded. "Yes, the books came this morning. I was worried they wouldn't get here in time."

"How many did they send?"

"Two hundred and fifty."

"Well, that should be enough. Forty-nine is the most he's sold at any event so far."

"I think so," Jill agreed.

"Don't send the extra stock back. You'll need it."

Jill laughed. "Aren't you the optimist."

Amanda smiled. "Well, I'd better be since I represent the author."

Five minutes later when Ryan and Rich arrived, ten or fifteen more spectators had taken their seats. Amanda felt relieved, as now there was a respectable crowd for the event. When seven o'clock rolled around Jill got up and introduced Rich. He thanked her and took the podium.

"I want to thank all of you for coming out. It's nice to be back in Texas. If you've ever traveled to the Northeast, you know Texans aren't always welcomed there. I don't know why that is. Some say it was the Kennedy assassination, and others say it's the general perception that Texas is populated by hordes of illiterate cowboys."

The crowd stirred.

"Anyway, I didn't exactly get a friendly welcome in the Big Apple, so I'm glad to be back here in Texas where people are more hospitable."

The crowd murmured their agreement.

Rich picked up a copy of *The Pact*. "I wrote this book almost twenty-five years ago with the intention of trying to get it published immediately. But when it was all finished my wife asked me not to publish it because she wanted to keep the intimate details of our courtship and marriage private. Because of the trial and media coverage surrounding it, far too much about it had already been made a matter of public record and she wanted it to stop.

"Since Erica meant more to me than fame or fortune, I acquiesced to her wishes. But enough time has now gone by that those concerns are no longer as important as they once were. So, when Amanda asked if she could present *The Pact* to potential publishers, after careful thought, Erica and I agreed. What shocked us was how quickly she made it happen and I can honestly say one year ago the manuscript was gathering dust in our attic and I had no plans to ever publish it.

"So, it's a little surreal to be here today before you talking about *The Pact*. Anyway, I thought I would read an excerpt from the book and then when I'm done answer any questions you might have."

The rest of the book signing went well and when it was over, Rich had sold ninety-two books, which Jill said was the best signing she'd had in months. After the signing Ryan and Amanda took Rich and Erica to the airport for their flight to LA. Rich was in a good mood, as it had been his best book signing yet, but Erica was quiet and appeared nervous.

After letting them off they drove to Red Lobster in Grapevine and had dinner. When they finally got home it was nearly ten thirty p.m., so Amanda turned on *The Tonight Show*.

Amanda said she wanted to see if Leno would announce the fact that Rich and Erica would be on the show the following night. She wasn't disappointed as he twice advised his listeners that Rich Coleman and his wife, Erica, would be guests the following night to discuss Rich's "new true crime book, *The Pact*."

After that they went to bed. Ryan fell asleep immediately, but Amanda couldn't relax enough to go to sleep. Instead she ran the events of the day through her mind over and over again. She worried about the cars that had driven through the alley while she was burglarizing Rich and Erica's house, Sylvia's article, and whether Jay Leno's writers would hear about it in time to take advantage of it. Finally, she worried about Rich and Erica's return and how quickly they'd point the finger at her for their debacle.

The next morning Amanda went by Sylvia's office to pick up a copy of her article the moment it came off the press. She waited about fifteen minutes until someone finally showed up to stock the newspaper stand in front of the building. She bought several copies and then went back to her car to read the story. Adrenaline pumped through her system as she read every shocking word. Sylvia had outdone herself. The story was scandalous! When she was done reading she took a deep breath trying to relax. In just a few hours Rich and Erica's life would be rocked to the core and she'd become the hottest new agent on the planet.

The afternoon and evening crawled by as Amanda waited and wondered what was happening in LA. She wondered if they'd made it to the studio on time and if the writers for *The Tonight Show* had gotten a copy of the *Inquisitor* yet. Sylvia had arranged for their West Coast distributor to have a copy delivered by messenger by noon. Amanda looked at her watch and saw that it was two p.m., so it would be noon in LA. She could just imagine how Jay's staff would be scrambling to rewrite the script for the interviews.

At five thirty she turned on NBC 5 to see if the story had hit the networks yet and was relieved when nothing was said about it. She assumed that NBC hadn't let the story out so it would be a big surprise to everybody watching Jay Leno that evening. Amanda was about to turn off the TV when a commercial came on.

"Tonight on Jay Leno: Will Rich Coleman get away with murder? Jay talks to Erica and Rich Coleman about their suicide pact."

"Oh, shit!" Amanda gasped.

Fortunately for her Ryan hadn't gotten home yet. She hoped he hadn't heard about the promotional spot. He'd be very upset and immediately try to get in contact with his parents. She didn't want that to happen, as she wanted to see the show without any distractions. To ensure this would be the case, she dressed in something very provocative, made his favorite dinner, and the moment he got home shut off his cell phone.

"We're going to have a nice quiet dinner, have a few drinks, and then celebrate your father's first network appearance," Amanda said excitedly.

"Wow!" Ryan replied. "My father needs to be on more talk shows."

"Yes. That would be great for both of us."

After Ryan had eaten she made them both a drink, put on some soft music, and cuddled up next to him on the sofa. She'd taken the phone off the hook because she was afraid the media or Ryan's parents would be calling soon. By now *The Tonight Show* would have already been taped and Rich and Erica would be reeling from the *Inquisitor* article. There was no telling what they would do once the show was over, but she was fairly certain they would be calling.

They kissed for a while and then began taking off each other's clothes but were interrupted by a loud knock at the door. Amanda cursed under her breath.

"Oh shit. I forgot I invited Matt and Candy over to watch *The Tonight Show*," Ryan said as he quickly put on his shirt and pants and stumbled to the front door. Amanda shook her head and escaped into the bedroom.

Ryan looked into the peephole, saw that it was Matt and Candy, and opened the door. Matt walked in carrying a large brown bag and Candy followed.

"Hey, you decided to come," Ryan said.

"Of course."

"What's in the bag?" Ryan asked.

"Beer."

"Oh. Good thinking . . . How are you, Candy?" Ryan asked.

"Fine. Where's Amanda?"

"I think she went to change. I forgot to tell her I had invited guests over."

"Oh, no. I hope she's not upset."

Amanda came back in the living room dressed in jeans and an SMU T-shirt. "Hey, I'm glad you two came over. Now we can have a real party."

"Well, this is a big day, so who better to celebrate it with than the person who made it all possible," Matt said.

There was more knocking on the door. Ryan looked over at it and frowned.

"That's probably the girls—they wanted to come. I hope you don't mind."

"No. The more the merrier," Amanda said.

Ryan opened the door and Jenni, Gina, and Sharon walked in, each carrying a bag of drinks and snacks for the party. Amanda showed them a table where they could set them out and then went into the kitchen to get some plates and napkins. Everyone seemed in a good mood, so she assumed no one had listened to the six o'clock news or picked up a copy of the *Inquisitor*.

They drank, talked, listened to music, and danced until ten p.m. when Ryan made a move to turn on the TV. Amanda jumped up and intercepted him.

"Leno doesn't come on until 10:35," Amanda said.

"Well, I thought we'd catch the news."

"No. You'll spoil the party. Come dance with me."

Amanda took Ryan's hand and led him over to the makeshift dance floor where Matt and Candy were in a tight embrace dancing to "Moon River." Amanda liked classic sixties music, especially for dancing, and managed to keep Ryan occupied until ten thirty.

"Okay. Now you can turn on the TV," Amanda advised.

Ryan picked up the channel changer and turned on NBC 5. The news was just wrapping up, and then *The Tonight Show* began. Jay took the stage, greeted his fans, and then gave his monologue. When he was done he announced his first guest.

"Well, tonight we are fortunate to have as our first guest Richard Coleman to talk about his new book, *The Pact*, just released from Thorn Andrews Publishing. Let's welcome Rich Coleman."

"What happened to Mom?" Ryan asked.

"I don't know," Amanda replied. "Maybe she backed out of the interview for some reason."

Rich walked onto the set, shook hands with Jay, and took his seat as the crowd applauded.

"Now your wife is here, too, and we'll bring her on in a moment, but I wanted to talk to each of you separately because it seems you have slightly different accounts of what transpired back in 1981. So, my first question to you, Rich, is why you waited so long to publish this book?"

Rich shrugged. "Well, it all was pretty much a nightmare for both of us and when it was over we didn't have any desire to relive it right away."

"Then why did you write the book in the first place?" Jay asked.

"Well, for me it was therapeutic. I just wanted to put it all down in writing before I forgot the details. When it was finished I was ready to publish it but Erica wasn't, so I put it in mothballs."

"Probably a good decision, but why publish it now? There are things that happened that you couldn't be proud of, like entering into an illicit affair with a minor?"

"Yes. I was twenty-nine at the time and Erica was seventeen. I'm not making excuses, but I had lost my first wife a year and a half earlier and Erica had just lost her father. When fate brought us together we were both desperately in need of companionship and understanding, and we fell in love."

"But you knew it was wrong, yet you still allowed it to happen?"

"That's true. I tried to resist her, but whenever we were together my resolve would quickly falter. And it didn't help that she didn't care about the law, or my fiduciary duty, or whether I lost my job or not. She knew she loved me and our love was the only thing that was important."

"Now despite the age difference you two were very happy except that you had to keep the relationship secret," Jay said.

"Yes. That didn't bother me that much, but Erica was a social person and wanted to get out and be with other couples, go to church, shopping, you know, do all the normal things that couples did."

"So, your relationship was finally discovered?"

"Yes. Erica talked me into taking her dancing one night and someone from the office saw us. That person told Peter, my boss, and he confronted us while we were vacationing in Barbados."

"And how did Aunt Martha find out?" Jay asked.

"Well, Erica hated her aunt Martha, so she hadn't told her she was going on vacation. Being a busybody, Martha checked up on Erica from time to time and when she couldn't contact her on this occasion she used that as an excuse to break into our apartment. When she did she found out Erica and I were living together."

"Don't you just love meddling relatives?"

"Yeah, well there was bad blood. Aunt Martha had been very hateful to Erica's mother and Erica blamed her for running her off."

"Hmm. I bet. . . . Now in your version of the story, your wife was caught by the police fleeing from the crime scene?"

"What do you mean my version?" Rich asked.

"Well. Did you see the *Inquisitor* story that came out this morning?"

Rich grimaced. "No. What article?"

"Well, there was a story in the *Inquisitor*—do we have a picture of it?"

A copy of the *Inquisitor* flashed on the screen. The headlines read: DID RICH COLEMAN GET AWAY WITH MURDER?

The crowd gasped in shock. Ryan looked at Amanda.

"What's going on? Have you seen the *Inquisitor* article?" Ryan asked.

"No," Amanda lied. "I can't believe there was an article."

Back on the TV Rich said warily, "I haven't seen that."

"Well, according to the story Erica has a different version of the events. So, let's get Erica out here so she can explain what really happened. Ladies and gentlemen, please welcome Erica Fox Coleman."

The crowd gave Erica a round of applause as she tentatively walked out on the stage. She appeared a little confused and disoriented. Jay walked over to her and guided her to the first guest seat.

"So, I take it neither of you have seen the *Inquisitor* article."

Both Erica and Rich shook their heads.

"Well, it just came out today and according to the article, Erica, you read Rich's novel right after he wrote it and had a different take on what happened."

"No," Erica protested. "I concur with the book as it is written."

"Well, the writer at the *Inquisitor*, Sylvia Sams, claims

that you made extensive revision to the manuscript that tells a completely different story than what's printed in Rich's book."

Erica just starred at Jay in shock and said nothing.

"In fact, Ms. Sams claims to have compared known samples of your handwriting to these notes and verifies that they are a match. So, do you deny making these revisions to your husband's manuscript?"

Erica looked at Rich and then back at Jay. She looked like she wanted to bolt. Finally, she sat back in her chair and sighed.

"No. I did make some revisions, but what you have to understand is that my version of what transpired is no less valid than what Rich wrote. You see I didn't witness Aunt Martha's murder, so I don't actually know what happened."

"But in your revisions you state that you found Rich unconscious next to your aunt's dead body."

Many in the crowd gasped in shock.

"True, but he was unconscious. If he had killed Aunt Martha he would have fled the scene. The only thing that makes sense is that another person killed Aunt Martha and knocked Rich out to make it look like he was the killer."

"But why did you and Rich's friend Joe move Rich and dump him in an alley miles away so he'd have an alibi?"

"Because I loved him and I couldn't stand the thought of him going on trial for her murder."

"So, you decided to take the fall and then plead temporary insanity?"

Erica nodded.

"And it worked out pretty well. The jury found you innocent by reason of temporary insanity."

"Yes."

"But had you been convicted, would you have gone through with your death pact?"

"Yes," Erica said emphatically. "Neither of us wanted to live without the other. We both had cyanide capsules ready to swallow."

The crowd stirred.

"Well, now that we've heard both Rich's and Erica's versions of Martha Collins's death, let's get the opinion of the detective who handled the Martha Collins murder case in 1981. Please welcome retired detective Vincent Perkins, formerly of the Dallas Police Department!"

Erica's mouth dropped and her face turned ashen. Rich gave her a concerned look and took her hand as they shifted seats. The crowd erupted in excitement as Detective Perkins made his way to the first guest chair. He was a tall, imposing man with green eyes, grey receding hair, and a thin mustache. He smiled briefly, but his face returned to what appeared to be a permanent scowl.

"So, Detective Perkins, you were the investigative officer in the Martha Collins murder case?"

"Yes, that's correct."

"So, what do you think of these new revelations from Rich Coleman's book and Erica Fox Coleman's extensive revisions to the original manuscript?"

"Well, I can't say I'm surprised. I never thought much of Rich Coleman's alibi. It seemed rather convenient."

"So, if you didn't buy his alibi, why didn't you pursue him as a suspect?"

"Well, once his wife pled innocent by reason of temporary insanity, the DA told us to back off. They were very confident that they could successfully prosecute her and didn't want us to create reasonable doubt by finding more evidence against Rich Coleman."

"I see. So, they didn't care who took the fall as long as one of them did?"

Perkins shrugged. "I don't know what was going through their heads. I thought whatever it was stunk, but I had no choice but to follow orders."

"So, what went wrong in the trial? How was it that the

jury found her innocent?"

"They had a slick attorney and an even slicker psychiatrist who brought in all this old family feud crap. It was bull****[bleep], if you ask me." The audience laughed. "They painted Erica as some poor victim of the hatred between her father and the victim, Martha Collins. And they portrayed Martha Collins as a jealous bitch out to create as much misery as she could."

Jay laughed. "I see. And the jury bought it?"

"Hook, line, and sinker," Detective Perkins acknowledged.

"So, you heard Erica say that neither she nor Rich know who killed Aunt Martha."

"Yes."

"Do you believe them?"

"Not on your life," Perkins spat. "They probably both planned the whole thing."

Erica gasped and put her hand to her mouth. Rich stiffened and glared at Perkins. The crowd went wild while Jay smiled gleefully.

"So, why do you think they decided to come clean now?"

"Arrogance. They figured they committed the perfect crime and wanted the world to know how smart they were."

"Do you really think so? Isn't that a bit dangerous?" Jay asked.

"Well, they probably think since Erica was found innocent by reason of insanity that they are both safe, but I've got news for them. There's no statute of limitations on murder, and I'm going to make sure the Dallas Police Department reopens the Martha Collins file. With Erica's version of the events on the day of the murder, convicting Rich should be a slam dunk!"

Rich turned beet red and Erica looked like she was going to faint. The crowd seemed confused, some yelling for Rich's conviction and others sympathetic to Rich and Erica. It was pandemonium for several minutes until the director cut the scene and went to a commercial. When they returned to the set Rich and Erica were gone.

"What the fuck was that?" Ryan asked. "How did this happen?"

Amanda, as pale as milk, didn't respond.

"Oh, my God!" Matt said. "I bet Mom and Dad are devastated. Do you think they could really reopen the investigation?"

Ryan frowned. "A case that is over twenty-five years old? I seriously doubt it."

"What about Mom's revisions? Where are they?"

"I hadn't known that there were any," Ryan said, "but I think we'd better get over there and find those revisions before the police get their hands on them."

Matt sighed deeply. "You're right. Come on, they could already be trying to get a search warrant."

Ryan and Matt took off without further debate. Matt drove fast, ignoring posted speed limits and stopping at red lights only to avoid an accident. When they rounded the corner and started down their parents' street, their hearts sank. Rich and Erica's home was surrounded by police cars.

"Fuck!" Ryan screamed.

"Oh, my God," Matt moaned.

They pulled to the curb and parked, not knowing what to do. They just sat there in horror as their childhood home was ravished by the police. Finally, they turned around and drove home, depressed and defeated.

Chapter 19
Media Frenzy

Rich and Erica took the first flight they could get on out of LAX after the taping of the Jay Leno show. They were angry, depressed, and scared. Their flight was uneventful until they deplaned and were mobbed by reporters and TV news crews just outside the luggage pickup area at DFW.

"Mr. Coleman, do you think you'll be indicted for Martha Collins's murder?" a reporter asked.

"No comment," Rich replied, trying to muscle his way through the dense crowd of reporters.

Erica hung on to Rich's arm and followed him through the crowd that seemed to be pressing harder and harder.

"Were you surprised when Detective Perkins showed up as a guest last night on Leno?" another reporter asked.

"No comment," Rich repeated, pushing the reporter aside.

"What do you think about *The Pact*'s climb to number one on Amazon's Best Seller list?"

Rich stopped a moment and stared at the reporter. "Seriously?"

That was good news, but it didn't mean a lot since Amazon was just one bookseller. True enough, it was the most important bookseller, but being number one didn't mean anything unless a book maintained that position for some time. Amanda had told him many an author had purchased hundreds, if not thousands, of their own books so they could boast that their book had once been number one on Amazon. He wondered if the position could be sustained.

"Yes, within thirty minutes of your appearance it was

number one," the reporter replied.

Rich looked at Erica, who didn't seem impressed by the news, and then started up again. "Let us through, please. We have no comment."

When they finally cleared the mob of reporters they rushed to a cabstand and got in the first one that was available. Rich put his arm around Erica and squeezed her tightly.

"I'm sorry, honey. You were right. Publishing this book was a big mistake."

"I had a feeling it would be," Erica said. "You know how the media has to find some new scandal every week for the public to feed on. I was afraid it would end up being us."

Rich shook his head. "I just thought it had been so long ago that it wouldn't be such a big story."

"It wouldn't have been had my revisions not been leaked."

"Who do you think leaked it?"

"It could have been only one person."

"Who?" Rich asked.

"Amanda, obviously," Erica said.

"No. She wouldn't do anything to hurt us. She's like family."

"She probably thinks she's doing us a favor by setting off this media storm. Now your book will be number one on the *New York Times* Best Seller list."

"No it won't," Rich protested.

"Yes it will, and we'll make hundreds of thousands of dollars, but the question is what will be the cost of that fame and fortune. Or, will we even survive what Amanda has unleashed upon us."

Rich shook his head. "Don't jump to any conclusions. It's possible Amanda had nothing to do with this."

"Oh, yes she did. She's going to be a very successful literary agent because she'll do whatever it takes to put her clients on top."

Thirty minutes later, when the cab rounded the corner near their house, they were shocked to see two police cars parked in front. When the cab stopped Rich got out and approached one of the policemen, who was standing in the driveway.

"What's going on here?" Rich demanded.

"Are you Rich Coleman?" the officer asked.

"Yes."

"We were instructed to stay here until you arrived. I'm afraid your door has been destroyed. Someone will be by in the morning to replace it."

"What are you talking about? How was it destroyed?"

"Since you weren't here to open it for us when we executed the search warrant, the door had to be forcibly opened."

"Search warrant? Who got a search warrant?"

"The district attorney applied for it and got a judge to sign off on it, I guess," the officer replied. "That's the usual procedure."

"Did you have to break the door down? You couldn't have simply picked the lock?"

The officer shrugged.

Rich shook his head angrily and stormed inside with Erica on his heels. He gasped at the mess the police had left. Erica pushed on past him.

"Oh my God!" Erica exclaimed. "What have they done to our house?"

"Somebody's going to pay for this," Rich promised, looking back at the officer watching them.

Erica walked briskly through each room of the house, inspecting the damage done. Then she rushed upstairs, pulled down the attic ladder, and climbed up. The contents of all the boxes and drawers and chests had been spilled onto the floor. She rummaged through the piles then looked up at Rich who had just climbed up into the attic.

"It's not here! The envelope with the revisions is gone!"

Rich swallowed hard. "If they pick us up for questioning

don't say a word to them. Even with your revisions they can't prove anything. Only your testimony could convict me."

"What about Joe?"

Rich shrugged. "Joe wouldn't say anything. He's my best friend."

"But if he lies to them they could charge him with being an accessory or even pin the murder on him. He had as much motive to shut up Aunt Martha as we did."

"Shit!" Rich said. "I can't believe this."

"What if they offer him immunity if he testifies against you?" Erica asked desperately.

"I don't think he'd go for it."

"You better call him and tell him to keep his mouth shut."

"Okay. I will," Rich said as he descended the attic stairs.

Just as he was picking up the telephone he heard Erica screaming, "Don't use the house phone!"

He dropped the phone back on the receiver. "What?"

"It's probably bugged. Don't use your cell phone, either. You'll have to go over to Joe's house and talk to him there. Not in his house, though. Go outside and take a walk."

Rich laughed. "I thought I was the attorney," he said.

Erica smiled. "You may be the attorney, but I'm the more cunning one in the family."

"I won't argue with that," Rich agreed.

"Go find Joe. I'll start getting this place cleaned up."

"I should get a piece of plywood and seal up the front door first."

"No. You can do that when you get back. The officer said they'd be here until the front door was replaced. I'll be safe."

Rich nodded. "All right. I'll be right back."

Rich drove across town to Joe Weston's house. He didn't call ahead because he wasn't sure his cell phone line was secure. He couldn't believe that he had to worry about his phones being bugged. What was next, a tail? He looked in his rearview mirror and saw a car a hundred yards behind him. Since he hadn't been paying attention to his rearview mirror, he didn't know how long the vehicle had been there. At the next corner he turned left, went two blocks, and turned left again. He was going around several blocks and if the car stayed within him he would know he was being followed. When he looked back, the car was still following him.

"Fuck!" he said, pounding the steering wheel.

He wondered if there was any way he could lose the tail. He wasn't trained in that sort of thing, but he'd seen plenty of movies where it had been done. The coolest trick he had seen was when a car thief would pull into an alley or hide behind another vehicle while his tail would go right on by, the driver scratching his head. He looked for that kind of opportunity and saw it almost immediately.

He was coming up on a McDonald's, and there was a big eighteen-wheeler unloading adjacent to the drive-through window. The McDonald's was on the corner, so he accelerated past the fast food restaurant and then took a hard right at the next corner. Immediately, before his tail could see what was happening, he pulled into the alley, sped around the McDonald's, and got in the drive-through line, which was hidden by the big truck. When the tail turned the corner the car went on down the street past the alley. The moment the tail was out of view Rich backed up and tore off in the opposite direction.

Rich felt proud of himself for successfully losing his tail, but his delight quickly turned to anger and frustration as he neared Joe's house. There were unmarked police cars parked out front. He knew they were police cars because they had government license plates, fancy antennae, and a portable set of lights on each dash. They no doubt had expected him to go see Joe immediately and were waiting to ask him why he'd decided to visit his old friend in the middle of the night.

Rich drove on past, cursing himself for not anticipating any of this. In retrospect he should have realized the district attorney would be very interested in his book to see if it incriminated him or anybody else. Now he'd put himself and Erica in jeopardy. Sure, Erica couldn't be prosecuted, but she'd be just as devastated if he were tried and convicted as a co-conspirator in Aunt Martha's murder.

Rich wondered about Joe. He'd been a wonderful friend over the years. Would he consider an immunity deal to rat his friend out? It wasn't likely, but still a concern. Joe had a wife and children to consider, and they trumped an old friend. Rich wondered what he'd do in the same circumstance, but he couldn't see himself testifying against Joe. It would be unthinkable. He hoped Joe felt the same way.

When he got home Erica had made great progress on the house and, except for the front door, it almost looked normal. After complimenting her on her work, he went into the garage and found a piece of plywood to seal off the front door until morning. After measuring the doorway and cutting the plywood, he nailed it securely in place. At a little after two a.m., they went to bed.

They were awakened at six a.m. by the sound of big trucks going down the street. Rich figured it was the trash pickup trucks coming by to empty garbage cans, but then he heard voices. He got up and looked outside.

"What the hell?" he said.

"What is it?" Erica asked sleepily.

"Media trucks setting up. I think our life is about to change forever."

Erica got out of bed and looked outside. There were three media trucks from each of the three networks, a crowd of TV and news reporters, and cameramen everywhere. "Damn it. I won't even be able to take a shower without worrying about somebody filming me through the window."

"Don't worry. The bathroom windows are fogged."

"Yeah. Great. What about our bedroom?"

Suddenly a head stuck up, and a cameraman flashed their picture.

196

"What the fuck!" Rich yelled quickly, closing the blinds. "Damn it!"

"Rich, what are we going to do?"

Rich took Erica in his arms and held her tightly.

"I don't know, honey. Maybe we should go stay in a hotel for a while—until the dust settles."

"No. I will not be driven from my own home," Erica declared.

"All right. Just keep all the blinds closed. I'll hire some security to keep the press out of our yard."

"Good. Go do it right now."

Rich nodded and went to the phone. After a few moments he turned and said, "It's done. They'll be here in twenty minutes."

"Good. Come on. Let's go eat some breakfast."

As they were eating breakfast Rich's cell phone rang. "Hello?"

"We're here from Sentinel Security."

"Oh. Right. Come around back. The gate's unlocked."

A few moments later two men knocked on the back door. Rich opened it. They shook hands and introduced themselves as Dave Hood and Walter Shockley.

"Come on in."

The two men walked in.

"Can I get you a cup of coffee?" Erica asked.

They nodded.

"Have a seat," Rich said.

The two men sat down and Erica gave them each a cup of coffee.

"So, thanks for coming by," Rich said. "I'm going to need somebody here 24/7 to keep the press out of our yard."

"Sure, no problem," Shockley said. "I'll handle that. I've had experience with media types."

"Really?"

"Yes. I'm retired Secret Service."

"Oh, excellent. We're probably going to have to have the

house swept for bugs, too, and our phones are most likely tapped."

"That's my specialty," Hood said. "I'm a good hacker, too, if you need any of that done."

Rich laughed. "Yeah, that's good to know. That kind of talent could come in handy."

After they'd finished their coffee, Hood and Shockley went off to do their work. As they were leaving Ryan and Matt showed up.

"We came by last night but the police had the place cordoned off already," Matt said. "We were going to clean out the attic but it was too late."

"I don't know why I didn't burn those goddamn revisions," Erica moaned. "Now we're in serious trouble."

"It's not your fault," Ryan said. "You had no idea someone would get ahold of them."

"Yeah, I wonder how that happened?" Erica remarked, looking at Ryan.

"Hey. Don't look at me," Ryan said defensively. "It was probably stolen during your break-in."

Erica thought about that for a moment. "But nobody even knew about the revisions."

"I knew about them," Matt confessed. "You and Dad used to talk about the revisions. I never really understood what you were talking about until last night."

Erica shook her head. "But how did they know they were in the attic?"

Ryan sighed. "I told people you had a manuscript in the attic and Amanda, I'm sure, did also. Nobody knew that it was a big secret."

"Did Amanda read the revisions?" Erica accused.

"No! She would have told me. She was as shocked as the rest of us when we were watching Leno."

"You didn't hear about the *Inquisitor* earlier. It came out at noon, I understand."

Ryan paled. "No. I don't read the tabloids, but it is a little strange we didn't hear about it. We had a TV-watching party, but we didn't turn on the TV until Jay came on."

"Why?"

"Amanda wanted to dance and party," Ryan said slowly. He swallowed hard. "But I'm sure she had nothing to do with this."

Erica sighed. "Jesus Christ! You are so goddamn naive!"

"Okay. Don't go accusing anybody without proof," Rich said. "Amanda may be completely innocent."

"Uh-huh," Erica spat. "I bet."

Ryan's phone rang. He looked at the caller ID and then put it to his ear. "Amanda?" he said as he got up and walked into the dining room.

"How are your parents?" she asked.

"Not so good," he replied and then explained the situation.

"They think I leaked the story to the *Inquisitor*, don't they?" Amanda asked.

"My mom does."

"It's not true. I was as shocked as you were about it," Amanda lied.

"Well, that's what I told her, but she's a little paranoid right now, so I'd stay clear of her for a while."

"If you say so."

"I do. We don't need any family squabbles right now."

"Okay . . . Hey, I got a call from Jill. They've completely sold out of *The Pact* and have ordered another hundred books."

"Great."

"And it's number one on Amazon and BarnesandNoble.com as of ten o'clock a.m. Eastern Standard Time."

"That's good news. When do they publish the *New York Times* Best Seller list?"

"That will come out Sunday, but it's a little early to be on that list. It might make the *Dallas Morning News* local best seller list on Sunday depending on what stores they poll this week."

"Have you talked to the editor at Thorn?" Ryan asked.

"Yes. Of course, she loves all this publicity. It's all free advertising to her."

"I bet. Do you think she had anything to do with the leak?"

Amanda hesitated. "I don't know how. She did know the manuscript had been kept in the attic, but I can't see a major publisher doing something like this."

"All right. I'll be home in a little while to take a shower and get dressed to go to the office. I've got an appointment this afternoon with Cindy Sharp."

"Okay. See you later."

Ryan hung up and went back into the kitchen to report the latest sales news to Rich and Erica. They didn't seem all that impressed, so he let them know he was going home and then to the office. Just as he was leaving, a carpenter came to install a new door. Ryan helped the man carry the door to the front porch and then left. He was mobbed by reporters as he went to his car, but he ignored their questions. When he got to the office an hour later Matt was already there, and he didn't look like he was in a good mood.

"What's wrong?" Ryan asked as he went by his office and noticed him staring out the window.

Matt turned and took a deep breath. "You're not going to believe this."

"What?" Ryan said.

"RMS just filed suit against Cindy Sharp for the wrongful death of Lucius Jones!"

Chapter 20
New Management

Several days after Lucius Jones's funeral Shelly's secretary advised her that Jones's widow, Samantha, had arrived and had immediately gone into Jones's office. Shelly hadn't received any instructions about future management of the company, so she went to see Samantha to see if she knew what was going on. The door to Lucius's office was closed so she knocked.

"Come in," Samantha said.

"Hi. I'm Shelly Simms."

"Oh, hi, Shelly. I'm Samantha, Lucius's wife and the new CEO of RMS. The board met this morning by telephone."

"Oh, really? I was wondering who was going to replace Lucius."

"That's me. I used to work for the company before I married Lucius several years ago."

"Yes, I heard that."

"I'm glad you stopped by. I was going to come and see you."

"Oh. Okay. What can I do for you?"

"Lucius told me you were one of only a few who were trusted enough to know everything that was going on around here."

Shelly nodded. "Right. Actually, nobody in this office other than Lucius and I knew everything."

"Good. We need to keep it that way in case the feds start snooping around."

Shelly raised her eyebrows in surprise. "Are you

expecting that?" she asked.

"There have been threats and rumors about an investigation looming, but I don't think there is any substance to it."

Shelly wanted to ask her why she felt that way but decided it wouldn't be appropriate to grill her on the subject the first day on the job.

"So, since I've been away from the game awhile," Samantha continued, "I'm going to need a lot of help from you to get me on top of everything, particularly litigation. I can't believe all the lawsuits that we're defending."

"Well, with the real estate market crashing and so many people losing their homes, it's only natural that people are bitter and lashing out."

"Do you know what our policy has been regarding settling these lawsuits?" Samantha asked.

"From what Lucius told me he doesn't settle them, he fights them tooth and nail. He believes most of them are frivolous and only filed to delay foreclosure or get revenge if the foreclosure has already taken place."

"Right. That's true. They're looking for a quick settlement, so we have to draw the litigation out and make them wish they never filed it."

"Right," Shelly acknowledged. "I think Lucius called that 'Rambo litigation.' "

"Exactly. Like this Cindy Sharp case—trying to blame her husband's suicide on us. Can you believe that?"

Shelly could believe it, actually, and felt it was probably true. She'd spent hundreds of hours while she worked in the customer service department for the old company listening to dozens of stories just like Cindy Sharp's. When you messed with people's homes there were bound to be deep emotions ignited. Getting kicked out on the street had to be one of life's most traumatic setbacks. She kept these thoughts to herself, however.

"It's definitely a stretch," Shelly commented.

"I told the police they ought to look into her whereabouts on the day of Lucius's murder. It wouldn't surprise me if she wasn't the killer."

"Are you serious?" Shelly asked, startled by Samantha's statement.

"As serious as a heart attack. I figured it was a good opportunity to cause her a little grief. The detectives said they'd talk to her. I just wish I could be there when they do it. I'd like to see the bitch squirm."

Shelly didn't reply.

"So, I talked to our attorneys this morning and told them to stick with the Triple D strategy."

" 'Triple D'?" Shelly asked.

"Deny, delay, dissuade. Deny everything—make them come prove their case on their own. Delay—don't agree to anything and do whatever can be done to drag out the litigation. Dissuade—make the cost of prosecuting their case so high that they are forced to give up or settle cheap at mediation."

"What about the company's legal expenses? Isn't that approach pretty expensive?"

"It would be if we used law firms in the traditional fashion, but instead Lucius set up our own company legal department with its own attorneys who defend everything from one central location no matter what jurisdiction it's actually filed in."

"I could see where that could have its advantages, but the logistics of going to all those different courts all over the country would be staggering," Shelly noted.

"Well, we have to hire local counsel to actually practice before each court, but the local counsel rarely do much of anything other than depositions and the rare case that goes to trial."

"We spend a lot of time and resources responding to discovery requests," Shelly complained. "It's a horrible waste of time and resources."

"I know. If the government would stay out of our business we wouldn't have to be fooling around with all these modifications. We could just foreclose on the deadbeats who got behind and move on. Now everybody thinks they have a right to a modification and if we don't give it to them they have a right to sue us."

Shelly sighed. "That does make it difficult."

"It's just a bad time to be in the mortgage business, and wouldn't you know Lucius would up and die and leave me with this mess."

"Well, I'm sure you'll do fine," Shelly said, taking a step toward the door. She'd heard enough to be sick to her stomach. "Let me know if you need any help with anything."

Samantha nodded, and Shelly made her escape. She went back to her office still reeling from the revelation that Cindy Sharp was being interviewed by the police. Wondering about whether there was any substance to Samantha's statement, she went to see Sally to see if she knew anything about it. Sally was just hanging up the phone when Shelly stepped up to the reception desk.

"Hey, Sally. I've got a question for you."

Sally smiled. "What's up?"

"On the day of Lucius's murder, were you here your full shift?"

"Yes. I left at five just like always."

"Did you happen to see Cindy Sharp at all during the day before you left?"

"No. Can't say that I did."

"Hmm. Samantha told the police that they should be looking at Cindy Sharp as a suspect, and I was just wondering if there was any reason she'd believe Sharp had anything to do with it."

"No. I haven't heard anything about Sharp, but Walter Savage called three times that day and when Lucius finally took the call, I heard them arguing."

"What about? Do you know?"

"No. All I heard were raised voices."

"Did you tell the police?"

"Of course."

"So, who do you think did it?"

"You just talked to her," Sally said.

"Samantha?"

"Well, yeah. She wanted a divorce but didn't file yet 'cause the value of the business was way down. Now she's rid of her husband, owns the entire business, plus gets a nice fat salary while she's waiting for things to turn around."

Shelly nodded. "Not to mention the group life insurance and the company pension plan."

"Right. Like I said. Samantha's got my vote."

Shelly thanked Sally for the info and returned to her office. At lunch she sent a coded message to Rich calling a meeting and then met him at Starbucks. She told him what she had learned from Samantha and Sally, and they discussed how that would impact their civil suit.

"It sounds like Samantha is as ruthless as her husband," Rich observed.

"If not more so. She has absolutely no sympathy for the home owners. All she's interested in is her bottom line."

"That's good for the lawsuit. We'll just have to put her on the stand and make sure the jury realizes that. I don't think they will have much sympathy for her—grieving widow or not."

They discussed Sally's suspect list for a few minutes and who each thought was good for the murder, then Shelly indicated she had one more thing she wanted to talk about.

"You know, I have been thinking, now that Lucius is dead and Samantha has taken over, that it would be a good time for me to quit. I can still testify for you. I certainly know what's been going on and will be a good witness."

"You're worried about the FBI investigation," Rich suggested.

"Well, a little."

Rich sighed. "You're probably right. There's no need for you to take any more risk."

"So, you're okay with me quitting."

"Absolutely. I'll feel better, actually. I've been worried about you."

"Good. I'll give my two weeks' notice this afternoon."

They talked a few more minutes and then left separately. A wave of relief came over Shelly knowing she'd soon be turning in her letter of resignation. She couldn't wait to deliver it to Samantha and see the look on her face. Hopefully she'd tell her to leave immediately and not make her work two more weeks. Then she started to worry about Samantha's reaction to her resignation. If Samantha was Lucius's killer, she might decide it was too risky having someone out on the street who knew the company's dirty secrets. If that were the case Shelly would have to consider getting a bodyguard.

When she got back to her office she typed up a letter of resignation, signed it, and went to Samantha's office. The door was closed so she knocked. There was no answer, so she went to the reception area and asked Sally where she was.

"Oh, she left and said she wouldn't be back today."

"Damn!" Shelly exclaimed. "Wouldn't you know she'd quit early on her first day."

"I think she was going to see the company's attorney to go over pending litigation."

"Listen, Sally. I'm tendering my resignation," Shelly said, holding out the envelope containing the letter she'd just typed. "Would you give it to Samantha when she comes in tomorrow?"

"Sure, but aren't you giving notice?"

"Well, in my letter I told her I would be happy to work another two weeks if she wanted, but that I knew it was company policy to escort employees who quit off the premises immediately. So, I'm not coming back unless requested."

"Right," Sally said. "You think I should bail, too? Is this place going down?"

Shelly laughed. "No. I don't know that it's going down and I doubt you are in any jeopardy if you stay. This is just a personal decision on my part."

"Well, okay. I'll miss you, girl," Sally said.

"I'll miss you, too, but you'll be the only one I'll miss," Shelly said and then went back to her office.

Twenty minutes later she exited the building with a file box containing her personal property and drove to her apartment. The phone was ringing when she went inside, so she dropped the box on a chair and answered the phone.

"Hello?"

"What's this letter of resignation?" Samantha spat.

Surprised, Shelly asked, "How do you know about my letter of resignation?"

"When I called in to see if I had any messages, Sally told me," Samantha said tersely. "I thought you were going to help me get up to speed and be my right-hand man."

"Well, that's what you said, but I never agreed to it. I think with Lucius's death and new management coming in it's a good time for me to leave."

"Listen, you ungrateful bitch! You better keep your mouth shut. Lucius trusted you with all the company's trade secrets and proprietary information. He paid you handsomely so you'd be loyal and keep everything he told you confidential. I better not find out that you've betrayed his trust."

"Or what?" Shelly asked angrily.

"Or, I'll tear you a new asshole, you motherfucker!"

"Oh my God!" Shelly gasped. "Don't talk to me like that."

"I'll talk to you any way I damn well please," Samantha said, "and you can't do a damn thing about it."

"There is one thing I can do," Shelly said and hung up.

Shelly was shaking badly after the exchange and just sat

there looking at the phone for a full minute. It rang again, and she nearly jumped out of her skin. She didn't answer it, assuming it was Samantha again. After it rang about twenty times she picked the receiver up, set it back down, and then took it off the hook. She'd have to change her telephone number the next day, she decided—and maybe consider moving somewhere where Samantha couldn't find her.

Chapter 21
Wrongful Death

Matt was tied up with his parents for a few days after the Jay Leno fiasco. He'd helped them get their home put back together and retain criminal counsel. They needed to prepare for the possibility that an indictment would be coming down against Rich for the Martha Collins murder. Nothing had happened since the execution of the search warrant, so Matt decided it was time to go back to work on Cindy Sharp's lawsuit against Reliable Mortgage Servicing. It was after lunch when he went downstairs to pick up the mail. As he sorted through it he discovered a large envelope from Richmond & Richmond. He held his breath as he opened it.

"What the hell!" he exclaimed.

The pleading was entitled *Defendant's Petition for Wrongful Death*, and Samantha Jones was the plaintiff. The letter from Marvin Richmond accompanying the petition stated that this was a courtesy copy and asked that Matt accept service of process. Matt squinted, trying to fathom what he was reading. The petition alleged that Cindy Sharp intentionally caused the death of Lucius Jones, the CEO of RMS, by stabbing him to death with a letter opener. What this meant was that Samantha Jones had brought a civil claim against Cindy Sharp for allegedly causing Lucius Jones's death and wanted a long list of damages. Matt looked up when Ryan walked by his office.

"Look at this bullshit," Matt said.

Ryan stepped into the room. "What?"

"Cindy is being sued for wrongful death."

"What?" Ryan exclaimed. "Let me see that." Ryan read

the pleading and shook his head. "I've never heard of anything like this before. You're right, it's bullshit—but brilliant bullshit. Even if they can't prove Cindy did it, it puts our client in a bad light and creates a lot of suspicion."

"They probably know that the police don't have enough to convict Cindy for murder since it requires the prosecution to prove its case beyond all reasonable doubt. But the standard for a civil action is much less stringent—to prove a case requires only a preponderance of the evidence."

"So, what do we do?" Ryan asked.

"Talk to Cindy and see if she wants us to represent her and accept process, I guess."

"Right. Like she can afford it. This will be pro bono work."

Matt shrugged. "So we can't let them get a judgment against her. It would ruin our lawsuit."

After discussing the situation awhile they took the letter and petition to Rich to get his opinion.

"Actually, this could be a good thing," Rich said.

Matt and Ryan frowned. "A good thing?" Ryan asked.

"Yeah, anything as unique as this will draw media attention. I mean, this is almost like a counterclaim by RMS against Cindy. The media will eat it up."

"Okay," Ryan acknowledged. "And how will that be a good thing?"

"It will be great for Matt's campaign against the mortgage servicing industry. Cindy's civil case will get ten times the media attention because of this."

Matt nodded thoughtfully. "That's true. I guess this is a good thing, unless we lose."

"Well," Rich said, "we can't let that happen."

"Isn't this defamatory?" Ryan asked.

"No. You can't defame someone in a lawsuit," Rich explained. "What we have to do is catch Samantha telling people that Cindy is a murderer. We need witnesses, or even better, we need to catch her on camera telling people Cindy is a murderer."

"Marvin Richmond has surely told her to keep her mouth shut," Matt said.

"That's true," Rich agreed. "I know she's already told Shelly Simms that she thought Cindy had killed her husband. That's one witness. I'm sure there are others."

"How about the receptionist. What's her name?" Ryan asked.

"Sally Sterns, I think," Rich said. "Talk to Shelly and see if Samantha told Sterns that Cindy was a murderer."

Matt nodded. "I'll do that and then we can counterclaim for slander."

"Also, check and see if there have been any news stories or TV interviews where she may have slandered our client."

"Will do," Matt said.

Ryan scratched his head. "What if Cindy is arrested and charged?"

Rich thought a moment. "Well, then we'll have the civil trial for wrongful death abated until the criminal case is over."

Matt and Ryan nodded and went back to their offices. Matt got on the phone and called Cindy. He told her the situation and asked if she wanted Coleman & Sons to represent her.

"I don't have any money to pay you."

"We know, but we'll let you run a tab until you get some money."

"Yeah, right. Like I'd ever get enough money to pay you."

"Well, you might come into some money if we win the lawsuit. Anyway, we don't have any choice but to defend you to protect your other lawsuit."

"Okay, I'll pay you when I can," Cindy said, sounding on the verge of tears. "Will there ever be an end to this?"

Matt smiled. "Yeah. That's a guarantee. One day it will be all over. I just can't tell you exactly when that day will come, but it may be sooner than you think."

"I hope so; I don't know how much more of this I can take."

"Hang in there, girl," Matt said. "I'll keep you posted on what's going on."

Matt hung up, feeling bad for Cindy. She'd been through so much—loss of both her and her husband's jobs, bankruptcy, her husband's suicide, and now being charged with wrongful death. He could understand how she was at the end of her rope. He just hoped he could keep her from letting go.

Chapter 22
Best Seller

Amanda closed her eyes as she pulled up the *New York Times* Best Seller list on her computer. When she opened them she gasped for joy. *The Pact* was number ten on the nonfiction list. She printed out the list and took it into the kitchen where Ryan was eating breakfast.

"Honey, guess what!"

Ryan looked up at her in anticipation. "What?"

"*The Pact* is number ten on the *New York Times* Best Seller list."

Ryan's eyes widened. "Seriously?"

"Yes!" Amanda exclaimed. "My first placement is a *New York Times* best seller! I'm so excited."

"I can see that," Ryan said, laughing. He got up and they embraced. "I am so proud of you!"

They sat down across from each other at the breakfast table.

"Well, it wasn't my doing, exactly. It was that unfortunate *Inquisitor* article and the Jay Leno appearance."

"Yes, I still can't understand how the *Inquisitor* got ahold of Mom's notes."

"The break-in, obviously."

Ryan frowned. "I don't know about that break-in. They didn't take the notes."

"Well, they probably just photographed them and put them back so it wouldn't be obvious what they were after."

"I guess, but something is not right about it. I just can't

put my finger on it."

Sensing she was walking on thin ice, Amanda changed the subject. "So, is there any chance you can get Matt to write *his* story?"

Ryan laughed. "No. Not a chance. If he told his story he'd be going back to jail, too."

Amanda's eyes widened in alarm. "You think your father is going back to jail?"

Ryan shrugged. "He could if the DA elects to prosecute him."

Fear and guilt swept over Amanda. She'd never seriously believed Rich would be charged with murder. She thought he'd be embarrassed and humiliated, but that would be the price of fame and fortune. But would the DA really try him for a crime that had taken place over twenty-five years ago? Her head began to throb and the muscles in her neck and shoulders tightened, causing her to wince in pain.

"Are you all right?" Ryan asked.

She forced a smile. "Yeah, I'm fine. I think I strained my neck jumping up and down. I'm going to go lie down."

She went to the bathroom adjacent to the master bedroom and took some aspirin. Looking in the mirror, she thought she looked a little pale. Was she getting sick, or was this sickly look the price of her ambition? She finally decided it was the lighting and assured herself that everything would work out okay in the end.

On the following Monday Sheila Samson called to see how Rich and Erica were holding up and to report that over a hundred thousand hardcover books had been sold in the first two weeks since its release. She also wanted to know if Rich or Erica were available for any more appearances.

"I seriously doubt it," Amanda replied.

"Well, that's a shame. I've got over a dozen request for appearances. One is even offering money for him to appear."

"Seriously?" Amanda asked.

"Yes, the *Inquisitor* is offering $50,000 for an exclusive interview and follow-up story to their initial exposé."

Amanda's heart sank. "Well, forget that."

"Why? It will be an opportunity for Rich to get some compensation for all the hassle he's going through."

"No. I don't think so."

"You have an obligation as his agent to advise him of any offers."

"I'll mention it to him. Who else wants him?"

"More talk shows: *Good Morning America*, *The View*, *The Late Late Show*."

"Okay. I'll try to get him to consider doing more shows, but don't hold your breath."

"I won't. But getting a author's book published is just part of your job, you know. You need to be putting deals together to increase the demand for his book."

"I think from his perspective he's got way too much exposure already."

"All right. See what you can do. I hope you don't disappoint me," Sheila said and hung up.

Amanda took a deep breath and let it out slowly. She felt a stress headache coming on and was hoping to short-circuit it. She'd have thought Sheila would be ecstatic with how everything had turned out and not putting heat on her for more promotion. The phone rang and she picked it up.

"Amanda Sherman?" a male voice said.

"Yes."

"This is Roy Stanhouse. I'm a foreign-rights agent and I've done work for your boss in the past. If you ask her I'm sure she'll vouch for me. "

"Okay. What can I do for you?"

"Do you have anyone soliciting foreign rights for *The Pact*?"

"No. Not yet. I was about to start looking for someone."

"Well, you're in luck. I've been checking around, and

Unconscionable

I'm pretty sure I could arrange a number of foreign-rights deals if Mr. Coleman would hire me."

"Who do you think might be interested?"

"My people in London tell me that there would be considerable interest at a number of publishing houses in Great Britain, France, and Germany. Japan is a possibility as well."

"Okay. Send me a proposed contract and I'll talk to my client about it. . . . What kind of advance do you think they will offer?"

"Probably $10,000 or so for each country."

"Oh, that much? I'll definitely talk to Mr. Coleman," she said and hung up.

Talking about money got her to thinking about Sylvia and the $50,000 offer the *Inquisitor* had made. She decided to go visit her friend Sylvia and talk to her. They met at Denny's near Sylvia's office.

"What exactly would Rich have to do for this $50,000?" Amanda asked.

"He'd have to sit down with me and answer all my questions."

"Doesn't the book answer all your questions?"

"No, there are a lot of holes I need filled in."

"He doesn't have any memory of the murder, so you're not going to get him to confess to it."

"I know, but there's a lot he will remember, I'm sure. I'm also interested in how our story and the Leno interview has impacted him."

"Okay, I'll let him know about the offer and let you know."

"Good. I appreciate it. Oh, congratulations on the *New York Times* Best Seller list."

"Yes, that is incredible, isn't it?"

"It is."

"So, did the story do anything for your career?" Amanda asked.

216

Sylvia nodded. "Yes, I've finally earned a little respect around the office. This follow-up will do even do more for me—not just a flash in the pan, you know?"

"Right. Well, that's good. I was hoping it would benefit us both."

On the way back to her office Amanda worried that while Rich was being interviewed, Sylvia might accidentally or intentionally reveal where she found out about Erica's notes. She didn't think Sylvia would do that, but the thought dogged her. *A reporter never reveals her sources,* she kept telling herself over and over again.

When she got back to the office she decided to call Rich to advise him of the talk show offers as well as the *Inquisitor*'s proposal. She was half-afraid to call him as she hadn't talked to him since the police had searched his house and he'd learned of a possible indictment for Aunt Martha's murder. She held her breath as she dialed the phone. Suzie answered the phone and said she'd put her through.

"Rich. This is Amanda."

"Oh, hi, Amanda. How are you?"

"Good, actually. I guess you saw you're number ten on the *New York Times* Best Seller list."

"Yes. I saw that. Can you believe it?"

"No. It's totally amazing."

"So, what's up?"

"Well, since you are now a best-selling author there have been requests for you to make appearances all around the country."

"Really? Any good ones?"

"Yes, *Good Morning America*, *The Late Late Show*, and others."

"Do they want me or both of us?"

"They'd like both, but they'd be happy with just you."

"I don't know. With the grand jury looking at me for a possible indictment it might not be a good idea to stir up more publicity."

"Well, if you don't, the press isn't going to get your side of the story and you may end looking guilty. Don't you think it would be better to tell people what you think happened? If Erica and your friend don't talk, the press won't have any way to refute what you tell them."

"I guess. I need to talk to Erica and my attorney about it."

"Oh, and the *Inquisitor* wants to do a follow-up story as well. They are willing to pay $50,000 for it."

"How much?"

"Fifty thousand."

"Whoa! That's a lot for an interview."

"You should do it. It will give you a chance to do some damage control and stop all the wild speculation."

"Okay. You may be right, and I could use the money to pay my attorney. I know he's going to want a big retainer."

"You don't have to give me a cut of the money. Technically I should get fifteen percent, but I'll talk to my boss. We didn't solicit the story so we—"

"Nonsense. I'm not going to take advantage of you just because you're family. You've done a great job. I'm a *New York Times* best-selling author for godsakes. I hope you make a million bucks."

"Right," Amanda laughed, "because that would mean you made eight million."

"Well, that's true," Rich agreed, laughing.

Amanda hung up, shocked at Rich's upbeat mood. She guessed it was due to the success of his book and felt relieved. *He's obviously not worried too much about being indicted, so why should I lose any sleep over it? Everything I've done has been for Rich and Erica's benefit as well as my own.* A feeling of pride and accomplishment swept over her, but it didn't last. No matter how many times she told herself everything would be okay, the throbbing in her temples and dull pain in her stomach wouldn't go away.

Chapter 23
Cold Case

When Detective Perkins returned from LA he was summoned to the chief of detectives office for a meeting. After he'd said hello to some of his old friends he stepped into Lt. Ben Edmonton's office. An attractive brunette in a business suit who looked to be in her early thirties sat in one of the side chairs, so he took the other. The lieutenant was on the phone, so he just smiled at the young lady and waited. When Lt. Edmonton got off the phone he turned to them.

"Well, Detective Perkins. It's been a while."

"Yes. It has."

"This is Detective Alice Longoria. She's been assigned to the Richard Coleman case."

Detective Perkins nodded. "So, you decided to open up the case again?"

"Well, with all the publicity from your appearance on Leno we didn't have much choice."

"Sorry about that. They called me at noon and put me on a private jet to LA. I didn't have time to call you and tell you what was going on."

"It's all right. Seeing the look on Coleman's face when they paraded you on stage was priceless."

"Yeah, I rather enjoyed that myself," Detective Perkins admitted.

"Anyway, I'd like you to brief Detective Longoria on what you know about the case that wouldn't be in the file. She'll be in charge of the investigation from here forward."

"Sure, be happy to."

Longoria stood up. "Let's go to my office."

Perkins got up and followed Longoria to her small but nicely decorated office. She pointed to a chair and asked Perkins if he wanted some coffee. He said he did, so she went down the hall and got them both a cup.

"Okay, I pulled the cold case file and have gone through it," Longoria said. "There's not much in there about Rich Coleman. It seems everyone bought his alibi."

"Well, they did. He was found unconscious in an alley near his office and rushed to the hospital. It seemed like an airtight alibi at the time."

"Didn't you think it was rather convenient?"

"Yes, I was bit suspicious and talked to a lot of people, but nobody saw Coleman at the motel."

"What about his friend, Joe Weston?" Longoria asked.

"He didn't have an alibi, but we didn't think he had much of a motive at the time. Of course, now with the book we know he had been executing illegal trades and knew of the illicit affair, so once Martha Collins found out what was going on she was as much a danger to him as to Coleman."

"I went to see Joe right after the *Inquisitor* article, but he refused to talk with me—said it was ancient history and his attorney had told him he didn't have to talk to anyone about it, including the police."

"It's too bad we can't get him on the illegal trades, but I suppose the statute of limitations has run out on that," Perkins said.

"Yes, about eighteen years ago, but we could still get him for murder if we can prove he and Coleman were in on it together."

"That will never happen unless one of them turns on the other."

"I was going to offer Joe that option, but he's as hard as nails. He wouldn't even look at me. He just turned away every time I asked him a question and kept his mouth shut."

"That figures. They've know each other since college."

"What about Coleman's secretary, Suzie?" Longoria asked.

"I doubt she'd talk. She's been his secretary longer than Erica's been his wife."

"So, no brilliant ideas for me, huh?" Longoria asked.

Perkins shrugged. "Well, Coleman claimed his law partner and the victim's son had motives. And there was the son's lover who Martha Collins was trying to run off."

"Really? The report didn't mention them."

"No, I didn't seriously consider any of them since I thought Coleman was just trying to distract me from his wife's prosecution."

"Hmm. What was the victim's son's name?"

"Arnold Collins, I believe," Perkins replied. "He's an attorney. He filed a lawsuit against Coleman but when Erica was found innocent by reason of insanity they settled the case."

"What did it cost Coleman to settle?" Longoria asked.

"Fifty grand, if I remember correctly."

"And Arnold's lover?"

"Ralph, I think. Ah. Benitez, Ralph Benitez."

"Ralph?" Longoria snickered.

"Yeah. That's why mom was trying to run him off."

"So, Coleman thought Ralph didn't like Martha's interference with their relationship and took her out of the equation?"

"Something like that," Perkins said.

"Okay, and the law partner?"

"Peter Phillips? Erica's father appointed Coleman as trustee of the trust the law firm had drafted. Coleman claimed Peter may have murdered Martha Collins to protect the firm from liability if it came out Coleman had breached his fiduciary duty while employed by the firm."

"Sounds like a lot of persons of interest," Longoria noted. "Maybe if we put some heat on them they will tell us something useful."

Perkins nodded. "Good idea. Did you find anything when you searched his house?"

"Yes, we found Erica's notes. They say exactly what was reported in the *Inquisitor*, but without Erica's testimony explaining and interpreting them, they don't do us much good."

"Why not?" Perkins asked. "Aren't they like a confession?"

"No. They could just as easily be fiction without Erica's testimony explaining them."

"Well, anything else?" Perkins asked.

"No," Longoria said, standing up and extending her hand. Perkins stood up and shook her hand. "Thanks for your help. If you think of anything that might be helpful, let me know."

Perkins nodded and left Detective Longoria alone. She studied her notes for a while and then picked up the telephone and called Grace Godwin, one of her investigators who was particularly good at tracking down people. She gave her all the names Perkins had mentioned and asked her to get current addresses for each and run their names on all their criminal databases. Grace said she'd do it and get right back to her.

Longoria took a deep breath and let it out slowly. Working a twenty-five-year-old cold case was not her idea of detective work. How could she possibly find witnesses and evidence so long after the murder had taken place? Finally, she stood up and marched back to Ben Edmonton's office.

"Sir," she said, peeking into his office.

"Yes. Come in," Edmonton said irritably.

"Sir, I talked to Perkins, but all he has is a bunch of names of other people with motives to kill Martha Collins. He doesn't have anything on Richard Coleman. It seems Coleman was doing more detective work than the DA's office."

"So, what's your point?"

"My point is why are we wasting our time on this impossible case? There is no way we're going to prove Coleman is the murderer after twenty-five years. So, why bother?"

Lt. Edmonton glared at Detective Longoria. "I'll tell you why, Detective. Because when Richard Coleman published that book he was thumbing his nose at the Dallas DA's office and the Dallas police. He was announcing to the world that he and Erica had gotten away with murder and we couldn't do anything about it."

"Right. We can't allow him to do that."

"Exactly. Do you know how much money he is going to make off this book?"

"No. How much?"

"It was reported he got a $50,000 advance, but now that the book is on the *New York Times* Best Seller list his royalty could be ten times that, not to mention subsidiary rights."

"Okay, I won't let that happen, Lieutenant. I'll get the evidence we need to put the bastard away for the rest of his life."

Lt. Edmonton nodded. "Now, that's what I want to hear. Keep me posted."

Detective Longoria turned around and went back to her office feeling a bit sick. The lieutenant's pep talk had been inspiring but hadn't got her any closer to nailing Richard Coleman. Now, not only did she have an impossible case, but she was now responsible for restoring the honor and reputation of the DA's office after Richard Coleman had dragged it in the gutter in his *New York Times* best seller.

Chapter 24
Lawyering Up

Rich surveyed the paparazzi out in front of his house. It had been over a week and they were still out there in force. He wondered how long it would be before they got bored with his case and moved on. He shook his head and then headed for the garage. Erica followed him, and they both got into their black Mercedes Benz SL 500. Rich pushed the garage door opener and the instant it was opened accelerated out of the garage. Several journalists moved quickly to block the car's exit, but Rich swerved and drove over the grass and off the curb. He accelerated away, but in his rearview mirror he saw several cars and vans hustling to catch up.

He didn't try to lose the paparazzi. He'd tried that before and almost got into a car wreck. By the time he got to his destination a dozen vehicles were on his tail. After parking in the underground parking garage, he and Erica made a quick exit from the Mercedes and took the elevator up to the lobby.

It felt like déjà vu going to see Bruce Pierson at Bradley, Pierson & Jones LLP. Rich had just been there a few months earlier to start the ball rolling on Matt's appeal and reinstatement to the bar. Now he had Erica with him and it was a much more somber occasion. Bruce took them into the firm's conference room and a secretary brought them a cup of coffee.

"So, I see you're a *New York Times* best-selling author now," Bruce said. "Congratulations!"

"Thanks. I think," Rich replied dejectedly.

"Did you get your home restored back to normal?"

"Yes," Erica replied. "We got a lovely new door, a new

security system, and our house swept for bugs."

"Did they find any?"

"Only a dozen or so? One in each telephone and every main room in the house."

"Wow. I wonder what they thought you'd be talking about in your own home."

"It beats me," Rich said.

"So, have the police tried to contact you yet?"

Rich nodded. "Yes, they came by and wanted to talk, but I told them I had nothing to say until I had talked to you."

"When they searched your house, did they find anything?" Pierson asked.

"Well, they found Erica's notes."

"The notes contradicting your version of Martha Collins's murder."

"Right," Rich replied.

"Well, as long as neither of you testify you should be okay on the notes."

"So, why do you figure they bothered with the search warrant?" Rich asked.

"They don't like it when it appears someone got away with murder. It was bad enough that Erica was found innocent by reason of temporary insanity, but now the idea that you were the actual murderer, or had a part in it, really makes them look bad."

"So, it's just a matter of someone's pride?" Erica asked.

"Pride, and the reputation of the police and the DA's office. You didn't paint them in a very good light in your book."

"Hmm. So, do you think we should talk to them?" Rich asked.

"No. Absolutely not. No good could come of it. Just tell them your attorney has advised you not to talk to anyone about the events surrounding Martha Collins's death."

"What about interviews for the book? Supposedly they will only be asking about what's happened since its publication—nothing about the contents of the book."

"If you're very careful you could do that, but it's risky. Who wants to interview you?"

"I've got requests from *Good Morning America*, *The Late Late Show*, and an interview request from the *Inquisitor* magazine. The *Inquisitor* says they will pay me $50,000 and won't talk about the content of the book or the notes, but instead concentrate on how we are coping with the investigation and sudden attention from the media."

"Well, that's what they say, but you can bet they will be trying to trick you into saying something controversial or incriminating."

"Yeah. You're probably right," Rich agreed. "I guess I shouldn't do it."

"You're already a *New York Times* best-selling author," Erica noted. "You don't need to be out promoting the book anymore."

Rich nodded. "Okay. It's just hard to turn down an invitation from *Good Morning America* or $50,000."

"I know," Bruce said. "But it's the smart thing to do if you value your freedom."

"Yes, take Bruce's advice," Erica urged. "We don't need to be taking any more chances."

"What about Joe?" Rich asked. "I'm going to a ball game with him tonight. Can I talk to him about what's going on?"

"No. He may be wearing a wire."

"No, not Joe," Rich said. "He'd never do that."

"If his freedom is in jeopardy he might," Erica said. "Don't go to the game tonight."

"I have to go, but I won't talk to him about Martha's murder. We'll just talk about baseball."

"Be very careful," Bruce urged. "Even if Joe isn't wearing a wire, there might be somebody close by eavesdropping. There are a lot of directional listening devices now that allow you to pick up specific conversations from quite a distance away."

Rich took a deep breath and let it out slowly. "I can't

believe this. I have no privacy anymore."

"Well, you're a celebrity now. Wherever you go the paparazzi will be there. So get used to it."

After the meeting Erica and Rich encountered the paparazzi in the building lobby on the way to their car.

"Mr. Coleman, were you here to visit your attorney?" a reporter asked.

Rich nodded. "Yes, that's correct."

"Are you expecting to be charged in the Martha Collins murder?" a second reporter asked.

Rich shook his head. "That's not my call."

"Mrs. Coleman. Do you dispute the implication of your notes that your husband killed Martha Collins?"

Erica shook her head. "No comment."

Finally a security guard helped Rich clear a path back to the parking garage and escorted them to their car. As they were leaving, the paparazzi picked up their trail and followed them back home.

That night Rich called a cab but gave the dispatcher the address of a friend three blocks away. When Rich left, he went out the back door and down the alley behind their house undetected. When he got to his friend's house the cab was there waiting for him. He told the driver to take him to the ballpark at Arlington where he was to meet Joe in the stands at their seats. Joe was there when he arrived.

"You made a clean escape, huh?" Joe said.

"I think so, but you never know. It wasn't easy."

"How you holding up?"

"I'm okay, but Erica isn't taking it too well. She's scared to death I'll be arrested again."

"That couldn't happen, could it?"

"I don't know. What did the cops say when they visited you?"

"How did you know they came to see me?" Joe asked.

"I went over to your place the night they searched my

house. There were a couple of squad cars in front of your place."

"Well, you don't have to worry. I didn't say a word to them."

"I figured that, but what did they say? Did they give you any useful information?"

"They were real interested in some notes Erica wrote. I told them I knew nothing about them, so they started reading excerpts to me."

"What excerpts?" Rich asked.

"They were particularly interested in the part about me helping Erica move you to the alley behind Adair's Saloon."

"Don't mention specifics. Someone could be listening," Rich warned.

"Right. I just told them I knew nothing about Erica's notes and what they meant. I suggested that she might have been thinking about making the book into a novel instead of true crime. These notes may have been the things she'd wanted to change to make the story more interesting. I told them they should talk to her."

"Good. I don't think they could possibly have any evidence to substantiate that story. Unfortunately, I have no memory of anything between curling up with a bottle of Jack Daniels and waking up in the alley."

"So, what I want to know is why in the hell you wrote a fucking book that's apt to get us all in deep shit," Joe spat. "That's got to be the stupidest thing you've ever done."

Rich nodded. "That's true. Almost as stupid as shacking up with Erica when she was seventeen, huh?"

"Yeah, that was right up there, too."

"In retrospect I know it wasn't such a great idea, but for some reason I felt compelled to write it."

"You need to learn to control your compulsions. They may one day be your undoing."

"You mean like today."

Joe nodded. "Exactly."

Unconscionable

On the cab ride home Rich felt much relieved. His old buddy seemed to be as loyal as ever. He had never doubted his old friend, but it was always good to get reassurance. Rich wondered what he could do to derail the DA's efforts to put together a case against him but couldn't think of anything. Finally he decided the only sure way to avoid being arrested and charged with murder would be to find out who actually did kill Aunt Martha. He'd tried to figure that out once before and had failed. He wondered if twenty-five years later he'd have any better luck.

Chapter 25
Finding the Killer

After pondering the wrongful death suit against Cindy Sharp for hours, Matt finally decided the only way to clear Cindy's name and put the lawsuit against RMS back on track would be to find out who actually had killed Lucius Jones. At the firm's weekly staff meeting he brought up that topic.

"Even if Cindy isn't indicted people are going to wonder if she killed Lucius Jones. The only way to dispel that nasty rumor is to prove someone else actually killed him," Matt argued.

"So, how do we do that?" Ryan asked.

"We identify who had motive and opportunity and then figure out which one of them did it."

"So, who do you think had motive and opportunity?" Ryan asked, looking at his father.

"I don't know. Shelly Simms likes the wife for it," Rich replied. "They were separated, and apparently Samantha was just waiting for the most lucrative moment to file for divorce. But with the mortgage business in such disarray she may have gotten tired of waiting and decided to settle for the insurance proceeds on her husband's life."

"How much insurance?" Ryan asked.

"At least $250,000 but probably a lot more."

"So, Dad. Why don't you follow up on Samantha and I'll check out Jones's ex-partner, Walter Savage?" Ryan suggested.

Rich nodded. "What's Matt going to do?"

"I'm going to see who else is out there who may have wanted to see Lucius dead."

"You may need to hire a private investigator for that," Ryan suggested.

"Maybe. I'll do a little snooping around on my own first, but if I don't get anywhere I'll hire some help."

After the meeting broke up, Matt started thinking about how he could find additional suspects. He remembered Shelly had said Sally, the receptionist out at RMS, knew more than anyone about what was going on around the office. Sitting out front and screening phone calls put her in a position to know everything about everybody. Matt called Shelly and set up a breakfast meeting with her and Sally the next morning at the Richardson IHOP. Shelly and Sally were seated in the waiting area when Matt arrived. They stood up, and Shelly introduced Sally to Matt. A moment later the hostess took them to their table and a waiter brought them coffee.

"Thank you for coming, Sally," Matt said.

"No problem. I was actually excited when Shelly called. I hated Lucius Jones but I hate his wife even worse."

Matt laughed. "Really?"

"Yes. So, how can I help bury the bitch?"

"Well, we're looking into the obvious suspects, including Samantha and Walter Savage, but I wanted to see if there is anybody else out there who hated Lucius enough to kill him."

Sally thought a moment. "Well, Lucius was pretty much an asshole, so he didn't have a lot of friends. But aside from Walter and Samantha I don't know anyone who hated him enough to kill him."

"What about people who would benefit from his death?"

"He had several companies and partnerships that fed off the company. One of his partners in those enterprises may have had a motive."

"Really? What kind of companies and partnerships are we talking about?" Matt asked.

"Well, he had a real estate company that bought foreclosed properties and another one that handled evictions."

"How did that work?"

"A company called Southern Real Estate Investments LP bought all the foreclosed properties, fixed them up, and then sold them."

"Was that profitable?"

"Yes, because they'd get the properties at least thirty percent below market value, so they almost always made money. If they couldn't turn the property right away they'd sell them to Prime Holdings Ltd., who'd rent them out to cover the interest on the loans. In the interim while they were waiting for the market to turn around, the investors would get a nice tax write-off."

"I see. Any other companies that, as you say, fed off RMS?"

"Yes, there was the eviction company and a company called Consolidated Document Retrieval."

"You knew about CDR?"

"What do you mean?"

"Do you know what they did?"

"No. Not exactly. Why?"

Matt looked at Shelly.

"Nothing. What about the eviction company?"

"Metro Realty. They handled the evictions and the Cash for Keys program. It was their job to inspect all property put up for foreclosure, get an appraisal done, and get the home owners out of the property after foreclosure."

"So, they offered money to evicted owners to induce them to leave peacefully."

"Yes, because if a home owner contested a foreclosure or eviction it could cost the company thousands of dollars and delay liquidation of the property."

"Who ran Metro Realty?" Matt asked.

"Ron Goddard. He's an independent real estate agent, but more importantly, he's six foot two and weighs 320 pounds."

"Seriously?"

"Yes," Sally replied.

Shelly nodded. "He's a scary son of a bitch. He worked for the old company when I was head of customer service. You don't know how many calls I got from people after he dropped by to encourage them to leave peacefully."

"Will Samantha still use him, you think?"

Sally nodded. "She's already talked to him and he's agreed to continue on."

"What about CDR?"

"Actually, CDR was Samantha's idea," Shelly noted. "Lucius said he got the idea for that company from his wife."

"What does CDR do, anyway? I've always wondered about that," Sally said.

Shelly looked at Matt. "Should we tell her?"

"Why not," Matt replied. "Listen, this is strictly confidential and before we'll tell you CDR's purpose, we need to be sure you'll keep the information to yourself. This is as much for your protection as ours."

"Okay. My lips are sealed."

"CDR is the company's forgery division," Shelly said. "Whenever the company needs a document that doesn't exist, CDR will create it for us."

Sally nodded. "That doesn't surprise me. I always wondered how you guys always seemed to find the documents you needed for court at the last minute."

"Uh-huh. Documents on demand," Shelly said. "One of my jobs was to provide the specifications for the documents we needed from CDR and then check them when we got them back for compliance and accuracy."

Sally shook her head. "I'm working for a bunch of crooks."

Matt smiled. "We'll put a good word in for you with the FBI when they take RMS down."

"Thanks. Maybe I should get out like you did, Shelly. Get off the ship before it sinks."

"That's your decision, but if you want to 'bury the bitch'

like you said earlier, there is no better way than to stay where you are and provide us intel."

Sally sighed. "Oh what the hell. They didn't prosecute Bernie Madoff's receptionist, did they? And he stole billions."

"No, I don't think the feds will go after you."

"All right, then. I'll stay."

"Good. Thank you," Matt said. "Now, one more thing. I know you need to get to work so I'll make it fast." Matt looked down at his notes. "Did Lucius have any other partners or friends who came around that weren't involved in CDR, Metro Realty, Southern Real Estate Investments, or Prime Holdings Ltd?"

"Well, just one comes to mind. Rick Shafer and Lucius had lunch at least two or three times a month. They were old college roommates and went to football games together sometimes."

"Can you get me contact information on Rick?"

"Sure, I'll email it to Shelly."

"Email it from your house, not the office. Someone might be monitoring your email."

"Of course," Sally said with a big grin. "I'm a spy now. I know the routine."

Matt swallowed hard. He wondered if Sally realized how dangerous a situation she was in. She seemed a bit cavalier, but he figured that might be just for show. Deep down she was probably scared to death. At least he hoped she was so she wouldn't make any fatal mistakes.

When Matt got to the office he saw unopened mail on his desk. As he rummaged through it he noticed an envelope from Richmond & Richmond, so he opened it first. When he read it his heart nearly stopped. The title on pleading read *Final Summary Judgment*.

"What the fuck! You've got to be kidding!" he exclaimed.

Ryan, who was in the library, heard Matt and rushed in. "What's wrong?"

"The court granted RMS's motion for summary judgment."

"What? We haven't even had a hearing yet."

"Apparently there was a hearing and Marvin Richmond didn't bother to give us notice."

"That bastard! He can't get away with that."

"No. But now we'll have to file for a rehearing and it will delay the trial for months."

"What a scumbag!" Ryan exclaimed. "I can't believe this."

"Believe what?" Rich said as he walked in to find out what all the commotion was about.

"Richmond got a summary judgment against us. He got a hearing, and it was held last Friday."

Rich sighed. "There was nothing on my calendar."

"No. We didn't get notice," Matt said. "It's total bullshit!"

"Well, I bet you Richmond has a green card saying we got notice."

"But how could he, if we didn't get notice from him?"

"RMS has their own forgery department, remember?" Rich said.

"Oh, shit. Do you think they would do that?" Matt asked, incredulous.

"Well, if they file fraudulent documents in court, what's to stop them from forging a return receipt?" Rich replied.

"For one thing, their attorneys would have to be involved," Matt said.

Ryan shrugged. "It wouldn't surprise me if Marvin Richmond were in on the entire RMS scam. In fact, I bet he engineered a lot of it. You'd need an attorney's assistance to pull off what RMS has been doing."

"So, what do we do?" Matt said.

"File a motion to strike the judgment for lack of notice. In case that doesn't work, file a motion for a rehearing. Luckily you can't get a summary judgment by default, so at the rehearing the court will have to consider all our evidence and legal authority."

"So, should I file a response to motion for summary judgment?"

"You didn't file a response?" Rich asked.

"No. They are supposed to give us twenty-one days notice and I don't have to respond until seven days before the hearing."

Rich sighed. "I know. But how many times have I told you not to wait until the last minute to file things? You should have filed that response a while ago."

"It's just about ready," Matt said dejectedly.

Rich shook his head. "Well, get it filed immediately."

Matt sat in his office completely deflated by what had happened. He felt sick and angry. *How could something like this have happened?* He picked up the phone and called Marvin Richmond.

"What's this crap about a judgment!" he spat.

"Oh. Matt Coleman. Is that you?"

"Yes, it's me."

"What happened? Why didn't you answer my motion for summary judgment?"

"You son of a bitch. I never got notice of it!"

Richmond chuckled. "Sure you did. I've got a green card right here."

"Who signed for it?"

"Rhonda Wilson, I think it says."

"I've never heard of her," Matt said.

"Well, the address is correct, so you must have had someone at your office by the name."

"Yeah, well I'm pretty sure we don't."

Matt hung up and went to see Suzie, who was responsible for personnel.

"Have you heard of someone named Rhonda Wilson?"

Suzie grimaced. "The name does ring a bell."

"So, did she work for us?"

"Well, we did have a temp a few weeks ago when Debbie was sick."

"Oh, shit! Look it up. I need to know if she was on duty in October."

Suzie nodded and went to a file drawer. She opened it up and pulled out a file.

"What am I looking for?"

"Her name, address, and telephone number. Then call her and find out if she signed any green cards."

Suzie nodded and went back to her desk. Then she got up abruptly and went to the desk where Rhonda had sat and rummaged through it. The left drawer was full of unopened mail.

"Matt! Look at this," Suzie yelled.

Matt came over and looked at the stack of mail. There in the pile was a letter from Richmond & Richmond. "Goddamn it! How could this happen? She wasn't authorized to open mail or sign green cards."

"I know. I don't understand it," Suzie agreed.

"I bet somehow Richmond got to her," Matt said. "Contact the temp agency and find out her address and telephone number."

"Yes, sir. Right away."

Rich walked in and looked at Matt. "What happened?" he asked.

Matt explained what they'd figured out. When Suzie returned she looked pale.

"What's wrong?" Matt asked, fearing the worst.

"The temp agency claims they didn't send over any personnel. They claim we canceled the request."

Matt turned beet red, barely able to contain himself. "Then who the hell came and worked here for a day!" he screamed.

"Okay. Okay. Calm down," Rich said. "We've obviously

been set up. Our offices must be bugged. Don't say another word until we get someone over here to sweep this place."

"Bugged?" Suzie repeated. "But—"

"Don't say another word," Rich repeated.

Twenty minutes later two technicians from Sentinel Security were on-site sweeping all the offices for listening devices and hidden cameras. After about five minutes one of the technicians found a listening device in one of the plants in the reception area.

"This could be the culprit right here," the technician said, holding up a small wafer-like object.

Rich shook his head. "Damn. Anybody who has been in our reception area could have planted that bug, and whoever was listening at the other end could have overheard that we were hiring a temp."

Matt slammed his fist on the reception desk. "Jesus! I can't believe Richmond would stoop to this."

"You don't know that it was Richmond. It could have been someone at RMS. Richmond might not know anything about it."

"So, you're saying we can't do anything about this?" Matt asked.

"No. Don't mention it to anyone. Unless we have proof it just makes us look desperate."

"But what about the summary judgment?"

"As long as we can show the failure to respond was inadvertent and without conscious intent, the court should grant us rehearing or a new trial."

Matt just looked at Rich in utter dismay.

"Just get your response filed along with the motion for a rehearing ASAP."

"All right, Dad, but this is bullshit!"

"I know. But RMS has a lot of dirty secrets to hide and they'll do anything to keep us from exposing them. We'll all need to be on our guard."

Unconscionable

That night Matt worked until midnight on his response and motion for a new trial. When he finally got to bed after one a.m., he couldn't sleep. All he could think about was explaining to Cindy Sharp how they'd screwed up her case and ruined any chance of getting justice for her dead husband. He'd never had to notify their insurance carrier of a possible malpractice claim and didn't relish the idea of starting now, but for Cindy's sake he'd have to do it. If he didn't put their insurance carrier on notice they might not pay the claim later if one actually materialized. He cursed RMS and Marvin Richmond and vowed to make them pay for their unscrupulous tactics.

Chapter 26
DNA

Erica could tell something was wrong when Rich walked in the door. His face was somber and when their eyes met he turned away.

"What's wrong?" she asked.

"We underestimated our adversary and got burned."

"Which adversary?"

"Richmond or his client, Samantha Jones. I didn't figure Lucius's wife would be more cunning than he was."

Rich explained to Erica what had happened.

"Well, you'll recover from this. It's going to be a pain dealing with it, but in the end you'll still kick their ass."

"I don't know. They don't play by the rules. That makes them doubly dangerous."

"So, what are you going to do?"

"Matt is taking care of it for now. I left him at the office finishing up his response and putting together a motion for a rehearing. I just feel sorry for him. He's blaming the whole thing on himself."

"It doesn't sound like it's his fault."

"It isn't, but when you fall into someone's trap it's humiliating."

"Maybe I should call him," Erica said.

"No. That will just make it worse. He'll be all right."

There was a knock at the door.

"Who could that be?" Rich asked.

"Don't you remember? You're being interviewed by the *Inquisitor* tonight."

"Oh, shit. Not tonight."

"Yes, I'm afraid so."

Erica went to the door and let Sylvia and her photographer in. "Good evening," Erica said evenly.

"Hello," Sylvia said as she stepped inside and looked around. "You have a nice home."

"Thanks," Erica replied.

"Where are we doing this?" Sylvia asked.

"In the study, I think," Erica replied. "It's the most suitable place."

"All right. Lead the way."

Erica led Sylvia and her photographer into their elegant study. She pointed to two big brown leather chairs at one end of the room. "Will this work?" Erica asked.

Sylvia nodded. "Yes. Quite nicely."

The doorbell rang.

"Who could that be?" Rich asked for the second time that evening.

"That's probably Amanda," Sylvia said. "She insisted she be present for the interview."

Rich nodded. "Good idea. I'll get it."

Rich left the room and a minute later came back with Amanda and Ryan. Erica's eyes brightened at seeing Ryan, and they immediately embraced.

"How are you, honey?" Erica asked. "I heard you didn't have such a great day."

"No. We didn't."

"Don't worry. These things happen. You'll get through it."

"What happened?" Sylvia asked.

Erica's face stiffened. "Oh, nothing. Just personal stuff. Nothing you'd be interested in."

Sylvia nodded skeptically. "Well, I'm ready when you are."

The doorbell rang again and Erica sighed. "Who could

that be?"

Erica looked at Amanda, who just shrugged. "Would you see who it is, Amanda?"

"Sure," Amanda said and left the room.

There was the sound of a scuffle at the front door and heavy feet approaching. A nicely dressed woman and a man in a suit entered the study followed by several uniformed police officers. The woman flashed her badge.

"Detective Longoria, Dallas Police Department," she advised, looking at Rich.

"What's the meaning of this?" Erica protested.

"We're here to arrest your husband," Longoria said.

Erica gasped.

"Richard Coleman. You are under arrest for the murder of Martha Collins. You have the right to remain silent; anything you say will be used against you in a court of law. You have the right to an attorney; if you cannot afford an attorney one may be provided to you by the court."

The male detective swung Rich around and cuffed him while the photographer snapped several pictures of the arrest. Erica threw herself at Rich and wrapped her arms around his neck. Longoria gingerly pulled her away.

"You can't do this," Erica protested. "I killed Aunt Martha. I've already been tried for it."

"You may have, but your husband helped you. He's as guilty as you were, and I doubt a temporary insanity plea will cut in this trial," Longoria spat.

"What possible evidence could you have to justify this arrest?" Ryan protested. "It's been twenty-five years and there are no witnesses."

Detective Longoria smiled. "Well, Mr. Coleman. In the last twenty-five years there have been great advances in medical science, particularly in the area of DNA evidence. Back when the murder took place we couldn't put your father at the scene of the crime, but today we can. You see, his DNA has been on the lamp

243

in the motel room all this time, and had we not reopened the case he would have gotten away with murder."

Amanda gasped and started to wobble. Ryan grabbed her and set her down in a chair. Erica just starred at Longoria in shock. Rich closed his eyes and took a deep breath. The photographer kept flashing pictures of the scene while Sylvia smiled broadly. Finally, Longoria nodded and the arrest team quickly escorted Rich out to a squad car.

"Call Bruce," Erica barked. "He'll have to work quickly to get bond posted so Rich won't have to spend the night in jail."

"There is no way to get him out of jail tonight," Ryan said. "That's why they waited until tonight to arrest him. They wanted to be sure he'd have to spend the night behind bars."

"Why?" Erica complained. "Rich gets people out of jail at night all the time."

"Not for murder. There will have to be an arraignment and a bond set. Unless Bruce can get a judge to set bond tonight, he'll have to wait until morning."

"Maybe he can. Call him."

"I will," Ryan said, "but don't get your hopes up."

Ryan got out his cell phone and called Bruce Pierson at his home. They talked for a minute and then Ryan hung up.

"Okay. He's on his way to police headquarters."

Erica nodded, tears streaming down her cheeks. "How could this have happened? After all these years how could Richard be charged with murder?"

Erica then turned around abruptly and pointed at Amanda. "This is all your fault! You caused this, you goddamn bitch! You couldn't take no for an answer. All you cared about was your fucking career! I told you we didn't want the manuscript published. Why in the hell did you read it anyway? It was private. You're not part of this family. You had no right!" Erica wailed. "You had no right!"

Ryan put his arms around Erica and held her tightly. "It will be okay, Mom. Calm down. It's not Amanda's fault."

Amanda fell into one of the stuffed chairs and began to sob. The photographer kept taking pictures. Ryan turned to Sylvia and the photographer. "Get the hell out of here. The show's over."

Sylvia nodded to the photographer, and they gathered their things and left.

"Why don't you go lie down, Mom," Ryan suggested.

Erica shook her head. "No. I'm going to the police station."

"No," Ryan protested. "That's not a good idea. I'll call Matt and send him over there. Amanda and I will stay here with you."

"No!" Erica screamed, turning to Amanda. "Get that woman out of my house. I never want to see her face again."

Amanda got up and hurried out of the room. Ryan watched her leave, obviously torn as to what to do. "Okay, I'll send Amanda home. But you need to go lie down. I'll call Matt right now."

Ryan took out his cell phone and called Matt. After a minute he hung up. "Okay. Matt's on his way to the police station. Come on. Let's get you to bed."

"No!" Erica exclaimed, pulling herself away from him. "Drive me to the police station or I'll drive myself."

Ryan sighed in frustration. "All right, I'll drive you."

Ryan went to find Amanda, and Erica followed, afraid he'd leave without her. When they couldn't find her in the house they went outside. Just as they stepped onto the porch they saw her driving away in Ryan's car.

"Shit!" Ryan spat. "I guess we'll take your car."

Erica nodded and they went back through the house to the garage and got took Erica's car to the police station. Matt and Bruce Pierson were already there when they walked into the waiting room. Also, standing on the other side of waiting room was Sylvia and her photographer. Erica dreaded to think of what would be in the next issue of the *Inquisitor*. They went over to

Pierson.

"What's happening?" Erica asked.

"They're booking him now. I've already got my bondsman running a writ, but the trick is going to be getting a judge to set bond. The ADA on the case has already said he wants a full hearing in the morning. I don't know what I can do about that. This is a high-profile case, and no judge is going to do anything to compromise it."

Erica sighed. "Will they keep him separated from the general population? I've had some experience in the Dallas County Jail, and it wasn't pleasant."

"The ADA said they would as long as he is here at the police station, but there are no guarantees once he goes to the county jail. That's up to the sheriff."

They waited impatiently while Pierson made phone calls and finally talked to Detective Longoria. When he was done he came back over with a somber face.

"I couldn't talk the judge into doing anything tonight, and Longoria says the ADA won't budge on waiting until tomorrow."

As they were talking a TV news crew came into the waiting room. Erica winced at seeing them.

"Who's the ADA?" Ryan asked.

"Frank Baldwin," Pierson replied. "He's their number-one prosecutor."

"That figures," Erica moaned. "Okay, let's get out of here before every media crew in the county gets here."

Ryan nodded and took Erica's elbow. Matt scrambled to get ahead of them and help forge a path through the growing crowd of reporters and TV news crews.

"Mrs. Coleman? What do you think of your husband's arrest for Martha Collins's murder?"

"No comment," Erica said, glaring at the reporter.

"Mrs. Coleman. Did you anticipate this new DNA evidence?"

"She has no comment," Matt spat, pushing a reporter

aside and opening the door for Erica.

They walked briskly down the long flight of stairs to the street and across to the parking lot. The press followed them and tried to cut them off as they crossed the street, but Matt angled away from them and managed to get Erica to her car before the crowd cut them off. Ryan got in the driver's seat while Matt put Erica in the shotgun seat and closed the door.

"Back off or you're going to get run over," Matt warned.

The crowd reluctantly backed up as Ryan gunned the engine. When they were clear Ryan eased out and away from the curb. Erica looked back at the mob and shook her head in despair. *How could this have happened? I thought this chapter of my life was over. That goddamned Amanda. I'd like to kill that little bitch.*

Chapter 27
Arraignment

Matt and Erica sat in the courtroom of the 195th District Court at the Frank Crowley Courts Building in Dallas waiting for Rich's arraignment. Bruce Pierson sat at the defense table with Rich while Frank Baldwin and another ADA sat at the prosecution table. There were several arraignments on the docket, and Baldwin was handling them all for the Dallas District Attorney's office. The court considered two of them before they finally called Rich's case.

"The State of Texas vs. Richard Coleman," the judge announced.

Pierson, Rich, and Baldwin all rose. "Frank Baldwin for the State, Your Honor."

"Bruce Pierson for the defendant, Your Honor."

The judge studied his docket sheet for a moment and then said, "All right. Mr. Coleman, you are charged with participation in the murder of one Martha Collins. How do you plead?"

"Not guilty, Your Honor," Rich said earnestly.

The judge gave Rich a hard look and then said, "Does the state have a bail recommendation?"

"Yes, Your Honor. As you know, this is an unusual case in that Mr. Coleman has written a book about this murder. In his book there is a lot of talk about fleeing the jurisdiction and hiding out in South America. Mr. Coleman is a wealthy man and there is a substantial flight risk. The state opposes bond."

The judge nodded. "Mr. Pierson? What say you?"

"Your Honor. This is a frivolous indictment. This crime took place more than twenty-five years ago and Erica Coleman

249

has already been tried for the crime and found to be innocent by reason of temporary insanity. I know the state supposedly has some new DNA evidence that puts Mr. Coleman at the crime scene, but that doesn't necessarily prove anything."

The judge nodded. "Yes, I'm a little skeptical of the state's case myself, but I'm not inclined to dismiss it quite yet. What do you have to say about bond?"

"Well, Mr. Coleman has no priors, he's an attorney who has practiced law for thirty years, he has a family here and owns real property in Dallas County. And as to his book, although flight was discussed by Erica Coleman and she did flee the jurisdiction, the record will show that Mr. Coleman tracked her down and brought her back before the trial was concluded. We don't believe there is any flight risk and ask that Mr. Coleman be released on his own recognizance."

The judge sighed. "Well, I don't think we are going to do that, but I believe bail should be allowed. Bail is set at two million dollars. The prisoner will be remanded into the custody of the county sheriff until such time that bond has been posted."

"Thank you, Your Honor," Pierson said.

Rich was taken back into his holding cell and Pierson left the courtroom. Erica and Matt were outside and intercepted him as he was leaving.

"Do you have bail arranged?" Matt asked.

"Yes, we should have your dad out in an hour or so. If you can wait it shouldn't be long."

"I'll wait," Erica said. "Matt, you can go back to the office."

"Just hang out in the jail waiting room," Pierson said. "He'll be coming out there."

Erica nodded and Pierson left.

"Are you sure you don't want me to stay?"

"No, it will just be a waste of your time. I'll be fine."

"Okay," Matt said, hugging his mother.

"Call me if anything comes up."

"I will. Get out of here."

Matt reluctantly left and headed back to the office. When he got there his secretary, Melissa Curry, intercepted him as he was walking by her desk and advised him that she'd been successful at getting him a setting on his motion for rehearing in the Sharp case and it was to be held in ten days. She handed him a notice of setting to sign. When he got back to his office he put the hearing date and time on his calendar and programmed it to remind him three days before the hearing.

Now it was just a matter of waiting, something Matt was used to doing, having spent over a year in prison. But he knew there was only sixty days left until all the discovery in the case had to be done, so he decided to work on Cindy's defense while he waited. In that regard he needed to talk to Walter Savage. Savage was one of several who had a strong motive to kill Lucius Jones, and Matt needed to know if he had an alibi. He put a call into him and was surprised when his secretary scheduled an appointment for ten the following morning and indicated that Savage was anxious to meet him. Matt thought this was a bad sign, as it indicated Savage had nothing to hide. The following morning Savage confirmed that feeling.

"I was picking up my daughter from school. My ex-wife and I have joint custody. She got out at three thirty, and we went to dinner at Wendy's afterward."

"Which Wendy's?" Matt asked.

"The one in Plano on Fifteenth Street."

"So, a long way from downtown Dallas."

"Oh, yes. Twenty miles at least."

"What did you do after dinner?"

"I took her to my apartment. My girlfriend was with me, so you can verify everything with her."

Matt took down the girlfriend's information. "So, that doesn't put you completely in the clear. You could have hired someone to kill Jones."

Savage shook his head. "Okay, I'll admit I was pissed off

the way Lucius split up the company. He took advantage of me and cost me a lot of money, but frankly I was glad to get rid of the delinquent accounts. Foreclosures are never very pleasant and the government makes you go through so many hoops now before you can foreclose, it's ridiculous."

"What did he do exactly that upset you?" Matt asked.

"We were supposed to sit down and divide up all of our customers in an equitable fashion. Then each of us would contact the accounts we were going to maintain and get their okay on the transfers to the new entities that we were each establishing."

"So, did you do that?"

"Yes, that went fine until I went to call my accounts and found out that Lucius had already contacted them and told them I wouldn't help them with any of their troublesome loans."

"What do you mean, 'wouldn't help them'?"

"Well, in other words, he was offering to do whatever it took to cure any paperwork deficiencies they might have with their accounts, whereas I would do whatever I legally could to help them resolve those issues but nothing more."

"So, this turned out to be a problem?"

Savage laughed. "Oh, yeah. About thirty percent of the accounts I was supposed to get refused to come with me. So, effectively I lost a third of my business."

"And how does that translate into annual sales?"

"Two hundred grand a year, easy," Savage replied.

"Ouch!"

"Right. Tell me about it."

"So, the thought of killing Jones didn't cross your mind?"

"No. But the thought of suing the bastard certainly did."

"That would be consistent with what I have been told about you."

"So, you believe me?"

"Yes, as much as I'd like you as a suspect, I can't really see it."

"Thank you."

"So, when I called your secretary she said you were anxious to see me."

"Yes, I wanted to offer my services in prosecuting your case against RMS."

"Really? That's an attractive offer, but with Lucius dead, why would you still want to help?"

"Because if RMS is perceived to be in trouble I may get some of my customers back."

"And some of Jones's, too, perhaps."

"That, too," Savage agreed with a grin.

"Well, any help you can give us behind the scenes will be appreciated; however, I won't be putting you on the stand. That could backfire on us."

"So, what do you need to know?"

"Actually, our biggest problem in this wrongful death case is the fact that Cindy Sharp is a person of interest in Lucius's murder. So, what we really need is to find out who actually killed Lucius."

Matt went over all the suspects they had identified so far and filled Savage in on what they knew about each of them.

"I wouldn't be surprised if Samantha was involved. I can't see her actually killing Lucius, but I doubt she'd have any qualms about hiring someone else to do it."

"How well do you know her?"

"Not that well. My ex-wife and I met with Lucius and Samantha socially from time to time, but my wife and Samantha never got along. They weren't friends."

"So, did Lucius have any friends that he was close to?"

"Not too many. In fact, the only one that comes to mind is Rick Shafer."

"Yes, someone else mentioned him. So, they were close friends?"

"Yes, they hung out together a lot and, more importantly, their wives were friends."

"So I should talk to Rick, then. He'd probably know if

253

there was anybody out there who had threatened Lucius."

"Yes, he'd probably be the only one that Lucius would talk to about that type of thing."

Matt thanked Savage for talking with him and went back to the office. He told Melissa to find Rick Shafer and see if they could meet up sometime. She said she'd get right on it. Just as he hung up the phone, it rang again.

"Matt Coleman."

"Matt," Erica said. "I just wanted you to know your father and I are home."

"Oh. Great. No problem with the bond?"

"No. The bondsman took care of everything. I only had to wait a little over an hour."

"How's Dad?"

"He's shaken up a bit, but that's to be expected. Knowing him he'll be back to work tomorrow."

"Okay. Well, tell him there's no rush for him to come back to work. We have everything under control."

"Okay. I will."

Matt hung up and a moment later Melissa came on the intercom. "I talked to Mr. Shafer, and he said he could come to our office tomorrow morning or he could meet you for happy hour at Benihana on Banner Drive."

"Happy hour sounds good, say five fifteen p.m."

"I'll tell him."

Matt was pleased that he'd been able to link up with Shafer so quickly. He guessed Shafer was as anxious as anyone to find out who killed his best friend. When the staff left the building at five he locked up and headed over to Benihana. When he got there the parking lot was full, so he had to park in the hotel parking lot across the street. Shafer was short but had an athletic build. He'd already downed a Coors Light and was working on his second one. Matt sat down next to him at the bar and ordered a bourbon and Coke. After Matt had his drink they went to a booth where they could talk privately.

"I am sorry for your loss," Matt said. "I understand Lucius Jones and you were good friends."

"Yes, since high school. I couldn't believe it when I heard on TV about his murder."

"So, when was the last time you saw Lucius?" Matt asked.

"Oh, just a few days ago. We usually hang out on the weekends. Lucius was pretty busy during the week running his business."

"Did he mention that he was having problems with anyone?"

"No, other than his ex-partner, Walter Savage."

"What did he have to say about Mr. Savage?"

"He said Mr. Savage was threatening to take him to court if he didn't quit contacting his clients and interfering with his business."

"How well do you know Savage?"

"Quite well, actually."

"So, do you think Savage had anything to do with the murder?"

"No. Probably not."

"How about Samantha? I understand she and your wife are good friends."

"They are."

"Has she mentioned anyone who might have wanted Lucius dead?"

Shafer laughed grimly. "You mean other than Samantha?"

"Right."

"Well, there was Lucius's mistress, Pamela Sands."

"Pamela Sands?" Matt repeated, writing down the name.

"Right."

"So, why would his mistress want him dead?"

Shafer sighed. "I don't know that she did, but the way Lucius was murdered with a letter opener to the neck just sounded like Pam."

"What do you mean?"

"Well, killing someone with a letter opener sounds like a crime of passion. They were arguing, things got out of hand, and she picked up the first thing she saw that would work for a weapon."

"Huh. That's a good point," Matt said. "That reasoning could work for Samantha, too."

"Not really. Samantha is cool and calculating. If she wanted Lucius dead it would probably look like an accident."

Matt laughed. "You should have been a detective."

"No, no. I just know both women. Pam is very emotional and spontaneous. I've seen her pick up a frying pan and throw it at Lucius. She's Italian."

"Well, I'll have to track down Pam and talk to her. Do you know where she lives?"

"Yes. In the condo that Lucius bought for her."

Matt laughed and took down Pam's address and telephone number.

"So, what about Lucius's business partners?"

"You mean his network of parasites?"

"I guess you could call them that."

"Well, Lucius was smart and always maintained a fifty-one percent ownership so that he could maintain control over them. I'm not sure what happened to them if he were to die. There could have been buy-sell agreements or key man insurance policies that might be motive for murder, but I wasn't privy to that kind of information."

"Well, I guess I'll have to check each one of them out."

"You probably should."

Matt thanked Shafer and then headed to his car. He called Candy and told her he was through with his meeting and she suggested he come to her place for dinner. She said there was someone there she wanted him to meet. He said he'd be there in half an hour. When he arrived Candy met him at the front door and escorted him into the den. A beautiful woman with a dark complexion and dazzling brown eyes was sitting on the leather sofa talking to Sharon. She looked up and smiled when Matt and Candy walked in.

"Matt. This is Mia Meyers."

Mia didn't extend her hand, so Matt nodded. "Hi. Mia."

"Mia just signed on last week, and it turns out Lucius Jones used to hire her to accompany his banking and mortgage lender clients when they were in town."

"Really? That's a nice coincidence. You don't happen to know anybody who wanted him dead?" Matt asked jokingly.

Mia shook her head. "No. His clients seemed pretty happy. They did a lot of partying and were usually in a good mood."

Matt sighed. "Too bad. I could use a good lead right now."

"Actually, I'm booked later this month with one of his business partners. Is there anything you need to know?"

"Who is your client?" Matt asked.

"Brett Smith. He owns a company called Prime Holdings, I think he calls it. They buy foreclosed properties."

"Right. I've heard about that company."

"So, what do you need to know?"

"As much about his business as possible and, of course, see if he has any theories about who killed Lucius Jones and why."

Mia smiled. "No problem. Give me your cell number and I'll call you after the date."

Matt told her his number and then thanked her. He didn't expect her spying to lead to anything earth shattering, but she could probably learn a lot more than he could if he went to Smith directly. Men had a way of opening up to pretty women, particularly if they'd had a few drinks and were hoping to get laid.

"Dinner's ready," Gina yelled from the kitchen.

Matt smiled and got up eagerly. "I'm starving. I was so busy I skipped lunch."

"Matt. You can't be missing meals. It's not good for you," Candy scolded.

Matt shrugged as he headed for the dining room. "I know. I don't usually do that, but everything's been so crazy lately."

Candy came up from behind him and began massaging his shoulders. "Oh, my God. You're so tight. After dinner we can sit in the hot tub and relax."

"Ohhh. Now, that sounds good," Matt replied.

They all streamed into the dining room and sat down. The table was already set, and there were several bottles of wine and steaming baskets of french bread. Gina walked in with a big salad and set it down on the table. Jenni came in next with a big bowl of pasta and a plate of Italian sausage. Before long everyone was enjoying the meal, talking, and drinking wine.

"So, how is your father holding up?" Candy asked.

Matt shrugged. "Ah. He's okay. It's my mother that I'm worried about. She's been very depressed."

"Well, that's to be expected, don't you think?" Sharon asked.

"Sure, but when she was on trial for murder she got so depressed she talked my father into agreeing to commit suicide."

"Oh, my God!" Gina exclaimed. "You don't think she'd do something like that now, do you?"

"I don't know," Matt replied. "With my mother you never know what she's thinking. My dad's watching her pretty closely and Ryan and I are watching Dad. If we get a hint of anything extreme like that going on we'll . . . I don't know . . . do something to prevent it."

"Well, the situation is different now. Your parents are much older and more mature," Jenni observed.

"True. I'm worried about my father being convicted more than anything else. With the DNA evidence putting him at the murder scene I'm afraid it's going to be hard to convince a jury he didn't do it."

"But nobody saw him do it," Candy argued.

"True. But he's an attorney, and juries hate attorneys. You know that."

Candy sighed. "That's true. I am so sorry, Matt."

"And I know what it's like to be in prison," Matt said, tears welling in his eyes. "I was in federal prison and that was no picnic. But they'll send my father to Huntsville. Do you know what a hellhole that is?"

Jenni began to weep. Matt looked at her and swallowed hard. "I'm sorry. Let's change the subject," Matt suggested, forcing a smile. "This sausage is awesome!"

After dinner the party moved to the hot tub. Matt soon forgot his despair when he found himself surrounded by Candy, Sharon, Jenni, Gina, and Mia. Candy and Sharon were topless, but Jenni, Gina, and Mia hadn't bothered with clothing at all. A combination of steamy water, pampering hands, and extreme visual stimulation did wonders for the stiffness in Matt's back. His only regret was that Ryan hadn't been there to share in his good fortune.

Chapter 28
Rehearing

On Friday of the next week Ryan had scheduled the deposition of Samantha Jones in her wrongful death case against Cindy Sharp. Since Samantha wasn't likely to talk to Matt or Ryan they decided the only way to get needed information out of her would be to take her deposition. Presumably she would tell the truth rather than risk a charge of perjury.

As was the custom Ryan went to the offices of Richmond & Richmond for the deposition. The court reporter he had hired was already there setting up. The receptionist brought them coffee. A moment later Samantha walked in flanked by Marvin Richmond.

Samantha was dressed conservatively in a navy blue suit and was noticeably restrained. Normally she was extremely talkative, but on this occasion she didn't say a word. Richmond looked dashing in his $2,000 suit and fiery red power tie. Ryan wondered why he had chosen to dress up for a nonvideo deposition. Ryan often didn't even bother to wear a suit to a deposition; however, today he had, figuring it might make it look like he wasn't taking the lawsuit seriously if he came in casual attire.

The court reporter got the names of the parties and the attorneys and then said she was ready.

Ryan cleared his throat and then began by asking Samantha about her background, education, work history, and relationship to Lucius Jones. After forty-five minutes he got to the crux of the matter.

"Now, you have claimed in your original petition that Cindy Sharp killed your husband, is that correct?"

"Yes. That's correct."

"Did you see her kill him?"

"No."

"Do you know someone who saw her kill him?"

"No."

"Were you in your husband's office on the date he was killed?"

"No."

"So, why do you think Cindy Sharp killed your husband?"

"She was recorded on a video surveillance camera a block away about the time he was killed," Samantha replied evenly.

"Okay, I'm going to show you what has been marked as 'Exhibit 1,' " Ryan said, handing her a single sheet of paper. She took it.

"Yes."

"Can you identity this?"

"It says it's a subpoena duces tecum."

"Right. Was that served on you recently?"

"Yes. I believe so."

"It's a list of things you were to bring to this deposition, right?"

"Correct."

"Please read item number one."

Samantha sighed. "Ah. 'Any videotapes in your possession that depict any facts relevant to this lawsuit.' "

"Okay. Did you bring any videotapes with you today?"

"No."

"Why not? You just testified that Cindy Sharp was captured on a video camera near the scene of your husband's murder about the time he was murdered."

"I don't have the tape."

"Who does?"

"The police."

"What police?"

"Ah. I don't know. The Dallas police, I guess."

"Have you ever viewed this video recording?"

"No."

"So, what makes you think there is one?" Ryan asked.

"Detective Morin mentioned it."

"But you don't know for sure what's on it?"

"No. I haven't seen it," Samantha admitted.

"What other facts support your claim that Cindy Sharp killed your husband?"

"She threatened him once over her foreclosure."

"Were you there when she threatened him?"

"No."

"What makes you think she threatened him?"

"Lucius told me."

"When did this alleged threat take place?"

"A few days after she was foreclosed."

"What did she allegedly say that you thought was a threat?" Ryan asked.

"She said he would pay for treating people the way he did."

"And you think that's a threat to kill him?"

"Sure, what else could she have meant?"

"Ah. Maybe that a jury might award her a million dollars' damages?"

Samantha laughed. "Well, that's not what she meant."

"In your opinion?"

"In my opinion and lots of other people's."

"Okay. So, what other evidence do you have that Cindy Sharp killed your husband?"

Samantha shrugged. "I don't know. I'll leave that up to my attorneys."

"So, right now you don't know of any other evidence to

link Cindy Sharp to the murder."

Samantha looked over at Richmond, who was holding up a finger. "Oh. I think there are fingerprints."

"Fingerprints? How do you know there are fingerprints?"

"Detective Morin told me about them."

"Where were the alleged fingerprints found?"

"I don't know. You'll have to ask Detective Morin."

"You testified that Cindy Sharp had threatened your husband, right?"

"Yes."

"Where did that happen?"

"She came by his office."

"Right after she was foreclosed, right?"

"Yes."

"So, she could have left her fingerprints then, right?"

"I don't know. You'll have to ask Detective Morin," Samantha repeated.

"Has Cindy Sharp been charged with your husband's murder?" Ryan asked.

"No."

"Why not?"

"I don't know."

"So, the police don't have enough evidence to charge Cindy Sharp, yet you brought this lawsuit. Why is that?"

"Because it's easier to prove your client killed my husband here in this civil court rather than in a criminal court."

"So, you believe that the evidence you've testified to today is enough to prove in this court that Cindy Sharp killed your husband."

"Yes. That's right."

"Isn't there another reason?"

"No. That's it."

"Didn't you really bring this lawsuit to distract attention away from Cindy Sharp's lawsuit against Reliable Mortgage Servicing?"

Samantha shook her head. "No. Not at all. She killed my husband, and she's gonna pay."

"Does that mean you're going to kill her if she's found innocent?"

"No. Of course not. I mean the jury will award me money."

"Isn't that what Cindy meant when she said your husband would pay?"

Samantha didn't answer.

"Did you husband have insurance on his life at the time of his death?"

"Ah. Yes."

"How much?"

Samantha looked at Richmond, but he just shrugged. Objections weren't generally allowed in deposition, fortunately. "Ah. Well. He had $250,000 group insurance and a half-million-dollar whole life policy."

"So, $750,000 total insurance?"

"Yes."

"Doesn't that give you more of a motive to kill your husband than Cindy Sharp's foreclosure?"

"I loved my husband," Samantha spat. "I wouldn't have killed him."

"Weren't you getting ready to divorce him?"

"No."

"So, you hadn't seen a divorce lawyer?"

"Well. Yes, I had a consultation."

"So, where were you when your husband was murdered?"

"At the beauty parlor having my nails done."

"That's kind of late to be having your nails done, wasn't it?"

"Well, the shop stays open for us working girls who can't get off during the day."

"What's the name of the shop?"

"The Clip Shop on Knox Avenue. Rita Shipley is the

owner. You can ask her."

"I will. Thank you, Ms. Jones. No further questions."

The deposition went on and on as depositions do. Fortunately there was a six-hour maximum according to the agreed discovery plan that controlled the deposition. When it was over Ryan was wiped out but relieved. He had been right—Samantha didn't have any evidence that they didn't already know about. Still, a video putting Cindy near the crime scene, threats toward the victim, and fingerprints in the reception area of the victim's office might be enough to convince a jury that Cindy was guilty—not beyond all reasonable doubt, but possibly by a preponderance of the evidence, which was the standard in a civil trial.

That night Amanda had gone out to meet a potential client. Ever since his father's arrest Ryan and Amanda's relationship had been strained. It was no secret that Erica blamed the arrest and indictment on Amanda. And as much as he tried to fight it, Ryan was leaning in that same direction himself. He was pondering the situation when his cell phone rang.

"Ryan?"

"Yes."

"This is Mia."

"Mia?" Ryan repeated, trying to place the name.

"I'm a friend of Matt."

"Oh. Okay."

"Matt had me doing a little undercover investigation for him."

Suddenly Ryan remembered Matt telling him about Mia and the hot tub. Ryan pictured a slinky naked brunette stepping into the water.

"Ryan? Are you there?"

"Oh, right. Okay. Yeah. I remember him saying something about it.'

"Well, I'm ready to give you my report. Matt is tied up so he said to call you."

William Manchee

"Sure. Right. Ah. How do you want to do it? I mean—"

"I'm at a club right now but it's too noisy to talk. Plus I'm famished. How about meeting me at the Cheesecake Factory on Northwest Highway?"

"That's great. When?"

"It will take me ten minutes to get there."

"Hmm. I'm probably twenty minutes away."

"Good. Then see you in twenty."

"I'll be there," Ryan said and hung up.

As he was freshening up to go meet Mia, Amanda walked in the front door. He smiled at her and took a deep breath. "Ah, I'm just leaving. Meeting a witness."

Amanda looked at her watch. "At 10:22 at night?"

"Uh-huh," Ryan said, not feeling like explaining himself.

"What's her name?" Amanda spat.

Ryan gave her a hard look, anger welling within him. Who was this woman? He thought he had known her and loved her, but now he wondered. She'd become secretive and evasive and had lost the sparkle in her eyes that he'd loved so much. He thought of Mia waiting for him.

"Mia," he said. "I'll be late, so don't wait up."

Amanda scowled at him, but before she could say anything he had rushed past her and was out the door. Traffic was light on Central Expressway so he made good time to Northwest Highway. The usually heavy crowd at the Cheesecake Factory had dwindled down, so Ryan found Mia without any trouble and they were quickly seated in a booth. Ryan looked across at Mia and smiled. His mental picture of her hadn't been far off. She wore a short black cocktail dress with a large diamond hanging from a gold chain. But the diamond wasn't the focus of Ryan's attention. He couldn't get the image of Mia in the hot tub out of his head.

"So, I just left Brett off at his house. He was hammered so I had to drive him home."

Ryan nodded. "I guess that happens a lot in your line of

work, huh?"

"Yeah. But that's okay. If he were half-sober he'd have wanted to take me to bed, and then I would have had a problem."

"I bet," Ryan said with a wry smile.

"Anyway. I got him talking about his business, like Matt asked, and he spilled his guts to me."

The waitress came over and took their orders. Mia ordered a full dinner and Ryan got cheesecake and coffee.

"So, what did Mr. Smith have to say?"

"It turns out he's Lucius's brother-in-law, Samantha's younger brother."

"Really? That's interesting."

"Lucius and he set up Prime Holdings, I think they call it. They buy the property that Lucius's company forecloses on."

"Right. I knew that."

"It's a pretty lucrative business, I guess, because all they have to do is bid enough to pay off the note."

"Right. So they get all the equity in the property, if there is any."

"He says they only buy property if it will at least break even."

"That makes sense, but I would think they'd want to make a profit."

"Well, they get money under the table, apparently," Mia explained.

"How does that work?"

"I don't know for sure, something about real estate commissions, title company fees, inspection fees, legal fees . . . and something else, I don't remember what it was . . . oh, rehab?"

"Right. When they foreclose they often have to go in and fix the place up to make it saleable. Did he mention the contractor who did that?"

"Yes. He owns part of that company, too."

Ryan laughed. "Jesus! He has his finger in everything."

"Yes, I think his cousin runs the construction company."

"I wonder how many foreclosures they do in a year?" Ryan mused.

"He said over two hundred in the Dallas Metroplex alone," Mia said, "and over five thousand nationwide."

Ryan shook his head. "Damn."

The waitress came with their orders. Mia began eating eagerly. Ryan fixed his coffee with two Splendas and a little cream and started working on his strawberry cheesecake.

"Well, you're quite the detective," Ryan complimented.

Mia smiled as she took a bite of a dinner roll and chewed it slowly. When she was done chewing she said, "It was fun. Usually listening to businessmen drone on about their work puts me to sleep, but since I needed to report back to you guys on what I heard, it was actually kind of interesting."

"Well, we really appreciate what you did. Send us your bill."

"No. I'm not sending you a bill. I did it as a favor to Matt."

"Well, can we do something for you? Any legal work you need done?"

"Yeah. You handle divorces?"

"Well, occasionally. They're not really my cup of tea."

"Mine would be uncontested. I haven't seen my Charlie for over a year. We don't have any children or property so it would be pretty simple."

"I can handle simple," Ryan said. "You'll have to come by my office, though. My secretary does all the paperwork. I just go with you to the courthouse when the time comes to prove it up."

"Great. I'll feel better when Charlie is history."

Ryan really didn't want to hear about Mia's relationship with Charlie, but he knew women liked to talk about those things, so he resigned himself to becoming a good listener.

"So, he beat you up or something?" Ryan asked.

"No. He cheated on me."

269

Unconscionable

"Hmm. Men. You can't trust them."

Mia smiled. "What about you? Are you trustworthy?"

Ryan thought about that. "Generally, but my girlfriend and I are starting to drift apart, I think."

"Really? How come?"

Ryan looked at Mia, wondering if she really wanted to hear about his crumbling relationship with Amanda. "It's a long story. I'd hate to bore you with it."

"Well, from what Candy tells me, anything involving the Colemans will be far from boring."

Ryan shrugged. "Okay, but stop me if it becomes tedious."

Mia smiled broadly. "If my eyes close and I slump over and start snoring you'll know I'm bored."

Ryan laughed and then started telling Mia everything that had happened from the day he'd met Amanda. As he talked she looked him in the eyes and listened attentively. Occasionally she'd laugh or ask a question, but mostly she just listened to Ryan release pent-up emotions that had been festering for months.

"Wow," Ryan said, looking at his watch. "I can't believe I've been ranting for over an hour. I'm sorry. You should have stopped me."

"No. It was fascinating. Don't you feel better?"

"Yes. I feel wonderful, actually," Ryan said and then frowned.

"What's wrong?"

He sighed. "Oh, I'm not looking forward to going back to the apartment and being confronted by Amanda."

"Hmm. You're right. That would be bad," Mia said, seeming to be struggling with something in her head. Finally she said, "I guess you could come crash at my place."

Ryan looked up at Mia, trying not to show the shock and excitement he was feeling. "Seriously?"

"Sure, why not? You can crash on my sofa."

Ryan smiled. "You don't have a hot tub, do you?"

Mia laughed. "No. Sorry."

Ryan shrugged. "That's okay. Matt's told me about some nice hot tub parties over at Candy's place."

"Ah, right. Well, I suppose I could throw in a massage."

Ryan's eyes lit up. "Really?"

"Yes. But just a massage," Mia stressed.

Ryan nodded. "Don't worry. That's a hell of a lot more than I'd get if I went home."

Chapter 29
A Daunting Task

Ever since posting Rich's bond and bringing him home, Erica had been in a panic. Although Rich and Bruce Pierson seemed optimistic about Rich beating the murder charges against him, she didn't see how he could escape conviction. She had been lucky to escape conviction by pleading temporary insanity, but now with her notes being made public no jury would believe anything Rich said.

Because of this ominous feeling about the upcoming trial, Erica wanted to make a run for it and had suggested to Rich on more than one occasion that they should flee to Argentina. When she had brought it up he hadn't said no, but he hadn't embraced the idea, either. When Rich came home from the office that night, he surprised Erica by bringing up the idea of running.

"You know we have considered every possible person who would have had reason to kill your aunt but can't find any evidence to prove any one of them did it."

"I know. It's so frustrating," Erica agreed.

"The only way we're going to figure this thing out is if I can remember what happened."

"Well, if you didn't remember it twenty-five years ago, how could you possibly remember it now?"

"I was thinking about that and wondering if I should go under hypnosis."

"Hypnosis? Do you think that would work after all this time?"

"I don't know. It's possible, and I'm running out of ideas. I need to know if I'm guilty or not. If I am, then we should escape while we can. I was foolish bringing you back to Dallas the last time and nearly lost you as a result. I'm not going to take that kind of chance again."

"I agree. Let's just pack our things right now and leave."

"If I'm innocent and can prove it, we don't need to run. That's why I have to find out as quickly as possible. Is there anything you haven't told me?"

"What do you mean?"

"You said you found me unconscious, but is that the truth?"

"Yes, I swear. I don't know if you killed Aunt Martha."

"Then we should go see the psychiatrist as soon as possible and try hypnosis. In the meantime we need to plan our escape. It won't be easy."

"No," Erica agreed, "but Matt knows a guy who can get us new identities and transport out of the country."

"Maybe. If he is still in business. There was some trouble when Matt and his friends left last time. I'm not sure if that connection is still viable."

"I'll call him and see," Erica said. "You call and see if Herman Beckman is still in business after all these years."

"Probably not. He'd be in his eighties if he were still alive, but he had some younger associates, if I recall correctly."

Rich went off into the kitchen to check the telephone book for Dr. Beckman while Erica called Matt to invite him to lunch. They met at Dickey's Barbeque not too far from their offices. She wanted it to be a public place where it was noisy and they'd not likely be overheard.

"So, this is a real treat to have lunch with you. What made you think of it?" Matt asked.

Erica cleared her throat and looked around to be sure no one was listening. "Your father and I need your help."

"Really? What kind of help?"

"In case the situation deteriorates we need to have an escape plan in place."

Matt swallowed hard. "You're thinking about running?"

"Yes. Argentina, maybe. Your father's not going to rot in prison the rest of his life."

"But it's going to be hard for the prosecution to convict him."

Erica shook her head. "No it won't. They have his DNA at the scene of the crime, and now people think his true crime book is a bunch of lies. Even if he testified, nobody would believe him."

Matt sighed. "Okay. You may be right. I'll call Eduardo and see if he can steer us in the right direction. I'm sure he's got new people handling that kind of stuff now."

"You've kept in touch with him?"

"Uh-huh. We go out and have a few beers from time to time. He's a good guy once he's your friend."

"Good. Come by the house on the way home if you're able to get the information. Your father is going under hypnosis to see if he can remember what happened that night. If his memory can be restored, then maybe we won't have to run."

"I hope he figures it out. I'd hate to have to visit you in Argentina."

"I know. I'd much rather stay in Dallas, believe me."

After they'd eaten lunch Erica went home and found Rich anxiously awaiting her arrival.

"Dr. Beckman is retired, but his associate Dr. Marcus Rothberg agreed to see me."

"Today?"

"Yes. He had a cancellation so it worked out well. We need to leave now."

"Okay. Let's go."

They drove out the back and down the alley hoping to escape the paparazzi, but several cars started up and followed them. Soon they were heading a caravan of media cars and vans. They parked quickly in the parking lot of Richardson Psychiatric Services and went inside immediately before any reporters could accost them. Rich checked in and Erica found them a seat.

"It should be about ten minutes," Rich said as he sat down next to Erica.

"What are we going to tell the reporters we were doing here?" Erica asked.

"Nothing. Just say 'no comment.' "

"Then they'll speculate and think you're pleading temporary insanity."

"Well, what do you suggest?" Rich asked.

"Just tell them I was getting therapy for all the stress we're under."

"You sure?" Rich asked. "They may make a big deal about it."

"It's all right. I don't mind sending them down a rabbit trail. They deserve it."

They continued to talk while they waited, and about thirty minutes later they were told the doctor would see them. Dr. Rothberg was a stout man of medium height, with a receding hairline. He directed Rich to a big stuffed chair, and Erica sat on a brown leather side chair. The doctor took a seat behind a small desk and opened a file.

"All right," Dr. Rothberg said. "As I recall from our phone conversation, you would like to try to resurrect some memories in the past through hypnosis."

"Yes, Doctor," Erica said. "Dr. Beckman helped me with my temporary insanity defense, but I didn't actually kill my aunt Martha. The truth is I don't know who did it."

"And I don't remember anything," Rich added. "I was found in an alley behind a tavern near my office building. I don't remember anything after taking a few swigs of Jack Daniels in my boss's office."

"All right, so you would like to know what happened between drinking the Jack Daniels and when—"

"Ah. When I was found in alley the next morning and taken to the hospital."

"Well, of course, there are no guarantees. It has been a long time and memories fade, even if they are repressed."

"I understand," Rich said. "But I need to try."

"So, what if you discover you did kill this Aunt Martha?"

Rich shrugged. "Then I will know not to testify in my trial."

Erica had told Rich not to disclose their plans to run to South America to the doctor as Detective Longoria would be sure to question him about their session. She remembered from many hours with her attorney when she was on trial for murder that there was some doctor-patient privilege, but it was limited and might not apply if a new criminal act was being planned. Because she was being allowed to sit in the session with Rich, that could taint the doctor-patient privilege, too.

Erica thought about waiting outside while Rich was being hypnotized but couldn't bring herself to leave. She had to make sure whatever Rich remembered was real, and the only way she could make that evaluation would be if she witnessed him being hypnotized.

"Fair enough," Dr. Rothberg said, taking out a small penlight. "What I'm going to do then is count to ten, and when I am done you will be back in your boss's office drinking some Jack Daniels."

Dr. Rothberg pointed the light toward Rich. "Focus on the light . . . one . . . two . . . three . . . You're feeling very relaxed . . . four . . . five . . . six . . . Your eyes are getting very heavy. . . . seven . . . eight . . . nine . . . Now you're going to wake up and be back in your boss's office the same night you discovered Erica's aunt Martha had broken into your apartment . . . ten. Now wake up."

Rich's eyes opened.

"Tell me what you see."

Rich took a deep breath. "It's dark. I'm on the floor leaning against the wall of the bar in Peter's office. I have a bottle of Jack Daniels in my hand. There's a noise. I put the lid on the

Jack Daniels and try to stand up. I'm wobbly from drinking too much, but I'm on my feet now."

"What's the noise?" Dr. Rothberg asked.

"Vacuuming. The janitors are starting to clean the offices."

"So what do you do?"

"I'm getting up and slipping out of the office. I don't want the janitor to see me because he might call security, so I'm very quiet. Once I'm out of the office I feel very much relieved until I hear the elevator chime. No. I can't let anyone see me, so I rush to the stairwell and climb down to the street level. Luckily, no one sees me as I rush to my car.

"Shit! It won't start. I crank the engine again but all that comes of it is a whine and a clicking sound. I recognize the sound to be a dead battery, so I call Erica on my cell but there is no answer. Then I check my messages and there is one from Erica, so I listen to it.

"The message says that Erica has gone to see her aunt at the Starlight Motel, where she is staying. I don't know what to do. I know it could get ugly if Erica confronts her aunt. I decide I need to get there first to stop them from killing each other, so I call a cab.

"The cab is taking me to the Starlight Motel. It's late and there's not much traffic. When I get there the motel is quiet and I wonder if Erica has already come and gone. The message has said she was in room 237, so I'm climbing the stairs and heading for that room number. I see it in the distance and study it for a moment before approaching. Finally, I get up enough nerve to walk up and knock on the door, but I don't have to. It's already ajar.

"Warily, I open the door and look around the room. Oh, my God. It's Martha. She's on the floor with her eyes wide open. I rush over and kneel down beside her. I check her pulse but don't feel anything. Now I'm feeling her forehead. It's cold and clammy. She's dead. There's a shadow coming up behind me.

Who's—"

Rich slumped over. Erica looked at Dr. Rothberg, who didn't look concerned. "What happened?" Erica asked.

"I think this is where he got hit over the head. . . . Rich, I'm going to count to three and snap my fingers. When I snap my fingers you will wake up and remember everything you've been exploring in your mind these last few minutes. . . . One . . . two . . . three . . . *Snap!*

Rich woke up with a start and looked around, seemingly confused.

"Do you remember now what happened?" Dr. Rothberg asked.

"Ah. Remember?"

"Yeah. Do you remember going to Aunt Martha's motel?"

Rich nodded. "Oh, that. Right. I do."

"Good. So, does this help you?"

Erica sighed. "Yes, it helps a lot. It means Rich is innocent. The problem is, however, we still don't know who killed Aunt Martha."

"Well, I am sorry to say I can only help you recall what is in your subconscious mind. If it isn't buried there somewhere, then you're out of luck."

"I know," Erica said. "You did exactly what we needed you to do. Thank you."

"No problem. Happy to help."

On the way back home Erica and Rich discussed what they had learned.

"So, I was at the crime scene, you were there, and then there was Joe," Rich said.

"Right," Erica agreed.

"Now, we know I didn't do it and you didn't do it, so who does that leave?"

"Joe," Erica said reluctantly.

"Joe. Yes. Joe. I always thought it was quite a

coincidence that he showed up just in time to help you move me away from the crime scene."

Erica nodded. "I wondered about that, too, but I can't image Joe killing Aunt Martha."

"Why not? He would have lost his job had it come out that he'd helped me do illegal trades with your money. Plus he didn't want our secret to become public. He obviously cared about us."

"True. That's why I ignored what should have been obvious," Erica said. "So, what should we do?"

"We can't turn him in," Rich said. "He's like family."

"I know, but what choice do we have?"

"We can't turn him in. None of this would have happened to him had you and I not asked him to break the law. It wouldn't be right. We have enough money to live comfortably in Argentina, so that's what we'll have to do."

Erica sighed deeply. "I guess you're right."

"But we should confront him with it and see if he'll come clean with us."

"Yes. We need to be sure we're right."

Rich altered his course from home to Joe's house. They were there in twenty minutes. They got out and slowly walked up to his front door, dreading their imminent confrontation. Joe answered the door and did a double take.

"Well, you two are the last visitors I would have expected today."

"We would have called, but it was a spur-of-the-moment decision to come by."

Joe backed up and let them come in. He directed them to a sofa. They sat and he took a seat in a overstuffed chair across from them. He smiled tentatively. "So, what happened?"

Rich explained how he had gone to see Dr. Rothberg to be hypnotized.

"So, did it work?" Joe asked.

"Actually, it did," Rich replied. "I learned that I had been at the motel the night of the murder, but that Aunt Martha was already dead when I got there."

Joe swallowed hard. "You were there all right. I saw you."

"Right. So Erica says."

"But how do you know she was already dead?"

"Because I can remember now checking her pulse and there wasn't any."

"Huh. That's weird. So, now we still don't know who did it."

Matt sighed. "Come on, Joe. You might as well come clean."

"What do you mean?" Joe protested.

"What he means," Erica interjected, "is that you got there before both of us and killed Aunt Martha."

"No!" Joe exclaimed. "I got there after you."

"Don't worry. We're not going to turn you in even if you did kill Aunt Martha."

"I didn't," Joe said meekly.

"But if you don't come clean we'll have to assume you're telling the truth and keep searching for the killer. If we do that we can't promise how it will end."

Joe shook his head. "I didn't do it."

"You know what I think happened," Rich said. "Aunt Martha called you to see if you knew where Erica and I were. During the conversation she probably told you she was going to break into our apartment. You knew that if she broke in she'd find out that Erica and I were living together and probably search the place to find out whatever she could."

Joe looked down and sighed.

"Partially for our benefit but also fearing that she'd discover that you were handling my reckless trading in Erica's account, you rushed over there to retrieve the records before she got there. Unfortunately, she was already there with the police."

Joe slowly nodded. "Right. So, I followed her back to the

281

motel. I had no intention of hurting her. I just wanted your records back."

"So what happened?" Erica asked.

"She refused to give me the records, so I forced myself into her room and tried to physically take them. But she was a feisty little bitch and started beating me with her purse. It hurt like hell. I think she must have had a brick in there."

"So, it was an accident?" Rich asked.

"Her death was an accident. I wasn't trying to hurt her, but she was definitely trying to kill me, so I had to defend myself. Then she started screaming, I panicked, and one thing led to another."

Rich took a deep breath and let it out slowly. Erica turned away and wiped a tear from her eye.

"Okay. That's what we needed to know. Like I said, we're not going to turn you in, so don't worry about it."

"But what are you going to do?"

Rich shrugged. "We don't know yet," he lied. "Hopefully the prosecution won't be able to prove their case beyond all reasonable doubt."

Joe smiled. "Hopefully."

They got up, thanked Joe one more time for the confession, and then left. They didn't tell him their plans to escape, as they feared he might tell someone about it. When they got home Matt's car was parked in front of the house. He was waiting for them in the living room.

"So, how did it go?" Matt asked eagerly.

"Great," Rich said without enthusiasm.

"Then why the somber face?" Matt asked.

"Your father didn't do it, but that only leaves Joe."

"Oh, really? What about your ex-partner, Aunt Martha's son, and the gay boyfriend?"

"There's no solid evidence putting any of them at the crime scene. It's got to be Joe."

"So, what are you going to do?" Matt asked warily.

"We can't point the finger at Joe, so we'll have to run."

Matt sank back onto the sofa, shaking his head. "I can't believe this. You're really going to have to flee the country."

"Yes. Did you talk to Eduardo?"

Matt nodded. "Uh-huh. He gave me the name of a man."

"Good. Just give us his name and number and leave everything to us. The less you know the better."

Tears welled in Matt's eyes. "But I don't want you to go, and Ryan is going to be crushed if you two disappear."

Tears began to stream down Erica's cheeks. "I know. Tell him we love him."

"Being a fugitive from the law is not any fun," Matt moaned. "Trust me. I've been there."

"It's better than languishing in prison, though, right?" Rich asked.

"Yes, that's true," Matt agreed.

"Then we have no choice."

Matt reluctantly got up and embraced Erica and Rich and then left. When he had gone, Rich called the name Eduardo had provided to give them fake passports and transport out of the country. After he made the necessary arrangements, they planned how they would slip away from the paparazzi. By eight o'clock their bags were packed and loaded into Rich's car. At 8:05 p.m. Erica drove out of the garage in her car and drove to the north entrance of Northpark Mall. The windows in her car were darkly tinted, and at night the paparazzi couldn't tell who was in the car, so everyone followed Erica to Northpark. When Erica got to the mall she parked in the garage and then hurried through the mall, quickly losing the paparazzi who were now just realizing Rich was not in the car. When Erica reached the south side entrance to the mall she stepped outside just as Rich was pulling up. She got in and they drove off with no one in pursuit.

They drove to Fort Worth where they stopped at a Holiday Inn. Erica, wearing dark glasses and a wig, checked in using her maiden name and a phony address. Rich snuck in the side entrance so nobody would see him. They stayed there until late Saturday when their passports were ready.

While they were waiting Rich decided to work on the Cindy Sharp case. If Matt was going to win he had to prove Cindy hadn't killed Lucius Jones. Matt had told him they had interviewed almost all of the principals in the various affiliated companies that were feeding off RMS's foreclosures and had come up empty. He thought that if he tracked some of the actual foreclosures that were taking place he might spot something.

Since he was in Fort Worth, he decided to search some local foreclosures. The firm subscribed to a real-property database that allowed him to search through the Tarrant County Deed Records. First, he pulled up all the foreclosures for the month Cindy had been foreclosed. Then he narrowed his search to RMS foreclosures. Two hundred and eleven foreclosures showed up, and he pulled up the records on each one and went through them.

Each transaction was nearly identical. First, there was notice of foreclosure signed by the same attorney at Park & Howard PC on behalf of RMS; second, a trustee's deed conveying the property to RMS or one of the subsidiary companies; and finally, a sale to a new home owner. Everything looked in order except one thing. Of the 211 special warranty deeds conveying the properties to the new home owners, thirty-nine were different from the rest. When Rich saw it he knew who had killed Lucius Jones and why. He emailed the information to Matt and told him how to prove it up at trial.

Chapter 30
Breakup

       Amanda shut off the TV after *The Late Late Show* was over at twelve thirty a.m. She wondered who Mia was. Was she really a witness, or was Ryan on a date? Thinking about their deteriorating relationship, she realized they hadn't made love in weeks. She knew it was her fault. She'd been so obsessed with making *The Pact* a best seller she had neglected Ryan. But more than neglect, it was her own guilt that was obviously showing through. She was so afraid that Ryan would find out what she'd done and break up with her that she'd become somber and ill tempered. Then it hit her. He already knew. Her own behavior had given her away. She doubted he could prove she'd been behind the *Inquisitor* story, but he knew in his heart that it was her doing. Their relationship was over.

       She went to the bedroom and began packing up her things. There was no way she was going to be there when Ryan came waltzing in gloating over his date with Mia. She didn't need him anymore, anyway. She'd made her first client a best-selling author and now writers would be lining up to have her represent them—a lot better writers than Rich Coleman. In an hour she was packed up and had everything loaded in her car. She'd soon be through with Ryan Coleman forever. But when she tried to leave and slam the door behind her past life, she began to cry and collapsed on the sofa in despair. What had she done?

       Depression fell over her like a dense fog. Her head began to ache and her shoulders got so taut she squirmed, trying to ease the pain. Then she remembered she had a bottle of pain medication that had been prescribed for a sprained ankle. Most of the pills were still in the bottle, as the injury had healed more quickly than expected. She wondered if there were enough in the bottle to kill her and how Ryan would react if he found her dead in their bed. But perhaps pills weren't the answer. He should come home and find her in a pool of blood. Yes, a bloody, smelly scene would be much more traumatic. He'd be scarred for life . . . or would he? Did he really love her? He'd said he did, but hadn't wanted to commit to marriage. His precious law practice meant more to him that their relationship. They had no future, she realized. Their split up was the best thing for everyone. None of the Colemans appreciated what she had done for them. *So, screw them! I'm out of here.*

Amanda got up and stormed out of the apartment. She got in her car, started the engine, and peeled rubber as she took off to no place in particular. In her haste to leave she hadn't thought out where to go—a motel, to her office, to her parents' house? She finally opted for a motel. She couldn't sleep very well at her office, and if she were discovered, it wouldn't look very good. She thought of her parents, but they'd ask too many questions. As she drove down Central Expressway she spotted an extended stay motel. It looked brand new so she exited and drove up to the front entrance. After checking in, she brought up what she needed for the night and then collapsed on the bed. After just lying there for half an hour brooding, she got up and turned on the TV. A replay of Channel 11's ten o'clock news was just starting. The anchor, Jessica Nichols, smiled as the camera began to roll.

"We have breaking news. Dallas attorney Richard Coleman is apparently missing. Authorities reported late this afternoon that the whereabouts of the accused accomplice in the Martha Collins murder and author of the best-selling true crime book, *The Pact*, is unknown. Members of the paparazzi who had been following Coleman around since his arrest last week have reported that he has not been seen in over twelve hours. Somehow he and his wife, Erica Fox Coleman, managed to slip away from their house undetected, and their whereabouts are unknown.

When we learned of Coleman's disappearance we sent our roving reporter, Dan Shipley, to track down Detective Alice Longoria, who is in charge of the Coleman investigation. He reached her earlier this evening as she was coming out of a performance at the Dallas Theater Center. Dan?"

"I'm here with Detective Alice Longoria of the Dallas Police Department. . . . Detective. Do you have any idea where Richard Coleman is at this time?"

"No, but that doesn't necessarily mean anything. He doesn't have to report in until Monday," Longoria replied calmly.

"But doesn't it bother you that nobody knows where he is? Could he be fleeing the jurisdiction?"

She shrugged. "I don't like it when a defendant goes off the grid, but it doesn't mean he's running. He and his wife may have just gotten tired of the paparazzi shadowing their every move. They could be holed up in a hotel somewhere."

"So, you're not going to go looking for him?"

"No, I didn't say that. Since there is concern about his whereabouts we will try to locate him. We've already contacted his attorney."

"What did his attorney say?" Dan asked.

"That he wasn't sure where he was but he'd try to track him down."

"What about the bond? If you can't find him will you revoke his bond?"

"No, I can't revoke his bond. But if he doesn't appear in court on Monday the judge might do it."

"All right. You heard it. Nobody knows where Richard Coleman and his wife have gone, but it doesn't appear much will be done about it until Monday when Coleman is due to report in to the court. Dan Shipley, at the Crowley Courthouse in Dallas."

Nichols turned toward the camera and said, "Well, has Rich Coleman gone on the run to avoid prosecution for the murder of Martha Collins? Will his two-million-dollar bond be revoked? We'll keep you informed on this breaking story as more

287

information develops—"

Amanda shut off the TV and rummaged through her purse to find her cell phone. She wondered why nobody had called her about Rich's disappearance. When she tried to turn on the phone she realized the battery was dead. Looking at her watch, she saw it was almost two in the morning. She thought a moment and realized if anyone had tried to call her on her cell and didn't get through they'd have probably tried her at the office. She went to the motel phone, dialed her office number, and punched in the password. There were over fifteen messages, including calls from Brenda Colson, Sylvia Sams, and Rich Coleman. She played the one from Rich.

"Amanda. By the time you listen to this message Erica and I will be out of the country. We have gone somewhere far away where no one will ever find us. I have assigned all of my contract rights and copyright to *The Pact* to the American Red Cross, as I have no interest in the money. Erica blames you for the misfortune that has befallen us. I hope she is wrong for Ryan's sake, but if she is not, then I hope you rot in hell!"

"Oh!" Amanda gasped. She dropped the phone and backed off, as if fearing a snake would jump out of it and bite her. Pain stabbed at her neck and shoulders, and her head began to throb. Tears welled in her eyes and came gushing down her cheeks. When she reached the bed she collapsed, curled up in the fetal position, and cried for a long time.

When her eyes ran dry and she'd regained her composure, she went over everything in her mind from the day she had learned of Rich Coleman's manuscript to his sudden disappearance. She hated herself for what she had done but wasn't sure that if she had to do it again she would act any differently. Rich hadn't put up that much resistance to publishing his manuscript. It was obvious he wanted the book published and therefore she wasn't responsible for his arrest and exile. She felt bad for Erica who had adamantly opposed publication, but blamed her for writing revisions to the manuscript in the first place.

Why did you write the revisions if you didn't want the book published? And why didn't you destroy them once it was clear the book would never be published? Leaving around incriminating evidence was stupid. And now, because of your stupidity, I've lost Ryan.

Amanda hadn't anticipated losing Ryan. Somehow, she thought she'd escape blame for what had happened, but everyone immediately assumed she was guilty. That had hurt her feelings even though they had been right. She wondered if they thought she was responsible for the break-in. Was she that transparent? *It was almost like I did exactly what they expected.* She began weeping again, feeling a bit sorry for herself, perhaps, but mainly feeling for the first time an emptiness without Ryan in her life.

In the morning she woke up feeling disoriented. For a few moments she didn't know where she was. Then the events of the previous day came streaming into her consciousness. Her body deflated at the horror of it. What was she going to do? She felt dirty and sticky from sleeping in her clothes, so she decided a shower was in order. She needed to think, anyway, and a shower was a good place to do that. As the hot beads of water eased the tension in her shoulders and neck she pondered the situation. Should she call Ryan and tell him his father and mother had skipped the country? No, she and Ryan were through. There was no reason to call any of the Colemans. Rich had severed the last connection between them, and she needed to move on. There was one problem, however: she was broke.

Her commission from Rich's advance had long been spent, and Ryan had been picking up all her expenses. There would be royalties coming in since Rich's book was a best seller, but they wouldn't be starting for another four or five months. How would she survive until then? Then she got an idea. After she'd gotten out of the shower and was dressed in a fresh outfit, she returned Sylvia Sams's call.

"Hello," Sylvia said sleepily.

"Sylvia? This is Amanda. You called?"

"Yes. Right. Thanks for calling me back. I was wondering if you knew anything about Rich Coleman's disappearance."

"I do, and you're going to want to hear it."

"What is it? Tell me."

"Not over the phone. We should meet."

"Sure. At the usual place in twenty minutes."

"Yes, and bring $25,000."

"Twenty-five thousand dollars? But—"

"Don't argue. You've got it in your budget. You never had to pay Rich the $50,000 for that last interview, and what I've got for you is much better."

"I don't know. I'll have to call my editor."

"Call whoever you want, but I won't say a word until I've got twenty-five grand in cash in my hand."

"All right. Give me a half hour, then."

Amanda smiled. "See you in thirty."

A rush of relief and satisfaction washed over Amanda. It felt good after all the fear and regret she had felt the night before. She was a survivor and knew better than to wallow in self-pity. Ryan Coleman hadn't been a mistake. Hell, he'd led her to her first big literary contract, but he wasn't anyone special. She'd find Mr. Right down the road when she was on top of her game and would have a large field of suitors to choose from. But for now she needed to regroup and focus on the opportunities that lay before her.

When she got to Starbucks Sylvia wasn't there, so she ordered her favorite coffee and took a seat. When thirty minutes came and went, Amanda began to wonder if she'd miscalculated the *Inquisitor*'s interest in her information. She wondered what she'd do for money if that were the case. The thought occurred to her that perhaps the story had already broken and everyone knew Rich had skipped out on his bond.

As she was about to search the news feeds on her cell

phone for stories on Rich Coleman, she spotted Sylvia rushing in from the parking lot. When she walked through the door Amanda raised her hand and waved her over. When Sylvia saw her she came over, dumped her purse on a chair, and took off her coat.

"Sorry I'm late, but it takes time to get cash."

Amanda smiled. "It will be worth the effort, I promise you."

"It better be," she said. "Let me get some coffee and then you can lay it on me."

"Sure. Take your time."

When Sylvia returned she sat down and looked at Amanda expectantly.

"Let me see the money."

Sylvia nodded and reached for the purse she had brought. Looking around first to make sure nobody was watching, she opened it and showed Amanda the contents. Amanda smiled when she saw numerous stacks of one-hundred-dollar bills.

"Okay, I've got Rich Coleman on my voice mail telling me he has left the country. Is that worth $25,000?"

Sylvia thought about that a moment and then nodded. "Yes, I think that would be."

Amanda dialed in to her office phone, punched in the password, and then called up Rich's message. She handed the phone to Sylvia. Sylvia put the phone to her ear and listened. Her eyes widened as she listened to the message.

"Just punch seven if you want it to repeat."

Sylvia nodded and punched SEVEN. After she'd listened to the message several times she gave Amanda her phone back.

"Okay, I'll need a copy of the message," Sylvia said as she reached for the purse.

"No problem," Amanda said, accepting the purse.

"Don't take the money out. Just take the whole purse. I bought it for ten dollars at Walmart."

"Okay. Thanks. If I hear anything else I'll let you know, but information may be a little scarce, as Ryan and I have broken up."

"Really? How come?"

"I think he suspects I leaked Erica's notes."

"Hmm. Sorry about that," Sylvia said. "Oh well. You must have known he'd figure it out eventually."

"Yeah. I guess, but it doesn't make it any easier."

"Well, I've got to go. My editor is waiting for this scoop with bated breath."

"Right. Go ahead. Don't let me hold you up."

Sylvia smiled sympathetically and then rushed out of the café, leaving Amanda feeling a little lost. Then she remembered she had $25,000 in cash that she ought to get to the bank. After finishing her coffee she headed for Bank of America, where she had her business account. After depositing the cash she went to her office and filled Brenda in on what was going on. Then she called Sheila Samson at Thorn to tell her about Rich's message on her answering machine.

"He did *what*?" Sheila asked.

"He assigned all his contract rights with Thorn to the American Red Cross. Apparently we will be getting the contract assignment in the mail. He didn't say exactly how it would happen."

"Wow. That's a surprise. . . . Well, none of this can hurt sales. As long as he's a fugitive he'll be in the news often, so if that's the way he wants to play it, I guess that's his business."

"It's a move to sway public opinion his way, I suppose. He doesn't want Matt and Ryan to be hurt by his actions."

"I hope his strategy works for their sakes."

"Me, too. Although, his son Ryan and I have broken up, so I won't have a close connection with the Colemans anymore."

"Oh. That's too bad. What happened?"

"It was inevitable. I should have known you can't mix your personal life with business."

"Hmm. That's true," Sheila agreed.

"So, that's all I have. I'll keep you posted if anything else develops."

"Do that, and thanks for the update. Sorry about you and Ryan."

Amanda hung up and sat back in her executive chair. It had been a whirlwind of a day but it had all ended well—for her, anyway. She wondered where Rich and Erica were at that moment and if they really could find a safe place to live out the rest of their lives in peace. She fought off feelings of guilt that tried to creep into her mind. No, this wasn't her fault. Rich and Erica had killed Martha Collins, and now they were paying for their crime. This wasn't her fault. At least that's what she kept telling herself.

Chapter 31
Opening Statements

On Monday when Matt came to work he was surprised to see a large manila envelope on his desk. It was from his father and addressed to him and Ryan. A cold chill went through him seeing the ominous package. He called Ryan on the intercom and told him to come to his office. In less than a minute Ryan was at his side.

"What's in the package?"

"It's from Dad."

"Huh? From Dad?"

"Right."

"Well, that's weird. What's in it?"

"We're about to find out," Matt said, taking his letter opener and slitting the top of the envelope. Matt looked at Ryan and then pulled out a stock certificate in Coleman & Sons PC, a deposit slip, a warranty deed, and a letter addressed to them. Matt read the letter.

Dear Matt & Ryan,

Your mom and I have decided it is too risky to hang around for a trial. By the time you read this letter we'll be out of the country. Don't try to find us. We'll find a way to communicate with you in a few months, but I'm not sure exactly how right now. Don't worry about us, we have plenty of money and will be living quite comfortably wherever we end up.

One of my greatest regrets is having to resign from the firm. Practicing law with my two sons has been a dream come true and it pains me that it must come to an end. I have assigned *my interest in the firm to both of you and deposited $200,000 into the firm bank account as a parting gift so you won't be strapped for cash.*

Finally, we have deeded our home to both of you. It's paid for so you can sell it or one of you can live in it. Your choice.

Good luck, we'll miss you.
Love,
Dad

Ryan ripped the letter out of Matt's hand and read it again angrily. "No! This can't be happening. That goddamn Amanda. I could kill the fucking bitch! Look what she's done."

"You blame Amanda for this?" Matt asked.

"Yes. I'm sure she's the one who leaked Mom's notes to the *Inquisitor*. Who else could have done it?"

Matt shrugged. "I don't know."

"I can't believe they left the country," Ryan moaned.

"I actually knew they were thinking about it," Matt confessed. "Dad came to me and wanted my help in getting new identities and transport out of the country. I got him the information, but I didn't think they'd act on it so quickly."

"Why didn't you tell me? I might have been able to talk them out of it."

"Do you think that would have been wise?"

Ryan didn't answer.

"Well, there's nothing we can do about it now and we've got Cindy's trial coming up next week, so we'll have to put it out of our minds. After the trial we can brainstorm and perhaps look into who else might have killed Aunt Martha. If we can find the actual killer, then that would clear Dad's name and he and Mom could then come home."

Ryan nodded dejectedly. "I know you're right, but it's not going to be easy to focus with Mom and Dad as fugitives."

"I know, but you read Dad's letter. They have plenty of

money and they will be fine."

Ryan left, and Matt started to work on his trial outline. He had to make a final decision on his witnesses, decide in what order to call them, and work up an outline of the questions he wanted to ask. When that was done he had to work on an opening statement. This didn't sound all that complicated, but in reality it was a lot of work and could take several days. Thoughts of his own exile after being released from prison tried to push their way into his mind, but he took a deep breath and concentrated even harder on the task at hand. Several hours later Melissa informed him he had a call from Sylvia Sams of the *Inquisitor*. He frowned, wondering what she wanted.

"Mr. Coleman. We are about to publish a story about your father's failure to report in with the court this morning. Our sources tell us that your father and mother have left the country."

Matt sighed. "What sources?"

"I can't say, but is it true? Have they left the country?"

"Yes," Matt spat. "Apparently they have."

"So, how did you find out?"

"I can't say. I have to protect my sources."

Sylvia laughed. "Okay. I understand. Thank you."

The line went dead and Matt slowly hung up the phone. He couldn't wait to see the *Inquisitor* story. It was sure to be a gem.

On Thursday Matt called the court to announce to the court coordinator that they were ready for trial. The coordinator told them they were number one and would definitely be going to trial. A wave of anxiety washed over Matt, as this would be the first trial for both him and Ryan. It would have been bad enough even with their father there to guide them, but now they'd be alone. He wondered how that would work out, but then thought of the challenges he'd faced in prison and was able to meet. In comparison this was nothing. Win or lose, he and Ryan would walk out of the courtroom just as healthy as ever. The only thing at stake was money and their reputation, both of which could be restored in time.

On Saturday before the Monday trial setting, Matt, Ryan, and Cindy met to go over Cindy's testimony. In a criminal case she wouldn't have testified, but since she was the plaintiff in the civil suit she had no choice but take the stand. It was risky since Richmond could take her on cross-examination and try to make it look like she had killed Lucius Jones. Therefore, Matt and Ryan were taking particular care to make sure she was fully prepared.

They did this by Matt taking her through her direct examination and Ryan handling cross. In direct examination, Cindy had to be somewhat emotional and get across to the jury what horrible things RMS had put her through and the damages she suffered, but on cross she had to be calm, attentive, and unemotional to avoid being led astray.

Ryan did his best to hit her with the hard questions that he knew Richmond would be throwing at her. At first, Cindy had trouble with this line of questioning, but they kept practicing until Cindy seemed to have it down. Of course, Matt knew that there was a big difference between practicing and actually being in trial. Often clients would get completely rattled during the heat of trial and forget everything they'd been taught. He prayed this wouldn't happen to Cindy. At the end of the session Cindy asked how they thought the trial would go.

"I think it will go all right," Matt replied. "I think once we tell the jury the whole story they've got to be outraged."

"What about the accusations that I killed Lucius?"

Matt shrugged. "You didn't kill him, right?" he asked, knowing what her response would be but wanting to hear her profess her innocence one more time.

"No, but it looks bad that I was in the neighborhood when it happened."

"The reason we have jury trials is that juries are good at reading witnesses. A witness may deceive one or two people, but it's hard to deceive a dozen. If you didn't kill Lucius Jones, the jury will know it."

Cindy sighed. "I'm so worried. If we don't win this trial I don't know how the kids and I will survive. It's bad enough not having Tony around to help out, but with not enough money to pay our basic necessities . . . Shit! Have you seen the price of gasoline?"

"Yes. Three dollars a gallon. I never thought I'd see that," Matt laughed. "My dad said when he was a kid gasoline was twenty-nine cents a gallon and if there was a gas war it dipped to nineteen cents."

"Jesus. That's hard to believe."

"I know."

"How is your dad, anyway? I heard he skipped the country."

"I don't know, but unless he gets caught, I'm sure he'll be fine."

"I guess everybody's got problems," Cindy mused.

"That's for sure," Matt said, smiling at Cindy. "Don't worry. I have a good feeling about your case."

Cindy took a deep breath. "I hope you're right."

On Monday Matt arrived at eight a.m. at the Dallas County Courthouse. The case had drawn more media attention than would normally have been expected for a civil case because of the allegations from RMS CEO Samantha Jones that Cindy Sharp had killed her husband. Not wanting to face the media, Matt arrived early and came in through the parking garage to the courthouse and climbed the stairs to the fourth floor where the trial was to be held. Ryan and Cindy Sharp arrived about a half hour later. Richmond, Samantha Jones, and two associates at Richmond & Richmond arrived about eight forty-five a.m. and set up on the defense table. The gallery was full of media and spectators.

Samantha had dressed in a black silk dress, matching shoes, nylons, and purse, and dark glasses. She looked very much like the grieving widow, although Matt knew she had shed few tears after Lucius's death. She looked over at him, but he couldn't read her expression behind the dark glasses.

At nine a.m. the judge made his appearance and called the case. Both parties announced ready, so the judge passed out jury packets. It took all morning and into the midafternoon to pick the jury. Many people had strong opinions about mortgage companies, and an equal number disdained deadbeats, making the jury pool a minefield for both sides. When the last juror took his seat, the judge looked over at Matt and said, "Mr. Coleman, you may give your opening statement."

Matt rose. "Your Honor, ladies and gentlemen of the jury. First, let me thank you again for your jury service. Cindy Sharp is very appreciative of the contribution and sacrifice you are making by being here today. Now, during voir dire you learned a little about what this case is all about, but now I'm going to tell you what we expect to prove as we call our witnesses over the next couple of days. Before I begin, though, I want to remind you that what I tell you and what Mr. Richmond tells you is not evidence. Only what you hear from witnesses or can glean from the exhibits that are admitted are evidence that you can rely upon.

"This case is brought under a law enacted by our state legislature called the Texas Debt Collection Practices Act or what I will refer to as Unfair Debt Collection Practices. We are also suing under the common law tort of unreasonable collection. At the end of the trial you will be asked to answer a series of questions designed to determine if this statute has been violated or if the defendant is guilty of unreasonable collection. If you determine that there has been a violation or the defendant has committed the tort of unreasonable collection, then you will also be asked to determine what damages should be awarded to her. So, listen to the witnesses carefully and review the exhibits placed into evidence so you will be prepared to answer the questions at the end of the trial.

"Now, our first witness will be the plaintiff, Cindy Sharp. She will testify that she is a schoolteacher and has three small children. She was married to a wonderful man, Tony Robert

Sharp, a master bricklayer working at the time for Arrow Construction Company. They had been married for eight years and were happily living the American dream with a beautiful car, wonderful children, and a bright future ahead of them. Tony had worked for Arrow for fifteen years but when the construction industry collapsed last year, Arrow filed for bankruptcy relief and Tony was laid off.

"Tony was a proud man, so it was with great regret that he went on unemployment. Unfortunately, unemployment compensation was only about a third of his normal pay, so the Sharps struggled to pay their bills. Even so, they cut their expenses way back to make ends meet and were doing okay until Tony's unemployment ran out. Then they began to get behind on their bills.

"Luckily, the Sharps had good credit, hadn't maxed out their credit cards, and were therefore able to make ends meet for a while by taking advances on their credit cards. This allowed them to keep their house note current. And it remained current until their mortgage company, North American Servicing, or NAS, sold their note to Reliable Mortgage Servicing, known to its customers as RMS. Unfortunately, by the time the notice of the sale to RMS got to them they had already made their May payment to North American Servicing. Since they had paid the payment by money order, they couldn't stop payment on it. Cindy, of course, immediately called North American Servicing to explain the situation and were assured that the payment would be promptly forwarded to RMS. But that didn't happen.

"Instead, they immediately started getting late notices and telephone calls claiming they were a month behind. So, Cindy will testify that she called the customer service line at NAS again and the person answering the phone acted like she had never called them before. So, she had to start all over again and explain what had happened a second time. This, obviously, was exceedingly frustrating and caused the Sharps much mental anguish. Finally, after being left on hold and transferred from one representative to another, someone finally checked their computers and acknowledged that they had received the check but that the funds hadn't been remitted to RMS as of yet, although it had been nearly ten days. Again, Cindy Sharp was assured the payment would go out the following day.

"But that didn't happen, and the Sharps continued to get late notices; each time, they got one a new late fee or charge was added to the balance due. But what really upset them was when they got a notice that RMS had paid their property taxes three months before they were due and were increasing their house payment by $350 per month! Obviously, if they were struggling with a $1,202 house payment, you can imagine how a $1,552 payment looked to them.

"If all this wasn't enough, in January Tony had been diagnosed with prostate cancer and had to have surgery right away and was out of commission six weeks. During that time Cindy had to put the kids in after-school care. Between that expense and the deductibles for Tony's medical treatments, the Sharps used up their tax refund and missed another house payment.

"Being a responsible woman, at this point, Cindy called RMS and explained the situation but got little sympathy. She will testify that they passed her around for a while until she finally talked to a representative, Joan Londry in the modification department. She said they had a hardship program for people in situations like theirs and she didn't see why they wouldn't be eligible for it. She said the way the program worked was they would take the delinquency and tack it on to the end of the note so once the modification took place they would be current and only responsible for regular monthly payments. Needless to say the Sharps were greatly relieved by this news and thought they were finally seeing the light at the end of the tunnel.

"So, Joan Londry sent them the paperwork, and Cindy filled it out and sent it back along with lots of other documentation they wanted. Cindy later called Joan to be sure she

302

had received the package and she acknowledged that she had all RMS needed to start the loan modification process. When Cindy asked how long it would take, Joan told her it would be no more than thirty days to process and that during that time the Sharps didn't need to make any mortgage payments, as whatever was outstanding would be tacked on to the end of the note at closing.

"Well, when thirty days passed and there was no word on the approval of the modification, Cindy will testify that she called Joan, but Joan wasn't available so Roger Wynn, the representative who finally took her call, checked the computer but couldn't find any record of the modification package ever being received! She, of course got very upset, but Roger assured her if she would just send in a new application everything would be fine and he would note in the computer that a modification was in process.

"Angry and frustrated, Cindy sent them another modification package by FedEx and tracked it to make sure they got it. Then, just to be sure, she called Roger, who confirmed that RMS had the application and supporting materials and everything was okay.

"But a week later Cindy was shocked and dismayed to get a letter from an attorney advising them that they were sixty days past due on the mortgage, RMS had no proof of insurance on the dwelling, and that they were considering accelerating the note and foreclosing.

"Cindy will testify that she had been handling this mess as Tony was sick, but when Tony saw this letter he went absolutely crazy. He was recovering from surgery and already a mental wreck from losing his job, so this undid him. At first it was anger, then depression, and finally withdrawal. He'd just sit on the sofa all day with a somber look on his face. He quit shaving, hardly spoke to the children, and would only get up to go to the bathroom and go to bed. Cindy wanted him to see a psychiatrist, but he refused.

"Angry and frustrated, Cindy told Tony he had more time

to deal with the mortgage company than she did, so he should call them, but she got little reaction. He just didn't seem to care anymore.

"When Cindy finally found time to call RMS again, a man named Ahmad Sheik took the call and said not to worry about the attorney letter, as it was just routine. He said the computer automatically sent any account over sixty days to their attorneys but as long as they were processing a modification, they wouldn't have to worry about foreclosure.

"But by this time Cindy didn't trust them, so she asked for something in writing. In response she got a form letter acknowledging the receipt of the modification package and stating that as long as it was being processed RMS would not foreclose. This letter eased her concerns and, having other problems, she tried to put it out of her mind, concentrating now on getting Tony out of bed and functioning normally again.

"Another few weeks went by and, not hearing anything, she called Ahmad, but he was not available and she finally ended up with Tom Jones. She wondered if this was his real name, but didn't say anything. Again, Tom advised her that there was no record of her modification being in the works. . . . Angry and frustrated beyond imagination, she asked for a supervisor and a Lois Ross came on the line. Lois agreed with Tom that they had no record of their modification application. As you can imagine, when she said that, Cindy was so outraged she could hardly maintain her composure. When Lois asked her to send in another modification packet she wanted to cry, but she had no choice but to do it.

"The next day she faxed the packet to them for the third time and got a confirmation that it had been received. But just when she had begun to relax a bit she got the mail and there was a notice of certified mail at the post office. The notice scared her, but it was impossible for her to get to the post office until the next morning. Neither she nor Tony slept a wink that night wondering what was in the certified notice. When she finally opened the certified letter the next day she discovered it was a default letter and a notice of trustee's sale!

"When Cindy got back home she immediately called the supervisor, Lois Ross, whom she had talked to two days earlier, and Ms. Ross acknowledged that she had the paperwork and not to worry about the foreclosure notice. Ms. Ross assured her the modification application would stop the foreclosure.

"But it didn't. Several weeks later Tony noticed a man taking photographs of their house. That upset him so he confronted the man, who identified himself as Simon Artis, and was told that RMS had hired him to do an appraisal of the property. When he asked him why they would do that, he advised him that their house had been foreclosed and that RMS was putting the property on the market for sale.

"Tony told the man they had a modification in progress and that RMS had promised not to foreclose, but Artis just laughed at him and said they had ten days to get out or he'd go to the justice of the peace and file an eviction suit. At that point Tony got mad and told Mr. Artis that if anybody set foot on his property he would shoot them.

"Of course, he wouldn't actually have shot anyone. He was just angry, frustrated, very upset, and worried about what was going to happen to them. They had no money and if they were evicted they'd probably be out on the street.

"When Cindy found out what had happened, she called Lois at RMS again and asked her why they had foreclosed when they had agreed not to. She apologized and said it was just a mistake and that Cindy should send them a letter explaining what had happened and asking for them to set aside the foreclosure sale.

"It seemed like a colossal waste of time to Cindy, but she did what Lois asked. Unfortunately, the letter did no good and RMS still filed the eviction suit and set it for hearing in ten days. At the hearing Tony told the judge what had happened, but the judge said his hands were tied and gave the Sharps seventy-two hours to get out of the house.

"Unfortunately, the Sharps didn't have money to rent a storage unit until Cindy got her next paycheck at the end of the month, so they weren't able to move out. After the seventy-two hours expired, the family slept at the Kamona Motel. It wasn't a very nice place, but it was cheap. The next day when they went to the house to start packing they found it padlocked.

"At that point they called Simon Artis, but only got his voice mail. They slept another few days at the motel, but by the fourth night they were out of money and had to sleep in the park. On the fifth day they went by the house and the constables were there removing everything and placing it out in the yard for scavengers to pick up. When Tony saw them throwing their stuff out on the lawn, he became outraged and started yelling and arguing with the constables. They told him to back off, but instead he took a swing at one of them. Of course, with that he was arrested and hauled off to jail."

Several jurors frowned and squirmed in their chairs. Matt took this to be a good sign. Perhaps the horror of Cindy's story was sinking in.

Matt continued. "Cindy and the kids slept in the park again that night. In the morning Cindy took them to school and then went to work. Later that day she got a call from someone at the jail informing her that they were letting Tony out and that she should come pick him up. But when she got there he was gone. Panic stricken, she drove around looking for him, but never thought of going back to their house. Late in the afternoon the police called and told her they'd found Tony back at their house. He'd broken in, climbed the stairs, tied a rope around his neck, secured the other end to a railing, and then jumped off."

There was a gasp from someone in the gallery, and one of the jurors put her hand to her mouth. Cindy wiped a tear from her eye, struggling to maintain her composure. Matt paused to let the scene sink into the jurors' minds.

"Tony was dead when the officers found him."

Matt took a deep breath, feeling his voice starting to crack, and then continued. "Of course, they wanted her to come to the morgue to identify his body. You can imagine Cindy's reaction."

The gallery stirred, and the judge banged his gavel. "Keep your emotions to yourself or you'll be asked to leave the courtroom," the judge warned. Matt looked at the judge, who nodded that he could continue.

"Now, no amount of money can compensate Cindy for what she has gone through and for the loss of her husband, but money is all you have as jurors to work with. If you find RMS acted in a manner that violated the law, all you can do is make sure Cindy Sharp gets enough money to compensate her for her loss and that RMS pays enough to deter them from violating the law and acting so callously in the future.

"Mr. Richmond, the RMS attorney, will point out that there were other factors that caused Mr. Sharp to commit suicide, and we do not dispute that. But one thing we are sure about, and we believe you will also be equally certain when you begin deliberations, is that had RMS honored their forbearance agreement Tony would be alive today.

"RMS has also done something rather ingenious. You've all heard the saying that the best defense is a strong offense. Well, RMS's CEO has taken that to a new level by filing a lawsuit against the plaintiff for the wrongful death of her husband. I'm sure you have all read the newspaper stories about Lucius Jones's murder. In order to distract you from what this lawsuit is all about and gain sympathy for RMS, Samantha Jones, RMS's CEO, has filed a lawsuit and instituted a media campaign trying to prove the plaintiff, Cindy Sharp, killed Lucius Jones.

"But don't believe a word of it. Believe this: When the government mandated that mortgage companies try to do everything they could to help home owners keep their homes, Lucius Jones, with his wife's blessing, instituted what is called dual processing. What that means is RMS would comply with the government mandate and take modification applications but would continue the foreclosure process—hence 'dual processing.' The problem with this was since RMS controlled the application process for modifications it could make sure the foreclosure would be processed before the modification. In reality what this meant was the government-mandated modification program was a sham.

"We will call witnesses who will show how Lucius Jones and, now his wife Samantha, profited from these foreclosures in a way that was completely and manifestly unconscionable.

"Now, that's a summary of what's to come. Unfortunately, to present all of this evidence to you will take time and might get a bit tedious. Let me apologize for that in advance, but it's necessary to prove our case by a preponderance of the evidence, which is the standard you will be applying when you start deliberations. Please be patient and attentive no matter how redundant it may seem. All the pieces of the puzzle will fall into place in the end. I promise you. Thank you."

Matt sat down, and the judge looked at Richmond. "Counsel, do you wish to give an opening statement?"

"Yes, Your Honor," Richmond said, getting to his feet. "Your Honor, ladies and gentlemen of the jury, Samantha Jones and the other owners of RMS would also like to thank you for your sacrifice in serving as jurors today, but also express their regret that you have to be subjected to the fiction and fabrications of the plaintiff's counsel. Of course, we know writing fiction runs in the Coleman family."

There was laughter in the gallery. Anger welled in Matt, causing Ryan to put his hand on Matt's arm to keep him from getting up and responding with his fist.

Richmond looked at Matt and smiled. "Now we are exceedingly sorry that Cindy Sharp and her family suffered from the collapsed economy, but that's hardly the fault of the defendant. Millions of Americans lost their jobs, and millions more had their homes foreclosed, but you can't blame all their suffering on the mortgage lenders. That is simply irrational. Who knows who was at fault for our economic collapse—the president, Congress, greedy corporate executives, or imprudent consumers?

"We are all sorry that Tony Sharp got prostate cancer, but you can't blame his prostate cancer on RMS. That's simply silly. And you can't, with any degree of credibility, contend that RMS is responsible for Tony Sharp committing suicide, either. It is simply impossible to determine what went on in his mind and what precisely caused him to take his life. It could just as easily have been something Cindy Sharp did that threw him over the edge. We're not blaming it on her, of course, but simply saying that there is no way to know why he committed suicide.

"What we have here is a simple contract situation. Pacific Glen Partners lent money to the Sharps to purchase their home. North American Servicing serviced the loan. That loan servicing was later assigned to RMS, who now acts on behalf of Pacific Glen Partners. The loan was secured by a deed of trust. When the parties closed the loan, the terms were set in concrete and couldn't be changed. Before closing the Sharps could have objected to the loan documents, but they didn't, so they had an obligation to comply with the note and deed of trust as it was written.

"We will show that the deed of trust does not allow any modification of the loan without the written consent of both parties. We will show that the document specifically states that any modification negotiations do not relieve the mortgagor of any obligations under the note and there is no waiver by the mortgagee of its rights and remedies provided in the deed of trust, including foreclosure. Therefore, the fact that RMS was considering a modification didn't prevent it from continuing its foreclosure proceeding. It's unfortunate that there were delays in the modification process, but we will show those delays were unavoidable and not intentional as plaintiff's counsel would suggest.

"We will also put on testimony that the plaintiff, Cindy

Sharp, become so obsessed with blaming her problems on RMS that she threatened Lucius Jones, the CEO of RMS who was later murdered. And we will show that Cindy Sharp was within a block of RMS's offices at the time of the murder and that she is a person of interest in that criminal investigation.

"It's sad but not uncommon for someone to try to blame their troubles on another. In this case Cindy Sharp sees RMS as her ticket to a bright financial future. We are sure that once the evidence has been presented you won't buy into Cindy Sharp's well-calculated scheme to rip off RMS. Thank you."

The judge looked at his watch. "Okay. It's nearly five so we'll reconvene tomorrow morning at nine."

The judge left the bench, and the gallery began to empty. Richmond looked over at Matt and whispered something to his associate. She laughed.

Matt turned to Cindy and smiled. "Well, what do you think?"

"I don't know. When you were giving your opening I felt good, but when I heard Richmond's argument I felt like shit. Do you think he's right, that I'm trying to blame all my troubles on RMS?"

"No. I think they violated the law and caused your husband to commit suicide."

"Let's just hope the jury feels that way," Cindy said worriedly.

Chapter 32
Plaintiff's Case

That night Matt and Ryan went over their witness list. They had talked to most of their witnesses but hadn't taken their depositions because they didn't want Richmond to know what their trial strategy would be. There were potential problems with not taking a deposition. One was the danger that a witness might change his or her testimony and another that they wouldn't show up for trial. If either happened, their entire case could be jeopardized. Since many of the witnesses had relationships with RMS, both of these were a distinct possibility.

Ryan had the task of making sure each of these witnesses showed up on time. They had all been subpoenaed, but if they didn't show up the judge wasn't likely to continue the case until they were found. Ryan called each of them on Monday night and told them to appear at nine a.m. on Tuesday. He reminded them that they could be arrested if they didn't show up on time. Fortunately, they all did, so the first order of business when court convened was to swear each of them in and let the judge instruct them to wait in the hall until they were needed.

After the witnesses were sworn in Matt called Cindy as their first witness. For most of the morning and afternoon she testified pretty much as Matt had predicted in his opening statement. Matt felt good about how she had performed but wasn't anxious to let Richmond take her on cross. A lot was riding on how she would hold up and he was afraid she'd get tripped up. Eventually, however, he had no choice but to stop asking questions and give the lectern to Richmond.

"Mr. Richmond, your cross," the judge said.

Richmond got up and walked to the lectern. "Ms. Sharp. Isn't it true that you and your husband signed the real estate lien note and deed of trust that has been introduced by your counsel and admitted into evidence as Exhibits 1 and 2?"

"Yes, sir."

"And isn't it true that you had a real estate agent represent you when you bought this property?"

"Yes, sir."

"And isn't it true you had a loan broker who helped you get the financing for your property?"

"That's right."

"Now, when you signed these two documents, had you read them?"

Cindy looked over at Matt. "Well, not really. I looked them over, but I'm no attorney. I can't say I understood them."

"Did your real estate agent or loan broker read them over?"

"I don't know. The loan broker probably did. I doubt our real estate agent did."

Richmond picked up a document and held it up. "Now, I'm going to show you what has been marked 'Defendant's Exhibit A' and ask you to identify it."

Richmond looked at the judge and asked, "May I approach the witness, Your Honor?"

"Yes, you may," the judge replied.

Richmond took Cindy Exhibit A and handed it to her.

"Now, can you identify this document?"

"Yes, this is the sales contract we signed for the house."

"Yes. And you and your husband signed it?"

"Yes."

"Did you read this document?"

"No. We didn't understand it. We relied on our real estate agent."

"I would like to direct you to Article 27 of that contract.

Do you see it?"

Cindy looked through the document. "Yes, I've found it."

"Now, read that for the jury, would you?"

"Yes. Ah. It says: 'You should have an attorney review this contract and all closing documents before you sign them.' "

"Yes. So, did you have an attorney review the contract and the closing documents before you and your husband signed them?"

"No," Cindy replied.

"Why not?"

"We couldn't afford one, plus we thought between the real estate agent and the loan broker we should be all right."

"I see. Do you think you and your husband understood the note and deed of trust?"

Cindy shrugged. "More or less."

"You knew you would have to make monthly payments, right?"

"Yes."

"And you knew you would have to keep the property insured?"

"Yes."

"Did you know you had to pay the taxes each year?"

"Yes. We always used our tax refund for that. "

"I see. Did you know that if you didn't keep your payments up the lender could exercise its right to foreclose?"

Cindy sighed. "Yes. We knew that."

"So, you will agree RMS had a right to foreclose your property for your failure to timely make all the payments on your note."

"No. They agreed they wouldn't."

"So, your only defense to the foreclosure is this alleged forbearance agreement."

"That and their repeated assurances that they would not foreclose until the modification had been accepted or rejected."

"Those representations were verbal, is that correct?"

"For the most part, but there was one letter."

"You're referring to Plaintiff's Exhibit 13?" Richmond asked.

"Yes. I believe so. And it specifically said they had received our application and that it was being considered."

"Right. But read paragraph twenty-three."

Cindy squinted. "You mean in the fine print at the bottom?"

Richmond smiled. "Just read paragraph twenty-three, please."

" 'Nothing in this letter shall be construed as a waiver of any right or obligation contained in the note and/or deed of trust.' "

"So, that letter didn't prohibit RMS from foreclosing, did it?"

"It seemed like it did to me, but I'm no lawyer," Cindy said.

"Objection, nonresponsive as to being a lawyer," Richmond said.

"Sustained," the judge said.

"All right. Ms. Sharp. Now after the foreclosure you were upset with RMS and the RMS CEO Lucius Jones, is that correct?"

"Yes. They'd lied to me and then took my house, what do you expect?"

"And, you in fact brought your protest to the offices of RMS, didn't you?"

"If you mean I went to see Mr. Jones, that's correct."

"And when you couldn't see him you left him a note, didn't you?"

"Yes."

Richmond picked up another document. "I'm going to show you what has been marked as 'Defendant's Exhibit B' and ask you to identify it. . . . May I approach, Your Honor?"

"You may."

Richmond took the exhibit to Cindy and then returned to the lectern. "All right. Could you identify Exhibit B for the jury?"

Cindy took a deep breath and let it out slowly. "Okay. it says:

"Dear Mr. Jones,

How could you foreclose on our home after you promised us in writing that you wouldn't do it while our modification was pending? We trusted you and believed you were acting in good faith, and now my husband is in jail because you wrongfully evicted us.

What kind of a company do you operate? Do you really think you can get away with lying to people and taking advantage of them the way you do? It is clear now that you never intended to modify our loan and only offered the modification option to shut us up.

I know you think you're pretty smart, but one day you'll pay for the way you treat people. That's a promise.

Cindy Sharp"

"So, what did you mean when you said one day Lucius Jones would pay for the way he treated people?"

"I mean evil people eventually get what's coming to them."

"Like a letter opener stuck in their throat?"

"Exactly, but I wasn't the one who delivered justice to Mr. Jones. I'm not a violent person. I wouldn't have done that."

"Your husband committed suicide, right?"

"Yes."

"You blamed that on Lucius Jones, didn't you?"

"I didn't even know Lucius Jones. I was mad at RMS."

"But he's their CEO and he's the one you threatened."

"I didn't threaten him. I just stated a fact that bad people eventually get punished for their sins. Not by me but by God."

"But isn't it true you went to RMS's offices on the day of

Lucius Jones's murder?"

"No."

"But you were a block away?"

Cindy nodded. "Yes, I bank near there and I went to the ATM."

"Just coincidentally on the day and near the hour that he was murdered."

"Yes. Coincidentally. Lucius Jones was the last person on my mind that day. I was getting money from the ATM to go shopping."

"Right. So you say. Pass the witness."

Matt thought about trying to rehabilitate Cindy's testimony but then figured it was better to get her off the stand before any more damage was done. "No further questions."

"You may stand down," the judge said. "Mr. Coleman, call your next witness."

"Yes, Your Honor. We call Joan Londry."

"Bailiff, bring in Ms. Londry."

"Yes, Your Honor," the bailiff said and went out into the lobby. A moment he returned with a tall, stout, middle-aged lady with black hair. She walked to the stand without smiling. All the witnesses had already been sworn in, so she took a seat in the witness stand.

"Please state your name," Matt said.

"Joan Londry."

"And how are you employed?"

"I work as a supervisor in the division 301 customer service department of Reliable Mortgage Servicing Company."

"And as supervisor do you run the division?"

"Yes. It's my responsibility."

"I assume the 301 designates some particular type of cases that you handle."

"Yes, we handle collections, modifications, and forbearance agreements," Londry replied.

"So, how many people do you supervise?"

316

"A dozen or so."

"And how many loans does RMS manage?"

"Twenty thousand, roughly."

"And how many land in your division 301?"

"About ten percent."

"So two thousand accounts?"

"That's correct."

"And how many of these customers are seeking a modification?"

"Most of them want some sort of modification. Probably eighty percent."

"Who handles modifications?"

"We take the application and then send it to underwriting."

"Now, when you get an account, what do you do first?"

"We log it into our Foreclosure Documentation and Processing software, or FDP, as we call it."

"Explain how that works," Matt asked.

"Well, it's an automated system that sends out all the required notices prior to foreclosure to each home owner who has been put into the system."

"Okay. What happens after all the notices are sent out?"

"The account is turned over to our attorneys who complete the foreclosure process."

"So, how would a home owner learn about the modification option?"

"One of the first letters that goes out is a government-mandated notice advising the home owner that they have various options rather than just let their property be foreclosed."

"And what options are those?" Matt asked.

"Short sale, deed in lieu of foreclosure, deferral, and modification."

"Okay, so if someone wanted a modification they would do what?"

"They would call the number in the letter, which would

come to the 301 division."

"So, when you got the call you would start the modification process?"

"Yes," Londry replied.

"Would you stop the foreclosure process while the modification was being processed?"

"No. The foreclosure continues, but if the modification is completed before foreclosure occurs, then the note would be cured and the foreclosure stopped."

"This is called dual processing, right?"

"I've heard it called that."

"So, do you explain to the home owners seeking modification that you are still going through with the foreclosure even though they have provided you a modification application?"

"Ah. We're not supposed to bring that up, but if they ask us specifically about it we tell them the truth—that if the modification is approved before foreclosure, then the process will stop, as the default will have been cleared."

"So, how long does the foreclosure process take?"

"In Texas it is about ninety days."

"And how long does the typical modification take to process?"

"That varies usually from ninety to 120 days."

"So, not many modifications get approved prior to foreclosure, do they?"

"A few make it through."

"During your employment at RMS—do you mind if I call it RMS?"

"No. That's fine."

"While you were working at RMS in the 301 division, did you have occasion to work with a customer named Cindy Sharp?"

"Yes. I believe I did."

"Did she inquire as to the possibility of a modification of her loan?"

"Yes, she did."

"Did you tell her a modification might be possible?"

"Yes, I explained the program and sent her a packet to fill out."

"And did she fill it out and send it in?"

"Yes, eventually."

"Eventually?"

"Yes, she says she sent it in but we couldn't find it, so she sent in another packet."

"Didn't she in fact send you the packet three times?"

"Well, I wouldn't know. I've only seen one copy."

"So, how much time was lost when her first packet was lost?"

"Objection," Richmond spat. "Assumes facts not in evidence."

"Sustained," the judge replied.

"I'll rephrase," Matt said. "How long was it between the first default notice when you advised Ms. Sharp of her right to apply for a modification and when you finally received a modification application from her?"

"Thirty to forty-five days, according to the dates in the file."

"So, by your timetable, a thirty- to forty-five-day delay would effectively eliminate any chance that the Sharps' application could be processed in time to beat the foreclosure?"

Ms. Londry shrugged. "I guess that's true unless the foreclosure date is reset."

"Did you tell her that she was wasting her time in continuing to pursue a modification?"

"No. I don't have authority to tell someone they are wasting their time. All I can do is tell them that if the modification is approved prior to the scheduled foreclosure date, then the foreclosure will not proceed."

"What would cause a foreclosure date to be reset?"

"If the account were escalated."

"What does that mean?"

"If the home owner demanded to speak to a supervisor and the supervisor found a defect in the foreclosure process, he could recommend a reset."

"What kind of defect?"

"Usually it would be the notices going to the wrong address or a third-party intervention."

"What's a third-party intervention?"

"Like the home owner hires an attorney or calls his congressman or something, then sometimes the account is reset to allow more time for the modification."

"So, resetting is . . . ?"

"Starting the foreclosure process over, which you have to do to comply with state law."

"But there was no intervention in the Sharps' case?"

"No. They asked to contact me, but they didn't claim a defect in the foreclosure process. They got their proper notices."

"But didn't you assure them that there would be no foreclosure?"

"No. I always tell them the same thing. I've got it memorized. We won't foreclose if the modification is approved before your foreclosure date."

"What if Ms. Sharp remembers differently? What if she says you told her not to worry about the foreclosure notice?"

"I wouldn't have said that to her."

"What about the employees you supervise?"

Londry shrugged. "I don't know. I didn't listen in to their conversations with Ms. Sharp."

"But you could have?"

"Yes."

"Are records of those phone calls available?"

"No. They are only kept for ninety days."

"Well, that's convenient. No further questions of this witness at this time."

The judge nodded. "Mr. Richmond. Your witness."

Richmond took Ms. Londry on cross and tried to undo the damage her testimony had done with limited success. Matt called Lois Ross, another supervisor at RMS and the person who had signed the affidavit attached to RMS's motion for summary judgment.

"Ms. Ross. How long have you worked at RMS?"

"Since the beginning, and before that, I worked for North American Servicing for seven years."

"And what is your position?"

"I am a supervisor in operations and also custodian of records for RMS."

"Now did you have occasion to talk to Cindy Sharp about her account?"

"Yes I did, but only after her property had already been foreclosed."

"I see. Did you tell her the foreclosure was a mistake?"

"No. I told her that if she thought it was a mistake she needed to put her thoughts in a letter and send it to the company—a phone call wouldn't help."

"I see. So, you didn't think the foreclosure was a mistake?"

"No. Not at all. We did everything right."

"Is that why you signed the 'Affidavit of Lois Ross in Support of Defendant RMS Motion for Summary Judgment'?"

"Yes. That's right."

"So, knowing that Cindy Sharp had concerns about the propriety of the foreclosure, did you conduct an investigation to be sure she wasn't right before you signed that affidavit?"

"Ah. Not a formal investigation. I looked over the paperwork the attorneys had sent to her and what was filed in the deed records. Everything seemed in order."

"What about the payment that was sent to North American Servicing? Did that get properly applied to the account?"

"Ah. I don't know about that."

Unconscionable

"You don't? So, how could you testify to the balance that the Sharps owed on their account if you hadn't dealt with the missing payment?"

"I'm sorry. I didn't know about it."

"You mean you didn't review all the correspondence and telephone conversations on the account?"

"I thought I did."

"What about the premature payment of property taxes? How do you justify paying taxes before they were even due when the Sharps had been paying their taxes all along themselves?"

"Oh, well, under the deed of trust we have the right to pay taxes if the home owner doesn't pay them."

"Right. But they weren't due until January, and you paid them the previous November and immediately increased the Sharps' house payment by $300. Isn't that correct?"

"Ah. Well, the computer did that automatically because the account was in default."

"Right. In default because you hadn't applied a payment properly made to North American Servicing before you were assigned servicing of the account."

"Well, I had nothing to do with that."

"Okay. How do we even know that RMS owns the note?"

"Huh? What do you mean?"

"Well, RMS sends a letter and says they own the account and you certify that RMS does own it and it's in default, but where is the paper trail? Where are the assignments of the note and deed of trust to North American Servicing and then to RMS?"

"The attorneys handle that. I don't have anything to do with it."

"So, you certify something that you have no way of knowing is true or not?"

"No. I know we own it."

"How? Where are the assignments?" Matt asked.

Lois swallowed hard.

Matt picked up a document. "Your Honor, may I approach the witness with a couple of exhibits?"

"Yes," the judge replied.

Matt took the document, walked up to Ms. Ross, and handed it to her. "Ms. Ross. I'm handing you what has been marked as 'Plaintiff's Exhibit 3' and asking you to identify it."

"It says it is an assignment of lien."

"Okay. And would you examine it more carefully—look at the legal description and confirm that it is an assignment of the original lien on the Sharps' homestead from Pacific Glen Partners LP to North American Servicing?"

"Yes. That appears to be correct."

"Have you seen this document before?"

"Yes, I believe I have."

"Is there another assignment from North American Servicing to RMS?"

"I would assume so, but I'm not sure I've seen it. Our attorneys probably have it."

"Yet, you certified that RMS owned the Sharps' note?"

Ross sighed. "Yes, well I've probably seen it, but I deal with so many properties you can't expect me to remember every single one."

"You mean it's okay if you foreclose on a property where RMS doesn't own the note?"

"Objection!" Richmond said. "Argumentative."

"Overruled," the judge said.

"You may answer," Matt said.

"No. I'm sure we owned all the notes on the properties we foreclosed on."

"All right, who signed the assignment of lien which is labeled as 'Plaintiff's Exhibit 3'?"

Ms. Ross squinted and said, " 'Thomas J. Hamilton, vice president of PG Managers LLC, general partner of Pacific Glen Partners LP.' "

"Now would you take a look at Exhibit 4. It is under

Exhibit 3."

Ms. Ross took a deep breath and then fumbled with the documents until she found Plaintiff's Exhibit 4. "Okay."

"Please identify that document," Matt said.

"It's the certificate of formation of Pacific Glen Partners LP."

"Objection, Your Honor. This document is irrelevant," Richmond complained.

"If the court will give me a little leeway, its relevance will become quickly apparent."

"I'll allow it," the judge said.

"Now, did Thomas J. Hamilton sign that document?"

Ms. Ross squinted again. "Yes, he did at the bottom."

"Now compare his signature with the one on the assignment of lien from Pacific Glen Partners LP to North American Servicing. Are they the same?"

"Objection, Your Honor. Ms. Ross is not a handwriting expert."

"Your Honor," Matt replied, "I'm only asking for her lay opinion."

"Overruled. You may answer."

Lois Ross's mouth dropped, and she turned a little pale. She looked at Richmond and then at Matt. "Ah, well. No. Actually, they look quite different."

The gallery stirred and Matt smiled.

"So, which document bears the real signature of Thomas J. Hamilton?" Matt asked innocently.

Richmond squirmed in his chair. "Objection! Assumes facts not in evidence. She's not an expert."

"Fair enough, withdrawn," Matt said. "No further questions of this witness at this time."

The judge looked at the clock and said, "We'll take a fifteen-minute break. Be back at ten thirty p.m."

The courtroom suddenly got noisy as the spectators reacted to a witness on the ropes and the revelation of a forged document. Matt kept one eye on Richmond and noted a look of concern on his face. This confirmed that his case was going well, which gave him much relief, particularly since the best was yet to come.

Chapter 33
The Unthinkable

Matt took advantage of the break to go check on his witnesses. They were all there minus his star witness that he was holding back for the following day. On the way back into the courtroom he looked around to see if there was anyone unexpected in the gallery. There were reporters, of course, some members of the DA's staff, Cindy's family, and employees of RMS—nobody out of the ordinary. A moment later as Matt returned to his seat, the door next to the bench opened and the bailiff yelled, "All rise."

Everyone stood up as the judge entered the courtroom and took the bench. "Be seated," the judge said. "Mr. Coleman, your witness."

"Ms. Ross, when you actually received the modification packet from the Sharps, was it promptly sent to the modification department for processing?"

"Yes."

"Did anyone instruct you to delay or sabotage the processing of the modification?" Matt asked.

"No. I would never do that."

"Did you know Cindy Sharp or her husband before she called you on the phone to ask about a modification?"

"No. I did not."

"So, the Sharps' application was treated just like the hundreds of similar applications you receive each week."

"That's correct."

Unconscionable

"And did you make any representations to Ms. Sharp about whether or not the foreclosure process would be abated pending the modification?"

"No."

"Does the company monitor the phone calls that come to you?"

"Yes, they do."

"Are they recorded for later access?"

"Yes."

"Did your attorneys produce the transcripts of those telephone calls?"

"I don't know."

"Well, I will represent to you that they did not. The explanation was that they were routinely deleted every ninety days. Is that consistent with your knowledge?"

Ross frowned. "Well, I didn't know that."

"Have you ever accessed a telephone conversation that took place more than ninety days earlier?"

The witness squirmed in her chair. "Yeah. I think so, but I may be mistaken."

"It's too bad we can't listen to that actual conversation just to see whose recollection is correct. You're sure you didn't assure Ms. Sharp that the foreclosure wouldn't go forward?"

"No. Like I said, I only told her that if the modification was approved prior to the foreclosure taking place, then the note default would be cured and the delinquent payments tacked on the end of the note."

"But the modification was not approved or declined? Is that right?"

"Not to my knowledge. I never saw anything one way or the other."

"If it had been approved, how would you have been informed?"

"The file would have been transferred to the modification department and the modification department would have

328

contacted the Sharps directly by email, with a copy to me, giving them information about closing on the modification."

"So, when you got that email you would have closed the account."

"Correct."

"And had it been rejected how would you have been informed?"

"I would have gotten an email notifying me of that fact."

"But you didn't get any such notification?"

"Correct."

"So, would it be accurate to say the modification at that time was still pending?"

"That would be my understanding. Yes."

"Thank you, Ms. Ross," Matt said. "No further questions."

"Mr. Richmond, your witness?"

"No questions, Your Honor."

"Then call your next witness."

Matt called Simon Artis, who testified that he worked for a firm called Metro Realty who was hired routinely by RMS to handle the eviction of home owners whose homes had been foreclosed. Richmond objected to the relevance of the testimony, but Matt explained that the amount of profit Lucius Jones was making from all the foreclosures RMS was turning out was relevant to its alleged failure to promptly turn around and approve modification applications. The judge agreed and overruled the objection. Then Matt asked Artis about his conversation with Tony Sharp.

"When Mr. Sharp told you that he had a forbearance agreement while the modification was being processed, what did you do?"

Artis smiled. "I laughed. That's what they all say."

"Really?"

"Yes, but I told him he didn't read the fine print. It clearly states that although RMS will consider a modification, it is not waiving any right or remedy under the deed of trust nor abating any foreclosure that has already been commenced."

"I see. So, why does RMS hire you? Why not just hire its law firm to file the eviction suit?"

"Because attorneys are expensive and going to court takes time. Plus I can usually get the home owners out voluntarily."

"How do you do that?"

"I explain to them how contesting the foreclosure is a costly and futile effort. Most people are realistic and practical, particularly when I offer them cash for keys."

"Cash for keys?"

"Yes, I'm authorized to give them up to $1,500 for moving expenses if they will surrender the property without any fuss."

"And that usually works?"

"Ninety percent of the time. Fifteen hundred dollars is better than a stick in the eye, as they say."

"Right. So, how much does Metro Realty get paid for handling the Cash for Keys program?"

"Per property, $1,250."

"And how many foreclosures did you handle last year?"

"Ah, I don't know exactly, but around two thousand in Texas."

"So, that's about $2.5 million?"

"That sounds about right."

"And how much of the profits from Metro Realty went to Lucius Jones?"

"Twenty-five percent."

There was a buzz in the courtroom, and the bailiff glared out at the crowd.

"Thank you, Mr. Artis," Matt said. "No further questions at this time."

"Very well. Mr. Richmond, your witness," the judge said.

Richmond briefly cross-examined Artis, trying to

downplay the profit Lucius was receiving from Metro Realty and bolster the need for Metro Realty's services.

"All right, Mr. Coleman. Call your next witness."

"Yes, Your Honor. The plaintiff calls Brett Smith."

Smith took the stand and explained how he and Lucius Jones had set up Prime Holdings Ltd. with him owning 49 percent and Jones having the controlling 51 percent interest.

"So, what is the purpose of Prime Holdings?" Matt asked.

"Well, most of the time when you held a trustee's sale, there wouldn't be any bidders due to the first lien note on the property, outstanding property taxes, and the condition of the property. So, Lucius and I set up Prime Holdings to buy the potentially profitable properties, fix them up, and sell them when the market was right."

"I see. So, what do you mean by potentially profitable?"

"Well, properties where there was sufficient equity that it was likely to eventually sell for a profit."

"So, what was the average profit on these properties when you sold them?"

"On average we made about a twenty-five percent profit over the purchase price."

"And how was the purchase price determined?"

"It was the greater of the first lien note balance plus the foreclosure costs or sixty-six percent of appraised value."

"Were these new appraisals?"

"Yes, we always had the property appraised prior to foreclosure."

"Did Lucius Jones have an interest in the appraisal company you used?"

"No. It was owned by his nephew."

There was laughter in the gallery.

Matt shook his head in disgust. "So, how many properties did Prime Holdings purchase last year?"

"Five hundred and twenty-four, I believe."

"Were they financed?"

"Yes, we have a line of credit with Happy State Bank."

Matt laughed. "Happy State Bank?"

"Yes. It's out of Amarillo."

"Okay. How much did you finance?"

"Roughly $138,000 per unit, or about seventy-two million, give or take."

"And how many were sold?"

"None. The market has been bad, so we're waiting for it to turn around."

"So, on seventy-two million, if your twenty-five percent profit model holds up, you should make about eighteen million."

"Well, there will be expenses, so it will probably be more like fifteen million if the market turns around. If it doesn't, our profit margin could disappear entirely."

"Understood," Matt said. "No further questions of this witness."

Again on cross Richmond tried to justify the need for Prime Holdings Ltd. in order to spare RMS from having to hold large inventories of property. It actually made sense, but Matt could see the jury was getting annoyed at all the profit Lucius Jones had been making on the foreclosures.

"Call your next witness," the judge said after Richmond had ended his cross.

"Thank you, Your Honor. The plaintiff calls Juan Rubio."

Matt had gauged Juan Rubio to be the less vocal of the owners of CDR and the one more likely to tell the truth. The judge reminded him he was under oath.

"Please state your name for the record," Matt asked.

"Juan Rubio."

"And for whom are you employed?"

"I work for Consolidated Document Retrieval, or CDR for short."

"And what does CDR do for its customers?"

"We find missing documents."

"How do you do that?"

"Well, it depends on who we are working for and what kind of documents are missing."

"Is RMS one of your customers?"

"Yes."

"Let's say they needed an assignment of lien," Matt said.

"Well, if it were an assignment of a deed of trust or mortgage lien, we go to the county where the property is located and find it in the deed records."

"What if it hadn't been filed in the deed records?"

"Well, then we would contact the assignor and the assignee of the lien and see if one of them had an unfiled copy."

"Let's say after a diligent search you couldn't find it?" Matt persisted.

"Well, it has to be somewhere. We just keep looking until we find it."

"What if it wasn't ever drafted and signed?"

"Ah. Well, then our customer is out of luck, I guess."

"You realize you're under oath, don't you?"

"Objection!" Richmond spat. "Counsel is badgering the witness."

"Overruled," the judge said. "It doesn't hurt to remind witnesses that they are under oath for their own protection."

"Thank you, Your Honor. You may answer, Mr. Rubio."

"What was the question?"

"Do you realize you're under oath?"

"Yes, of course."

"So, isn't it true that if you cannot locate a document you create it?"

Rubio looked at the judge and then Richmond. "Ah. I think I need my lawyer."

The judge studied Rubio. "You're a witness, Mr. Rubio, not a defendant. You can consult with an attorney if you wish, but unless he is in the gallery or can get here in the next fifteen minutes, we don't have time to allow you to consult with him. What is your concern about continuing to answer questions?"

"I'm afraid I might be getting myself in trouble."

"You mean your answers may tend to incriminate you?" the judge asked.

"Yes. Possibly."

"Well, you can exercise your Fifth Amendment right not to answer a question on the grounds that it might tend to incriminate you, but only if you legitimately believe that is the case."

"Yes, Your Honor. I want to take the Fifth."

"Very well. Please read the last question posed to Mr. Rubio."

The court reporter spoke. "So, isn't it true that if you cannot locate a document you create it?"

"Do you understand the question, Mr. Rubio?" the judge asked.

"Yes, sir."

"So, you want to take the Fifth on that question? Is that right?"

"Yes," Rubio said.

"All right. So noted. Now, if Mr. Coleman wants to keep asking you questions he can do so, and you can only take the Fifth if you are genuinely concerned that answering the question might tend to incriminate you. Do you understand?"

"Yes."

Matt picked up another document. "Mr. Rubio, I'm going to show you what's been marked Exhibit 4. . . . May I approach, Your Honor?"

"You may," the judge said.

Matt took Exhibit 4 to the witness. "This is what an earlier witness identified as the assignment of lien from Pacific Glen Partners LP to North American Servicing. Does that look correct?"

"Yes. That's what it says."

"Now, was this document created by CDR?"

Rubio reviewed the document carefully and then sighed.

"I think I'm going to take the Fifth."

"You're refusing to answer on grounds it may tend to incriminate you?" Matt asked.

"Yes," Rubio said tentatively.

"Thank you. No further questions of this witness."

"Mr. Richmond. Cross?"

Richmond thought for a moment then looked at his co-counsel. "Ah. No questions of this witness, Your Honor."

The judge looked at the clock. "It's nearly noon. We'll adjourn until one thirty p.m."

The judge stood up and left the courtroom. The gallery erupted in conversation as people began to wander out into the hall. Matt got up and began packing everything into his briefcase. The courtroom was supposed to be secure, but he didn't like leaving critical papers and evidence lying around.

"I've never been to a trial before. That was quite interesting," Candy said.

Matt, recognizing the voice, turned around quickly and smiled. "Candy! Hi. So, how long have you been here?"

"All morning."

"Wow. What did you think?"

"I think it's a good thing Lucius Jones is dead. I doubt he'd enjoy seeing his company torn apart piece by piece."

"Well, I'm not sure that's what's happening. The plaintiff's case always looks good until the defendant puts their case on."

Candy raised her eyebrows. "Well, you're doing a hell of a job."

"You want to grab some lunch with Ryan and me?" Matt asked. "We've got time to go to the West End."

"Sure, I've got Sharon with me."

"Bring her along. Ryan will be thrilled to meet her."

Ten minutes later the foursome was walking briskly past the Kennedy Memorial toward the West End. Sharon insisted they eat at Gator's Croc & Roc because she loved their fried pickles. Fortunately, there wasn't a line and they were seated quickly.

"So, how do you think it is going?" Sharon asked.

"Pretty good," Matt said. "So far all the witnesses have testified pretty much as expected."

"What was that about the signatures that didn't match?" Candy asked.

"Well, we think, or I should say know, that it's RMS's practice to create any documents that they don't have but need in order to prove a chain of title."

"Is that legal?" Candy asked.

"No," Ryan said. "It's fraudulent and a crime to forge someone's signature."

"How do they figure they can get away with it?" Sharon asked.

"Well, most people think RMS is a reputable operation and complies with the law, so they never even suspect that the documents they come up with are fake."

"Wow. How did you know they were crooked?" Sharon asked.

Matt looked at Ryan. "Well, let's just say we have our sources."

As they were talking the waitress came over, took their drink orders, and gave them menus.

"Excuse me, I'm going to the ladies' room," Sharon said.

"Oh, I think I'll join you," Candy said, getting up.

Matt nodded, picked up the menu, and started reading it. A minute later the waitress returned with their drinks. As she was leaving Sharon returned.

"So, Ryan. How's the criminal law business?"

"What criminal law business? So far all I've been doing is working on this case."

"You haven't had to get any of the girls out of jail?"

"No. What's with that?" Ryan teased. "You girls been paying off the cops?"

Sharon smiled wryly. "No, Candy runs a tight ship. She's very careful and screens our clients very well."

"Well, that's good. Sitting is a jail cell isn't much fun."

"Amen to that," Matt interjected.

Sharon grinned and took a sip of her iced tea. Everyone was studying their menu when a young blond-headed boy ran up, handed Matt a folded piece of paper, and ran off. Startled, Matt nearly knocked over his drink.

"What's this?" Matt asked irritably, but the boy was gone. Matt looked at the paper warily and then cautiously opened it. A note had been printed in capital letters.

COLEMAN,

YOU'RE GOING DOWN A DANGEROUS ROAD. STOP NOW BEFORE IT'S TOO LATE AND KEEP YOUR MOUTH SHUT ABOUT WHAT YOU THINK YOU KNOW. I'VE TAKEN CANDY AS INSURANCE. IF YOU WANT TO SEE HER ALIVE AGAIN HEED THIS WARNING. NO COPS OR FBI AND DON'T TRY TO FIND HER. I'VE KILLED ONCE TO PROTECT WHAT'S MINE SO I WON'T HESITATE A SECOND TIME.

Matt's heart sank. Memories of his wife's kidnapping and brutal murder raced through his mind.

"What the hell?" Ryan exclaimed.

"Where's Candy?" Matt asked.

"She was in the ladies' room a minute ago," Sharon said.

"Go check on her," Matt said urgently.

Sharon rushed to the ladies' room with Matt on her heels. She went inside and came out almost immediately. "She's not in there. What are we going to do?"

"Search the restaurant!" Matt ordered. "I'll check out the front.

Sharon went one way and Ryan the other, but they soon returned to their table with frightened looks on their faces. Matt sat down and studied the note again. He wondered if he should call the FBI. He hadn't contacted the police when his wife Lynn's life had been threatened. He'd caved into the threats and intimidation, assuming that if he did what the thugs asked, they would leave her alone. But giving in to them hadn't worked and they'd murdered Lynn and her sister anyway. He wondered if Candy was already dead, or if she was alive, whether capitulation would save her.

"We should call the police?" Ryan urged.

"No. The note said no cops or FBI."

"So? How would he know?"

"He may have someone watching us."

"So, what are we supposed to do, then?" Ryan asked, fear in his voice.

"I don't know. I need to think."

"We've got to find Candy!" Sharon moaned, tears running down her cheeks. "We can't let anything happen to her."

"I know, I know. We'll find her," Matt assured her.

"So, this guy is Jones's killer?" Ryan asked.

"Obviously. He figured out we knew who he was and were about to expose him."

"Damn it!" Ryan exclaimed. "I can't believe this is happening. I wish Dad were here. He'd know what to do."

"You know who killed Lucius Jones?" Sharon asked.

"Yes. We've figured it out and we were going to expose the killer tomorrow."

"So, what are we going to do?" Ryan asked frantically.

"We can't call any more witnesses," Matt noted. "We'll have to close with what we've got or try to settle."

"You think they would consider settling?" Ryan asked.

"Maybe, if they think there's more damaging evidence about to come out."

"Then let's ask the court for the afternoon to try to settle and then maybe the asshole will let Candy go."

"That's our best bet, I guess," Matt agreed. "But I'm not going to make the same mistake I did with Lynn."

"What mistake was that?" Sharon asked.

"I believed if I cooperated with them they'd leave her alone."

"But isn't that exactly what you are doing by shutting down the trial?" Ryan asked.

"No. I'm going to make it look like I'm complying, but in reality I'm going to be doing everything humanly possible to get Candy back and bring the asshole down who kidnapped her."

"Good. What can I do to help?" Sharon asked.

"I don't know right now, but stick around. We might need you for something. And don't tell anyone what's going on."

"What if someone asks me where Candy is?"

"Tell them she had to go back to work but you wanted to stay and watch the trial."

"Okay," Ryan said thoughtfully. "So, you're bringing in the police and the FBI?"

Matt nodded. "Yeah. There's no way you and I could ever find the bastard alone."

"Good," Ryan replied.

They paid for their drinks and went back to the courthouse. Matt got off at the third floor, went into the law library, and found an empty typing room in which he could make a phone call without anyone eavesdropping. He didn't know anybody at the FBI, so he called Detective Finch, the female detective who was handling Lucius Jones's murder.

When Matt returned to the courtroom the gallery was nearly empty, as there was still almost an hour until the trial resumed. Matt scanned the room for Richmond but didn't find him. A few moments later they located him talking to the court coordinator. Matt walked up to him.

"We need to talk," Matt said, trying to hide his desperation.

"About what?" Richmond said.

"About whether you want all your client's secrets revealed to the news media covering this trial."

Unconscionable

Richmond studied Matt and then replied, "Okay, let's go into the attorneys' conference room."

Matt walked across the courtroom to a door that led to a tiny room with a small conference table. He opened the door for Richmond and then followed him in. They both sat down.

"All right," Matt said. "I think you can see where I'm going with this case. Bit by bit RMS's reputation is being trashed, and it's being reported all over the country."

"You haven't proven anything yet. Wait until I put on my case and show the jury your client is just a freeloading deadbeat trying to get rich off RMS."

Matt sighed. "Give me a break. You're not going to convince the jury of that. Accusing Cindy of the murder was just a diversion and you know it."

Richmond started to protest and thought better of it. "So, what do you want?"

"Give her a million, and your client can keep its little foreclosure cash cow from being gutted."

"A million?" Richmond gasped.

"Yeah, that's what? A few weeks' profit?"

Richmond rolled his eyes. "I'll have to talk to my client."

"All right. The offer is only good until court reconvenes."

"What?"

"That's what I said. It's now or never. My next witness is going to tell about the profit that is made rehabilitating the properties after they are acquired. Oh, and let's see—we haven't fully explored how much is made from the appraisals, inspections, and attorney's fees. You haven't paid referral fees back to Jones, have you?"

"No. Of course not."

"Good, so you don't have anything to lose other than, how much in legal fees each year?"

Richmond sighed, got up, and left. Matt followed him out, found Cindy, and brought her back to the conference room.

"What's up?" she asked curiously.

340

Matt took a deep breath, not sure what to day. "Well, I wanted to let you know that this is a good time to settle your case."

"Really? But everything is going so well."

Matt nodded. "I know. It looks great now, but once Richmond puts on his case and starts trying to prove that you killed Lucius Jones, things could change for the worse in a hurry."

"Hmm," Cindy said. "I just have such good feelings about how everything is going."

"If I could get you a half million dollars, would you take it?"

"A half million?" Cindy said, pondering the thought. "I don't know. That's not a lot, considering they killed Tony."

"Well, I've told you it's unlikely that we can prove RMS caused your husband's suicide. It's a very novel idea and not one that can be easily proved. I'm not saying we won't try, but you should be realistic."

"I don't know."

"It's your decision, of course, but a bird in a hand, you know."

"Right," Cindy replied, obviously struggling with the idea of settling.

"I know you're enjoying me ripping RMS a new asshole, but you've got to think about your kids. You don't have any money and if Richmond gets a couple of jurors to think you had something to do with Jones's death, you could lose everything."

"I know," Cindy said, tears welling in her eyes. "I just hate the idea of them getting away so cheaply."

"Cheap for them, but a half a million will tide you over until the kids grow up, if you're prudent with it."

"You're probably right."

"I'll try to get more, but I'm thinking half a million is the most we can expect to get right now."

Cindy nodded. "Okay. If you think that is best."

"No. It's not what I think. It's your decision. I just want you to know you have a narrow window of opportunity to settle the case right now and avoid losing everything, or if we win, having the judgment appealed and tied up in appellate courts for two or three years."

"Okay. You're scaring me now. Go ahead and settle it."

Matt sighed in relief. "Good. Go ahead back to the counsel table. I'll join you in a minute."

Matt sat there awhile, worrying about Candy, wondering where she was, and praying she was okay. He was about to go looking for Richmond when the door flew open and Richmond walked in with a scowl on his face. Matt judged the look to be a good sign.

"So, what did your client say?" Matt asked.

"Two hundred and fifty thousand and not a dime more."

Matt shook his head in disgust. "Give me a break. Two hundred and fifty thousand dollars is all that the future of RMS is worth?"

"That's our offer, take it or leave it."

Matt half smiled. Attorneys always relished telling an opponent to take it or leave it, but that was usually a bluff. Matt figured that was the case now.

"Okay. Time is short. The judge will be taking the bench in about two minutes. I'm authorized to go down to $750,000."

"What? That's ridiculous."

"It is? I don't think so. I think it's a good deal for your client. You should take it to them—like right now."

Richmond studied Matt. "This is against my recommendation, but I'm authorized to go to $500,000. But that's it, and we want an airtight confidentiality agreement signed by your client, and you and Ryan, too."

The door burst open and the bailiff poked his head in. "The judge is about to take the bench."

"Thanks," Matt said, and the bailiff left. "Okay, it's a deal. Let's go announce the settlement to the court."

Matt knew the confidentiality agreement could be a problem, but he'd have to deal with that later. When the judge had taken the bench, Matt rose. "Your Honor."

The judge looked over at Matt. "Yes, Mr. Coleman?"

"Can we have a sidebar, Your Honor?"

The judge nodded. "Come on up."

Matt and Richmond walked up the bench. The judge leaned in. "Yes, what is it?"

"Your Honor," Matt said, "plaintiff and defendant have reached a settlement."

The judge sat back. "Really?" He looked over at Richmond. "Is this true, Mr. Richmond?"

"Yes, Your Honor. We just reached an agreement during the lunch break."

"Well. All right. Step back."

Matt and Richmond went back to their tables, and the judge informed the jury and the gallery that the trial was over. He thanked the jury for their service and told them they hadn't wasted their time, as their presence had been instrumental in forcing the parties to reach a settlement. One of the jury members asked how much the settlement was for, but the judge explained that the settlement would be confidential. The gallery let out a collective groan of disappointment.

As the judge left the bench, Matt and Ryan followed him out his private entrance, rushed past him to the end of the hallway, opened the door to the stairwell, and went down two stairs at a time. Three minutes later they were tearing out of the courthouse parking garage in their separate cars, Ryan heading for Candy's place in case she called there and Matt going back to the office. They both had lots to do but nobody could know what they were up to.

Chapter 34
Break in the Case

Detective Jill Finch was out of leads in the Jones murder case. They'd scrutinized all the usual suspects: the wife, the ex–business partner, the unhappy home owner who blamed her husband's suicide on RMS and Jones, but it didn't appear any of them could have been the killer. There were other persons of interest, but none of them had a motive to kill Jones. None of them inherited Jones's interest in the various enterprises, so there would have been no reason to want him dead. For most, the loss of Jones was an inconvenience and would likely cause a disruption in the cash flow the businesses were enjoying. Nor did any of them have insurance on Jones. Only his wife was the beneficiary of insurance and she had provided an airtight alibi. The phone rang. Finch picked it up.

"Finch here."

"Detective," Matt said. "This is Matt Coleman."

"Matt Coleman. Right. We met in your office."

"Yes, we represent Cindy Sharp."

"Okay. What can I do for you?"

"Listen very carefully. I only have a minute to talk to you. We're in the middle of trial."

"Right. The civil trial. Your client is suing RMS."

"That's correct. A few minutes ago the judge gave us a lunch break, and my brother Ryan and I went to lunch with two women, Candy Kane and Sharon Sparks. They are friends."

"Okay," Jill said, wondering where this was going.

"While we were eating, Candy and Sharon went to the restroom, and while they were away a boy delivered me a note.

By that time Sharon had come back, but not Candy. I don't have time to read the note, but it was a demand that I end the civil trial immediately or Candy would be killed."

"What?" Jill said, not quite believing what she was hearing.

"Yes, it said they would kill her if we didn't end the trial immediately. When we went looking for Candy we couldn't find her."

"Okay. I'll call the FBI and get someone over to the restaurant right away. What's the name of it?"

"No! The note said no police or FBI. You have to work this in the background. If you send someone to the restaurant or to Candy's house, the kidnapper will know I contacted you and they will kill her!"

Jill took a deep breath. "Okay, so why do they want the trial stopped?"

"Because I know who killed Lucius Jones."

Jill's mouth dropped. "You do? Who is it?"

"Rick Shafer."

She shook her head. "No. We've interviewed Shafer. He and Jones were best friends."

"He's the murderer, and if you track him down you might be able to save Candy's life," Matt said emphatically. "Please find him before it is too late."

"But—"

"That's all I can tell you now. I've got to go settle this case or Shafer will kill Candy. I'll call you when the case is settled. Hopefully in less than an hour."

"But—"

"Sorry, got to go. Talk to you later."

The phone went dead. Jill slowly lowered it, just staring at it in shock. Her partner, Detective Tom Morin, seeing the look on her face, asked if she was all right.

Jill grimaced, blinked a few times, and then replied, "Yeah, fine. Ah. Listen, we've got a kidnapping and a lead on the

Jones murder."

"Huh?"

Jill explained the situation to Morin and the urgency in finding Rick Shafer. They checked their notes, found his address and telephone number, and headed out to their unmarked Chevrolet Impala and exited the police parking lot with Tom driving. According to their notes Shafer lived in Grand Prairie and worked in downtown Fort Worth. They decided to check Shafer's home first.

"So, do you think Coleman knows what he's talking about, or is this just speculation?" Tom asked, turning onto the on ramp to I-30 going west.

Jill shrugged. "He seemed pretty sure about it. I think he believes he knows who the killer is. Whether or not he's right, I wouldn't hazard a guess at this point."

"What do we know about the victim?" Tom asked.

"Nothing. I'll call in and get somebody checking her out," she said, pulling out her cell to make the call.

"So, don't you think we should give the FBI a heads-up? That's protocol."

"Yeah. But let's wait until we hear from Coleman. I don't want to get his girlfriend killed if we can avoid it."

Jill's cell phone rang. She flipped it open and put it to her ear. "Finch here," she said and listened to the caller. A moment later she hung up.

"Okay, Candace Kane owns an escort service and runs about a dozen girls. She has one arrest for solicitation, but the charges were dropped. She claims her girls don't sell sex, just companionship."

"Yeah, I've heard that one before." Morin chuckled. "Look but don't touch."

"It's possible," Jill said.

"No it's not. If a guy hires a companion he's going to want sex before the night is over."

"You're an expert, huh?"

"Damn straight," Tom said as they got to the Grand Prairie exit.

Ten minutes later they pulled up in front of Shafer's house on Ola Drive. It appeared to be a relatively new single-story house, nicely landscaped, with a two-and-a-half-car garage. The house was dark, and there were no cars in the driveway. They got out of the Impala.

Tom went around back, and Jill went up to the front door and rang the doorbell. Chimes rang throughout the house, but there was no response. A minute later Tom came around from the back.

"Nobody's home. Should we go in?" Tom asked.

"No. Not without a warrant. I don't think Candy is here."

"Okay, how about the neighbors? They might have some information."

"Good idea. You go across the street and I'll check next door."

They split up with Jill going to the house to the west. Shafer's home was a corner lot, so he only had one next-door neighbor. Jill went up the front door and knocked. A young white female wearing shorts and a TCU T-shirt answered the door. Jill showed the woman her badge.

"Hi. I'm Jill Finch with the Dallas Police Department. We're looking for your neighbor, Rick Shafer. Have you seen him today?"

"Yeah. I saw him leave early this morning. I guess he was going to work."

"How well do you know him?"

"Not that much. We don't socialize or anything. If we see each other we say hi and that's about it."

"How long have you been neighbors?"

"About five years."

"Does he own any other houses besides this one anywhere nearby? Rental properties, lake lots, or anything like that?"

"He has a old farmhouse he bought at Lake Lavon. He keeps his boat there—says it's not much more expensive than paying for a slip on the lake."

"Really? Do you know where it is?"

"No. Sorry. Like I said, we're not friends."

"Okay. I appreciate your help."

Jill and Tom got back into their car, and Jill immediately called in to get someone to locate Rick Shafer's place at Lake Lavon. When she hung up, her phone immediately rang.

"Finch," she said.

"Detective," Matt said. "Okay, the trial is over."

"It is? How did you manage that?"

"We settled, so the kidnapper should be happy. Maybe he'll let Candy go now."

"I hope you're right, but don't count on it."

"I think he'll let her go," Matt said. "If he doesn't he knows I'll talk."

"But you are talking," Jill noted.

"Right, but he doesn't know that."

"Okay, whatever. Tell me why you are so sure he is the killer."

Matt explained what the lawsuit against RMS was all about and how Lucius Jones had been profiting from the record number of foreclosures over the past few years. Then he briefed her on the situation with Samantha wanting a divorce but trying to time it just right to maximize her final settlement.

"A greedy bunch," Jill noted.

"You got that right," Matt agreed. "Anyway, to summarize, Jones had his finger or one of his relatives' fingers in all the pots—Metro Realty who handled evictions, Prime Holdings who bought the properties that were underwater, Southern Real Estate Investments who bought the properties with equity, Ascot Construction who fixed the properties up for resale, CitiTitle who did the title work, and I don't know about Richmond & Richmond, their law firm, but I wouldn't be surprised if someone in the family worked there."

"Okay, so how does Shafer fit in?"

"Oh, well, you know Rick Shafer was Jones's best friend, right?"

"You said that."

"Well, the strange thing is, he is not involved in any of these affiliated companies that are feeding off RMS's foreclosures. So, why is that?"

"I don't know," Jill confessed. "You're right. It doesn't make sense, unless Shafer is a law-abiding citizen and didn't want any part of it."

Matt laughed. "Yeah, right. No, we thought about it a lot but could never figure it out, but my father finally did. He took some oil and gas classes in law school and had a few clients in the business, which enabled him to make the connection."

"So, what is it?" Jill said impatiently.

"Okay, it turns out there is a company that Rick Shafer and Lucius Jones owned. A company called Seismic Engineering."

"Seismic Engineering?" Jill repeated. "How could that company possibly have anything to do with RMS foreclosures?"

"Right. It was brilliant. . . . Have you ever heard of the Barnett Shale?"

"Sure, a natural gas field in north Texas."

"Right. One of the largest natural gas fields in North America, and it runs right under Fort Worth and the cities around it."

"Uh-huh."

"Well, Chesapeake Energy and its partners have spent several billion dollars developing this field in north Texas, and part of the process is getting thousands of home owners who own property above the shale to sign a lease so Chesapeake can drill its wells and produce the gas. These leases often offer a large signing bonus and then a long-term royalty once production begins. An individual home owner, let's say, might be offered a ten-thousand-dollar signing bonus and then a small percentage royalty on production. The problem is production often doesn't start for five or ten years, so the home owners often sell their interests cheap, cutting the overall market value of the interests dramatically."

"Okay, so how does Seismic Engineering fit in?"

"Seismic Engineering is a company Shafer has owned for years. I guess he was in the seismic engineering business at one time. The company was dormant for years but was reactivated about the time Chesapeake began developing the Barnett Shale. Anyway, Seismic Engineering has been buying any foreclosures that are situated over the Barnett Shale and then flipping them, much like Southern Realty. The only difference being when the properties are sold, Seismic retains the mineral interests."

"Clever," Jill said thoughtfully.

"So, if you make a really conservative estimate of the stream of income from each mineral interest over thirty years, it would be, say, $60,000."

"That much?"

"Well, it's a wild guess, but the people I've talked to say it's on the low side."

"Okay."

"So, take $60,000 over the 887 properties that Seismic has flipped, and you have over $53 million."

Jill was too stunned to respond. Finally she said, "Damn! Okay, that's impressive, but why does that make Rick Shafer the killer?"

"Because Samantha doesn't know about Seismic. This was Lucius Jones's private stash, but it wasn't in his name and he had no intention of disclosing it as an asset in his divorce. He trusted Rick and knew after the divorce Rick would fork over his half of the pot and he'd be set for life. The problem was, in the divorce Lucius Jones would have to lie under oath, and attorneys and accountants would be poring over RMS's books and records if there was a divorce. Do you think Rick wanted that?"

"Probably not," Jill agreed.

"Now, I can't say for sure exactly what motivated Shafer to kill his friend, but I would suspect it was because he realized if Lucius Jones were dead, he'd own the entire $53 million and nobody could challenge him."

"Right. So, he had a 26.5 million dollar motive to kill Lucius. Well, I don't agree that he is definitely the killer, but he does go to the top of the suspect list."

"You think?" Matt said sarcastically.

"So, he kidnapped Candy so you wouldn't bring all this out in court?"

"Exactly. He couldn't afford for Samantha to find out about Seismic. That's why I think he'll let her go now."

"Because if he doesn't, you'll give Samantha a call."

"Now you're with me," Matt said.

"Well good, I hope you're right. In the meantime, we are on our way to Lake Lavon. Apparently Shafer has an old ranch house he bought to stay at when he went fishing."

"Good. You can call me on my cell if you need me."

"Will do," Jill said and hung up.

Tom looked at Jill expectantly. She filled him in on what she'd learned.

"Sounds like a hell of a motive. Why don't you get someone to look at those surveillance tapes we caught Cindy Sharp on? Maybe Rick Shafer's face will show up."

"Good idea," Jill said as she pushed a speed dial number on her cell phone. A moment later she told someone to check the surveillance tape and hung up.

"We've got a lot of unidentified fingerprints at the crime scene," Tom noted. "Maybe we'll get lucky and find one of Shafer's."

"Yeah, but since he's Lucius's best friend I'm sure he goes by the office from time to time. He'll just say he left the prints at an earlier meeting."

"Maybe, but I'm sure the offices are cleaned every night,

so that excuse may not fly."

When they got to Shafer's property at Lake Lavon it appeared deserted. They got out of their car and approached the house warily. Tom looked down at the ground.

"These are fresh tire tracks. Someone has been here today," he said.

"Maybe he picked up his boat and went fishing," Jill speculated, looking over at an outbuilding to her right. "Bet that's where he keeps his boat."

They walked over to the outbuilding. The door was ajar, so they walked in. A spare outboard motor was lying on the ground amid an assortment of engine parts, an old anchor, and a torn life jacket. Tom saw a beer can sitting on a workbench.

"I bet this will have Shafer's fingerprints and maybe some DNA," Tom said.

"Leave it alone; we don't have a search warrant."

"Perhaps we should try to get one," Tom said.

"You're right. It's getting late. Shafer should be getting back pretty soon. I'll get someone working on a search warrant and we can stake the place out until he gets here."

"Right. If we grab him and take him in for questioning before he touches anything, we'll have some good evidence."

"We better call the Collin County Sheriff's office since we don't have jurisdiction out here."

"I'll do that," Tom said, "while you're getting the evidence."

They went back to their car and drove it out of sight where they could see the house but they couldn't be seen. A detective at the sheriff's office agreed to come out and stand by a short distance away in case they were needed. A half hour later the search warrant was issued and an officer was dispatched to bring it out to them. Now it was just a matter of waiting.

Just after dark they heard a vehicle driving up the dirt driveway. As it got closer they saw it was a Ford F-150 towing a Bass Tracker. As the truck got up to the house, Tom turned on the lights and drove up behind the boat, blocking any attempt at an escape. Jill got on the radio and called for backup from the Collin County Sheriff's office. Tom got out and approached the driver's side door warily as a sheriff's car pulled up behind them.

"Police officer! Step out of the car!"

A sheriff's deputy ran up behind Tom, and another joined Jill on the passenger side of the truck. The door slowly opened, and Shafer stepped out with his hands in the air. He was a middle-aged white man of medium build, with thick brown hair and blue eyes.

"What's this about?" Shafer demanded.

"We have a few questions for you about Lucius Jones and Matt Coleman," Tom replied.

"Didn't I talk to you guys a few weeks ago?"

"Yes, you may have," Jill interjected, "but there's been some new developments."

"So, what do you want now? I told you all I know."

"We have a search warrant for your house and outbuildings," she explained. "We're going to search your house first and then ask questions. These deputies will take you to the sheriff's office in McKinney and we'll be there shortly after we are finished with the search."

"A search warrant? What the hell for?"

"We'll explain it all to you at the sheriff's office."

"I want a lawyer," Shafer said.

"We are not arresting you, Mr. Shafer. We just want to ask you a few questions."

"Like what?" Shafer spat.

"Like, do you know where Candace Kane is?"

"Who?"

"Candace Kane. She was abducted this afternoon from a West End restaurant in Dallas."

"I've been fishing all day. I don't know anything about it."

"Was anyone with you?"

354

William Manchee

"Sure, Luke Meyers came along. I dropped him off at his house ten minutes ago."

"Okay, give the sheriff's deputy the information on Luke Meyers and we'll check it out."

"So, is that it?"

"No, I'm afraid not. . . . We have other questions for you, but we want to conduct our search first."

"What are you looking for?"

"Anything to tie you to Ms. Kane's abduction."

"I told you, I didn't have anything to do with it."

"I know. Just hang tight."

The officer took Shafer away, and Jill, Tom, and the remaining sheriff's deputy began searching the premises and the outbuildings. An hour went by and they hadn't found anything relating to Lucius Jones or Seismic Engineering until the sheriff's deputy announced he'd found a pair of shoes with blood spatter on them. Jill rushed over and examined the shoes without touching them. It looked like Shafer had made an attempt to wipe the blood off the outside of the shoes but hadn't noticed that blood had gotten in the seams.

"He should have thrown these in the fire," Jill said, laughing.

"Well, you don't know that it's Jones's blood, or even human blood, for that matter."

"These are shoes you would wear fishing," Jill noted.

"Well, we'll have to see what the crime lab says. In the meantime we better get over and interview Shafer before his lawyer shows up."

Jill nodded, and they left the sheriff's deputy to wait for the crime lab unit to arrive. On the way to the sheriff's office Jill called Matt.

"Hey, we have Shafer, but he claims not to know anything about Candace Kane. He's got an alibi that looks solid, too. I'm sorry."

"Damn!" Matt said. "Who has her, then?"

355

"I don't know. Why don't you drive up to the sheriff's office in McKinney. We could use your help in questioning Shafer about the murder. I know you explained the whole thing to me, but it's pretty complicated. We can also get you with the FBI so they can start looking for your girlfriend."

"Okay. I'm on my way," Matt said and hung up.

When Tom and Jill got to the sheriff's office, they were told Rick Shafer was in an interview room waiting for them. Jill went in first while Tom and the sheriff's deputy watched from the viewing room. Shafer sat up when Jill came in and sat down.

"Finally. I've been here over an hour."

"I'm sorry, Mr. Shafer, but I wanted to thoroughly search your house before I talked to you."

"You didn't find anything, did you?"

"Not much," Jill said, not wanting to alarm Shafer and have him clam up.

"You talked about a lawyer earlier, so I presume you know your rights."

Shafer nodded.

"You have the right to remain silent; if you talk to us everything you say can and will be used against you should charges be brought. You have the right to an attorney and if you cannot afford an attorney, one will be provided for you."

"I've got several attorneys, and if I need more I can get them."

"Well, your alibi seems to check out. So, you're in the clear on the Candace Kane kidnapping."

"You're damn right I'm in the clear. I've never heard of the woman."

"We have some more questions about Lucius Jones's murder, though."

"Like what? I told you all I know."

"Well, at the time we were just gathering information, but now we have some concerns that you might be involved."

"Me? That's ridiculous. Lucius was my best friend."

"I know. Where were you on the day he was murdered?"

Shafer was silent a moment. "I don't know. Let me think.
. . . I was on my way home from a closing in Dallas."

"On one of your Seismic Engineering acquisitions?"

Shafer gave Jill a cold stare. "How did you know about Seismic?"

"I'll ask the questions, Mr. Shafer, if you don't mind."

"Okay."

"So, when did the closing end?"

"I don't know, three or three thirty."

"So, where did you go after the closing?"

"Home. I wanted to beat the traffic."

"How far away was the closing from Lucius Jones's office?"

He shrugged. "Ten minutes."

"So, you didn't stop in to say hello?"

"Ah. No. Like I said, I went straight home."

Jill gave Shafer a hard look, trying to see if she could unnerve him, but he just looked right back at her with cold eyes. She felt good that he didn't seem to have an alibi and was admittedly close by Jones's office just before the murder. She just needed something to force him into a corner so he'd make a mistake.

"So, tell me about Seismic Engineering. How long have you owned it?"

"Oh, God, forever. I formed it when I first got out of law school and was doing seismic testing out in west Texas."

"Do you still do that kind of work?"

"No. Oil prices dropped and drill activity came to a screeching halt, so I had to come up with another way to make a living."

"Hmm. So, what does Seismic do now?"

"I buy foreclosed properties from RMS, Lucius's company, fix them up, and then sell them."

"Was Lucius a part owner?"

"No. It's always been my baby."

"So, do you have to bid at the foreclosure sales?"

"Right."

"Do you ever have anyone bidding against you?"

"Not often. It's hard for people to bid on this property because they have to come in with cash or have financing already lined up."

"So how do you know what to bid?" Jill asked.

"Lucius would call me and tell me what it would take to acquire the property. Then I'd attend the foreclosure sale."

"How much have you made over the years buying houses from RMS?"

Shafer's eyes narrowed. "I don't know. Not that much. I'm mainly worried about losing money."

"So, why do it, then?"

"I don't know. I make enough money to make it worthwhile, but I'm not going to get rich."

"What about the oil royalties?"

Shafer's mouth dropped. He squirmed in his chair but said nothing.

"We know you have hundreds of mineral interests you've retained."

"So? That's not a crime the last I checked."

"What do you think Samantha would say about it?"

"Don't you dare tell that bitch. Seismic has nothing to do with her."

"You were worried about her finding out about Seismic, weren't you?"

"Of course I was. She's one greedy bitch, but it's my property and she has nothing to do with it."

"So, you couldn't take a chance on her finding out. Is that why you killed Lucius?"

"No. I didn't kill him. Why in the hell would I do that?"

"Because he was the only one who knew half of Seismic belonged to him. It was his stash in case she took him to the cleaners."

"No. No way. That's my business. That's my money."

"You know we've found your prints in Jones's office," Jill lied.

"So? I go there all the time."

"But we've checked, and the night janitors claim they wipe everything clean each night."

"Yeah. Of course they'd say that. What do you expect them to say, they do a half-assed job?"

"Did you plan to kill him or was it a spur-of-the-moment thing?"

"I didn't kill him!" Shafer protested. "He was my best friend."

"But he'd never cut you in on anything before. Only when he needed to hide money from his wife did he give you a piece of the action. That must have pissed you off, huh?"

Shafer face was red now with anger. Jill pressed on.

"We know you went to his office. A surveillance camera at the bank down the street caught you heading for his office," Jill lied again.

Shafer stiffened. He looked down, and his breathing became heavy. He began to sweat.

"So, were you two arguing about the divorce? Did he want you to do something for him? Give him some of the royalty money? What happened? Tell me. I'm going to find out sooner or later. Rich Coleman and his son have already figured it out. Matt will be here any minute to explain it all."

Shafer took a deep breath and shook his head. "Those bastards! God damn them. Okay, okay. Lucius wanted me to set up an offshore company in both our names and then transfer all the mineral interests to it. He said it would be safer, but I knew once it was in that offshore company somehow he'd figure a way to steal it from me. I told him no. I liked it right where it was."

"But he insisted?"

"Yeah. And I knew once he got his mind set on

Unconscionable

something there was no fighting him, so I had no choice."

"You figured nobody would know about Seismic if he were dead."

He chuckled, his eyes glazing over. "Yeah. That's right."

"So, you killed him?"

He nodded. "I saw the letter opener. So I picked it up and held it at my side so he wouldn't see it. Then I told him I'd go ahead and transfer the mineral interests. He was happy that I had relented and went over to fix us a drink. While his back was turned I came up from behind and stuck the letter opener through his neck. He gasped in pain, and blood came rushing out of his mouth. After I wiped the handle of the letter opener clean, I left and went home. I didn't think about surveillance cameras."

"Because you hadn't planned the murder in advance."

"Right. He forced my hand."

"Well, that's good. The court might be more lenient since it was a spur-of-the-moment thing."

Jill signaled to Tom, and he came in and cuffed Shafer. "You're under arrest for the murder of Lucius Jones." Tom turned Shafer over to the sheriff's deputy, who took him to a holding cell.

"Nicely done!" Tom said.

Jill smiled. "Yes, thanks to Matt and Rich Coleman. They did have it all figured out after all."

Chapter 35
Square One

When Matt got to the office Melissa advised him the phone had been ringing off the hook. The press wanted to know why he had bailed out of the RMS case when he was doing so well. He ignored those calls and got Detective Finch on the line. After he'd told her his theory of who had killed Lucius Jones he hung up. Melissa wanted to know what was going on, so he told her but cautioned her not to talk to anybody about it.

"I'm going up to McKinney to help Detective Finch out with her questioning of Rick Shafer and then talk to the FBI."

"Do you have any idea who has Candy?" Melissa asked.

Matt sighed. "No, I don't. I really thought Shafer had her. Now we're back to square one."

"Well, if I can do anything, let me know."

"I will. Thanks," Matt said, picking up his briefcase on the way out the door. "I'll call you if anything develops."

Matt left his office and went to the elevator. When he got to the first floor he walked past the security desk.

"Have a good day, Mr. Coleman," the guard said.

"Thanks. See you later."

Matt strolled through the sliding door that led to the parking garage and headed toward his car. Just as he emerged into the garage he saw movement to his right. Suddenly, a car lurched forward toward him with tires screeching. He froze momentarily but just as the car was about to hit him, he jumped out of its path. As the car went by it slowed, and he saw a man point a gun at him. Instinctively he raised his briefcase as a shield as three quick shots rained down on him. The first two hit the briefcase and he felt it slam against his chest. The final shot hit him in his arm as he fell to the ground. Tires squealed again as the assailant made his escape.

A second later the security guard came running around the corner. He saw Matt lying on the ground and ran over to him.

"Mr. Coleman! Are you all right?"

Matt felt excruciating pain coming from his arm and saw blood gushing from the wound. "My arm. I've been shot."

The guard pulled up Matt's sleeve and took a handkerchief from his pocket and used it as a bandage to stop the bleeding. "I'll call 911," he said as he whipped out his cell phone and hit the three digits. A moment later he hung up. "An ambulance should be here shortly. I heard three shots. Did the others miss?"

Matt nodded toward his briefcase. There were two large bullet holes two-thirds of the way down one side.

"What did you have in there that stopped those bullets, lead?"

"No. A book. *O'Connor's Texas Evidence*. It's pretty thick, thank God."

There was a siren in the distance, and soon an ambulance and fire truck arrived. A minute later two police cars pulled up. The ambulance took Matt to Medical City's emergency room and rolled him into a room. A nurse came in and took his vitals, and a moment later a doctor arrived.

The doctor looked at Matt's chart and then examined the wound. "You were lucky. The bullet went clear through without hitting any bones or muscles. A couple of arteries were severed. That's why you had all the bleeding, but it should heal okay."

"Good," Matt said, feeling a little relieved.

The doctor examined Matt's chest. There were dark bruises from where the briefcase had slammed into him. "What caused this?" he asked.

"Two shots hit my briefcase. Luckily I had a thick book inside that stopped the bullets."

"It's a good thing. If you hadn't had the briefcase, one of those bullets could have hit your heart and you'd be dead."

Matt swallowed hard. "Yeah. That's what I figured."

"So, do you know who shot you?"

Matt shrugged. "No. I don't."

As they were talking a well-dressed woman strolled in. She flashed her badge. "Matt Coleman?"

Matt nodded. "Yes."

"I'm Detective Alice Longoria."

"Right," Matt said, recognizing the pretty detective.

The doctor excused himself and left the room.

"You know who I am?" Detective Longoria asked.

"Yes. You're handling my dad's prosecution."

"Right. So, who shot you? Did you get a look at them?"

Matt shook his head. "No. All I saw was a late-model, dark blue Lexus coming at me fast. I jumped out of the way as the car passed by and saw a man stick a gun out of the driver's side window and point it at me. All I could think to do was use the briefcase as a shield, and fortunately, it took two of the bullets. I did get a partial plate number."

"Really? What was it?"

"DTR. I don't know what the numbers were. The DTR stuck out because I used to be a bankruptcy lawyer and 'DTR' stood for debtor."

"Okay. I'll call that partial in. Any idea who would want you dead?"

"I could think of a few candidates," Matt said. "As you probably know, I've just concluded a rather contentious lawsuit."

"But you settled it, right? That's what they said on the news."

"I did, but not by choice," Matt advised and then filled Detective Longoria in on the events of the day.

"So, the kidnapper decided he couldn't trust you, huh?"

"That would be my guess, although I followed his instructions to the letter. I just hope he hasn't killed Candy. She knew nothing."

"I'll call up to McKinney and explain what happened here to Detective Finch. Maybe they'll send somebody over here from the FBI."

Matt shook his head. "I'll die if anything happens to Candy. My wife was murdered two years ago. I couldn't take another loss like that."

"Candy means a lot to you?"

"Yes. I didn't realize how much until now."

Detective Longoria nodded and gave him a sympathetic smile. "I know, I followed your trial. It must have been excruciating for you to lose your wife after only a few months of marriage."

Matt took a deep breath, trying to maintain his composure. When the detective had left the room, Matt closed his eyes and tried to relax, but couldn't manage it. His body felt as if it had collided with a buffalo at full gallop. He had no energy and his mind was in a fog. Eventually he dozed off, but his slumber didn't last long. Footsteps woke him.

"Matt. Are you all right?" Ryan asked nervously.

Matt smiled. "Yeah. I'm fine. My arm is messed up a bit, but it will heal."

"Good. I almost died when I heard you'd been shot. Who do you think did it?"

Matt shrugged. "I didn't get a good look at him. Probably the same guy who kidnapped Candy."

"Man. First Candy and now you. I can't believe this."

The door opened again, and two well-dressed men walked in. They flashed their FBI badges.

"Matt Coleman. I'm Special Agent Ralph Rule and this is Special Agent Art Ramirez."

"Hi," Matt said. "Any word on Candy?"

"No. We've just been called in on the case. We need to ask you some questions."

"Okay. No problem."

Matt and Ryan filled them in on the trial and kidnapping and gave them the long list of persons who might have wanted to shut them up.

"Okay. We'll get out to the restaurant and canvass the area. Perhaps someone saw something. In the meantime I'll have Candy's picture released to the media. Perhaps somebody has seen her today."

"I'll give a hundred-thousand-dollar reward to anybody who provides information that leads to her safe recovery."

Agent Rule nodded. "Okay. I'll advise the media."

Agents Rule and Ramirez left, and Matt closed his eyes again. Ryan sat down in a chair and rubbed his temples.

Matt opened his eyes. "Samantha Jones has to be behind this," he said. "She's the only person with so much to lose that she'd do something this brash."

"How do you figure? She was at the trial all day."

"She must have hired someone. She wouldn't have done it herself."

"Well, if she did it would be a professional," Ryan said. "And I wouldn't have a clue how to figure out who that would be."

"But I know someone who might," Matt said thoughtfully.

"Your buddy from prison?"

"Right. Eduardo might be able to make inquiries in his circles and find out who hired a hit man to kill me."

"So, why don't you call him?"

"Get me my cell phone."

Ryan fumbled through Matt's personal belongings that had been shoved into a plastic bag and found his cell phone. He handed it to Matt, and a minute later Matt had Eduardo on the phone.

"Hey, man. I heard on the news someone tried to take you out. What's up?"

Matt gave him a brief rundown of what had happened.

"So, I need you to check with your sources and see if there are any rumors on the street about who put a hit out on me. It's probably the same guy who kidnapped my girlfriend."

"Sure. Anything for you, Matt."

"There's a hundred-grand reward to the first person who tracks the bastard down."

"Then I better get working. I'll get back with you."

"Thanks, Eduardo. Talk to you later."

A few hours later Matt was released from the hospital, and he and Ryan went to Candy's place to be with the girls until there was some word on Candy. Sharon, Gina, Jenni, and Mia were all sitting in the den teary eyed and obviously worried about Candy. Sharon jumped up when she saw Matt looking beat up and wearing an arm sling.

"What happened to you?" Sharon said, examining his arm.

"The bastard tried to kill me," Matt explained.

"Oh, my God!" Jenni moaned. "Are you all right?"

"Yeah. I was lucky. The bullet passed right through without hitting anything critical."

"Oh, geez!" Gina said. "Does it hurt?"

Matt nodded. "Yeah, it's kind of throbbing right now."

"So, has the FBI turned up anything?" Sharon asked.

"No. Not yet," Matt said and then brought them up to date on the investigation.

Matt's cell phone rang. He answered it deftly with one hand. It was Eduardo. "Hello."

"Matt. Okay. There was word on the street yesterday that someone was looking for an assassin and willing to pay top dollar for a kidnapping-murder."

Matt's heard sank. "Kidnapping-murder?"

"Right. That means it's got to look like a kidnapping but it's understood that there's not going to be any ransom. The target is grabbed, taken to a designated location, and killed."

"Shit! Any idea who picked up the job?"

William Manchee

"Yes. The word has it that a Cuban known as 'Cork' picked it up."

"Cork?"

"Yeah. Like on a bottle of champagne. If you saw him, you'd see the name fits."

"Okay. Where does this guy usually hang out?"

"There are a couple of bars he frequents from time to time, but he hasn't been seen since yesterday evening."

"Give me the names of the bars. That will be a place for the FBI to start looking."

"No, man. No FBI. No one who knows anything will talk to the feds. Meet me at Club Babalu on McKinney Avenue and we'll find your man."

"Okay. It will be about twenty minutes."

"See you then," Eduardo said.

Matt told Ryan what Eduardo had said and that they were supposed to meet him in twenty minutes.

"But this guy has already tried to kill you. Do you think we ought to be chasing after him?"

"We have to. We've got to find Candy."

"I know, but this is a job for the FBI."

"Eduardo said these people won't talk to the FBI. Plus Eduardo has a crew that won't let anything happen to us."

Ryan sighed. "Okay, let's go."

"Be careful," Sharon said. "Don't do anything stupid."

"Don't worry," Matt said. "I don't have a death wish."

When they got to the club, Eduardo was sitting on the hood of his car. Several of his men were with him. He got up when Matt approached him. They exchanged greetings.

"So, what do we do now?" Matt asked.

"We go inside and see if Cork is there. If not, we start asking people if they have seen him."

"Fine. Let's go."

The club was crowded, and the Latin music was deafening. Eduardo approached a group of guys and asked what

367

was up. After a little small talk he got to the point.

"So, you guys seen Cork here tonight?"

A couple of the guys shook their heads. One of them said, "No, haven't seen him for a couple of days."

"Hmm. My friends here need to talk to him. Any idea where he might be tonight?"

They all shook their heads. Eduardo thanked them and repeated the exercise with several other groups of patrons that he knew. Finally, they hit pay dirt.

"Yeah, Cork has a loft off Central near Citiplace."

Eduardo got directions, and Matt and Ryan followed him back out to the parking lot.

"Okay, so now you call the FBI," Eduardo said. "And if you find your girl you owe me a hundred grand."

Matt smiled. "No problem. I hope tomorrow I'm writing you a check, believe me."

Eduardo and his friends left, and Matt called Special Agent Ralph Rule.

"Hey, this is Matt Coleman. I've got a lead on Candy's kidnapper. He's a professional hit man who goes by the name of Cork. Word has it he accepted a contract on Candy and me a day or two ago."

"How did you find this out?"

"Well, I'm sure you know I was a guest at the federal prison at Texarkana for over a year. While I was there I developed a few contacts."

"Right. Okay. Got an address?"

"Yes," Matt said and then gave him the address and directions how to get there.

"Got it. We'll meet you there in ten minutes. Just stay in your car. Don't approach the place."

"Okay. We'll wait for you," Matt assured him.

Matt and Ryan beat the FBI to the location and parked across the street in front of an abandoned auto repair shop. It was old, run down, and dark inside. As Matt was looking the place over he heard a car pull up behind them. It was Agents Rule and Ramirez. Matt got out and walked back to their car. Rule and Ramirez got out and looked up at the three-story warehouse building that had been converted into lofts.

"Our team should be here in a few minutes," Agent Rule said. "We should have a warrant by then and we can go ahead on in."

A few moments later, three more cars drove up and an FBI SWAT team emerged. One of the agents came over and handed Rule his warrant.

"I'll deploy my men around the building, and then on your word we'll go in."

Agent Rule put his finger to his earpiece. "Just got confirmation there is a 2009 Lexus in the back parking lot with a partial plate number of DTR."

"He's here!" Matt exclaimed.

Rule nodded, and the SWAT team began swarming the building. A few moments later Rule and Ramirez went to the front door and went in while Matt and Ryan watched from across the street. After a while there were shouts and screams from the building. Then there was gunfire. Finally, several minutes later agents began coming out of the building. Several persons in handcuffs were put into an FBI van that had suddenly appeared. When Ramirez came out he went over to them.

"We got your guy, but there is no sign of Candy."

"Damn it! Where in the hell could she be?"

"I don't know, and he's lawyered up, so I doubt he's going to tell us anything."

Matt shook his head in despair. Then he took another look at the abandoned auto repair shop.

"You know," Matt said, "this old building would be a convenient place to stash someone."

Agent Ramirez pondered that idea a minute and then motioned for one of the other agents to come over. They talked a moment and then walked toward the building. Matt and Ryan followed them at a distance.

The door was nailed shut, but the wood was rotted, and one hard pull and it opened. The two agents pulled their Glock 17s and plunged into the darkness. After they yelled "Clear," Matt and Ryan followed them in.

It was dark but enough light filtered in so they could see fairly well. Matt heard the two agents go upstairs after they'd cleared the bottom floor, so he and Ryan walked around the bottom floor looking for any place someone could be locked away. Then Matt heard a faint pounding sound. He stopped Ryan.

"Listen."

The faint sound was like the steady beat of a drum. Matt began to move toward the sound until he almost fell into a oil-changing well. He looked around and found a ladder that went down into the well. As he quickly descended the stairs, the sound got louder and his pulse quickened. Finally he realized the noise was coming from a locked closet. Looking around for something to pry open the door, he spotted a rusty screwdriver and picked it up. Adrenaline pumping, he attacked the lock with brutal force until it gave way, and then ripped open the door to reveal Candy, tied and gagged.

"Oh, my God! It's Candy!" he screamed.

Matt carefully pulled off the gag, tears flowing down his cheeks.

"Oh, Candy. Are you all right?"

Candy gave Matt a weak smile, nodded, and then passed out.

"Get Agent Ramirez!" Matt ordered. "We need an ambulance!"

Soon Agent Ramirez was on the scene, and he helped Matt bring Candy out of the well. A siren could be heard in the distance.

"Is she going to be all right?" Ryan asked.

Matt nodded. "I think so. She's weak—probably dehydrated."

Matt rode in the ambulance to Presbyterian Hospital, thanking God for Candy's safe return. By the time they got to the hospital Candy had awakened and seemed better. Matt figured the oxygen and IV that was running were working and was optimistic that Candy would have no permanent physical injury. Mental anguish was another story. He'd had plenty of experience with that and knew that type of injury took years to overcome.

Within a week the settlement agreement and check for $500,000 arrived at Matt's office. After reading it and not finding anything too onerous contained in it, he called Cindy and had her come in to approve and sign it. It bothered him that they'd let RMS off so cheaply, but since Candy was now safe and Cindy Sharp had enough money to keep her off the streets for a few years, he had no regrets. That didn't mean he had given up on linking Cork to Samantha Jones, however. In fact, he could hardly think of anything else. Who had hired him? He figured it must have been Samantha Jones, but how would he prove it? She was a smart woman and probably hadn't left any kind of a trail to link her to Cork, but he vowed somehow she'd pay for what she had done.

As promised, his father finally called to report that they were settled in for a long exile somewhere in South America. Matt was pretty sure he knew where they were but didn't say anything in case the phone was being tapped. While Rich was on the phone he asked him for advice on how to prove Samantha had ordered a hit man.

"A kidnapping and hit like that would be expensive. I would bet she wired the money to an offshore bank account."

"Do you think a guy like Cork would have an offshore account?"

"Oh, most definitely. Assassins like to remain anonymous, so they don't like meetings and they don't want briefcases full of cash. An offshore bank account is almost a given."

"Well, the next time I talk to the FBI I'll mention that to

them."

"I'm sure they have already looked into that and came up empty," Rich said. "I'd guess a guy like Cork would have a business partner or broker who handled the money. What you need to do is find out who that is and give that information to the FBI. Then they will have something to work with."

Matt thought about the FBI and wondered if they were making any progress at their end. He hadn't heard from anybody at the FBI since the night they'd captured Cork. He figured since Candy had been found and was safe, nabbing the kidnapper wasn't a high priority anymore. So he decided it was time to turn up the heat on the investigation, and he knew exactly how to do it.

Chapter 36
Payback

When the Candy Kane kidnapping broke, Detective Alice Longoria volunteered to be the DPD liaison to the FBI. She had been stymied in her investigation of the Martha Collins murder when Rich and Erica Coleman disappeared. Besides being an interesting case, she thought since the victim was Matt Coleman's girlfriend that working the kidnapping might give her an opportunity to get a lead on Rich Coleman's whereabouts.

After Candy had been rescued and Esteban Corvallis, a.k.a. Cork, had been arrested for the kidnapping of Candy Kane and the attempted murder of Matt Coleman, the only remaining task was to find out who had hired him. One of Matt Coleman's contacts had supplied the identity of the hit man and whoever it was had even managed to provide an address. Longoria wondered if Matt's contact could also help them find out who had paid for the hit and kidnapping. One day she stopped by Matt's office and asked him.

"Okay. I'll call my guy. I've already paid him a hundred grand for helping me recover Candy, so I'm sure he won't mind snooping around a little bit more for me."

"That was incredibly generous of you," Longoria said.

"Well, I couldn't let anything happen to Candy."

Matt put his phone on speaker and called Eduardo.

"Eduardo, Matt here."

"Hey my man, what's up?"

"I've got Detective Longoria here with me."

There was silence. "Okay. Hi, Detective."

"Eduardo. What's your last name?" Longoria asked.

"Just Eduardo. I don't use a last name."

"The detective wanted to thank you again for helping get Candy back alive," Matt explained.

"Not a problem. I have been well paid for my assistance and I'm enjoying the fruits of my labor immensely."

"What did you buy?" Matt asked.

"A monster truck. Gonna start racing."

Matt laughed. "A monster truck?"

"Right. You should come out and watch me race, man."

"Yeah. Sounds like a blast. . . . Hey, I've been talking to ah, . . . people, and apparently these assassins like Cork often have a broker or middle man who handles the contracts and the money. Can you check around and see if Cork has a guy like that?"

"Sure. Shouldn't be a problem. I'll ask around."

"Great. Good luck at the races."

"Oh, ah . . . Eduardo," Detective Longoria said. "I could use someone like you as a CI. We'd pay top dollar and you could stack up some bonus points in case anybody in your crew got in trouble."

Eduardo laughed. "No thanks, senorita. I only help my friends, and I wouldn't do it for money. I would have helped Matt gratis, but he insisted on paying me, so what the fuck, right?"

Detective Longoria frowned. "All right. Just thought I'd ask."

"Thanks Eduardo, catch you later," Matt said.

Matt pushed the disconnect and looked over at Detective Longoria angrily. "Why in the hell did you do that? That was insulting."

"Sorry," Longoria said. "Just thought . . ."

Detective Longoria couldn't believe Eduardo had blown a hundred grand on a monster truck. A hundred grand was more than her annual salary. She imagined what she would buy with a hundred grand but then caught herself. She wondered how else she could find Cork's manager, so she asked Matt if he had any ideas.

"Sally Sterns, Samantha's receptionist. She doesn't like Samantha much, so she might be inclined to talk. Let me call someone and see if she knows how we might contact her without alerting Samantha. We can't call her direct because all the calls at RMS are monitored and recorded."

Matt dialed Shelly's number with the phone on speaker.

"Hello?"

"Shelly?"

"Yes."

"This is Matt. I've got Detective Longoria here with me. Does your friend Sally ever hang out somewhere after work where the detective and I could meet with her?"

"She goes for happy hour at Friday's every Thursday night. I'm sure you can catch her there."

"Oh. Perfect. Thanks for the info. How have you been doing?"

"Fine. I got a new job as customer service representative for an online computer retailer."

"Good. That sounds less dangerous than your work at RMS."

"Yeah. Tell me about it. Now I can sleep at night."

"Listen, the FBI is working this case with Detective Longoria, so I'm sure she would put in a good word for you to the FBI if you can help out in any way."

"Sure, anything I can do just let me know."

"Yes, of course," Detective Longoria assured her.

Matt hung up and put the phone in his pocket.

"I'd like the FBI to put the screws to Samantha and RMS," Matt said. "They've broken a lot of laws and now have tried to kill me and Candy to try to keep it covered up. Shelly can provide you with plenty of evidence to shut them down. I'd suggest you get the FBI to cut a deal with her to make that happen."

"What kind of deal?" Longoria asked warily.

Unconscionable

"Just immunity. She was going to quit RMS when she found out about their illegal activity, but I asked her to stay on to provide me information. She was invaluable in getting a settlement with them."

"Okay. I'll talk to Agents Rule and Ramirez about it. I doubt they'd have a problem with it."

"Good," Matt said.

The following Thursday Matt and Detective Longoria walked into Friday's on Greenville Avenue a few minutes before happy hour began. They took a booth that gave them a good vantage point of the front entrance to the restaurant. Matt ordered a cup of coffee and Longoria got a Diet Coke. Fifteen minutes later Matt saw Sally come in with several other women. After they were situated and had downed their first drink, Matt strolled by and feigned surprise at seeing her.

"Sally! Hey. Nice to see you."

Sally crinkled her nose a moment until recognition came. "Ah. Matt, right?"

"Yeah. How are you?"

"Fine, now that I have escaped the evil headquarters of the Queen Bee."

Matt laughed. "I trust none of your companions escaped with you."

Sally shook her head. "No. These are old friends from NAS. They were smarter than I was when the split up came along."

Matt nodded. "I see. Hey, if you have a minute I have some news I know you'll want to hear and someone I want you to meet. It will just take a minute."

Sally's eyes widened. "Really? Is it classified or can my friends listen in?"

"Well, it's classified for now, but you can fill them in later when the time is right."

"Okay. I'll be right back, girls," she said and followed Matt back to his booth. She sat down next to him and smiled at Detective Longoria. Matt introduced them.

"So, what's the big news?" Sally asked.

"Well, Detective Longoria believes Samantha might have ordered the hit on me and my girlfriend."

Sally nodded, not seeming to be shocked by the idea. "So, what makes you think that?"

Longoria leaned forward. "Well, from what Matt tells me, she had the greatest motive to want him out of the picture. He was about to expose her illegal activity when Candy was kidnapped and he was forced to prematurely settle the case."

"I wondered about that. She was scared to death Matt was going to hammer RMS, but then all of a sudden it was over."

"Right," Matt said. "So, what we need from you is help in finding out who she hired to do the hit."

"I'm afraid I wouldn't know. She doesn't confide in me."

"Right. I didn't figure you would know anything consciously but you may still have valuable information."

"How's that?"

"Well, she would have had to pay the assassin's handler a large sum of money. It would have probably been wire transferred to an offshore account."

Sally thought a moment and then said, "She uses North Dallas Bank for her wire transfers. She's got quite a few different accounts there. I know because I disburse the mail and I've seen the statements come in."

"Has she got her statements for last month yet?"

"No. They start coming in about the fifth of the month. She must get six or eight different ones."

"Okay. I'll have the FBI look into it," Longoria said.

"You're working with the FBI?"

"Yes. They have jurisdiction over kidnapping cases so they're leading the investigation."

"So, is Samantha going to be arrested?"

"I don't know," Longoria replied. "There's not enough evidence yet to prove she hired the kidnapper, but we are working hard to get it."

"Good. I hope she goes down for it."

"So, you'll help us get the evidence we need to do that?" Longoria asked.

"Oh, yes. That would be a dream come true."

They all laughed.

"Can you call me later with the names on those bank accounts and the numbers?"

"Sure, you got a card?"

"Yes," Longoria said and dug a card out of her purse.

"It won't be until the fifth of the month. I don't have access to them except for a few hours from when I get the mail and Samantha picks it up."

"How are you going to get the account numbers from sealed envelopes?" Matt asked.

Sally smiled. "Leave that to me. I had a big sister and I'm an expert at steaming open envelopes."

They all laughed as they got up and said their good-byes. Longoria thanked Matt for his help and went back to her car. Before she started the engine she called Special Agent Ramirez.

"Agent. This is Detective Longoria."

"Oh. Hi, Detective. What can I do for you?"

"I've got a couple of leads for you. Can we meet?"

The next morning Longoria, Rule, and Ramirez met for breakfast at Denny's off LBJ Freeway in North Dallas. The waitress brought them coffee and took their orders.

"So, why are you working this case?" Rule asked irritably. "You know you don't have jurisdiction."

"I know, and I'm not trying to tread on your territory, but I've been using this kidnapping as an excuse to spend time with Matt Coleman. I'm hoping I might get a lead on his father's whereabouts."

"Hmm," Rule grunted. "So, why are we meeting now?"

"Excuse Ralph," Ramirez said, shaking his head. "He's a little grumpy before he has his first cup of coffee."

"It's all right. . . . Anyway, I suggested to Matt that he get his friend Eduardo to check into who might have been brokering Cork's hits."

"What makes you think he had someone handling his hits?"

"Well, Matt thought so. He didn't say why, but I suspect he's been talking to his father."

"Right," Ramirez agreed. "His father's been around the block a few times. I understood he parlayed $50,000 into a million dollars in less than a year."

"Right. So, anyway Eduardo said he would check into it."

"Good. So, let us know how that works out," Rule said skeptically.

"That's not all," Longoria quickly added, now getting annoyed at Rule's attitude."

"Drink your coffee, for godsakes," Ramirez said. "Sorry, Detective. Go on."

Longoria took a deep breath. "Anyway, Matt thinks Samantha Jones ordered the hit on him, and he took me to meet the receptionist at RMS, Sally Sterns. She hates Samantha and agreed to cooperate with you guys. In fact, in a few days she's going to call me with the names of a half dozen or so companies that Samantha and RMS control."

"We already have all that," Rule spat.

"She's giving banking information and account numbers, too," Longoria added.

Agent Rule raised his eyebrows. "Really?"

"Yes, so if you can be bothered, I wanted to pass that information on to you. Matt thinks there may have been a wire transfer from one of the accounts to pay Cork for the kidnapping and the hit."

"That's excellent," Ramirez said. "Call me the minute you get that information and we'll check it out."

Unconscionable

"Good. I'll do that," Longoria said and sat back.

The waitress brought their orders and they all began eating. Longoria wasn't pleased with the FBI's attitude. In fact, she'd suddenly lost her appetite. Ramirez, noting that she wasn't eating, sighed.

"Listen, Detective. We appreciate your help on this investigation. In fact, I for one welcome it. Our supervisor gave us a good chewing out for not making as much progress as he had expected. You'd think the fact that we captured Cork would make him happy, but he wants the person who ordered the hit."

Longoria leaned forward. "Well, maybe I can help you get him off your back."

"How's that?" Ramirez asked.

"You know Coleman was investigating RMS and was about to expose not only considerable fraudulent activity but also some serious criminal conspiracies."

Ramirez nodded. "He mentioned that when he talked to us."

"Well, did he tell you he had a mole in RMS who knows the intimate details of what was going on and is prepared to testify in exchange for immunity?"

"Seriously?" Rule said, now keenly interested.

"Yes, he called her, a Shelly Simms, and she's agreed to cooperate. Apparently she knows a lot about RMS and a company called CDR and their principals Ross, Rubio, and Stafford. CDR is nothing short of a forgery mill, from what I understand."

"Is that right?" Ramirez said. "I've heard about them. That would be nice to take down one of those operations."

"So, can I tell Matt you're in?"

"Let us check with the US attorney's office and we we'll get back with you."

"Okay. Let me know."

When Longoria got back to the office she was surprised to have a phone message from Joe Weston. She wondered what he could want. She'd tried to talk to him several times, but each time he'd refused, citing advice of counsel. She wondered what had changed. He picked up on the second ring.

"Hello."

"Joe Weston?"

"Yes."

"Detective Longoria returning your call."

"Oh hi, Detective. Thanks for returning my call."

"No problem. Does your attorney know you've called me?"

"Yes. He advised me against it, but I just can't do this anymore."

"What do you mean?"

"Not over the phone. Can I come to your office?"

"Sure. You know where it is?"

"Yes. I'll be there in about twenty minutes."

Longoria hung up the phone, wondering what was up. Had Coleman contacted Weston? *Is he finally going to do the right thing and help them bring him in?* she wondered. Thirty minutes later he walked into her office. He looked pale and disheveled, like he hadn't slept in a while. She cleared off a chair for him to sit in.

"Are you all right? You don't look so good."

"I haven't been able to sleep ever since someone kidnapped Matt Coleman's girlfriend and then tried to kill him."

Longoria nodded. "Right. Well, that's understandable. You were friends with his father."

Weston sighed heavily, tears welling in his eyes. "Yes, and he needed his father and mother, but because of me he didn't have them."

"What do you mean? I don't understand."

"Because I'm a coward, they've had to run to God knows where to keep from being prosecuted for something they didn't do."

"You're telling me neither one of them killed Martha Collins?"

"Yes, that's exactly what I'm telling you."

"So, do you know who did it, then?"

"Yes . . . It was me! I killed Martha Collins."

Longoria's mouth opened. She tried to say something but nothing came out. Finally she said, "Okay, let's go into an interview room and you can tell me all about it."

Longoria ushered Joe Weston into an empty interview room and then went to get Lt. Edmonton. When she related Joe's confession he came to watch the interview. A moment later she took a seat opposite Joe.

"So, Mr. Weston. I must advise you that you have the right to remain silent. Anything you say will be used against you in a court of law should you be charged with a criminal act. You have the right to an attorney. If you can't afford an attorney, one will be provided for you. Do you understand your rights?"

"Yes."

"And you have an attorney but you are choosing not to have him present for this interview, is that correct?"

"Yes. I don't need an attorney."

"Okay, then. Why don't you tell us about the night Martha Collins was murdered."

Joe took a deep breath and began his confession. "Martha Collins had called Peter, Rich's boss, looking for Erica. Peter in turn called me and asked me if Rich and Erica had returned from Barbados yet.

"I was surprised by the call, because their affair was supposed to be secret. Peter shouldn't have known they were on vacation together. I asked him what made him think they were together, and he told me he had just returned from Barbados himself and knew they were having an affair.

"This upset me because I'd known for a long time about the affair and actually handled Erica's trust account. If Peter found out about the very risky trades we had been making, he would have had a stroke and probably filed a complaint against me with the SEC.

"Peter told me that Aunt Martha was looking for Erica and was on her way over to her apartment. I knew of Aunt Martha's reputation and feared she would likely try to break in if Erica wasn't home, so I decided to try to intercept her.

"Unfortunately, when I got there she was already inside and had called the police. When the police came she talked with them awhile and then they left. Continuing to watch, I saw her take several boxes of records out of the apartment and load them into her car. I knew the brokerage statements were most likely in one of the boxes and if she went through them she'd discover the risky trades Rich was making.

"I assumed she'd already figured out the two of them were living together. The situation was unbearable. I had to do something but wasn't sure what it should be. When Aunt Martha drove away I followed her all the way back to her motel.

"After she'd moved everything from the trunk of her car to the motel room, I decided to knock on her door and confront her. I thought perhaps I could reason with her and get her to voluntarily return Rich's records. Unfortunately, she was belligerent and completely irrational. The more I tried to reason with her, the more intransigent she became. Finally, I got so frustrated I decided to just go inside and take the records from her.

"So, I forced my way inside and tried to haul off the biggest of the three boxes full of files and records. That's when she began hitting me and screaming bloody murder. When she realized I was too strong for her, she said she was going to call the police and tell them I had tried to rape her.

"That really scared me. I'd heard of men's lives being torn apart by a false accusation of rape. And I wouldn't be able to explain what I was doing in her motel room without incriminating myself as well as Rich, so I couldn't let her make that call.

"I grabbed her arm and wrestled the phone away from her, but she began screaming. I knew it was just a matter of time before one of the neighbors would call the police, so I pushed her

Unconscionable

onto the bed and put a pillow over her mouth to shut her up. I wasn't trying to kill her, just stop the screaming, but I guess I held the pillow over her face too long and she quit breathing.

"When I realized she was dead, I became panicky and didn't know what to do. Finally, I decided just to leave. I didn't think anyone had seen me come, but as I was driving away I saw Rich drive up. I watched him go to Martha's room and knock. A moment later he tried the door and found it unlocked. I cursed myself for not making sure it was locked when I left.

"I didn't know what to do. Should I go in and explain to Rich what had happened or just pretend I'd never been there? But before I could do anything I saw Erica drive up in her car. After she went into the motel room I decided I'd better go in and explain what had happened. But when I got to the door Erica was standing over Rich's limp body looking rather bewildered.

"She explained she had walked in and seen a man standing over Martha's lifeless body. Instinctively she had grabbed a lamp and hit him over the head, not realizing it was Rich.

"She was frantic that Rich would be accused of murder and said she couldn't let that happen. That's when we concocted our plan to take Rich away from the crime scene so he wouldn't be implicated in Aunt Martha's murder."

"Wow! That's quite a story," Detective Longoria said. "It must have been very difficult for you to keep such a dark secret all these years."

Joe sighed. "Yes, you have no idea. Many times I tried to muster the courage to come forward, but just couldn't do it. I hated myself for it but rationalized that it was all Rich and Erica's fault and not mine."

"Yes. That makes sense. You were just trying to be a good friend and got dragged into Rich and Erica's mess."

"Right, but I didn't mean to kill Aunt Martha and had I come clean in the beginning, it probably would have been better for everyone."

384

"Probably so," Detective Longoria agreed as she got up and took out her handcuffs.

The next day Detective Longoria watched as Lt. Edmonton held a news conference. He announced Joe Weston's confession for the murder of Martha Collins and told the media gathered for the press conference that all charges against Rich Coleman had been dropped. Someone asked him if Rich Coleman would get his bond money that had been forfeited returned, but Lt. Edmonton said he didn't know. Longoria felt relieved that the Martha Collins case was finally solved and happy that Rich Coleman had turned out to be innocent. She didn't know him that well, but she had become fond of Matt and figured his dad must be a nice guy, too.

The next day Special Agent Ramirez called and said the US attorney had agreed to the deal Matt had proposed and that they were anxious to get their investigation of Samantha Jones and RMS under way. Detective Longoria said that was good news and she'd tell Matt right away and set up a meeting. After she hung up she called Matt.

"So, when will your father be coming home?" she asked.

"I don't know. As soon as they find out the charges have been dropped," Matt replied excitedly. "I can't believe Joe decided to confess."

"Actually, it was Candy's kidnapping and the attempt on your life that finally made him crack."

"Really? Wow. Joe's a good guy. He's been like an uncle to me. I hate to see him go to jail."

"Well, he got a free pass for twenty-five years. It could have been worse."

"Well, that's true."

"So, the FBI has agreed to immunity for Shelly, and they're launching an investigation into RMS."

"Oh. Awesome! I'm glad to hear it."

"So, they want to meet with you and Shelly as soon as possible."

"Okay, tomorrow afternoon, maybe?"

"That will be fine, I'm sure. Do you know where their office is?"

"Sure, in the federal building downtown, right?"

"Right. Two o'clock p.m. See you then."

"Thanks, Detective," Matt said and hung up.

Detective Longoria hung up the phone and then took a deep breath. She was excited about the new investigation and working with the FBI. Now that she had delivered them a couple of key witnesses and helped them expand their investigation to RMS, their attitude about her had changed dramatically. She didn't know how long it would last, but for now it felt good.

Chapter 37
Homecoming

A bright ray of morning light struck Matt's eyelid. He turned over to avoid the glare and felt Candy's warm body next to him. His eyes blinked open, and a feeling of immense gratitude came over him. He silently thanked God again for returning her to him. He cuddled up close and held her tightly. She sighed in satisfaction and took his hand in hers.

Now that he was awake Matt couldn't go back to sleep, but Candy felt so good next to him that he didn't want to get up just yet. He was enjoying the energy flowing between their naked bodies. It was a blissful feeling that he hoped would never end. Eventually Candy turned over and peered up at him.

"Can't sleep, huh?" she asked.

"No, but I'm enjoying just lying next to you."

"Hmm. Me, too. Let's stay in bed all day."

"I'm afraid we can't do that. We've got to pick up my parents from the airport."

She sighed. "Okay, but you can't make a woman wet with desire and then leave her longing for fulfillment."

Matt laughed. "Did I do that?"

"Yes. You've been squeezing and caressing me for the last twenty minutes. Didn't you think I'd notice?"

"I thought you were asleep."

Candy closed her eyes. "I was trying to," she whispered.

Matt rolled over on top of her and kissed her breasts gently. She moaned in delight and pulled him into her. They made desperate love, losing all track of time and the world around them. They were experiencing the enhanced pleasure that comes after being on the brink of losing it all. Matt hadn't believed he could ever find love again after Lynn's murder and hadn't allowed himself to fall in love with Candy. But now he had a new perspective. Love wasn't something you could control. He *had* found love again, and he promised himself he wouldn't squander a moment of it ever again.

The rude metallic ring of the alarm clock brought them back to reality. Matt had set the alarm because he had feared they might oversleep. He didn't want his parents standing on the curb at passenger pickup waiting for them. They got up, dressed quickly, and headed for DFW. When they arrived at the luggage gate where Rich and Erica were expected to emerge, they were met by a large contingent of media.

"Mr. Coleman, how do you feel now that your father has been exonerated?" a reporter asked.

"Very happy and relieved," Matt replied.

"Ms. Kane. Were you hurt at all when you were kidnapped?" another reporter asked.

"No. Not physically. I was just scared to death. I thought I was going to die," Candy recalled.

The reporter shook her head.

"Mr. Coleman. Will you be assisting the FBI in the prosecution of Samantha Jones and RMS?"

Matt smiled. "Yes. I'll help in any way I can."

The baggage belt began turning, and the American Airlines flight from Mexico City flashed on the screen. A few moments later passengers began streaming out into the baggage area. Matt spotted Rich and Erica and began moving with Candy in that direction. Finally they made it through the throng and embraced.

"Dad, thank God you're home," Matt said, smiling broadly.

"Oh, man. It's great to be back. Argentina is beautiful, but it's not America."

Candy and Erica embraced. "I'm so glad you're okay,"

Erica said. "I was devastated when I heard the news that you'd been kidnapped."

"Yes, there were moments when I thought my life was over," she confessed, tears flowing down her cheeks.

"Let's get your luggage and get out of here," Matt suggested.

"Mr. Coleman," a reporter asked. "How does it feel to be exonerated?"

Rich smiled as he hugged Erica. "Wonderful. Absolutely fantastic."

"Mr. Coleman," another reporter asked. "Are you angry that your old friend was going to let you take the fall for Martha Collins's murder?"

Rich shook his head. "No. I understand why he did it and I've already forgiven him."

Erica pointed to their luggage coming around, so Matt pulled it off the belt. A porter came up and offered to handle it for them. Matt nodded, and the porter had it quickly loaded and ready to go.

"Mr. Coleman," another reporter asked. "With a *New York Times* Best Seller under your belt, is there another book in the works?"

Rich laughed. "Not yet, but I certainly have plenty of new material for one."

Ten minutes later they made it back to Matt's car and were driving out of the airport. When they finally made it to Rich and Erica's neighborhood, cars were lined up all along the street. The paparazzi were camped out in front as usual, so Matt pulled the car into the alley and parked in the garage. When they came into the house there was a chorus of applause.

"Welcome home!" Ryan said, giving his mother a hug.

"Oh, Ryan. I have missed you so," Erica replied, squeezing him tightly.

Friends, neighbors, and family were everywhere and they quickly closed in around Rich and Erica to welcome them home.

Soon the party was under way and it went on for hours as a twenty-five-year nightmare was finally over. As the party was winding down there was a knock on the door. Ryan went to answer it and was shocked to see Amanda there.

"What are you doing here?" Ryan spat.

Amanda looked around nervously then replied, "Your father called and said I should come."

Ryan frowned. "What? My father called you?"

"Uh-huh. A half hour ago."

Ryan turned and spotted his father going into the kitchen. "All right. Come on in. Let's find out why in the hell he invited you."

Amanda followed Ryan into the kitchen where they found Rich opening a bottle of champagne.

"Amanda," Rich exclaimed excitedly. "I'm so glad you came."

Rich poured her a glass of champagne and handed it to her. She took it and smiled broadly.

"What's this all about, Dad?" Ryan said irritably. "Why did you invite Amanda after all that she's done to you?"

Rich smiled warmly. "Because I wanted to thank her."

Ryan grimaced and Amanda looked confused. "Thank her? What are you talking about?"

"For helping me solve Martha Collins's murder. What happened the night she was murdered has haunted me for over twenty-five years. You don't know the anguish that it has caused your mom and me over all those years. If Amanda hadn't come along and forced me into publishing *The Pact*, I'd still be having nightmares about it and I'd continue to have them until the day I died."

Amanda nodded.

"But Dad," Ryan protested. "She fed the story to the *Inquisitor* and had you ambushed on Leno."

Rich laughed. "That was brilliant. You're one hell of an agent, Amanda."

Amanda smiled tentatively. "But, if you approved of what I was doing, why didn't you say something?" she asked. "That certainly would have made my life a hell of a lot easier."

"But if I'd have let on that I knew what you were up to and approved it, the *Inquisitor* wouldn't have printed the story. They would have considered it just a publicity stunt. It was the fact that you believed you were going behind my back and that Erica and I were about to be humiliated on national TV that made it a great story."

"But what about the trial? You could have been convicted," Ryan said.

"I don't think so. I knew your mother didn't do it. She's not a killer and she's already been tried for it. And I knew I couldn't have done it, so I figured somehow we'd figure out who the real killer was."

"But you lost two million dollars when your bond was revoked. How can you forgive her for that?"

"Revoked but not forfeited. My attorney says since the charges were dropped before the bond was forfeited I'm not likely to lose a dime."

Ryan didn't say anything. He stood there in shock and disbelief.

"What about Erica?" Amanda asked. "Does she still hate me?"

Rich nodded vehemently. "Oh, yeah. I'd stay clear of her for a while."

They all laughed.

"But she's a woman who has always had an appreciation of money. She'll get over it as the big royalty checks roll in."

Ryan nodded and gave Amanda a hard look. She looked right back at him, and the two just stared at each other for a long moment. Then Amanda asked, "Can you ever forgive me? I know what I did was stupid and selfish, but I never intended to hurt anyone. I truly thought we would all profit by what I was doing."

Ryan thought about it a moment. "I guess if my father

can forgive you after everything you did to him, I should be able to. Just promise me there won't be any more secrets between us. I have to be able to trust you. And don't even think about representing my dad on a second book!"

Amanda shook her head. "No. No way . . . Unless, of course, he just begs me to do it."

Ryan shook his head, took Amanda's hands, and pulled her toward him. They embraced.

"I've missed you," Ryan whispered in her ear.

"Me, too," Amanda replied, tears rolling down her cheeks.